A Murder Most Fowl

A Murder Most Fowl

A FOOD TRUCK MYSTERY

Carmela Dutra

CROOKED LANE
NEW YORK

Books should be disposed of and recycled according to local requirements. All paper materials used are FSC compliant.

This is a work of fiction. All of the names, characters, organizations, places and events portrayed in this novel are either products of the author's imagination or are used fictitiously. Any resemblance to real or actual events, locales, or persons, living or dead, is entirely coincidental.

Published in the United States by Crooked Lane Books, an imprint of The Quick Brown Fox & Company LLC.

Crooked Lane Books and its logo are trademarks of The Quick Brown Fox & Company LLC.

Library of Congress Catalog-in-Publication data available upon request.

ISBN (hardcover): 979-8-89242-317-5
ISBN (paperback): 979-8-89242-318-2
ISBN (ebook): 979-8-89242-319-9

Cover design by Jesses Reisch

Printed in the United States.

www.crookedlanebooks.com

Crooked Lane Books
34 West 27th St., 10th Floor
New York, NY 10001

First Edition: September 2025

The authorized representative in the EU for product safety and compliance is eucomply OÜPärnu mnt 139b-14, 11317 Tallinn, Estonia, hello@eucompliancepartner.com, +33757690241

10 9 8 7 6 5 4 3 2 1

To my favorite twins, Mary and Martha.
Though you are no longer with us, your love, light, and inspiration live on.

And to my husband, David.
Whose unwavering belief in me, even when I didn't believe in myself, has meant more than words can express. Your support is my foundation, and your love is my strength.

Prologue

"All right, Big Bird. On your feet. Let's go." The officer who arrested me is standing in front of my cage. "Someone's here for you." His keys rattle against the bars as he unlocks my improvised coop.

I step over the cell's threshold when I remember my head. "Wait a sec." Scrambling back inside, I retrieve the top of my costume.

As we walk in silence down the hallway, the officer steals glances at me. I assume it's not every day he has the chance to arrest a giant chicken. But that's not all I notice. This officer is tall and has strong, broad shoulders and soft strawberry-blond locks—the kind you want to run your fingers through. Or, in my case, a chicken wing. Officer Pretty Boy is easy to look at, and I sneak just as many glances his way. Only mine are not so subtle because, well, I'm Beth, and nothing I do is subtle.

A deep clearing of a throat draws me out of my thoughts, and I see Officer Pretty Boy staring at me. Oh god, I'm not walking. At some point, I've stopped to lean against a wall and gawk at him.

Get it together, Beth. This man just arrested you. He's your nemesis.

"Ms. Lloyd, if you'll follow me."

"How do you know my name?" I spring off the wall as gracefully as possible. In retrospect, I should have moved a little slower, because I lose my balance and fall forward into my escort, wings flapping.

Officer Pretty Boy grabs me as I fall into him. His muscular arms lift my chicken body into a standing position. "It's my job to know who I'm bringing to the station. Plus, I met your brother. He's waiting just through there." He points toward a set of double doors.

"Of course. I knew that," I say, trying to maintain some dignity. But it's becoming harder the longer I'm here. "Lead the way, Officer Pretty Boy."

Oh god. Did I just say that out loud?

"Officer Pretty Boy?" another voice says. Another officer laughs at the man hauling me out of here. "Has a nice ring to it. Perhaps we found a nickname for you after all." The guy gives Officer Pretty Boy a hard slap on the back before he walks away, chuckling to himself.

I peek up at Officer Pretty Boy and his arched brow, but he says nothing. Instead, he walks toward the double doors, expecting me to follow. If the chicken suit had a tail, I'd tuck it between my legs.

"There's my chicken of a twin!" says Seth with his arms wide open as I push through the double doors. Seeing my brother, I burst into a sprint. "Wow, slow down, Beth. You're running around like a chicken with its head cut off."

"Really? You're making chicken jokes right now?" I stamp my foot at him.

"Don't stomp your drumstick at me, young lady."

"Can we just get out of here while I still have a shred of dignity left?"

"Ms. Lloyd!" Officer Pretty Boy calls out after me.

"Yeah, I think that ship has sailed." My twin points over my shoulder.

"You forgot your head," Officer Pretty Boy says from across the room.

Slowly, I turn around to see the head of my chicken costume sitting snug in his muscular hands.

I must've dropped it when I fell into his arms. I was in such a hurry to get out of this place that I'd left it behind without realizing.

A slow smile creeps across the officer's face. He's enjoying this way too much.

"Forget it. Let's go." I start to leave the precinct.

Seth grabs one of my wings, twisting me back. "You're the one who wanted Kluckin' Good. That costume came with the truck and belonged to Aunt Dolly. It's practically a family heirloom." He shoves me forward.

Shuffling toward the officer, I feel my face turn red. When I reach him, I don't make eye contact as I grab the chicken head. "Thanks," I mumble.

I pull away, but the chicken head doesn't budge. Officer Pretty Boy is giving me another lopsided grin. "You're welcome, Beth." The way he says my name makes my stomach do a small somersault.

Ugh, nope, not gonna happen. He's now as much my nemesis as Benji, I remind myself.

I feel my lip curl into a sneer at the thought of Benji.

Benji Mayhew owns The Dog House, a hot dog–themed food truck in the small town of Princemount, California, about twenty minutes north of my hometown of Clementine. Benji has an impressive amount of energy for a man in his fifties, even while doing grueling work in a hot food truck with no air-conditioning. He's also a perpetual source of irritation for me.

Our towns, although small, are in the heart of the Bay Area and are frequent destinations for tourists. Clementine's City Hall is a National Historic Landmark and a popular attraction that draws visitors from all over. From the observation deck, you can enjoy breathtaking views of the coastline, and if the weather is good, you might glimpse the Bay Bridge. Ever since I started running Kluckin' Good, I've been strategically positioning my food truck there to catch the foot traffic of the lunchtime crowd and tourists. Or I was, until two weeks ago, when Benji started infringing on my territory.

Just thinking about Benji makes my blood boil. I could kill him right now for all the trouble he's caused. Repeatedly, for the past two weeks, I've tried to calmly reason with him. Every time I mentioned he was in my spot, he replied with, "Oh, am I? I must've forgotten." I then would politely ask him to move to a different location, maybe go back to his town or try the piers between our cities. "Why would I do that when I'm making a killing right here?" he'd say. "The hot dogs are a hit, and your customers seem to love 'em."

Last week, he had the audacity to accuse me of being a spoiled brat! Claiming that, while he toiled away, building his business from the ground up, I was privileged to have inherited an established truck. He doesn't care that I own Kluckin' Good because my aunt died. Nor does he consider that I spent two years at community college taking business classes learning how to run things. All Benji sees is a woman more than twenty years his junior managing a successful business, and he credits all my success to luck and privilege. Neither of which are true.

Today, I thought I could outwit Benji by getting to City Hall earlier than I typically do. But he was already there. In my spot. Again.

With my assistant, Rylie, out sick, it was my job to wear the chicken suit for advertisement. Securing my head, with my beak held high, I strutted toward his truck to ask him once again to kindly move. He laughed—whether it was because I was in the giant chicken outfit or because I told him to leave, I don't know. Probably both. But I could see I was getting nowhere, so I tried a different approach.

"Why don't we share the space?" I suggested. "There's a lot of foot traffic and ample room for both of our trucks." His head drooped into his chest. "Benji?"

"Huh?" He looked up. "Sorry. I often doze off when I'm really bored."

"I'm trying to be reasonable here." I held out my wings. *Gimme something here, man!*

"It's so cute when you try to sound like an adult. Did you learn these negotiating skills in community college?" Then he had the audacity to reach out and *boop* my beak.

I struggled to suppress my simmering anger. "I do everything the best way I know how. Trying to be reasonable with you was my greatest mistake." Shaking out my wings, I jutted my beak in the air. "You know what? Forget it. You want this spot so badly, take it. You're not worth my time. I'll park somewhere else."

"That's right," he called after me. "Run away, Little Chicken Girl. You're just like your pathetic aunt, always running away from a fight."

I had tried to be reasonable. But calling my aunt pathetic was the feather that broke this chicken's back.

My face turned a deep shade of red as anger and sadness consumed me. Aunt Dolly wasn't pathetic. She was my mentor and inspiration, the one who taught Seth and me from a young age the secrets of making the perfect wings.

In a fit of anger, I chicken slapped his truck while expressing some colorful, creative swear words, if I do say so myself.

Word to the wise: If you get so angry that you're about to use poultry profanity, try not to be dressed as a larger-than-life fowl. Looking like a character from a fast-food commercial makes it hard to be taken seriously.

While I was angrily striking his front fender with my wings, the sound of police sirens suddenly filled the air. When I looked up, I saw Benji with his phone against his ear.

"You called the police?"

"You bet your feathers I did. See this dent on my front fender? That's the result of you damaging my property," he said, pointing.

"It's barely a scratch!" I glanced at the softball-sized dent. "For all I know, that's always been there."

"We'll see what the police have to say about it," Benji said, his phone still pressed to his ear.

As the officer walked over, Benji and I were still yelling at each other. Shouting at Benji wasn't the reason for my arrest. Apparently, it's considered "assault" if I ruffle my feathers in someone's face.

Now at the police station, I shake my head, clearing away the memories of the afternoon, and look at Officer Pretty Boy.

"Thanks again for grabbing my head." I attempt to yank the chicken face free.

"No trouble at all. It's not every day I meet Big Bird."

"Hopefully today was your first and last time. Have a nice day." I rip the costume top free. Holding my real head high, I walk out of the precinct, ignoring the whispered giggles from people in the lobby.

Seth bounds after me as I run down the steps and almost tumble to the sidewalk. I hardly ever wear this outfit, so I didn't remember how badly it affects my center of gravity. Cars are honking as they drive by. Standing in front of the Clementine Police Station dressed as an oversized bird, I'm about as subtle as a lightning storm. Someone even shouts, "Save the chickens! Eat beef!"

"Well, that wasn't the phone call I expected to receive at work today. C'mon, chicken girl, I'm parked right over here."

I trail after my brother toward the parking garage. "You'll need to take that off before you get in," he says gesturing to my outfit.

"I'm good, thanks," I say as we reach his Pontiac Solstice, and I attempt to shimmy into the front seat.

"No, seriously, you're not gonna fit."

"I've got this," I insist as I try a different approach, backside first this time. Why did he have to purchase the hardtop? If this was a convertible, I could just hop over the door.

"Take that monstrosity off, will you? Let me help."

I yelp as he grabs the zipper. "Seth, no!" I scream, twisting around and flapping my wings at his hands. "You can't do that."

"Relax, I'm your twin. Since when do you have any shame around me?" He reaches for my zipper again.

"Stop. You can't undo the zipper. I can't take it off."

"Why in the world not?"

"Because"—I look around to see if anyone might hear—"I'm not wearing anything underneath."

"What?"

"It's not like I stripped down in the food truck to put the costume on." I tug at the collar, avoiding eye contact. "Okay, well, maybe I did."

"WHAT?!"

"I didn't plan to spill Kluck-It sauce down the front of my clothing. It's not like I could put the suit on over my dirty clothes. What choice did I have?"

"Did it ever occur to you to go home and change? Or call someone to bring you a clean outfit?"

"Huh. Neither crossed my mind," I admit, more to myself than my brother.

"I would have preferred a call asking for a change of clothing than to leave work early to *bail you out of jail*."

"I'll keep that in mind for future reference."

"This better not become a new habit for you."

"What? Wearing nothing but a chicken suit or getting hauled off in the paddy wagon?"

"Both!" my twin says with an eye roll. "All right, my little chicken nugget, you've had a long day. Let's get you out of here."

"Did you remember to collect my personal items? I need my phone."

Seth takes my phone out of his suit pocket. "Here." I quickly snatch it from his fingers. For weeks, I've been checking my email obsessively. After my arrest today, I wasn't able to check for several hours, and I'm jonesing. I'm supposed to hear back any day now. "The thing was buzzing nonstop," he says.

As I open my email, I quietly hope for a positive response. And there it is. My stomach somersaults as I read each subsequent word.

Dear Beth,

We're pleased to announce you've been selected . . .

"Yes!" I pump my wing up in the air.

"What? Did Rylie find a rooster costume so you two can match?"

I reread the email, grinning, then take in Seth's words and roll my eyes. "I didn't know you were a lawyer who moonlights as a comedian. You're the total package."

"You're acting weird." Seth scrutinizes me. "Weirder than usual. What is it?"

"Let's just say a $50,000 opportunity has just presented itself."

"Bethany"—Seth pronounces my name just like our mother—"what have you gotten us into?"

"I'll explain on the drive home."

I'm about to attempt another shimmy into Seth's car when someone yells, "Beth!" Turning around, I see Officer Pretty Boy walking by with another cop. "As much fun as I'll have telling people I arrested a giant chicken, don't let me catch you around here again."

Chapter One

Two weeks later.

"I can't believe I let you talk me into this," Seth complains from the passenger seat of the truck. "I don't know how I'm going to survive the next eight weeks."

Seth, Rylie, and I are driving to the filming location for the first episode of *The Food Truck Showdown*, where we'll be joining seven other competing teams. When Rylie first showed me the online ad announcing that casting producers would be in town holding auditions, I knew we had to apply. One lesson I took away from my business classes at Clementine Community College was the value of unconventional marketing strategies, and there's no better marketing than being on national TV. The competitors' food trucks will be featured in the opening credits the entire season, even after elimination. Regardless of who wins, being shown on a national food network is fantastic publicity for all of us small-business owners.

"Does that really need to be there?" In the rearview mirror, I observe Rylie straightening the slightly crooked picture frame.

"You're the one who always says there's no such thing as bad publicity," she says, tilting it a little to the left.

"Okay, but I didn't mean *The Clementine Gazette* featuring me on the front page dressed as a giant chicken!" A girl has her limits.

The guys in the car that honked and shouted at me that day must've worked for the local paper. I glance at the framed full-color newspaper clipping of me exiting the jailhouse captioned "Local Chicken Flees the Coop!" and sigh. Clementine is a small tourist town, which means just about everyone knows everyone's business. In a small town, even a story like mine, getting arrested for attacking a rival food truck, becomes headline news.

"Admit it," Rylie says between mouthfuls of the gummy bears she's been pilfering from my bag. "The write-up has been a boon for business."

"That's because people are hoping to catch a glimpse of the crazed chicken girl."

She waves a gummy at me. "There really is no such thing as bad publicity. Besides, it's not like you were naked while wearing the suit. Well, it's not like anyone *knows* you only had underwear on. Other than Seth and me. And we didn't tell too many people."

"You suck at motivational speeches." I shake my head, recalling the events of that day. "It was all Benji's fault!"

Rylie rolls her eyes. "It's always 'Benji, Benji, Benji' with you. You need to find a way to get along. You're going to spend the next several weeks competing alongside him."

"We'll learn to get along when you learn to cook," I say under my breath, while approaching the parking lot, which is encircled by a chain-link fence.

Coming to a halt outside the lot entrance, I patiently wait for the truck in front of us to pass through the gates. Once the powder-blue truck ahead of us enters the parking lot, a man in a white button-down shirt and tie, sporting dark sunglasses, reads the side of our truck, checks his clipboard, then signals for us to proceed. Creeping forward, I slowly drive into the parking lot, and the truck jostles over a speed bump. While navigating the cone maze, I take in my surroundings.

In the back of the lot is an old, abandoned warehouse giving off eerie vibes. Maybe that's why we're starting filming here, for dramatic effect. That or the cost to shoot here was dirt cheap. Cameras are strategically placed around a makeshift film set near the old warehouse, ready to capture the action.

"I don't know how I let you talk me into these things," Seth complains again from the passenger seat. "This is the worst idea ever."

"It's going to be an adventure. Now hush up, I need to focus," I say, turning the truck to the right. A woman in a vibrant yellow vest is instructing the trucks on where to park. Her excessive pointing and gesturing make her seem better suited for air traffic control.

"I will not hush up! You forged my signature on the contracts with the network, forcing me to participate in this ridiculous reality show." Out of the corner of my eye, I catch a glimpse of Seth flailing his hands. "You had no right to do that!"

Sighing, I glance at my annoying brother. "First, I didn't forge anything. You—*the lawyer*—willfully signed the paper without reading it. Don't blame me for your negligence just because you were too busy watching the basketball game." Seth starts to protest, but I whip my head in his direction, and he stops. "Second, I'm the older twin. As per Aunt Dolly's will, I was the primary inheritor of the truck, with you as the next in line. Which means I hold greater authority in matters related to the business decisions."

"Don't speak legalese to me," Seth says in his lawyer tone. "You are not listed as the primary benefactor. Your name is listed first on our *joint* inheritance because the letter B comes before S in the alphabet, but it belongs to both of us."

Following the parking instructions, I pull alongside the other teams already here. Putting the truck in park, I kill the engine and smile. We've arranged our eight vibrant trucks in a semicircle around the stage. Only now, I feel doubts slowly creeping in, and Seth's persistent grumbling is only exacerbating my growing nerves.

"Fine, it was left to both of us," I say, unbuckling my seat belt. Twisting around in my seat, I look at my twin. "But I am older. By a whole month, in fact."

"No, you're not."

"Does February not come before March?"

"It does," he relents. "But if you want to be technical, you're actually seven years younger than me."

"I am not!"

"Were you or were you not born on leap day, while I was born on March first?"

I *hate* that he has this trump card and plays it regularly. I would *never* stoop so low.

"Stop being a grouch and drink your coffee." I side-eye my brother before opening the driver's-side door and leaving the truck. I don't have time for his attitude when I'm having a mild freak-out.

What was I thinking signing up for a food truck reality show? I don't even have half the experience as the rest of the owners here. I've already familiarized myself with a few of the other teams we'll be up against. Some of them have been running their trucks for decades. With their restaurant included, Fettuccine Bartolini has been in business for almost twenty years. Lumpia-Licious, a family business, is on the verge of reaching their fifteen-year milestone, with three trucks in operation.

Like me, two other trucks are from the Bay Area. Nacho Momma's Tacos and The Dog House. I'm not exactly on friendly terms with either of them. Then there's Dough Brothers. The three brothers are from Southern California. At the casting session, Rylie and I met Ben Quill and his two siblings. We got along really well, and they were super nice.

Rylie, Seth, and I make our way toward the stage to join the other competitors. Looking down at the paper in my hands, I read the overview once more.

"Wagons West! *The Food Truck Showdown* heads to the Wild West, where the Cooking Channel's legendary host Bobbi Taylor welcomes eight teams of food truck operators from across the country as they embark on the adventure of a lifetime. Each week, they'll race across the desert landscape to a new town where they'll face unique challenges, cook fantastic dishes, and, as always, try to outsell the competition. The food truck that earns the least will have to leave the wagon trail, but the two teams with the tenacity to make it to the end will face off for the $50,000 grand prize."

"Oh my god!" Rylie squeals as she jumps up and down. "Is that her? Is she here?"

"Rylie, can you tone it down just a little?" Seth plugs his ear. "Nothing is even happening yet."

"It's her. It has to be her," Rylie insists as she bounces from foot to foot while people gawk at her. It's hard not to notice Rylie. Inês Rylie Abril Cortes is her full name, but she prefers to be called Rylie. She and her siblings are first-generation Americans after her father left the Azores.

While I tend to blend in, Rylie catches everyone's eye, with her olive complexion and rich mahogany eyes framed by thick, dark lashes. A light dusting of freckles dances across her nose and cheeks like constellations in the night sky. Then there's her hair. Loose waves of rich chestnut-brown hair cascade down her back. Between all that, and her seamless transition between English and Portuguese, she's impossible to overlook.

With another loud gasp, Rylie draws the attention of three other drivers. "It's her. She's here!" She points toward a woman too far away to make out any precise details.

"Who in the world are you talking about?"

"Bobbi Taylor," I answer my brother.

"Do I know him?" he asks.

"Not him. *Her*," snaps Rylie. "She's the most fantastic chef there is. Have you not seen *Baking with Bobbi*?"

"Can't say I have, no," Seth says.

"It's only the best show on the Cooking Channel," Rylie scoffs. "She focuses on healthy things you can bake using everyday ingredients. As Bobbi always says, 'Good food, good mood.'"

"I don't recall asking about the show." Seth quirks an eyebrow as he knocks back the rest of his coffee.

Rylie opens her mouth to reply when a tapping sound draws our attention to the front of the crowd. A woman with tortoiseshell glasses and a cropped green mohawk is standing on the raised platform, tapping a microphone.

"Is this thing on?" she asks, and everyone chuckles. "Oh, you can hear me." She sounds embarrassed. "Well, that's good news. It means we set the equipment up correctly the first time," she jokes. "For those who don't know me, my name is Imogen Comestible. You'll see me running around at every taping. I'm one of the producers for this season of *The Food Truck Showdown*."

A woman with a short bob haircut whispers something to her. Imogen gives her a firm nod before returning to us. "All right, where was I?" Pushing her glasses further up her face, she scans her clipboard. "Oh right, as I was saying, my name is Imogen, and I'm here to assist with production and other odds and ends. If there are any problems, you can talk with my assistant producer, Sloane"—she gestures at the woman with the bob standing next to her—"one of the other people on set, or me, and we'll do what we can to handle any issues." Pausing for a moment, she covers the microphone with her palm as she leans over to an individual on her left.

As she pulls her hand away from the mic, she flashes everyone a sheepish grin. "Sorry, I'm used to being behind the scenes, assembling a coherent narrative, and handling the editing, not being the one making the introductions. We're all juggling multiple roles, dealing with a tight budget this season, and working against an even tighter deadline. But I won't go into the specifics and bore you." Pausing, Imogen waits for the camera crew. She smiles as a man nods, indicating filming is ready. "Without further ado, I would like to introduce all of you to the lady of the hour. She's the host of *Baking with Bobbi*, *Bobbi vs. Tommy: A Celebrity Cook-Off*, and *Bobbi's Brew House*. Please welcome your host, the one and only Bobbi Taylor!"

A full-figured woman with long dark hair, sporting a pair of the tallest black stilettos I've ever seen, takes the stage. The food truck owners cheer wildly as she waves. She gives Imogen and Sloane a quick hug before reaching for the mic. "Hello, hello, hello, everyone! It's great to be here with you today. How's everyone doing?"

Uncontrollable clapping and screams erupt from the group.

"Eek!" Rylie squeals once more while clapping. "*Eu simplesmente a amo!* I just love her!"

When Rylie learned who this season's host was for *The Food Truck Showdown*, she'd insisted we binge-watch all of Bobbi's shows. I knew next to nothing about the woman other than she's a celebrity chef and *The Food Truck Showdown* is her latest show. Rylie gave me a full history lesson about her cooking idol, which is hilarious when you think about it. Rylie can hardly boil a pot of water, yet her idol is a culinary genius. I expressed as much when Rylie was prattling on about Bobbi. She said that just because she can't cook doesn't mean she can't appreciate the art of cooking. Or eating.

"Is it just me, or does she look taller in person?" Rylie asks.

"Do you have a crush on this woman or something?" Seth asks. "She's just another person. Relax."

"Wrong. *You're* just another person. She's Bobbi Taylor."

"Would you pipe down?" I shush the two of them.

"If any of you have watched the show before, then you know eight teams are competing for a grand prize of fifty thousand dollars," Bobbi explains. "Each team is made up of a driver and one or two crew members who must staff the truck. You are responsible for cooking, shopping, and placing orders. Each team will start with no food, and everyone must make do with the seed money provided.

"Similar to previous seasons, we film on location and have a speedy editing time. Filming will take place from Friday to Sunday. Our filming, travel, and editing are all tightly scheduled to ensure episodes air on Wednesdays at 9|8c. The season finale results will be broadcast live. All of you are professionals with your own trucks, so you already understand the ins and outs of running your own business, or at least you should."

As the cameras spin, it films the crowd sharing a laugh with Bobbi. Mine is hollow. Although I've gone to school and earned the right to own Kluckin' Good, I don't feel like I have the same level of experience as the other food truckers here. Do I even know what I'm doing? Do I truly understand the ins and outs of running my own business?

"Are you ready to hear about your first challenge?"

Before anyone answers, a series of crashes startles the entire crowd.

"What the heck?" yells a man.

"Technical difficulties," Bobbi says, drawing our attention back to her. "Would someone please see what's happening?"

Sloane and a man with glasses leave to investigate.

"As I was saying," Bobbi continues, "each of you will receive five hundred dollars in seed money to buy all the ingredients needed to make your most popular dishes. For the first challenge, the first team to make three hundred in sales at Fisherman's Harbor is the winner. The winner will receive a custom cooking set from yours truly. You will have three hours to shop, get to the pier, and prep all your food before you open for business."

"That's easy," Seth says as he smugly folds his arms over his chest. "I've checked the records. We can sell that amount in our sleep."

"Not so fast, Mr. Yummy Scrummy," Rylie cautions. "It's never this easy. There's always more."

I can't help but roll my eyes when she uses one of her many pet names for Seth.

Bobbi's voice booms from the stage. "But wait, there's more."

Elbowing Seth, Rylie smiles. "Told ya."

"Since you'll be selling on the waterfront, it's only fitting we incorporate seafood into the menus." Bobbi pauses for effect, sweeping her gaze across the contestants.

"Each team must purchase fish and potatoes to serve their version of fish-and-chips. The first team to sell twenty orders will receive a set of my Renaissance Chef's Knives. Perfect for all of your slicing, chopping, dicing, and mincing needs." She winks, placing a manicured hand over her heart. "Perfect for busy food trucks."

A brand-new cooking set? My heart flutters. I'd kill for a new set for Kluckin' Good. Okay, maybe not literally, but I'd definitely consider a light maiming.

"May the best food truck win. Your time starts now!"

Cameras capture the chaos as an air horn blares and people rush to their trucks. Lucky for us, we're from this area, so I know which store will have everything we need.

"Okay, I wasn't expecting to serve fish-and-chips," Seth admits as he buckles up and I put the truck in drive. "But that's not too bad of a curveball. It could've been worse."

"Right. We could be a dessert truck like the Dough Brothers," Rylie says.

"Do you think they even know how to make savory food?" I ask.

"Not sure," Seth says. "But if they don't, this is one heck of a way to learn."

Turning onto Beach Street, I explain my plan. "I'm parking at the harbor first to get the best spot."

"Right in front of the pier?" Seth asks.

I nod. "It'll be the perfect place for us to set up."

Fisherman's Harbor is one of those cutesy beach areas that visitors explore before continuing their drive to San Francisco. This place is nowhere close to the size of Fisherman's Wharf. At most, the harbor spans only a couple of blocks. While it doesn't have anything like Pier 39, it has several charming shops, bistros, and a cute used bookstore. This place is perfect for a relaxing afternoon before heading to the beach.

"Once we park, where to?" my brother asks.

"Clover Market," I say. "It's just a short walk from where we'll set up. They'll have everything we need."

"Smart thinking, *irmã,*" Rylie says. "Plus, they work with the local fishers and have the best fresh seafood."

"My thoughts exactly." Pulling alongside the curb, I put the truck in park and unbuckle. "Seth, grab the tote bags under the prep counter."

My twin retrieves the bags with a mock salute. "I think we should split up once we get inside," he suggests as we sprint toward the grocery store. "We can cover more ground and get back to the truck to prep."

"Big Boy has ideas."

"How many times must I beg you to stop calling him that?" It's no secret that I find Rylie's nicknames for Seth repulsive. Ever since we were in our late teens and he discovered the gym, she's been calling him this one. What started off as something to irritate my twin has transformed into something I can't quite put my finger on.

Rylie winks at Seth and clicks her tongue. "Can you blame a girl for noticing? *Ele é gostoso!*" She fans herself with her hand.

As much as it disgusts me to admit, Seth is attractive. My brother is the tall, dark, and handsome type, which might compliment me if we were identical twins. We both have sparkling green eyes, but that's where the similarities end. A smattering of freckles covers my face like our mom's, and Seth has unblemished skin like our dad. His hair is thick and wavy. Mine is thin and straight.

When Seth isn't working or going to school, he spends his free time at the gym. In my free time, the only cardio I do is walk from the freezer to the couch holding a pint of mint chocolate chip. Seth enjoys hiking, and I enjoy shoveling popcorn into my mouth by the handful.

But this is my brother and my best friend we're talking about here. So, no. Gag, gross.

"I don't know why you're surprised," Seth says as we sprint across the parking lot. "I am a lawyer, after all. Having good ideas is in the job description."

"Not yet you're not," Rylie reminds him.

"Enough, you two," I say as we walk through the automatic doors. "We don't have time for whatever this is." I gesture between them, then pick up two handbaskets. "Here," I say, shoving one at each of them. "Rylie, you already know what type of produce we need. But get extra potatoes for the fish-and-chips."

"On it!" Rylie whizzes off in search of the needed veggies.

Grabbing a basket for myself, I turn to my brother. "Go to the butcher counter. I need ground beef and fresh chicken wings. Stick with grass-fed lean ground beef—either 90/10 or 93/7."

"How much?"

"Ask for Fred. Tell him you're picking up for Beth at Kluckin' Good. He'll know what to give you and how much. Also, tell him you need fresh cod, between four to five pounds."

"Got it. Anything else?" he asks.

"I'll get the rest. Meet at self-checkout when you finish." It's terrific shopping in a store where the employees know you on a first-name basis.

While running through the store, I slam into a stout yellow brick wall of a man. "Oof," I groan, as I fall onto my backside and drop several spice bottles. "I'm so sorry. I didn't notice you there."

"You're not the only one in a hurry."

I know that voice . . .

"Think you could watch where you're going next time?"

I definitely *know that voice.*

"Benji," I snarl.

"Beth." His beady brown eyes lock onto mine as he picks up the scattered items on the tile floor. "I see you're still running around like a chicken with her head cut off," he says, handing me several spice bottles.

Narrowing my eyes at him, I snatch the bottles away and put them in the basket. "Why, Benji, I see you've slithered out of your cave. Maybe you should head back. I bet the other slimy creatures miss you."

"I'd rather spend my time with slimy creatures than engage in pointless conversations with the likes of you."

"That tracks," I say. "I know you love being slimy."

Benji gives me a haughty laugh as he picks up the remaining bottles and tosses them into my handbasket. "What are you doing here, Lloyd? You can buy all the food you want, but it won't make a difference. You don't stand a chance. Accept it. You're mediocre at best."

Now it's my turn to laugh at him. "If you define 'mediocre' as becoming a successful businesswoman at half your age, then yes, I guess I am."

"Your 'success' results from the privilege of receiving a ready-made business. Best of luck to you out there. You're going to need it." As he reaches into his pocket, he retrieves a white slip of paper, causing a crumpled one to slip out, landing on the ground.

"Hey!" Bending over, I pick up the paper.

He gives me a vulgar gesture while striding away.

"You dropped something," I say weakly.

The problem with Benji is his personality. Anger, impulsiveness, control issues—he's bullish is what he is. It's impossible for him to be pleasant, even for a second, and he has a way of pushing all my buttons. But that's typical of Benji. He spreads his misery to those around him. From the moment he learned I was taking over my aunt's truck, he's been calling me Little Chicken Girl, and every time we see each other, our verbal sparring match only intensifies.

Kicking my foot in frustration, I send a stray spice bottle rolling. "I know someone whose head I'd like to cut off," I mutter while uncrumpling the paper to see what he dropped.

"What the heck?" The paper has a collection of random letters clipped and pasted onto it.

Back off unless you want to end up like your steamed buns.

"Steamed buns?" I say to myself. "Did Benji make this? Is this some kind of threat?"

"Excuse me?" Startled by the unexpected voice, I yelp, and the spice bottles fly from the basket.

"I'm sorry," says the voice from behind me. "You were so deep in thought you must not have heard me approach."

My heart races as I turn around and find Sloane, the assistant producer, standing before me, her arms full of iced coffee.

"Let me help you." She sets the coffee on an empty shelf, kneels to the floor, and starts picking up the bottles.

Apparently, my reaction to fear is to hurl spices in self-defense.

"Here you go." She extends two spice bottles to me. "Again, I didn't mean to scare you."

Shaking the fog from my head, I kneel beside her. "No, no, I should be the one apologizing. I hope none of these bottles hit you." Retrieving the bottle I accidentally kicked, I add it to my basket along with the others. "I wasn't expecting anyone to be right behind me," I say, reaching for the garlic powder.

"Well, I wasn't expecting to make a quick trip to the store for Bobbi." She shrugs, implying a sense of resignation. "Besides, you were in an intense, one-sided conversation. Something about steamed buns and cutting off someone's head?"

"Huh?"

"You said you knew someone's head you'd like to cut off?" Adding a hollow laugh and a suspicious glance, she drops a bottle into my handbasket.

"Oh, um . . ." *I didn't mean to say that out loud.* "I think you might have misunderstood me."

"What's there to misunderstand?"

"You heard me reading this." I pass her the crumpled paper. "Benji dropped it."

"Maybe it's his shopping list?" she suggests, taking it. As she reads the crumpled paper, her eyes widen.

"How many people do you know who hand cut letters to make a shopping list?" I ask, trying to decipher the note's meaning. "I think it might be a threat," I say, mulling over the words. *Back off. Back off from what? Or, from whom? Which team serves steamed buns?*

"It does look creepy," she agrees. "Like it belongs in a horror film. I'll examine this further to determine if it poses a threat and take appropriate action." She stands up, tucking the paper into her pocket. "You're right, though," Sloane says, shuffling the coffee bottles in her arms again.

"About what?" I ask, getting up from the floor.

"About Benji. He is a little on the angry side, isn't he?"

My mouth falls open. How much did I say? *How long has she been standing there?*

Sloane gives me a genuine laugh. "It's all right. A few of my coworkers are a little intense too. Besides, everyone is guilty of dreaming about getting rid of unsavory coworkers from time to time," she says with a wink.

"Um . . ." *What does that mean?* "Again, I think you misunderstood me."

"I'm going to assume you don't care for your fellow food trucker, Mr. Mayhew?"

"It's something like that," I confess, scuffing the tip of my shoe on the floor. "Benji and I know each other, but we don't get along."

"Why is that?"

"Honestly, it's been so long now, it's just the way things are. I'm Beth." I thrust a hand toward her, hoping to change the subject.

She shakes my hand. "I know who you are. You're Beth Lloyd, owner of Kluckin' Good."

"I am. And you're Sloane. The assistant producer."

"Yes, Sloane Owsinski," she says. "I'm technically a producer, but I'm more the glorified errand girl for Bobbi most days. Hence why I'm here, getting iced coffee for her." She sighs with a slight eye roll.

"I can imagine that could become very frustrating."

"It can, but it comes with the job when you work with major celebrities."

"Is Bobbi Taylor considered a major celebrity?" I ask.

"Don't let her hear you say that," she warns me.

"Why?" I ask, unsure of what I said wrong.

"Bobbi is certainly no minor celebrity. Her cooking skills are legendary, always have been. She's built an empire with her cookbooks, cookware, and restaurants. I've known her since before she even became Bobbi. She's worked hard for the reputation she's built. So, if Bobbi wants iced coffee, Bobbi gets iced coffee." Sloane pauses as she looks at her smartwatch. "It was a pleasure chatting with you, Beth."

As Sloane walks away, my phone buzzes in my back pocket.

It's a text message from Seth. Where are you? We're waiting at self-checkout.

Shoot! I have to get out of here. We have a challenge to win.

Chapter Two

The presence of a cameraperson makes the interior of my small truck feel even more cramped than usual as we scramble to finish the last details. I expected to be surrounded by cameras, but I didn't factor in a fourth person inside the truck filming us with a shoulder-mounted camera. I watch as Alex positions the camera strategically to capture a close-up of Seth removing a batch of sizzling sliders from the flat range. Then he quickly spins to capture Rylie arranging colorful baskets of chicken wings before transferring them to the hot holders.

"How do you know those are going to taste good?" Seth asks as he raises an eyebrow over the basket of fish-and-chips I've just prepared.

"I don't. That's what I have you for." I slide a basket across the prep counter for him to taste. "I think the flavor is good, but I want a second opinion."

"Me? Do I look like a guinea pig to you?" He pushes the basket back.

"You look like whatever I need you to be." I thrust the food basket in front of him. "Take a bite."

"No way," he says as he shoves the basket away in disgust. The camera pans back and forth, capturing our expressions.

Refusing to take no for an answer, I nudge the basket back. "You have to. Personally, I think the fish-and-chips are fantastic, but I need a second opinion. We will get eliminated if our food tastes bad. Is that what you want? For us to get eliminated, then go out of business because our truck becomes a laughingstock and I wind up homeless on the street?"

"You're overreacting."

"I wonder if the Eighth Street Bridge would be a good place to take up residency?"

"Bethany."

"I'd have to forward my mail to the YMCA. Are those still around?"

Seth's nostrils flare as he looks down at me, his arms folded over his chest.

"Please?" I bat my lashes at him.

Begrudgingly, Seth picks up a piece of breaded cod while grumbling about his aversion to seafood. After chewing, he consumes some fries. Picking up the fish once more, he dips it into my version of tartar sauce.

"Well?" I ask.

"I don't like fish."

"I know that, but Rylie is allergic to seafood. I couldn't ask her."

"I offered to try a small piece," she says.

"And I appreciate that." I give her arm a soft squeeze. "But I need you selling food, not running to the bathroom every two minutes."

If the bathroom trips didn't keep her busy, the noxious gas she produces after eating seafood would be enough to send people running toward our competition. I wasn't about to take that risk.

"Can you just tell me what you think?" I ask again.

"I already did. I don't like fish."

"You're just being difficult." Grabbing some sandwich wrap paper, I line the baskets for the fish-and-chips.

"I don't like fish," he repeats. "But it has good texture and a great crunch. If people enjoy eating seafood, they'll like what you created.

Just not me because I don't like fish. However, this avocado aioli you made"—Seth drags a few shoestring fries through the dressing—"is delicious. You should keep this as a regular condiment. I could see people dipping the Kluck-a-Doodle Classics in this stuff."

Bringing my hands to my chest, I beam. "You think so?"

"The sauce is great, and the fish . . ." He pokes it with his finger. "It's not awful. That's the best I can give you."

"I'll take it!" A burst of joy strikes me. I would spin around and dance in this truck if there was more room. "We're almost ready. I just need to finish the mac-and-cheese poppers."

"I wish there was something I could do to help." Rylie pouts as she watches my brother drop a batch of chicken wings into the deep fryer.

"You know, Rylie, there is something you could do. You could learn to cook rather than stand by bemoaning that you can't."

"Hear, hear!" Seth pipes up as he removes the previous batch of wings from the fryer. He gives the basket a good shake before adding the wings to the mixing bowl and tossing them with seasoning.

Rylie hikes up an eyebrow as she leans a hip against the prep counter. "Do you not remember the last time you tried to give me a cooking lesson?"

I wince at the memory. "The towels."

She mimes an explosion with her hands. "*Whoosh*."

"Right up in flames."

"I mean, if you want me to try, today of all days"—she shrugs—"that's up to you."

"You know what? You're right, never mind. Here." Alex moves his camera with me as I stand on my toes, capturing the moment I retrieve a bag from the overhead cabinet. He's good at what he does. Utilizing every corner of the truck, squatting to capture shots of ingredients being retrieved from storage, and smoothly rising to capture the overall atmosphere. I almost forget he's here. *Almost*. "Measure me out a half cup of breadcrumbs." I hand her the bag.

"I can manage that," she says with a perky smile.

"Hey, Beth, where's the habanero lime seasoning?" Seth asks as he searches the bottles on the counter.

"It should be with the rest of them."

"It's not."

Pushing Seth out of the way, I examine the seasonings myself. Alex pivots swiftly, hot on my heels to capture my expression, but I'm too focused to worry about how I look. I need to find those bottles. "It has to be here."

Where is it? I remember grabbing it before leaving the aisle . . .

"It's not here, the Cajun seasoning is missing too."

A faint ring interrupts us, prompting Alex to press a button on his camera then lower it. "Hold on a second," he says, taking out his phone and answering a call. "Hello? Yeah, I can come over." With a flick of his thumb, he puts his phone back in his pocket.

"Everything okay?" I ask, worrying my bottom lip.

"Yeah." He nods. "I'm needed at another truck. I'll be right back. But this is great footage and leaves viewers hanging."

"Let's keep looking," Rylie says once Alex exits the truck.

"Are you sure you grabbed the bottles?" Seth asks. "We were in a rush this morning. Is it possible you forgot to grab them?"

I shake my head vigorously. "Habanero lime was the last bottle I grabbed, then I made a beeline for self-checkout when . . ." I pause, recalling the sequence of events in the store.

"When what?" Rylie asks.

"*Benji*," I growl.

"What does Benji have to do with this?" Rylie asks as she slips on a pair of poly gloves before combining the breadcrumbs with the mac-and-cheese batter.

"I was in such a hurry that I didn't see him."

Seth shakes his head. "I'm confused. Why are we talking about Benji?"

"I slammed into him and dropped several bottles."

"Okaaay," Seth draws the word out. "And how is this his fault?"

"Because everything is!" At his glare, I throw my hands up. "Because he helped pick them up and made a snide comment about me running around like a chicken with its head cut off." Seth snorts and tries to cover the laugh with a cough. "Not funny. Anyway, he must've pocketed some of the bottles."

"Why would he do that?" Rylie asks.

"Because," I say, like it's obvious, "it's a competition, and Benji will do anything to win. Even if that means sabotaging me by stealing one of our most important spices."

"You don't know that, Beth. It's possible the bottles rolled away, and you just missed them."

"Two spice bottles, Seth? *Two?* No, this has Benji written all over it. I don't know what his problem is, but he and I will have words."

"You need to calm down."

"Don't tell me to calm down!" Pulling myself up to my full height, I poke my brother in the chest, which does nothing to intimidate him, considering he's a million feet taller than me.

"This is the first day, and already you're making accusations. You don't have any proof he's done something," Seth says. "Let it go. We'll regroup."

"How?" I ask. "The Crazed Chick and the Plucked Cajun are two of our best sellers. We need those spices."

"I'm back!" Alex's voice echoes as he reenters through the back of the truck. "What did I miss?"

"Nothing much," Seth says. "We were just discussing what wings to serve since we can't find the seasoning."

"Perfect!" Alex positions his camera for the shot.

Seth turns his attention back to me. "We already have the Kluckin' Greek made up. What about Klucked in the Bayou? It's primarily barbecue sauce. I doubt anyone will notice it's missing the Cajun seasoning."

"I'll notice," I pout.

"Well, get over it," Seth orders, as he tosses a batch of hot chicken wings into a warm metal bowl, coating them in sauce. The camera peeks over his shoulder capturing the steam rising from the bowl. "We're competing to win, and sometimes things don't always go according to plan."

"I know," Rylie says. "Take Seth's idea and make some Kluck-a-Doodle Classics served with a side of avocado aioli."

"That's a great idea." Seth smiles at her. "Plus, we have the Juan and Only Sliders. We're good."

"Okay, we can do this," I say. Seth's confidence is rubbing off on me. "Do you still think offering just one slider is enough?"

"I do. We don't want to show our full hand in the first round. We need to save some of our other items for the next challenge."

"If we make it to the next challenge."

"Get that negative attitude out of this truck, or I'll kick you out myself." My twin glares at me while Alex zooms in to capture the building tension. "I didn't take off from work to listen to a pity party the first time something goes wrong." The camera jostles as it pans to me. All the bright lights and camera equipment around make the already-cramped quarters feel even smaller.

"All right, all right, jeez." With Alex capturing our every move, I hope they don't edit me as a spoiled brat. A hard knock sounds on the outside of our truck, and I see bright green movement.

Imogen Comestible, the head producer, peeks in through the open back door, a camera trailing behind her.

"Just giving you a five-minute warning until you have to open for business. I hope you have everything you need because once you hear the air horn, you can't do any more cooking."

Rylie gives her a thumbs-up. "We're ready."

"Remember, the first team to sell three hundred dollars of food at Fisherman's Harbor is the winner."

"We remember," I say, adjusting my blue hat to cover my hair.

"Don't forget you must include fish-and-chips on your menu." Adjusting her glasses, Imogen smiles into the camera recording us. "May the best food truck win."

As I open the side partition, I prepare for the customers and onlookers who will want to see the filming up close. The plan is for Rylie to sell food on the street while Seth brings her refills as required. I'll be in the truck, since people will also order directly there.

Poking my head out the window, I spy a beige truck that looks like a giant dog. I feel Alex shift his camera behind me, likely to provide viewers with a glimpse of Benji's truck from my perspective.

"Don't worry. We got this, *irmã,*" Rylie whispers as she drapes an arm over my shoulders.

"His truck reminds me of the van from *Dumb and Dumber,*" I say.

"The shaggin' wagon?" Rylie asks.

"Yes! The truck looks like a mutt. A big ole ugly mutt."

"I think it's pretty ingenious," she says, wrapping a bandanna around her head. "I mean, the truck looks like an actual dog. It has a face on the front and a tail on the back."

"Did you notice he has to lift a leg to fill it with gas?" Seth moves the vibrant baskets of Kluck-a-Doodle Classics, which are accompanied by warm fries and sides of avocado aioli, to the hot holders.

I'll never admit this out loud, but Benji's truck is clever. There's even a sign on both sides that says *Our Dogs Are the Wurst.*

"The cuteness of that truck is likely the only reason Benji even made the cut," I sneer.

I'm so getting cast as the villan this season.

"Are you sure you're not just jealous that you didn't transform our truck into a giant chicken?" Rylie asks.

"I don't need to transform my truck when I have you." I thrust the chicken head into her hands at the exact moment the air horn sounds. "Time's up, chicken girl. Get outside and start struttin'."

Chapter Three

The first round passes in a blur. We're so busy that we sell out. Rylie is great as she struts up and down the pier, clucking and shouting, "My wings are kluckin' good! But don't take my *bawk* for it. Come have a bite and tell me how I taste." She might not cook, but boy, she is one heck of a hype woman.

"You were fantastic!" I say, pulling back into the production lot.

"I know, I'm awesome." She removes the bandanna from her head and pushes a black curl out of her face. "Did you hear all those cars honking at me? I even had people ask if I would pose for pictures with them."

Most of the walkups told me they'd come because the giant chicken told them to. Can you blame them? Who wants to anger a big chicken? I park the truck next to Porked 'n' Rubbed, a BBQ truck owned and operated by retirees Loretta Able and Ella Mae Parker. After locking the door, we follow the orange cones guiding us to the stage area.

"What about me?" Seth asks, wrapping his enormous arms across both our shoulders as we walk past the other food trucks. "Don't I get any love for all the running back and forth I did?"

"You were also the best. Rylie couldn't have sold as much product if you hadn't been replenishing her tray every few minutes." Who knew there would be so many hungry customers?

"My feet are killing me." Seth shakes a foot.

"Don't look at me. I'm not rubbing them," I say.

"Don't get any ideas," Rylie says as Seth turns to her.

"Why are you still wearing the suit?" he asks her.

"Psychological warfare," she says. "Nothing gets in people's heads like a *galinha maluca.*" Seth and I exchange glances. "It means crazy chicken. We've been best friends our entire lives, and you still don't know Portuguese." Rylie rolls her eyes.

"Beth, Seth!" Imogen calls to us as she walks up. "You're supposed to have a brief interview with Bobbi recapping today's challenge." The woman is petite. She couldn't be over five foot three, but you know she means business.

"We were just about to head to the stage area," I say.

"Not before you do your interview. Follow me. Oh, and bring the mascot with you." She points at Rylie before marching away.

"I'm not gonna lie. The tiny woman scares me a little," Seth says as we follow Imogen toward the warehouse.

"Here we are." Imogen looks around. "Sergio!" A man holding a stack of binders and sporting enormous glasses approaches. "Have you seen Bobbi?"

"She's running behind schedule," he says while juggling his binders. "I saw Bert on the bus. Try checking there." He must be talking about the giant bus with the show's name and network logo on the side. It is parked in the back of the lot.

"Who was that?" As I ask, I see the man stop and attempt to multitask by grabbing a doughnut from a table without dropping his binders.

"Sergio Romare, my personal assistant."

"And who's Bert? Does he help with the interviews?"

Distracted, Imogen murmurs to herself and sighs as she checks her watch. "I'll get the interview sorted out. Grab yourself a drink from the refreshment tent while I go look for Bobbi."

As Imogen heads off to find Bobbi, I spot Sloane, standing with her hands on her hips, staring up at the sky. "Anything yet?" she calls out to a man on a ladder.

"Nope," the man replies. He retrieves a screwdriver from his back pocket and fiddles with a camera on the warehouse building.

"What's going on?" I ask, my curiosity piqued. Squinting, I raise my hand to block the sun and gaze at the man on the ladder.

Sloane lets out a frustrated sigh. "We're encountering problems with the surveillance camera system."

"What kind of problems?" I ask.

While working on the ladder, the technician briefly glances down. "The cameras are acting up. I'm trying to get them back online, but it's a bit of a challenge with this old building."

"That's James." Sloane nods at the technician. "He's from Wiz Tech. According to Yelp, if he can't fix those cameras, then no one can."

Rylie furrows her brow. "But isn't it crucial to have proper coverage, especially with all this expensive equipment around?"

"Not to mention our trucks," I add.

Sloane nods. "Of course it is, but we're on a budget. And this warehouse was the most affordable option for this shoot. We'll just have to make do with what we have."

"What do you mean 'on a budget'?" I ask. "The Cooking Channel has some of the best ratings."

Seth snorts. "Oh, my little Beth. So naive to the ways of the world. Didn't you know the corporations with the deepest pockets are often the stingiest?"

James puts the screwdriver in his back pocket and descends the ladder. "That's the best I can do." He gives Sloane a sympathetic look. "The whole system is ancient. It's analog and predates Wi-Fi.

There's no footage being uploaded online. The cameras are working for the moment, but I think it's more than just an insufficient power supply." He claps his hands and brushes off the dust. "I've gone through all the power connections, power splitters, and cable connectors to eliminate any potential connection problems.

"It all boils down to the fact that the surveillance cameras are in shabby condition." James bluntly states. "The building is old, and the cameras haven't been maintained. It's a toss-up whether they'll record, and if they do, there's a chance the coverage will be filled with static and have no sound. Like I said, they're currently recording, but there's no way of knowing how long until they're down again."

Seth glances up at the malfunctioning cameras. "It's a good thing there's a security guard stationed at the gate's entrance."

"I suppose," Sloane says, nibbling on her bottom lip. "Thanks for your help, James."

"Should we be worried about the faulty cameras?" I ask, watching James pick up his tool bag from the ground before heading to a white van.

"We're only here for one episode. We'll be moving on to our next location soon." Sloane pauses, looking at her smartwatch. "There's a situation that I need to help with. See you when the winner of the challenge is announced. Good luck!" Sloane walks around the side of the building, leaving us behind.

I'm still squinting against the bright sun, scanning the top of the old warehouse, when I gasp. "Seth, Rylie, look! An owl! I thought owls were nocturnal."

"Not all of them are nocturnal," he says. "There are actually five species that are diurnal. I'm noticing some white patches on the wings. It might be a northern hawk-owl."

"God, you're such a dork," I say before cupping my hands around my mouth. "*Hoot, hoot!*"

"Really?" Seth folds his arms as he looks at me. "I'm the dork?"

"Yes," I say before trying my birdcall again. "*Hoot, hoot!* Why is he ignoring me?" I put my hands on my hips.

"Perhaps your accent offended him," Rylie teases.

"He needs a name," I state, gazing up at the owl.

"You don't have to give a name to every animal you encounter," Seth says.

"Yes, I most certainly do! Hmm, let's see." Tapping a finger to my chin, I study the bird. "The resemblance between the tips of its feathers sticking up and Wolverine's hair in X-Men is uncanny," I muse. "Between that and its stoic, disinterested look—"

"Beth," Seth interrupts, "you can't see the bird's expression from here."

I shoot him a playful glare. "I'm naming him Hoot Jackman."

Rylie laughs, shaking her head. "Hoot Jackman? Really?"

"Absolutely." I grin. "Hoot Jackman it is."

Hoot Jackman turns his head the other way.

"I don't think he likes it," Seth observes.

"Not that this wasn't entertaining," Rylie says. "But what now?"

"Let's get a snack from the refreshment tent," I suggest, giving up on my bird-watching for the day.

As we stroll to the tent, we hear shouting from inside The Dog House. Benji isn't the most pleasant person on any day of the week, but he sounds downright enraged now. I can't tell who the other voice is, but Benji is doing enough yelling for the both of them.

I put my ear to the siding.

"I know what you're trying to do! You won't get away with this!" he shouts. "You think you're so clever, but I caught you red-handed. Don't even try to deny it."

Before Seth can stop me, I bang on the side of the partition. "Everything okay in there?"

Benji pushes open the front door just enough to pop his head out and glare at me with his beady brown eyes. "What do *you* want?"

"I was just checking on you. After all, I do have one kind and decent bone in my body for you." I offer him a sweet smile. "Who are you talking to?"

He opens the door wider, moving to the lower step. "Mind your own business!"

"Would it kill you to be nice for once in your life?"

"If you know what's good for you, Lloyd, you'll stay out of my way." Stepping back up, he slams the door shut.

"Glad to know you're all right, Benji!" I yell.

Seth drags me away from the truck. "It's been one day, Beth!" he whisper-shouts while we walk away. "One day, and you're already fighting with him. That mouth of yours is going to get you—and by extension, *us*—in trouble."

"Hey"—I jerk my arm free—"it's not my fault he's difficult."

"It is, because he's like a scab you keep picking at."

"I heard yelling and wanted to make sure everything was okay. It's called being a good Samaritan."

"More like a nosy Samaritan."

"You know Benji is a hothead," Rylie says. "I'll bet that's the reason he cooks alone. Nobody wants to work in a confined space with him. I'm curious, what did you overhear?"

"It was mostly him shouting. I heard Benji say, 'I know what you're trying to do! You won't get away with this!'"

"That could have been about anything," Rylie comments.

"Then, 'You think you're so clever, but I caught you red-handed.' What do you think that meant?"

"Don't know, don't care," my brother says.

"How can you not care?" I ask.

"Because I'm not nosy like you," Seth says. "I didn't hear anything, and I'm not interested in finding out what was happening."

"I'm not nosy." I huff and cross my arms.

"Says the woman who has shushed me at Chili's not once, but thrice, so she could listen to another couple arguing."

"He confessed to his girlfriend that he was harboring feelings for her sister. For two years! What was I supposed to do? Eat my tacos and ignore them?"

"Most normal people would have focused on their own discussion and not nearly fallen out of the booth to eavesdrop."

"Well, maybe I'm not normal."

"Your words, not mine," Seth says, holding up his hands. "But I'm happy to hear you admit the truth to yourself."

"Beth, Seth." Imogen waves to us as she walks over. "We're going to have to push your interview back until after the elimination round."

"Why?" I ask, feeling dread welling up inside me.

Does this mean we're being eliminated?

"We're behind schedule. I need all of you to come with me to the stage. We're ready to start." Imogen doesn't wait for an answer.

Several minutes pass as we convene near the stage, and Bobbi still hasn't arrived. The group of drivers is getting antsy, and who can blame them? It's our first elimination round, and the air is thick with tension.

Sergio, Imogen's personal assistant, jogs over and speaks loud enough so all can hear. "Ms. Taylor will be here in another five to ten minutes."

Imogen winces at how loudly he speaks. "Thanks, Sergio." She pats him on the shoulder and sends him on his way. "I'm sure all of you heard Sergio." The crowd chuckles. "Apologies. Go grab a snack or drink from the refreshment tent and come back."

Ten minutes later, everyone is back with coffees and half-eaten doughnuts. Rylie smiles as she sees Bobbi. "Bobbi Taylor!" she cries out, shattering the silence. If only her admiration would inspire her to learn to cook.

The rest of the participants mimic the action, breaking into a chorus of clapping and cheering over her long-awaited appearance. Despite the attention, Bobbi remains composed and greets everyone with a friendly yet humble nod.

"Hello, foodies!" Bobbi's voice is smooth like warm honey. "How is everyone doing?" There are a few lingering cheers, but she doesn't seem impressed. "Let's try this again. How is everyone doing?"

The group cheers and claps in response.

"Much better." She gives a nod of approval. "I'm certain you're all eager to find out how you did in today's challenge—"

"Bobbi, wait!" A flash of bright green hair bolts across the stage.

"What is it?" Bobbi snaps at Imogen, who's now scanning the crowd.

"Not all the drivers are present." Imogen adjusts her glasses as if that will help her see the faces better. "Benji isn't here."

"Who?"

"Benji Mayhew, owner of The Dog House."

"The portly fella who speaks with a slight wheeze?"

"I would have found a better way to refer to him"—Imogen clears her throat as she corrects the host—"but yes, that would be him."

"Well, then someone needs to find him," Bobbi says.

Imogen gives a curt nod and motions to Sloane Owsinski, who's holding a clipboard to her chest. I notice her eyes are a little too large. I know how she feels about approaching Benji. He's not a pleasant person to be around.

"Now, Sloane," Bobbi orders. Sloane hesitates a moment before leaving.

"While we wait, we can use this time to better acquaint ourselves. When I call your name, tell us a little about yourself." Bobbi smiles and points at Seth and me. "Let's hear from our very first set of twins, Beth and Seth Lloyd. Tell us, how did you get into the food truck business? And the real question is, why don't the two of you look alike?"

"We're fraternal," we say in unison.

"Does that happen a lot?"

"What?" we ask.

"Speaking at the same time."

"Sometimes," we answer.

"I love it!" Bobbi claps. "How did the two of you become food truck owners?"

"We inherited the business from our late aunt. She passed away two years ago," Seth says.

"I'm sorry to hear that," Bobbi says. "I'm sure she would be proud to learn that both of you are carrying on her legacy. Tell us, what's it like owning a business with your sibling?"

"Well, just as with most siblings—"

A hysterical scream interrupts me as Sloane comes running through the crowd and crashes into Imogen Comestible. "He's dead." She sobs into Imogen's shirt.

"Who is?" Imogen asks.

"Benji." Sloane hiccups as she looks over at Bobbi. "Benji Mayhew is dead!"

Chapter Four

"What does she mean Benji's dead?" My mind swirls with confusion as I sit down on a folding chair.

"I think she means he's no longer alive, technically speaking," Seth says, shocked, taking a seat next to me.

"Thank you, Mr. Obvious."

"Ask a dumb question, get a dumb answer."

"What I mean is, I just talked to the man less than twenty minutes ago, and he seemed fine. How does someone go from being alive to just . . . dead?"

Seth shakes his head. "I'm not sure what to tell you, Beth. Death is sometimes inevitable. Aunt Dolly passing from a heart attack in her sleep is a prime example of how unpredictable life can be."

"I know," I admit, remembering the shock that swept through the family when we learned she'd passed away. "But something about this feels *different*," I say.

"How so?" Rylie asks.

"Benji sounded so angry in his truck." I think back to what I heard. "He said, 'You won't get away with this,' and now he's dead? Doesn't it strike you as too coincidental?" I ask Seth and Rylie.

"We don't know what happened yet. Not everything in life is sinister. Maybe, like Aunt Dolly, his death was unexpected."

Unexpected isn't the same as unplanned.

"You've been listening to too much *Murder and Mayhem*," Seth says, referencing my favorite true-crime podcast.

I watch as Imogen hands Sloane over to one of the production assistants, who walks her somewhere more secluded. Imogen takes action by instructing someone to send security to Benji's truck. While her assistant, Sergio Romare, leads Bobbi to a private area, Imogen pulls out her phone.

One of the runners who was handling miscellaneous tasks earlier today moves the contestants to the refreshment tent, where we wait for more information. While most of us are in shock, there are a few unsportsmanlike comments about there being one less competitor for the fifty thousand dollars.

"Poor Benji," Rylie says. "I know you didn't like him, Beth, but no one deserves to die unexpectedly in their food truck."

"Rylie!" Seth warns, scanning the area. "We both know how Beth felt about him, but we don't need to broadcast it."

"I've done nothing wrong." I'm not sure what my brother is implying.

"We know that"—Seth looks around the space once more—"but no one else does. Plus, we don't know how he died." Lowering his voice, Seth switches to lawyer mode. "The police will treat this as an investigation until the medical examiner determines a cause of death."

Rylie looks around the tent and says, "Out of everyone here, you might have despised him the most, Beth."

"You're not helping matters," Seth says, pinching the bridge of his nose.

"It's true, though," Rylie says to me. "You and Benji have been at each other's throats ever since Benji stole your spot outside of City Hall. I kept telling you to let things go, but you wouldn't listen to me, and now the man is dead!"

"I didn't kill him!" Standing up suddenly, I tip over the plastic folding chair.

"Bethany," Seth growls my name, yanking my arm. "People are staring."

Ignoring the whispers and side-eyes, I jerk my arm free and fix my chair. "Let them stare. I did nothing wrong. Last time I checked, it's not a crime to dislike someone."

Especially if that someone is poaching my spot!

"Can we focus here?" Seth's face looks like our mother's when she's about to count to five because you're in trouble. "Without more information about the situation or his cause of death, we remain silent. Nothing that would imply any of us had hostile intentions toward him." Seth fixes his gaze on me. "Especially you, Beth."

Deep breaths, Beth. In through your nose. Out through your mouth.

"How many times do I have to say it? I. Didn't. Do. Anything!"

"I know you didn't. You've been with Rylie and me all day."

"Right, we're your alibi," she says.

"You're my alibi now? A moment ago, you all but accused me of killing Benji. What type of friend are you, anyway?" I ask, narrowing my eyes at her.

"I'm the best type of friend," she says, ignoring my annoyance. "Who else would visit you in prison with a cake that has a file baked into it?"

"Not you," I say with a laugh. "You can't cook."

"True, but I know people who can."

"Enough!" Seth's loud voice causes some nearby individuals to turn their heads. "We know you're innocent. Unfortunately, it's best if we don't bring up the unpleasant history between you and Benji."

The sound of sirens fills the air as an ambulance pulls into the lot. A pair of police cars trail behind. Everyone stops and stares like rubberneckers on the freeway as two paramedics jog into Benji's truck. One medic goes back to the ambulance and grabs a gurney.

Short people have certain advantages. Slipping in and out of places unnoticed or buying clothing in the teen section, for example. But if you're five foot two like me, it's difficult to see important things in a crowd. I squeeze myself between Ness and Dane Jaxson, owners of Chowder Bowl on the Roll, and witness two uniformed officers cordoning off the area around Benji's truck with yellow tape, just like they do in the movies. Out of nowhere, an unmarked car enters the parking lot. The dash on the front window flashes red and blue lights.

Something about this doesn't feel the same as when Aunt Dolly died. I don't care what Seth says, I'm trusting my true-crime gut on this one.

"I can't wait any longer," Reyna Katapang declares. She's one of the three sisters who own Lumpia-Licious, a Filipino food truck. "C'mon, I need to know what's going on." She motions to her sisters, and they exit the tent to investigate.

Their journey is short-lived.

"Get your hands off me!" Lila screams at a security guard, stopping her and her sisters. As he leads them back to the tent, she shouts, "We have a right to know what's going on!"

While Lila continues to yell, Ula and Reyna follow behind. At least I think that's Lila. All of them are identical in height and have the same dark hair. It's hard to tell them apart.

With empathy, the security guard addresses the group. "I know this has been an exhausting day—"

"Can you tell us what's happening?"

"How did he die?"

"Was it a stroke?"

"Can we leave?"

The number of people speaking at once is overwhelming. It's impossible to determine who is asking what question.

The security guard seems to share the same sentiment, taking a deep breath before continuing. "We ask that everyone please stay here until the CPD removes the body and inspects the lot. Your patience is much appreciated. My name is Héctor, and we're doing everything we can to get you home soon."

Once again, the other competitors ask simultaneous questions about what happened and how Benji died. Héctor the security guard leaves without answering any.

Yeah . . . something isn't right.

"CPD?" asks Marco Bartolini, owner of the Fettuccine Bartolini food truck. He looks to his wife, Sofia, for understanding. The Bartolinis left their Italian restaurant behind to take part in the show, driving down from the Oregon coast.

"Clementine Police Department," answers Willa Garza, owner of Nacho Momma's Tacos. "Looks like the police want us to stay put."

I'd first met Willa when I was taking business classes at Clementine Community College. She was from Greendale, the town sandwiched between mine and Princemount. She'd parked on the campus lot, and I found her truck confusing. The word *nacho* was on it, but she didn't offer any nachos. Willa insisted it was a play on words. After much protest from the student body, she'd caved and added nachos to the menu.

Her food was always fresh, cheap, and delicious, and I was a regular patron until she learned who my aunt was and that I was the individual taking over her business. My aunt had a reputation for her creative chicken wings and sliders. The magazine *Best of the Bay* often featured her food truck. Willa's friendly demeanor changed, and she became yet another business owner who was unhappy I was taking over my aunt's truck. It was difficult to realize that several fellow food truck owners in the area were displeased that my aunt's business was staying in the family. Seth and I received multiple buyout offers. Refusing to sell made me a target in the food truck world.

Willa began accusing me of attempting to steal her ideas. Just because I'd asked her about running a food truck doesn't mean I wanted to turn my aunt's business into a taco truck. My homework had required me to speak with business owners. Despite my explanations, she wouldn't accept that I was fulfilling my aunt's wishes.

She went from pleasant to frosty in the blink of an eye, banning me from her truck.

One day, when I was craving some tacos al pastor, I'd disguised myself, thinking I could order unnoticed. I was wrong. After recognizing me in my disguise, Willa abandoned her truck and tackled me on the lawn. Many staff members and students witnessed our altercation, and a video went viral of Willa wrestling a community college student over a plate of tacos, resulting in the school banning her from selling at the campus. Willa blamed me for everything.

"What did the security guard tell you?" Marco asks the Katapang sisters.

"That we can't go near his truck, and an officer would be over shortly to speak with us," Lila answers.

"Why were you arguing with the security guard, then?" I ask.

"The way he spoke to me just wasn't right," Lila says as she flicks her dark-brown braid over her shoulder. "He overreacted when all we were doing was trying to get a closer look."

"Why are the police coming over to talk with us?" asks Ben Quill.

"Isn't it obvious?" Willa says. "We're the last people who were around the hot dog man. They must suspect something."

"Benji," I say.

Her head swings so fast in my direction that I'm surprised she doesn't give herself whiplash. "Excuse me?"

These are the first words we've exchanged since filming began this morning.

"His name is Benji," I repeat.

"You mean *was*," Willa says. "Besides, I find it interesting that you, of all people, would care how I speak of him."

"What does that mean?" Rylie asks while puffing her feathers and moving closer to me.

"It's no secret how the two of them felt about each other," Willa says. "The last time she had a run-in with him, she went to jail. Or do you not remember the write-up in the newspaper? It made the front page, as I recall. Above the fold."

"This isn't the time or place, Willa," Seth warns.

"It's ironic how you immediately highlight my differences with Benji but conveniently leave out yours." I turn the focus back to her.

"I don't know what you're implying," Willa says coolly.

"When I was in school preparing to take over my aunt's business, I had a homework assignment," I tell her and the group of people now listening in. "We were tasked with studying local businesses, and I learned your taco truck wasn't always a taco truck."

She scoffs. "What's your point? Businesses adapt to the changing times."

"True, but doesn't it seem a little suspicious that after working with Benji for less than a year, you quit and opened your own hot dog truck in the next town over?"

The tent is abuzz with whispers after hearing this juicy piece of information.

"It was Polish sausages, not *hot dogs*," Willa says to the gaggle of people gossiping around her. "And it's business. Here's some free advice for you, Beth: Oftentimes in business, in politics, in Hollywood"—she widens her arms to indicate the production lot—"you have to do whatever it takes to get ahead. Benji's truck was booming, so I tested the market to see if I could replicate his success. It didn't work, and I switched to tacos. So, sue me."

"Isn't that what Benji did, though?" I ask. "Sue you? If someone plagiarized my truck, I would be furious."

Seth gives me a warning look. "That's enough, Beth."

"You know nothing," Willa says with a haughty laugh. "What went down between Benji and me is ancient history now. He never sued me. It was just talk."

"Personal differences aside, Willa, a man is dead," I say. "We owe him some respect. It's the least all of us can do."

"Beth is right," says Ben, speaking to the group. "Benji Mayhew was a fellow food truck owner, just like the rest of us. Let's honor the fallen driver by taking a moment of silence."

A few seconds later, Ben clears his throat before continuing. "A conversation about the competition and how everyone did might help us feel better."

Before Loretta or Ella Mae, owners of Porked 'n' Rubbed, can answer, the paramedics bring a sheet-covered gurney out of Benji's truck, transporting him to the back of the ambulance. We still know nothing. But I can't help wondering whether or not the argument I overheard at his truck was harmless. If it wasn't, surely the camera crews on the lot must have captured something.

Chapter Five

"Can we please leave already?" Lila complains to no one in particular. "I need to eat actual food. I'm starving."

"It's been an hour already since Héctor told us to stay put," Ula whines. "I'm exhausted and my feet hurt!"

"Those two are annoying," Rylie whispers. "But if I have to smile at one more picture of Ella Mae's cats dressed up for their latest family portrait, I'm going to chicken slap someone."

"But Cat Sajak cuts a dashing figure in a tux," I joke.

"I need food!" Lila cries.

"Food?" Reyna scoffs at her sister. "Who cares about food? I'm not leaving until I know who won."

"Guys, someone just died. How can you worry about the competition—or your stomach—at a time like this?" Ness scolds the two sisters.

"Babe, take it easy on them," says Dane, grabbing his wife's hand. "It's been a long day for everyone."

"All I'm saying is that they could be a bit more considerate and less self-centered. Someone we know just died."

Marco says something in Italian while making a cross over his chest. "Can we talk about something else instead of death?"

"Would pretending Benji didn't die make you feel better?" Ula Katapang asks. "People die suddenly every day. There are a lot of undiagnosed medical conditions."

"You don't know," Lila says. "Maybe Benji was murdered . . ."

"Nobody said anything about Benji being murdered!" Dane shouts at the group.

As Dane argues with the Katapangs, I lean over and whisper to Rylie, "Give me your phone."

"Why?" she asks, removing her phone from the side pocket of the chicken costume.

"Because my battery is almost dead." Taking her phone, I open the Notes app and begin typing, recalling the words of my favorite podcast host. "On *Murder and Mayhem*, Inga Nevarez advises that when you suspect something, write it down." With a final tap, I hand her back the phone.

Nodding her chin toward the Katapang sisters, Rylie whispers, "You suspect them? They strike me as being gossipy."

"Gossip isn't always a bad thing," I say. "Sometimes, there's truth to what's being passed around."

"Is that what you think this is?" Rylie asks.

"I'm not sure," I admit. "But I know what I heard inside his truck. And the police are here. *And* I take things seriously because of my obsession with true-crime documentaries."

She looks around the space for a moment. "It's hard to believe something like a murder would go unnoticed with this many cameras floating around."

"I agree, but—"

"Fine!" Dane shouts, ending my side conversation with Rylie. "Let's talk about something else, please."

I point at the Katapang sisters. "Do you guys sell anything like a bao bun?"

"Siopao asado," Lila answers, nodding. "They're like pork buns. Why?"

"I guess I'm hungry, and steamed buns sound amazing," I reply, motioning for Rylie's phone. I jot it down on our Kluckin' Clues list, the gears in my mind turning.

Could Benji have written a threatening note to the Katapangs—and paid for it with his life?

"How does everyone feel they did today?" Rylie asks the group.

Marco answers while grabbing the back of his neck. "Things could have gone better. If I wasn't in such a hurry while shopping. I might've remembered the basil."

"We did fine." Sofia lovingly strokes her husband's arm. "Forgetting an ingredient was more stressful than the ingredient itself."

"I hear ya," Ben agrees. "Beckett forgot to grab maple syrup." He hooks a thumb toward his youngest brother.

"How many times do I have to tell you? I didn't forget the maple syrup," Beckett snaps. "I grabbed two bottles."

"Then where were they?" Ben spreads his arms wide.

"No clue. But I bought them. I'll find the receipt and prove it."

Two other food trucks also had missing ingredients? What are the odds of that?

Just as I'm about to delve deeper, Imogen and a stocky police officer with fawn-colored skin and salt-and-pepper hair appear at the tent.

"I'm Detective Hamstead. Thank you for your patience," he says in a monotone voice. "I recognize this day must be feeling quite lengthy for all of you. My partner and I needed to check a few things."

"Can you tell us what happened?" Marco asks, clutching hands with his wife.

"Were any of you acquainted with the man?" The detective ignores Marco's question. "Perhaps outside of the show?"

Seth and I share what our parents call "our twin look." We communicate several things with our eyes, without speaking a word.

Keep your mouth shut, Beth.

But he's asking if I know him.

Don't do it.

Remaining silent is not an option when it comes to someone else's life. With a small lift of my hand, I wiggle my fingers in the air. When I look around the tent, I see Willa is keeping quiet. Why? She has a longer history with him than me. I bet she knew Benji better than anyone.

"You there." The detective points at me. "What's your name?"

"Beth Lloyd." I lower my hand.

"You, stay. The rest of you are free to leave." Detective Hamstead dismisses everyone. "We'll be in touch."

Each person leaving the tent gives me suspicious looks. Seth, Rylie, Detective Hamstead, and I are the only ones left. Approaching the three of us, the detective lifts a bushy brow at my brother and Rylie, who is still wearing the chicken suit.

"This is my brother, Seth, and my assistant, Rylie Cortes. They operate the food truck with me."

Detective Hamstead grunts in approval while he sits down across from us. He pulls out a notepad and pen from his blazer pocket and scribbles something down. "How well did you know Mr. Mayhew?" he finally asks.

"Not very," I admit. "Sometimes our paths crossed at different food truck events, but we weren't close, if that's what you mean."

"And what truck do you own?" he asks.

"Kluckin' Good."

"And these two"—he motions with his pen between my brother and Rylie—"operate the truck with you?"

"Seth is the co-owner and fills in as needed. Otherwise, it's just Rylie and me on the truck."

"The giant chicken?" He points at Rylie.

"That's Ms. Giant Chicken to you." Rylie crosses her wings over her chest.

After giving Rylie a look, the detective scribbles something on his notepad. "Were you aware of any health conditions Mr. Mayhew might have had?"

"No," I answer.

"What about you, *Ms.* Giant Chicken?"

"No."

"So, as far as you're aware, he had no underlying health conditions or anything that may have run in his family?"

I shake my head.

"Health conditions?" Seth asks.

"Just covering the basics," Detective Hamstead says while keeping his eyes fixed on me. "Do you recall anything unusual with Mr. Mayhew today?"

Seth's voice flashes as a warning in my head, telling me to keep my mouth shut. But I can't keep silent. "I overheard yelling coming from his truck earlier."

"What kind of yelling?" Detective Hamstead asks.

"It was hard to hear everything," I admit. "But I remember something like 'I caught you red-handed,' and 'You won't get away with this!'"

"And did either of you hear this?" the detective asks Seth and Rylie.

"No," Seth says. "Beth was walking ahead of me when she stopped at Benji's truck."

"What about you, *Ms.* Giant Chicken?" Detective Hamstead looks at Rylie. "Can you confirm any of this?"

"No." Rylie gives me an apologetic smile. "I was with Seth. Beth walked up to Benji's truck without us."

"Hmph." Detective Hamstead taps his pen against his notepad. "Ms. Lloyd, was there anyone else near his truck who you can recall?"

"No."

"When was the last time you spoke to Mr. Mayhew?" he asks.

I resist the urge to squirm in my folding chair. "Earlier today," I answer.

"Was this at the same time you heard yelling?"

"Yes."

Detective Hamstead adds a couple more notes. Without lifting his gaze from his notepad, he asks, "And what did the two of you discuss?"

Seth and I exchange another silent conversation with our eyes.

Keep quiet, Beth.

I'm trying.

I'm serious. Not. A. Word.

"Ms. Lloyd?" The detective is looking at me again. "Would you mind telling me what the two of you discussed?"

"Umm . . . I was just . . . checking on him."

He quirks a bushy brow at me. "Checking on him?"

"I mean, I heard him yelling," I say.

"And why were you checking on him?" he asks. "Do you normally check on people you aren't close to?"

"It's called being a good Samaritan—"

"Why are you asking us these questions?" Seth interrupts. "Can you tell us anything about what happened to Benji?"

"Right now, we're just collecting statements."

Well, that's a non-answer if I've ever heard one.

"Is there anything else?" the detective continues. "How did Mr. Mayhew appear? Did anything strike you as odd or out of the norm with him?"

"No." I shake my head again. "Benji kept to himself. Besides, we competed in a competition today. I was more interested in selling my product than monitoring my competitors."

"Except for when you heard yelling?" Detective Hamstead comments. "Then you were interested enough to check on him?"

"I don't appreciate what you're implying about my sister," Seth says, slipping into his lawyer mode. "Is there something specific you wish to discuss? If so, we can make an appointment and come down to the station."

"No need for that," the detective says. "We're just having a conversation."

"This feels like more than just a conversation," Seth says.

"Why aren't you writing down what I said?" I ask. "Benji was yelling at someone." Then I remembered: "And he dropped a note!"

"A note?"

"Yes! A note that said, 'Back off unless you want to end up like your steamed buns.' I gave it to the assistant producer, Sloane Owinski. She said she would look into it and see if it tied back to the show. Now Benji is dead after the incident with that note and after arguing with someone in his truck."

"Can you tell me who that someone was?" he asks. "Can you tell me anything? Was there someone near his truck? Did Mr. Mayhew look distressed? Because right now, there doesn't seem to be much to what you're claiming. For all you know, Mr. Mayhew could have been listening to a radio—"

"I know what I heard!" I interrupt him. "Benji was yelling at someone and now he's dead! You're a detective. You can't tell me that doesn't seem suspicious."

"Ms. Lloyd." Detective Hamstead offers me a sympathetic look. "I can understand that today has been an emotionally draining day for you—"

"This has nothing to do with being emotionally drained." It's a struggle to keep myself restrained. "I know what I heard. I'm not making it up."

"You mean what you think you heard," the detective corrects me. "You said yourself the competition was keeping you preoccupied."

"Being preoccupied doesn't mean I'm oblivious to someone shouting."

"Mr. Mayhew might have been on the phone."

"Do you normally shout at people on the phone and say things like 'you won't get away with this'?" I ask.

"Yes, specifically when I'm having a conversation with my mother-in-law." The detective briefly pauses, possibly recalling said mother-in-law.

"If you don't believe me, check the cameras," I suggest.

"Cameras?"

"This is a TV show lot," I say. "There had to be a camera somewhere."

Detective Hamstead scans our faces briefly before giving a strained smile. "Thank you for your time." He stands, returning the notepad and pen to his pocket. "Either my partner or I will be in touch with you if we require additional information. Have a nice day."

"I guess that means we're free to leave?" Rylie asks, looking around the now-empty tent.

"He didn't believe me," I say. "How could he just disregard what I heard? Or that note?"

Seth gives my shoulder a squeeze. "It's not your fault, Beth. You told him what you know."

"This doesn't feel right," I say. "When Aunt Dolly passed away, we didn't face such intense questioning. And that note . . . if only you had seen it. It was creepy, with hand-cut letters pasted to the paper. It was trying to send a message."

Now I'm wondering if that message was *to* Benji and not *from* Benji.

"I agree." Seth stands up from his chair and scans the area. "The police wouldn't be so thorough if this wasn't serious. Both of you, but especially you, Beth"—Seth points a finger in my face—"*say nothing* to anyone about Benji."

"Why especially *me* and not her?" I gesture with my thumb toward Rylie.

"Because you have a condition known as 'Diarrhea of the Mouth.'"

It doesn't matter. Clearly the police don't believe anything I have to say.

Imogen walks into the tent, ending our conversation. Her green mohawk is a welcome sight. "How are you doing?"

"I don't know," I say with a shrug.

"Given the circumstances, I guess that's to be expected." She attempts a smile, but it comes off more like a grimace. "Production is requiring everyone to either go home or go back to your hotel and return tomorrow afternoon at two."

"Why then?" I ask.

"We need to let the police wrap up."

"Is the show going to continue?" Rylie asks.

"I can't answer that. A contestant died. We're all in uncharted territory here." Clearing her throat, she shakes her head. "If you'll excuse me, I need to inform next of kin about his truck and who they need to contact."

"He didn't have any family," I say.

When I'd first met Benji at a food truck night, I'd asked about his family. I was trying to be polite and thought we could be work friends. He was clear that he neither had nor wanted any family and told me to keep my intrusive questions to myself.

Imogen pushes her tortoiseshell glasses up her petite nose, giving her a clear view. "Even so, I still have some calls to make. You're free to take your truck or leave it on our lot. Just a heads up, the security cameras are experiencing some issues. Whatever you choose, please return tomorrow afternoon at two o'clock to hear the announcement." Imogen steps aside to talk with the tow truck driver who'd arrived to pick up The Dog House.

Chapter Six

The following day, it's a few minutes to two when Rylie and I pull into the lot, and only three other teams are here. Fettuccine Bartolini, Dough Brothers, and Chowder Bowl on the Roll are all parked neatly along the back fence. Seth is already here, leaning against the side of his car and talking on his phone. We park near the other trucks, exit, and cross the parking lot to meet my brother.

"How was your shift?" Seth asks as he tucks his phone into his front pocket.

"It was good. We had a few new customers." Since there was no filming, there was no point in missing a shift.

"So Rylie's idea worked?" he asks.

"What is that supposed to mean?" Rylie scowls at Seth, her hands on her hips. "I have some pretty good marketing ideas."

"Calm down, *irmã*." I smile, throwing her own words back at her. "He wasn't implying anything."

Rylie had come up with a brilliant idea! As soon as we'd found out our team was selected to compete on *The Food Truck Showdown*, she'd wasted no time and had flyers and a life-size cutout of Bobbi Taylor made to promote our truck. We began advertising for this season as soon as the network did.

I can't help noticing how the energy in the parking lot feels different compared to yesterday. Yesterday had marked the start of a new season, and the air had crackled with excitement. Cameras were in position, sound equipment was undergoing the last tests, and the production crew set the stage for the chaos to unfold. If only we'd known how chaotic things would get just hours later. Benji's death casts a depressing energy over the film crew as they complete tests and equipment checks for the announcement of the show's fate.

"Where should we go?" Rylie asks as she steps around a director sprinting past, his headset pressed against his ear as he double-checks details on a clipboard.

My stomach grumbles, reminding me I missed lunch to be here on time. "The refreshment tent. I'm starved."

Once we're inside the tent, I head straight for the snack table and snatch an apple. As I munch, I grab some other snacks and realize we're not the only ones here.

"What do you think is going on over there?" I nod to the group of contestants tucked away in the back corner.

"Whatever it is," Seth says, surveying the tent, "has them deep in conversation."

He's right. The entire group is sitting in a close circle, engrossed in a hushed conversation. Ness Jaxson and Sofia Bartolini are leaning their heads close together, whispering. They're so absorbed in their conversation that they haven't even noticed we're in the tent with them.

"*Vamos!*" Rylie says to us, her eyes brimming with curiosity. "I've got a feeling there might be some juicy gossip about Benji floating around here," she whispers, her eyes darting to the huddled drivers.

I agree at the same time Seth says no.

"Why not?" I whisper. "Don't you want to know what's going on?"

"Not really." He twists the top off a water bottle.

"Well, too bad!" I grab his hand as Rylie follows, and we move closer to the contestants absorbed in their conversation. Moving deeper inside, we stick close to the food and drink stations. To avoid attracting attention, we prepare ourselves coffee and plates of food without facing the huddled group. Quietly, we edge closer, eavesdropping.

"I'm curious how the producers will avoid featuring a dead body in the show," Dane Jaxson says.

"Maybe they won't even use the footage from yesterday's challenge," Ben Quill replies. "Or edit Benji out altogether. That's the beauty of filmography. You can delete what you don't want."

"I heard Benji was acting strangely during the competition," Dane's wife, Ness, says, casting furtive glances around. "He seemed aggressive."

He was always aggressive.

"Paranoid maybe," Ness continues. "Perhaps he thought someone was out to get him?"

Benji was a lot of things, but I never considered him paranoid. *And* who *would be out to get him?*

"Out to get him? Who would do that?" Sofia voices what I was just thinking.

"According to a showrunner I spoke with, Benji's casting was surprising," Ness says. "The showrunner claimed the executives felt Benji's vibe didn't mesh with everyone else. Maybe that's why he was murdered."

"What do you mean 'murdered'?" Sofia's husband, Marco, asks.

Chancing a look over my shoulder at them, I realize they still haven't noticed us. Spotting a garbage can near them, I quietly walk over and toss my wrappers, edging closer until I'm nearly upon them.

"We can't assume that," Marco continues.

"Think about it," Ness says, looking at Marco. "If his death was an accident, why would the police have questioned Dane and me?"

Ness folds her arms. "The detective said they were just gathering statements, but I've seen enough mysteries to know that's code for murder."

Marco mumbles as he makes a cross over his chest.

"Besides," Ness whispers, making me strain to hear. "I saw one of the Katapang sisters sneaking around his truck on the pier, and Benji caught her."

Sofia gasps, a hand flying to her chest. I can't tell if her reaction to Ness is because of gossip or genuine concern. "Then what happened?"

Gossip it is.

"Benji started swearing when he noticed his back door ajar and chased her away. He was shouting that he better never catch her snooping around his truck again or she'd be sorry."

Sofia shakes her head. "I can't believe he would say such a thing."

I can.

"If the sisters were really in his truck, there should be a recording of the incident, right? What do you think they were doing?" Marco's wife, Sofia, asks.

"If I had to guess, snooping," Ness says.

"What would that accomplish?" Sofia asks.

"Who knows what their reason was?" Ness shrugs. "When Benji approached, he found them next to his open back door. Maybe they went in, and maybe they didn't. All I can tell you is that Benji was furious and threatened them. If that isn't a motive, then I don't know what is. I said as much to the handsome, er"—Ness cuts her eyes to Dane, who raises an eyebrow at his wife—"I mean, to the detective."

Detective Hamstead handsome*? Barfff.*

Seth leans in close behind Ness and whispers to her. "That doesn't prove motive."

"Seth!" Ness jumps a little while Dane snickers over her reaction. "I didn't hear the three of you." She smacks her husband on the arm. "Stop laughing at me. He scared me."

"That's what you get for gossiping," Dane says, still chuckling.

"We didn't mean to scare you, Ness. We just got here." I mentally caution myself to be careful of what I say around her. "But how did you know Benji caught them with his door open? Did you see any of this?"

"It's not like I was eavesdropping," Ness says, defending herself. "While returning to our truck from a bathroom break, I witnessed Benji pointing at one of the sisters. He was yelling and carrying on about staying away from his truck."

"What did you do when you saw this?" Seth asks.

"I stepped to the side behind a tree to listen," Ness says.

"So, you were eavesdropping?" Sofia asks.

"No!" Ness shouts but quickly stops herself. "I wanted to make sure everything was all right. Competitions like these are stressful, and misunderstandings can quickly get out of hand."

Is that what happened with Benji? A misunderstanding gone wrong?

"What did the police say when you told them this?" I ask, wondering if Ness got the same brush off as me.

"Not much. The detective thanked me for sharing the information with him, then he left," Ness says.

"He said they would be in touch if there were further questions," Dane adds. "But I don't see what else there is for us to tell."

"Did they say what they think happened?" Marco asks.

"Nope." Ness shakes her head. "But I'm telling you, something isn't adding up. I've seen my fair share of murder mystery movies, and I can tell when the police are hunting for something more significant."

"There are two of you," Seth says, looking at me.

"What?" Ness asks.

"Nothing," I say, ignoring Seth's jab at my true-crime obsession. "Have you heard anything about the status of the show?" I ask the group.

"Not yet," Marco answers. "I don't suspect we will until everyone gets here." He checks his watch, making a tsk sound. "It's ten after two. Where is everyone?"

Marco strikes me as someone who values time and expects the same from others. We're still waiting for Nacho Momma's Tacos, and Lumpia-Licious to arrive.

"I still wonder how they'll deal with a dead contestant," Dane says. "I can't see them cutting Benji out. His death is going to be great for ratings."

"Dane!" Ness slaps his shoulder.

"Ouch!" he says, rubbing at the spot she hit. "What was that for?"

"How could you be so morbid? A man just died."

"I'm not trying to be macabre. I'm just saying that his death will leave the audience craving more. The producers won't remove something that enticing."

"This is too much!" Mumbling in Italian, Marco crosses his chest.

"Are y'all talkin' about Benji?" Ella Mae asks as she and her partner, Loretta, join our gossiping cluster. "Such a sad way to go, alone in your food truck."

"Poor man. He was a rooster one day and a feather duster the next," Loretta drawls.

I'm not entirely sure what she means, but I nod in agreement.

Loretta and Ella Mae are lively, gregarious older women. I'm discovering that Ella Mae has a keen sense of observation, while Loretta has a sharp tongue.

"What do you think they'll decide for the show?" Dane asks, squeezing his wife's shoulder. "I would hate to have to leave after one challenge. This wasn't a close drive for us."

"Nor us," Marco says. "We can't afford to turn around and go back home to Oregon so quickly. Besides the travel costs, we also had to pay for someone to manage our restaurant. Coming here was a bit of a gamble for us."

"We're fellow Oregonians too!" Dane tells Marco. "We don't have a restaurant like you, but we had to give up our regular spot at Portland's food truck market. It's terrible that Benji died, but we can't just leave. The financial loss would be too great."

Sympathizing with the Jaxsons' situation, Marco nods. If the show gets canceled, it won't hurt us like it would them.

"Is it *that* detrimental for us to cut our losses and leave?" I ask. "People are suspicious that Benji was murdered by someone here." I look around at the production crew milling about, then at the small group of participants before continuing. "We've already received advertising benefits to be grateful for."

"Don't take this the wrong way," Ness prefaces, "but are you genuinely concerned, or are you just trying to avoid getting caught due to your past with Benji?"

Wow! Is she suggesting what I think she's suggesting?

Ness puts her hand up. "Look, I don't know you, but I did some research on what went down between you and Benji after Willa mentioned it. A news article stated the police apprehended you for allegedly assaulting his truck."

"The police dropped those charges," Seth tells her. "I take offense to your suggestion that my sister has done something nefarious—"

"Seth, it's fine," I stop him. "People will think what they want. All that matters is I know the truth."

And if that means I must clear my name, I will!

Nacho Momma's Tacos interrupts our conversation with the cheerful sounds of mariachi music as the truck pulls into the lot, with Lumpia-Licious following behind. As soon as the music ends, Willa plays the lively tune again. At that moment, Imogen arrives asking us to move to the stage area.

Bobbi Taylor is sitting in a white director's chair on the stage, waiting for her cue, as a makeup artist perfects her look. She effortlessly rocks the business casual attire, something I could never do. The contrast between her white button-down top, dark skinny jeans, and shiny black pumps is perfect. With a thumbs-up from the makeup artist, the set director starts the countdown for filming. The crew members take their positions. The moment Bobbi stands, a stagehand promptly removes the chair, and the cameras roll, capturing every breathless moment.

"A terrible thing happened here yesterday," Bobbi says. "Benji Mayhew, owner of The Dog House, died. We will always remember him as a bold competitor."

It isn't until I wrinkle my nose slightly over her statement that I find a camera pointing right at me. In a split second, I change my wrinkled nose into a sniffle, hoping to appear solemn, but the camera has already shifted its focus. I'm definitely getting cast as the villain.

"We had a big decision to make, folks. Should we continue with the showdown, or should we end it right here? Before I share the network's decision, I would like to hear from you."

In a matter of seconds, multiple people shout their answers. Bobbi acknowledges a few of them before calling on Porked 'n' Rubbed owner Loretta Able. "I reckon we honor Benji by continuing the race." The camera crew does a slow spin, capturing the round of applause for her comment.

Bobbi asks Marco Bartolini of Fettuccine Bartolini for his answer. "We should continue! Benji wouldn't want us to stop." The applause over his words is deafening.

We weren't close, but I'm certain Benji would be indifferent to the show going on.

"All right." Bobbi smiles at all of us. "I would like to see a show of hands. Everyone who would like to continue, please raise your hand."

The crowd bursts into cheers after a majority vote in favor of continuing.

"We hear your answer." Bobbi turns up her dazzling smile even brighter for the cameras. "Now for ours." She pauses, the tension rises, and I suspect they will add suspenseful music during editing to this part. "The show will continue!" Loud cheers break out, and Bobbi has to bring the crowd back under control. "However, we had to make some unexpected changes in how this season will continue."

After a brief exchange of confused looks and whispers, someone speaks up and asks, "What do you mean?"

Bobbi glances to her left, where the stage director is standing. She gestures to him, and he shouts, "Cut!"

A clapboard snaps and the cameras stop recording.

"The police are looking into a few things regarding the sudden death of Mr. Mayhew—"

Ness Jaxson, one of the owners of Chowder Bowl on the Roll, cuts Bobbi off. "Tell us what's going on! How did Benji die?"

"Is it safe for us to continue?" Marco expresses his concerns.

"Of course it's safe for you to be here." Bobbi gazes at him in disbelief. "Why would you ask such a thing?"

"Then why are the police looking into things?" Marco asks.

"I heard Benji was acting strangely before he died," Ness adds. "Is that why he was murdered?"

"Let's pause for a minute." Bobbi raises her hands to silence the grousing crowd. "The cause of death hasn't been confirmed yet. According to the police, this is standard procedure following someone's death. We are in full cooperation with the local authorities. The paramedics said it appeared that Benji Mayhew had a heart attack. So, there's no need to panic. No more wild rumors. The show can go on, and the show will go on! For Benji!" With a triumphant gesture, Bobbi raises her fist.

Her words have a calming effect on everyone, and her speech generates more cheers and applause. "To best assist the Clementine Police Department, we will remain in the local area for the duration of the season. Therefore, we will *not* be traveling to Arizona."

There's an audible gasp. None of us expected this. "Despite the sudden change in our plans, we still need to accommodate the schedule already set by the network, which means there will be more off days from filming," Bobbi adds.

"What does that mean for us?" Ben Quill asks. "What are we to do with more off days? And where will we stay?"

Bobbi is all business as she answers his questions. "Permits are being arranged for those of you who live outside of California. This will allow you to sell your food when the show isn't filming." A sigh of relief washes over the drivers. "We understand this is your livelihood and you were not expecting to have a curveball like this thrown at you. You can operate your trucks outside of the show if you choose. Any of you who are staying in hotels will remain there for the duration of filming, courtesy of *The Food Truck Showdown*."

Bobbi waits for everyone to process the news. "Now, I'm sure all of you are wondering who was the winner of the fish-and-chips challenge and who will be advancing. But before I share the results, I want to congratulate everyone on completing the first challenge. You should be proud." Bobbi, Imogen, and a few other staff members are the only ones to clap.

Reyna Katapang raises her hand. "What do you mean? Is one of us going home?"

Bobbi scoffs. "Please don't tell me you assumed that because Benji died, the rest of you would be safe?"

"But someone has already been eliminated. Literally," Reyna says.

Her comment elicits gasps from everyone. I can't argue with her statement, but that doesn't mean she should have said it out loud.

"This is a competition. We can't all be winners," Bobbi says in a matter-of-fact manner. She glances at the director once more and gives a nod.

"Roll 'em!" he shouts and the clapboard snaps again.

"Now, I have the results of the fish-and-chips challenge. Does anyone want to hear who won the first challenge?"

The crowd gives an unenthusiastic cheer. "I can't hear you." Bobbi cups her ear with one hand. "Does anyone want to hear the *good* news?"

The audience responds, with Rylie at the forefront, shouting, "Yes!" directly into my right ear. I pop my jaw and massage my ear. I'm not sure I'll ever be able to hear out of it properly again.

"Much better." Imogen hands Bobbi a large envelope that she tears open and scans. "Congratulations to Chowder Bowl on the Roll! Your team was the first to sell twenty orders of fish-and-chips! For winning this side challenge, your team will receive a set of Renaissance Chef's Knives for your truck."

A round of applause breaks out as Dane pumps his fist in the air, grinning like he's just won the lottery.

Imogen hands Bobbi another envelope. "And now for the team who was the overall winner of this week's challenge." Bobbi rips open the second envelope with practiced flair, her eyes scanning the paper. "Oh, how interesting . . ."

"What is it? What's it say?" The suspense overwhelms Marco, leading him to shout out his questions.

"The winner of this week's challenge is . . . The Dog House." Lowering the paper, Bobbi looks at the contestants. "Since The Dog House cannot proceed, the alternate winner, having come in second place with the highest sales, is Chowder Bowl on the Roll!"

Ness lets out a delighted squeal and jumps into her husband's arms, their joy uncontainable after just winning two challenges. They receive congratulations from Bobbi, a smattering of polite applause, and tight smiles from the other contestants.

I'm happy for Dane and Ness. They've worked hard. Still, it's hard to ignore the sting of disappointment. Not winning either challenge feels like a gut punch, especially because I was hoping to impress this week. That's okay. There's always the next round.

"Again, we can't all be winners. The team that scored the lowest is . . ."

I brace for the bad news that our time on the wagon trail has come to an end.

"Lumpia-Licious."

Whew.

"However . . ." Bobbi's pause adds tension to the already anxious crowd.

Uh-oh.

"Lumpia-Licious, you are receiving a one-time free pass because of the unusual nature of this season and unexpected occurrences. If you want to avoid being sent home in the next round, I suggest you step up your game."

Can someone help me get off this emotional roller coaster?

"In other words," Bobbi says with a smile, "you're all advancing to the next round!"

Cameras swing around the area, capturing every facial expression and nuance, waiting for a reaction. There's a sudden understanding among the audience, and a loud cheer breaks out. Rylie jumps up and down, making chicken-like squawks as if ready to take flight. Her unexpected hug almost knocks my brother down.

Bobbi raises her voice above the cheers, calling out to Dane and Ness. "As the winners of today's challenge, you will receive a custom cooking set."

A set that would have gone to Benji if he were still alive.

Slipping the envelope and papers under her arm, Bobbi claps once more for everyone. "Go home and celebrate"—she points dramatically at a camera—"and we'll see all of you next week!"

"Cut!" the director yells as the clapboard slaps. The cameras halt, and Bobbi strides purposefully off stage.

We stand idly and exchange uncertain looks on what to do next, when Imogen Comestible replaces Bobbi onstage. "This must be a surprise for all of you," she says sympathetically. "We have a few last-minute things to sort out, specifically transitioning from a traveling show to a local one. Bear with us as we tackle these issues, and join us again on this lot on Friday morning at nine."

My hand shoots up in the air. "Yes, Beth?"

"Will we be remaining at this location?" I ask, lowering my hand.

"Is that a problem?"

"What about the faulty security cameras?" My question immediately elicits grumbles and concerns from my fellow competitors. "Should we film in a place with malfunctioning equipment?"

"Is there a guarantee that our personal property will remain safe on this lot?" Marco asks.

"Okay, everyone," Imogen says as she tries to soothe the worried group of contestants. "Everything will be fine. Clementine is a safe town. Just ask the Lloyd siblings." She motions to Seth and me. "Plus, another technician from Wiz Tech will inspect the cameras tomorrow. By Friday, they should be fully operational and functioning with no issues."

Despite the ongoing grumbling and exchanged looks, nobody offers any further comments. "All right, everyone, let's reconvene here on Friday," Imogen says before leaving the stage.

As the crew and other contestants depart, I say to Seth and Rylie, "This doesn't sit well with me."

"What doesn't?" Seth asks.

"Aunt Dolly." I chew my bottom lip. "She died from a heart attack."

Seth nods, our twin bond taking over. "That was open and shut. The police didn't linger or question everyone."

Exactly.

Then why *are* the police investigating things here?

Something is most certainly afoot.

Chapter Seven

Pulling up to the set Friday morning, I see the production crew has been busy. The parking lot we used over the past weekend had a gate and an old warehouse. The filming equipment was designed for the road, including RVs, buses, and cars. You name it; it traveled. Today, there's a security check booth, two places to get refreshments, and various areas with tables and chairs. A temporary trailer has replaced the network-branded RV bus. There's also a portable restroom. Not porta-potties. I'm talking about the fancy bathroom trailers with flushing toilets. The type of luxury bathroom trailer reserved for top movie industry professionals.

I feel Seth's breath on my neck as I turn the wheel and approach the Dough Brothers truck. "Careful. You don't want to clip their side mirror."

"You never drive the truck," I say, putting the truck in park. "Plus, you declined my offer to practice driving it." Unbuckling, I roll my eyes at Rylie. "That means you also forfeit the right to comment on my driving."

"That's not how being a backseat driver works."

"Rylie, please make a note of the day and time for me," I say to my assistant.

"Sure." She pulls out her phone. "What's this for?"

"I want to remember the date my little brother admitted he was wrong and is a backseat driver."

"I never said I was wrong."

Rylie taps a few times on her smartphone. "October 23rd, Seth Lloyd admits he is a backseat driver and a pain in his sister's you-know-what."

"I never said that!" Seth snaps as I laugh.

"It was implied." Rylie blows him a kiss as she gets out of the truck.

Their behavior is erratic; they argue like children one moment, then stare at each other as if they're in love. *They're not, but I should call a meeting to discuss employee conduct.*

As we make our way through the parked vehicles, a high-pitched shriek sounds from Chowder Bowl on the Roll.

Ness collides with me as she runs down the truck's steps, knocking me to the ground. Dane helps us up while apologizing. "Sorry, Beth. She's a little upset."

"Upset?" Ness spins around, poking her husband in his chest. "I have every right to be 'upset.'" She says the word using air quotes. "I'm on my way to lodge a formal complaint." Waving a crumpled piece of paper in the air, she stalks off.

"What was that about?" Seth asks Dane.

"We received our prize box of custom cookware, and Ness wanted to see them right away."

"Did she not like the color or something?" Rylie asks as we walk in the direction Ness is heading.

"The color was fine. It's what was inside that's the problem."

"What do you mean?" I'm trying to imagine what was in the box that would rattle her.

"There was a silly little note inside. I told her it was nothing to worry about, but she doesn't agree."

"I don't understand?" Seth says. "Was it a note about the cookware?"

"No . . ." Dane says, grabbing the back of his neck. "It was something else."

"Why are you being so cagey about this?" I ask him. "Are you uncomfortable with what the note said?"

"It doesn't bother me, but Ness has been a little high-strung lately. I think she's making too much fuss about it. All it said was 'Piss off' in block-style letters."

Block-style letters . . .

"Can I see what it looks like?" I'm trying not to seem too interested.

"Ness has it," Dane says.

"What did it look like?" I ask. "What do you mean by block letters?"

"I don't know." This conversation is making Dane agitated, and he squeezes the back of his neck again. "It looked like someone cut and pasted them onto the paper."

"That sounds creepy, like something a serial killer might do," Rylie says.

"Whoa!" Dane holds up his hands. "Serial killer is a bit of a jump, don't you think?"

"I don't know," I say. On *Murder and Mayhem*, Inga Nevarez always stresses the importance of paying attention to the smallest details. "Given what happened to Benji, I'm not sure I would blow that off as just a silly little note."

"But Bobbi said Benji's cause of death was a heart attack," Dane says. "That's why the show is continuing."

"Maybe," I say. "But what Bobbi actually said was the paramedics said it appeared that Benji had a heart attack. Either way, what you found in your box sounds like a threat." I pull out my phone and begin typing. "What do you think it meant?"

"We didn't know," Dane says. "Then when we removed the lid, we saw yellow liquid swimming at the bottom of the pan."

I automatically put my hand over my mouth without thinking. My gag reflex is strong, and what Dane just shared makes me want to vomit.

"That's revolting," I say, a little louder than I mean to.

"I'm pretty sure it was sour lemonade." Dane shrugs as if to say "What can you do?" "Like I told Ness, it's best that we not make a big deal of it." Looking to the left, he catches sight of her standing with Imogen. Unfortunately for Imogen, it looks more like Ness is talking at her rather than with her. "I gotta go," he says and jogs over to the two women.

Mumbling "piss off," I complete my notes.

If Benji had been alive to win the cooking set, would the same thing have happened to him?

"Are you seriously getting involved in this?" Seth asks.

"I'm not getting involved in anything." I shove my phone into my pocket. "There's nothing wrong with keeping detailed notes. On *Murder and Mayhem*, Inga Nevarez always says—"

"Not that true-crime podcast again." Seth shakes his head. "This is the real world, not an amateur sleuthing case, Beth."

"And that is why I added Rylie to my shared note list and not you." I raise my chin toward him. "She values the process and understands that having more information than needed is essential."

"She's right," Rylie agrees. "Plus, we're thinking of cowriting a book. This kind of thing creates great tension in mysteries."

"Cowriting a book?" Seth shakes his head again. "You can't be serious about this."

"Of course we are!" Rylie says.

"Let's not ignore the rumors circulating about my contentious relationship with Benji."

"Are they rumors if they're true?" Seth asks.

I tap my foot, unamused. "The note described by Dane matches the note Benji dropped in the store. If that note is linked to Benji's death, I'll uncover it! So, if you'll excuse us," I say, linking my arm with Rylie's, "we need to eavesdrop."

We creep up from behind, with Seth trailing us. He may deny it, but I think he enjoys drama. Ness is flailing her arms while shouting, "This is unacceptable!"

"I'm not sure what to make of this." Imogen tucks the note into her pocket.

"We're being targeted because we won the challenge. What are you going to do about someone vandalizing our cookware?"

"I understand you're upset—"

"UPSET?!"

I rub my ear as I pop my jaw again. I'm still recovering from Rylie yelling directly into it during the first challenge's results announcement, and Ness's shriek is loud enough for every dog in a four-block radius to hear.

"And you have every right to be upset," Imogen says, ignoring her outburst and continuing. "I assure you, I'll look into what happened."

Dane rubs a small circle on his wife's back to soothe her and asks Imogen, "Any idea who would've done this?" With a catlike motion, Ness bats his hand away as if toying with a peacock's feather.

"I don't." Imogen runs a few fingers along her green mohawk. "But I'll ask my assistant, Sergio. He delivered the box to you."

"No, he didn't," Ness says in a clipped tone. "The box was waiting for us on the ground next to our front tire. I saw it when I went back to the truck."

"You must be mistaken." Imogen shakes her head. "I told Sergio to hand the box directly to you."

"I think I would know if someone handed me a box of cookware." Ness impatiently taps her foot. "No one handed us anything."

"How would someone get urine into a sealed box?" I ask openly, coming out of hiding. "Are you sure that's what it was?"

"Oh, trust me." Ness gives a hollow laugh. "I know what urine smells like."

"Babe"—Dane looks at his wife—"your sense of smell has been a little off. It was sour lemonade."

Ness stomps her foot. "The point is, we're victims of vandalism!"

"The box wasn't sealed." Imogen ignores Ness and answers my question. "Bobbi handpicked the items herself. The collection included pots, pans, baking dishes, and mixing bowls. She selected the pieces while I was with her. After tucking the flaps together, I handed the box over to Sergio."

"Who did not give us the box." Ness crosses her arms as she looks down her nose at Imogen.

"Could I see the note?" I ask, hoping she's distracted enough to not notice my nosiness.

"Here." Imogen fishes the paper from her pocket.

"This note," I say, staring at the paper.

"What about it?" Dane asks.

I look up at them. "It's exactly like the one Benji dropped at the grocery store on the day of the first competition."

"Are you sure about that?" Imogen says, taking the note back from me.

"What did it say again?" Rylie asks.

"'Back off unless you want to end up like your steamed buns,'" I say.

"I'm sure you're mistaken—" Imogen starts, then is distracted by a black Tesla with tinted windows driving onto the lot.

"Hand-cut letters pasted onto paper aren't common outside of serial killers," I say. "Trust me, I know what I saw. I showed it to Sloane, who agreed it looked threatening. She told me she was going to investigate and take appropriate action if necessary."

"Today is the first I'm hearing about any threatening notes in circulation," she says. "I'll see what's going on."

"Has anyone checked the cameras?" I ask.

"What cameras?" Imogen looks perplexed.

"What do you mean?" I laugh. "You can't go anywhere in this place without being on camera. It's hard for me to believe that someone didn't capture what happened."

"Cameras aren't rolling yet," Imogen says. "If we aren't filming, there's nothing being recorded."

"What about security cameras?" Rylie asks. "There has to be a security camera somewhere."

"There is," I say. "Remember, James was working on them the other day. If I'm not mistaken, Imogen, you told us they would be fixed by now. Could you look at them and see if they caught anything?"

"The cameras are still being worked on," she says.

"You promised they would be completely functional once filming started again today."

"Correction," Imogen says. "I said they *should* be fully operational, with no issues. I didn't say they *would* be. These things can take time."

"Can't you check the other cameras?" I ask.

Imogen shakes her head. "To my knowledge, there are only two CCTV cameras. Both are on the warehouse building."

"How is it possible for a property this big to have only two cameras?" I ask.

"Maybe there are more," Imogen says. "But I've only noticed the two on the warehouse, and they're still glitching. Besides, if anything happened to the food trucks, those cameras wouldn't have caught it anyway. The refreshment tent and production trailer are blocking the cameras." Imogen's phone dings. Pausing momentarily, she takes out her phone to read the message before quickly returning it to her pocket. "There's a technician from Wiz Tech here trying to troubleshoot the issues. Hopefully, we'll find some solutions soon."

Seth and I exchange a glance.

"Keep in mind, the network is renting this site," Imogen continues. "State-of-the-art facilities equipped with around-the-clock cameras come at a hefty price. A price that's out of our production budget. We picked this place for that very reason." She gestures around the parking lot and toward the old warehouse building. "We didn't care if there were a few broken cameras. It was both affordable and available." She checks the time on her watch before continuing. "The only way to get the warehouse's CCTV footage is by requesting it from the property owner. I'll talk with our security guard, Héctor. Maybe he saw something. In the meantime, we'll get you a replacement set," she tells Ness. "Help yourself to some snacks. We'll begin filming in a few minutes."

Imogen leaves before Ness can argue, and we follow her advice and get a snack, leaving the Jaxsons quarreling with each other.

The aroma of freshly brewed coffee and sweet pastries wafts through the air, greeting me. The film crew has adorned the tent with white-and-blue decorations, adding a touch of elegance to the parking lot setting. A tempting spread of snacks and refreshments is meticulously arranged on tables. It's almost enough to distract me from the threatening note.

"*Two* threatening notes," I say aloud to myself, and Rylie and Seth exchange a glance.

"What about them?" Seth asks, grabbing a coffee with two creamers for himself.

"It just seems odd that there are two of them." I fix a coffee and grab the last sugar doughnut.

"But you don't know what happened with the note Benji dropped," my brother points out.

"True." I bite my doughnut. "But I'm going to find out."

"How?" Seth asks as we approach the area where some of our fellow competitors are seated.

"I'll ask Sloane."

Walking over, I observe the group of drivers. Lila Katapang is speaking loudly enough for everyone to hear. "Have you heard about what happened to Dane and Ness?"

"No, what?" Sofia eagerly asks.

"Whaddya talking about?" I ask around a mouthful of doughnut.

"Someone peed on the gift set they won," Lila tells the group, all too happily.

"Eww." Sofia scrunches her nose. "Why would someone do that?"

"Dane said it was sour lemonade," I correct Lila.

She shrugs a shoulder at me. "Either way, I think someone is jealous they won." Lila casts a suspicious glance around the tent.

Willa snorts while casually sipping her beverage. "And who are you? Little Miss Detective?"

Willa is a full-figured woman, and today she opted to wear too much makeup and too little clothing, paired with a set of red cowboy boots and a matching hat. If this is her plan to drum up more business, it's working. I certainly can't take my eyes off her gaudy ensemble.

Lila's mouth falls open. "I'm sorry for wanting to have a serious conversation about what's happening here. My sisters and I aren't here for fame and fortune like you. We want to create a reputation for ourselves."

"If you're going for the reputation of 'gossiping trio,' then bravo!" Willa salutes with her paper cup.

The Katapangs respond in their native Tagalog, firing off their replies.

"All right, everyone," Sofia interrupts. "No need to get upset with each other. We're a television family, after all."

Family is a bit of a stretch, but I get her point.

"What do you think is happening around here?" I ask the sisters.

"Someone dies, and now trucks are being vandalized—"

"I think 'vandalized' is too strong a word," Seth says to Lila.

"You say that now," she says. "When a vicious attack comes your way, let's see if you sing the same tune."

"Now hold on a minute—"

Sofia reaches out to touch his arm. "Seth," she says, "despite being in a competition, it's important to work together. Let's not get too upset."

"It must be sweet living in a naive bubble," Willa replies to Sofia. "Here's something important for everyone to remember. Unless you want your reputation to be that of an ass, never assume." After taking a long sip from her cup, she and her daughter, Bria, leave the tent.

"Good riddance to bad trash," Ula says to her sisters. "Understanding things requires a good gossip session. Take the note the Jaxsons received, for example—"

"How do you know about that?" I cut her off. "It's been less than ten minutes."

"We were by our truck when Dane told you what happened," Ula answers.

"I don't recall seeing your truck parked next to Chowder Bowl on the Roll." My comment is more of an accusation than a statement.

Have the Katapang sisters been snooping around the lot? I mean, sure, that's what I'm doing. But my reason is because Detective Hamstead doubted me when I told him about both the threatening note and Benji's outburst in his truck. What reasons do the Katapangs have?

"We're parked on the other side of them," Ula says.

"Yeah," Reyna agrees. "Not our fault you were too busy laying on your backside in front of Chowder Bowl on the Roll to notice us."

"Ness burst out of their truck like a charging warhorse, flattening me, and—"

Sofia interrupts my defense. "Ladies, arguing with each other won't accomplish anything. We should focus on the note."

"We got one of those notes too, and you don't see us carrying on like drama queens," Bryan Quill adds.

"That's not fair," Ben says to his brother. "We didn't have someone take a leak in our cookware."

"Again, sour lemonade," I say, taking the empty seat next to Ben. "And you got one of those notes too? What did it say?"

"Yep." Ben nods at me. "It told us 'Watch your steps. You're close to getting deep fried like your doughnuts.'"

"It was creepy," Bryan says.

"Creepy how?" I ask, even though I have an idea. Cradling the warm cup between my palms, I subtly glance at Rylie. Reading my thoughts, she takes out her phone to jot down notes.

"It looked like letters were cut from a magazine and stuck to the page," Bryan says.

Just like Dane and Ness's note. And Benji's.

"What do you suppose it meant?" Rylie asks.

Bryan taps his finger against his chin. "My guess is that it's a prank meant to scare us."

"Whoever wrote it will have to come up with something more creative than that, considering I grew up with these two lunkheads." Ben playfully shoves his brothers.

Things are amiss. Whatever is going on is more than just pranks—it's borderline sinister. I think someone is trying to manipulate their competitors by using psychological attacks.

But would someone kill to win this competition?

Before I can delve deeper into this line of thought, Sloane appears out of nowhere. She gestures for everyone to follow her to the stage.

"Hey!" I spring up from my folding chair and hurry over to her. "I have a quick question."

"No time," she says, walking at a brisk clip.

"It'll only take a second," I huff, trying to keep up. I have to double my strides as her long legs eat up the pavement from the refreshment tent to the stage area.

"Maybe later," she says, pulling away from me just as a showrunner guides me to the seating section.

Taking my seat, I observe as the crew sets up the cameras and the director gives orders.

"Any luck?" Rylie asks, taking the seat next to me.

"Nope," I mutter, watching the boom operator approach Bobbi. Above her, the microphone hovers just out of the shot. The operator must have some serious upper body strength and stamina to hold the boom for such extended periods of time.

"I'll try to talk with her before we leave for filming to see if she's learned anything from the note I gave her."

"And if you can't?"

"I'll wait until we find out the results from the next round, then I'll corner her. She'll have to talk to me eventually."

As the stage lights turn on and a clapboard snaps, Bobbi's face beams, and she transforms into the effervescent host we're used to seeing on television.

"Welcome back, foodies," she greets us while also addressing the viewers who will watch later. "Losing a fellow competitor makes it difficult for all of you to be here, and I understand that. It's hard not to wonder what the show would look like today if Benji Mayhew were still with us. His life being cut short is saddening, but let's appreciate the mystery of life and never forget that each day is full of surprises." Bobbi's eyes dart between the drivers. "Speaking of surprises"—she flashes her trademark dazzling smile for the cameras—"are you guys ready to hear about the next challenge?"

Whoops and shouts of excitement fill the air.

I lower my voice to Seth. "It feels strange to be excited, in light of what happened to Benji."

"It's what Benji would've wanted," Seth says as he claps, his eyes still on the stage.

Is it?

"As food truck owners, we all know it's impossible to be prepared for every situation. You have to roll with the punches." She throws a quick one-two punch. "That's the challenge for today. Each of you will receive an index card with an ingredient you *won't* be able to use. When shopping for supplies, this staple is not an option for your truck." She points a wagging finger at a camera.

The contestants murmur in response. I get ready for the worst-case scenario as I visualize making chicken wings with no chicken.

"Myself and two mystery judges will sample your food to determine how well you improvised for the missing ingredient. We will rate you on taste, ability to tell that the component is missing, and how much cash you earn for the challenge. The team with the most points and cash will win this round, plus immunity in the next challenge. Three hundred dollars in seed money will be provided to each team." Everyone complains about how minimal it is. "Oh, c'mon," Bobbi says with a laugh. "It wouldn't be a challenge if you didn't have to work for it."

Sloane hands out index cards and seed money to the contestants. Walking past me, she plants herself in front of my brother and hands him the card.

I read the card Seth is holding. "Meat? What does that mean? A singular kind of meat? If it's beef, that's easy. We can just skip serving sliders. Problem solved!"

Bobbi speaks as the rest of the contestants receive their cards. "To avoid any confusion, you can't simply remove an item from your menu just because you have to forgo an ingredient."

"Well, there goes that brilliant idea," I mutter under my breath.

"The point of this challenge is to test your creativity and ability to adapt under pressure. Something all of you must have in order for your businesses to operate."

Bobbi wraps up with a few closing comments before dismissing us. We have a tight schedule of two hours to shop, prep, and set up in downtown Clementine. Thankfully, we don't have to compete on the same street this time. We have the freedom to set up our trucks in any part of the downtown district. With the addition of dashcams in the trucks to capture footage while driving, we can begin immediately.

As Rylie floors the truck out of the parking lot, Seth asks her, "Why are you wearing that?"

"I'm getting into character." She adjusts the chicken head. "This competition is all about mind games, and I'm becoming one with the chicken."

"More like you're becoming a crazy chicken." Seth white-knuckles the prep counter as Rylie takes a hard right on Ocean Grove Street.

While Rylie drives to the store, I plan the menu. "No meat." Panic brews inside me, ready to erupt like a geyser. "Does that mean no chicken *or* beef?" I mimic a painting I saw as a child and slap my hands on my cheeks. "What if we can't serve either of those things?"

"Let's go without both to be safe." Seth acts like this isn't a big deal. "It's better to avoid meat altogether since 'Meat' could mean either."

"And what? Be a vegetarian meat truck? A chickenless chicken truck?"

"He's right," Rylie says, taking a sharp left turn onto Citrus Heights Avenue. "The card would have specified if we could use something else like pork or lamb." Seth and I jerk forward as Rylie slams on the brakes. She sticks her head out the window, then yells, "*Saia do caminho!* I have the green light, buddy!" Rylie's colossal chicken head startles a pedestrian glued to his phone. Looking up, he sees her costume and hurries across the street.

Rylie continues the conversation as if she didn't just scream at a man while dressed as a larger-than-life fowl. "I think we should set up in our usual spot in front of City Hall."

"Good idea. We already have a loyal customer base there. Plus, Fridays are the busiest day of the week for tourists visiting the observation deck." I chew on my bottom lip as I mull over what to serve. "For the sliders, let's go with black bean patties. What about the chicken?"

"Seitan," is all Seth says.

Pulling into Clover Market's parking lot, Rylie asks, "Who're you calling Satan?" She puts the truck in park and turns off the ignition, turning to look at Seth, aghast.

"Not Satan. Seitan. It has a mild flavor and texture similar to meat. If we season it, it will soak up all those flavors. Making it is also simple," he explains as he grabs our shopping bags. "All you need is wheat gluten, chickpea flour, nutritional yeast, and a medley of herbs like sweet paprika, onion powder, garlic powder, and salt."

"Looks like we aren't the only ones who decided to shop here," Seth says, watching Marco Bartolini locking his truck. Sofia, his wife, is standing to the side, sliding a few tote bags onto her shoulders while she waits.

Marco and Sofia begin talking, presumably to strategize for the challenge. They completely ignore us as they walk right past our truck heading toward the entrance.

Still wearing her giant chicken head, Rylie unfastens her seat belt and leans out of the driver's-side window. "Bagok!" She quickly moves her head back and forth, mimicking a chicken. "Bok, bok! Buckawk!"

Not only does this snap Marco out of his conversation, but it also nearly scares the man to death, judging by the way he grabs his chest and screams in Italian. Marco hurriedly takes Sofia's elbow as they run into the store, not looking back.

"Ms. One with the Chicken," Seth says, giving her a once-over after she's fully back inside the truck, her expression triumphant. "Are you going to wear that while we shop?"

After a brief pause, she takes it off and places it on the front seat. "I'll get fully dressed after we prep. Anyway, my hair needs a break." She fluffs her black curls a few times.

I'm jealous of how she can wear that chicken head all day without getting hat head. If I put on a baseball cap for just five minutes, I end up looking like I've electrocuted myself.

As we step out of the truck, Alex jumps out of a white van and starts capturing the moment with his camera. After ensuring the truck is locked, we sprint toward the store's entrance, with Alex in pursuit.

"How do you know so much about seitan?" Riley asks, clearly shocked by his knowledge of vegan substitutions.

"My ex-girlfriend Liza was vegan," Seth answers as we rush into the store. "I learned to cook for her when we dated."

"Who's Liza?" she asks. "Why don't I know her?"

"Because it was very short-lived," I say, grabbing a shopping cart. "Since the produce section is nearby, let's head there first. Seth, grab a bag of potatoes." I push the cart forward.

"Not that short-lived," he says, grabbing a ten-pound bag of medium, russet potatoes. "We dated for a couple of months."

"Why did you break up with her?" Rylie pinches a few avocados to see if they're ripe. "It's because she was vegan, right?"

"Why do you assume *I* broke up with her?"

"Now isn't the time for this!" Tightening my grip on the shopping cart, I shoot an annoyed glance at Seth and Rylie. "Grab a second bag of potatoes," I tell Seth. "I'll get the lettuce."

"Because I would totally break up with someone for being vegan," Rylie says, ignoring me.

"Can we focus on the competition, please?" I toss a bag of mixed greens and some green onions into the cart.

"You would?" Seth asks her, also ignoring me.

"I couldn't be in a relationship with someone who criticizes my food choices. Plus, I dress up as a giant chicken for work, for crying out loud!"

The camera zooms in on Seth's laughter.

"This is *not* the time for this conversation," I tell them. "We're here to win, not discuss our dating preferences. Focus!" I snap my fingers in their faces.

Seth nods, his eyes lingering on Rylie. "I get that. Sometimes people are meant for different chapters in our lives."

She looks at him, giving him a shy smile. "Sometimes, they've been there all along, but we're too blind to notice."

Alex skillfully adjusts his camera to capture the moment my brow furrows and my nose crinkles. "What is going on with the two of you?" I look between them as they look at each other. "You know what?" I throw my hands up. "I don't care. Just move!"

I don't wait for Rylie and Seth—I can't afford to. The cameras scramble to keep up, but I don't have time to care. Every second counts. We have to pack our dishes with flavor and be ready for the lunchtime rush. I spot a single bottle of berbere and snatch it off the shelf. With a triumphant grin, I look straight into the lens of the rolling camera.

Our next stop is Elm Street, where City Hall is located. Tucking my hair behind my ears, I lower my baseball cap in place and start working. Seth, Rylie, and I start the whirlwind of prep work. Rylie forcefully pushes potatoes through the fry cutter that's mounted on the prep counter. Alex gets intimately close with his camera, capturing everything we do. When the producers combine the footage with the narrative, I'm convinced viewers will almost taste what we're making. To make his chicken substitute, Seth marinates the "meats" in flavorful concoctions and simmers sauces on the stovetop. I'm occupied with making black-bean patties for our sliders.

In a medium bowl, I mash the black beans with a fork until they have a thick, pasty consistency. "Similar to traditional burgers, it's important to ensure the black-bean burger remains intact," I explain. Alex captures me breaking a couple of eggs over the bowl. Next, I pour in some panko breadcrumbs and mix it all up. "Black-bean patties can lack flavor," I mention to the camera, "so I'm adding a few dashes of berbere."

Putting my fork in the sink, I grab a wooden spoon and continue to mix the ingredients. "Berbere is a North African spice blend of cayenne, paprika, urfa pepper, chili, coriander, cardamom, ginger, and fenugreek. This mix of spices adds heat but also some complexity. It's perfect for enhancing my flavors in this challenge."

The camera zooms in to capture our synchronized movements as we move swiftly, showcasing our culinary skills. Well, mine and

Seth's skills. But Rylie's superb use of the fry cutter is also being captured. Our mom taught Seth and me the very basics of cooking at a young age. Our cooking creativity flourished when we started assisting Aunt Dolly on the truck as soon as we were old enough to work. Being on the truck together is second nature to us. It's tough to stay focused while giving quick instructions, sharing animated banter, and ignoring the camera.

Alex backs up to adjust the camera angle but stumbles and collides with the prep counter. A bowl of flour flips, landing on the floor right in front of Rylie.

"Phfft, phfft." She waves at the white puffy cloud drifting through the air.

"Oh, shoot!" He halts the recording. "I'm so sorry!" Pushing some sauce bottles aside, he sets down his camera. "I'll clean it." He reaches for the roll of paper towels, tearing off a few sheets.

"It's fine." I stop him. "We have extra flour for dredging the wings."

"Let me clean it," he insists. But he ends up spreading the flour even more.

"Really, it's fine," I say, grabbing his arm and tugging him to his feet.

"It was an accident," he says, looking around at the mess he caused.

"No harm, no foul." I kick some of the flour to the side. "But we don't have time to clean it."

"I've never done anything like that before. I'll be more careful." He goes to pick up his camera.

"Actually," Rylie stops him. "It's a bit cramped in here." She wipes at some residual flour on her chest.

"She's right," I say. "You've already gotten some great footage. Can we just use the dashcam for the rest?"

"Sure, no problem," he says, nodding, understanding he's being kicked out. "Let me just make sure it has enough power." He fumbles with a few settings on the dashcam, then repositions it closer to our workstation. "Good to go! Rolling!"

"Thanks," I say. "And maybe watch where you swing that thing?"

Alex grabs his camera and leaves through the back of the truck.

As the two-hour deadline approaches, we add the final touches. Seth meticulously arranges colorful baskets, adding garnishes and drizzling sauces before placing them in the hot holders. Rylie and I ensure the truck is spotless and ready for service.. Glancing at the clock, my heart pounds.

"We've done everything we can," I say, wiping sweat from my brow with the back of my arm. "Now it's time to show the judges what Kluckin' Good is all about."

Sloane knocks on the back door and peeks inside. "Permission to come aboard?" Her smile widens as she enters. "Wow!" she remarks, taking in the flour-covered floor. "What happened in here?"

"Alex happened." Rylie fusses with her flour-stained shirt.

That's why she should wear an apron like Seth and me.

"What can we do for you?" I ask, rolling my shoulders and stretching my neck.

As she looks around our tiny, messy kitchen, she pushes a few towels to the side and places her water bottle, bag, and clipboard on the far end of the prep counter. "You can open your window and begin serving in five minutes. Are you ready?"

"Ready as we'll ever be." I smile into the dashcam.

"Um . . ." Rylie looks at Sloane's stuff. "Can you move your things so I can disinfect the counter? It's not sanitary to set your items where we're preparing food. We've already made enough of a mess. We don't need more."

"Oh goodness, I'm sorry." As Sloane gathers her stuff, she knocks over a roll of paper towels. "I hope I didn't ruin anything," she says apologetically, picking up what she knocked over.

"You didn't," I assure her. "Rylie is right, though. We have specific regulations to comply with when preparing and serving food."

"I completely understand." Sloane steps down onto the back steps of the truck. "Cluck onward and upward!" She snorts, walking away.

Rylie slips into the chicken suit and pulls it up onto her shoulders. Once she secures her hair, I zip up the back and hand her the head.

My brother cracks his neck from side to side as he gears up for the challenge ahead. Leaning forward, he opens the serving window as Rylie struts out of the truck carrying a sign to attract customers. The air horn sounds, and things are underway.

Film crews gather outside the two other trucks that parked in the same area as us. The cameras are ready to welcome the first customers of the day. They position the cameras, capturing contestants' anticipation and the eager crowds forming around our bright-yellow food truck. You can't miss us driving down the street with our red, brown, and beige striped truck. Both sides of the truck feature a super cute, laughing cartoon chicken. The truck's name is written on the sides in a bold, eye-catching red script.

The interior of our truck is just as vibrant. The shiny chrome, vintage teal, and pops of red give our truck retro vibes. I'm glad Seth is here with me today because we're swamped with customers at the serving window. The lure of delicious aromas and the promise of an unforgettable culinary adventure is bringing in more people than we've ever served before. While we're serving dishes, I notice the cameras capture customers' ecstatic expressions as they savor each bite. Bobbi Taylor, standing nearby, is interviewing satisfied patrons about their food truck experience.

"And how does that dish taste?" I hear her ask a city worker.

"Amazing!" the worker answers. "The flavors are explosive!"

If only I knew which truck they were talking about.

An older lady with a little purse dog joins the queue for our truck. I suspect she may be one of the mystery judges. I put Seth in charge of the order window because of his charm with the older ladies. He has a way of chatting and smiling that instantly makes people his friends. If she is a judge and doesn't care for our food, maybe his charisma will sway her vote.

While moving sliders from the grill to takeaway baskets for an order, a boisterous laugh grabs my attention. "Here you go!" I pass the food through the serving window to the customer while trying to figure out where the laughter is coming from.

Outside City Hall, I spot Bobbi engaging in a lively conversation with a cheerful group of people, all sporting matching blue-and-yellow shirts. I watch as the cameraperson glides around the space, capturing every detail of Bobbi's interaction. The individual talking with her is holding a basket of food from our truck. Laughter and nods, hopefully in approval, punctuate their conversation.

"Here she comes!"

As I take a basket from the warming station, I smile and hand the order to a waiting customer, just as Bobbi approaches our truck. Her heels click on the concrete.

"Here I am, ready to try some food from Kluckin' Good." With a smile, she poses in front of our eye-catching yellow truck, hand extended toward the menu. The camera shifts from Bobbi's face to our chalkboard. "Hmm . . ." She taps a finger to her lips. "I'd like to try a basket of Kluck-a-Doodle Classics with the avocado aioli, Golden Oldie Sliders, and a side of Plucked and Truffled Fries, please." I grab the Kluck-a-Doodle Classics and a side of aioli from the mini fridge while Seth boxes the sliders and fries.

"Wait!" I stop him as he's about to give her the order. "You forgot to sprinkle dried chives on the fries." Frantically, I scour the bottles on the prep counter, feeling as though I'm searching forever (though it's probably just twenty seconds).

"I can't find them," I whisper in panic.

"We don't have time." He takes the boxes and hands them to her through the service window.

"Your arrangements are so colorful. I love it!" She takes a bite of a slider and hums a few notes. She directs her words to the camera. "Many people forget that sight is the first sense we use when eating. We imagine the flavor of our food before tasting it. Your baskets are appealing in both appearance and taste. Great job!"

"Thank you!" we say in unison.

Knowing that I gave her an incomplete order pains me. I pray this minor detail won't count against us.

"Let's hope the mystery judges share the same sentiment." Bobbi leaves as the air horn blares, signaling the challenge is over. I never discovered who the second mystery judge was.

Still pumped with adrenaline from the intense competition, I reach for a rag and get busy cleaning up. Utensils clatter, water splashes, and the sound of scrub brushes fills the air of our small truck. As I clean the prep counter, a roll of paper towels falls against the stainless-steel counter with a thud.

When I pick it up, I find the bottle of chives wedged deep in the paper towel roll. "What are you doing there?" I ask the inanimate object. "This is not where I put you." As I grab the bottle, it slips and spills everywhere. Shaking my head in frustration, I scoop the mess into the catch tray on the side of the counter to empty later.

"Mova isso!" Rylie yells out the passenger window, hoping to somehow will the cars in front of our truck to part like the Red Sea. "This is ridiculous! Can't they do roadwork at a decent hour?"

"We're already late, and now we're gonna be later!" Seth complains. He glances at his watch for the third time in five minutes. "Can't you go any faster?"

"Why aren't you honking?" Rylie shouts.

"I'm going as fast as I can!" Gripping the wheel, I stare at the endless stream of taillights in front of me. "The road is jammed with traffic, and honking won't make them move any faster."

Seth folds his arms, annoyance etched on his face. "We're gonna miss the results."

"No, we won't," I say, inching forward. "All teams need to be present for the announcement of the results. It's fine. We'll get there."

As we creep forward in the truck, the tension rises, and my thoughts fixate on the challenge. I hope the fake stuff was a hit. We could really use immunity in the next round.

Finally, we reach the lot. While passing the security booth, I see the guard shake his head and check his watch.

"I think we might have cut it a little close," I say maneuvering to our spot and putting the truck in park.

"I told you not to worry about cleaning up," Seth chastises me.

"We had the time," I defend. "I didn't know the roadwork would close an entire street."

"Vamos, menina!" Rylie says, unbuckling from the passenger seat.

"The roadwork wasn't the problem," Seth says, speed walking. "Why would you try to make a U-turn in an eighteen-foot truck?"

"I didn't try. I succeeded."

"After backing up five times."

"You know what—"

"There you are!" Imogen shouts, marching toward us. We're the last team to arrive and, from the look on her face, we're most definitely late.

She guides us to the seating area arranged in front of the stage, where Sloane and Bobbi finish up a quiet conversation. As we take our seats, someone off to the side counts down on their fingers before the camera rolls. Just as the clapboard sounds, Sloane steps out of the frame.

Bobbi grins broadly into the camera and gives a round of applause to welcome everyone back. "I just wanted to say how impressed I was with your performance in this week's competition. You must be wondering how well you all did. The scores are tallied, and we have the results." Bobbi presents two sealed envelopes for all to view.

"Hold on just a minute!" Loretta Able, co-owner of Porked 'n' Rubbed, hollers, waving both hands high in the air. "Ain't we gonna talk about what happened? I told Ms. Comestible I had ingredients snatched right outta my truck! Someone came waltzin' into my kitchen like they owned the place! It was dang near impossible to finish!"

"We also were missing ingredients," adds Reyna Katapang.

"Can you prove anyone was inside your trucks?" Bobbi asks the two owners.

"Well, no." Reyna shakes her head.

"You expect *me* to have cameras set up catchin' things?" Loretta snaps, standing up and pointing a finger at Bobbi. "It's *your* job to keep things fair on this show! Why don't you take a good, hard look at the camera footage"—she jabs her finger toward the camera filming her—"and tell me who went sneakin' into my truck?"

Bobbi gives her a withering look. "The network is not liable for your forgetfulness or lack of preparation. If you can prove someone was in your truck, then that's a separate issue. Based on what I'm hearing, neither of you had what you needed and are making excuses for being underprepared."

My mind drifts back to my chives. At first, I thought they were missing, but they weren't. Is it possible that's what happened to Loretta and the Katapangs? Did they just misplace their stuff?

Or is this just another example of how everything ties together? Does it all somehow lead right back to Benji?

I add a note to Rylie's and my Kluckin' Clues list about what just happened. Something isn't adding up.

"As I was saying"—Bobbi scans the crowd to see if anyone else will interrupt—"your ability to improvise was considered during the judging process, and we assessed you based on flavor and the ability to identify the missing ingredient. One team performed exceptionally well. Their taste, texture, and creativity were superb. But first, I want to invite our mystery judges out before announcing the winner."

"I knew it!" I whisper as the older woman appears, holding her purse dog. Unfortunately, I don't remember seeing the next person—a college-aged student wearing a red T-shirt with jeans ripped at the knees.

"Mrs. Larkin, Mr. Winters. Would you mind sharing your thoughts on the food you sampled today?"

There's a yip, then a small, fluffy white head pops up. Everyone coos, and a camera zooms in on the fluffy little pooch. Mrs. Larkin adjusts the oversized bag on her arm, shushing her miniature pup. "Every dish was full of flavor. It amazed me to learn that I had eaten a dish with no meat. Had you not told me, I wouldn't have known."

I grip Rylie's hand, and she squeezes mine back. I'm waiting with bated breath.

"Mr. Winters, what are your thoughts?" Bobbi asks the young man.

"Everything tasted great. I never thought I'd enjoy a doughnut with no sugar in it, but that was the bomb."

I peek around my twin to see Ben, Bryan, and Beckett all fist-bumping each other.

"So, tell us, what were your overall favorite plates?" Bobbi asks the mystery judges.

"Kluckin' Good."

"Dough Brothers."

The judges answer simultaneously.

A tie? What happens now?

"Thank you, and who did you find had the least appealing dish to offer?"

"The egg rolls from Lumpia-Licious," Mrs. Larkin answers.

"Hard agree," says Mr. Winters. "They had a bitter aftertaste."

"Thank you for your comments," Bobbi says to the mystery judges, signaling their exit.

Mrs. Larkin's pooch chooses this moment to become a star. A ball of white fluff escapes from her bag and runs around the stage.

The contestants laugh as a stage assistant chases the small dog while Mrs. Larkin makes smooching noises. All but the Katapang sisters, that is. Lila and Ula look devastated, while Reyna seems furious.

Bobbi catches the small white dog and scratches its head. "It's always a pleasure to meet a fan, even one as small and fluffy as you." Turning toward us, she continues. "You all did great improvising, but this is a competition. There can be only one winner. One team showcased real creativity and impressed the judges with their menu."

I tighten my grasp on Rylie's fingers.

"Ow." Rylie extricates herself from my grip and shakes out her hand.

"The winner is—" Bobbi pauses dramatically.

Bobbi needs to share the results soon, or I'll explode.

"—Kluckin' Good!"

Rylie and I leap up from our seats and do an awkward chicken dance. I yank Seth up by his collar to join us. His brilliant chicken wings idea helped us win, and he should be celebrating.

"Okay, okay," Bobbi says, chuckling. "Team Kluckin' Good, since you won today's challenge, you're granted immunity during the next round. Congratulations!"

Immunity! We can breathe and just enjoy the challenge.

"Sadly," Bobbi says in a solemn tone. "One team performed the poorest in the challenge. That team is—" She pauses dramatically again. "Lumpia-Licious."

Lila sobs and slumps in her seat, and Reyna's eyes hurl daggers at Bobbi.

"Your use of radicchio instead of cabbage may have seemed like a suitable substitution, but it left the judges with a bitter aftertaste. Between that and having the lowest sales of the challenge, I'm sorry to say it's time for you to leave the wagon trail." Bobbi's tone is gentle.

"You wouldn't know what a suitable substitution was if it came up and bit *you* on your bitter aftertaste." Reyna's words drip with venom.

Burn.

Well, kind of. She tried.

Bobbi gives a tight-lipped smile. "Thank you for your participation, and we wish you the best."

This is the Katapang sisters' cue to leave. A crew member steps in to guide them out of their seats. Imogen joins the assistant and escorts the sisters to the green screen for their postshow interview.

I wish I could be a fly on a wall getting Reyna's firsthand opinion on Bobbi and her bitter aftertaste. Perhaps Seth is right—I *may* be overly nosy. But it's not my fault. I'm powerless against the appeal of a good dose of drama. Lock me up and throw away the key if that's a crime, because I have no intention of stopping.

Bobbi directs the focus back to herself as the Katapangs leave. "I want all of you to give yourself a round of applause. You've done great." Bobbi leads the group clapping before smiling into a camera onstage.

"Psst!" Rylie says to me.

"Ow!" I rub the spot where she's just pinched me. "What was that for?" I whisper.

"Did you hear her?" she whispers.

"Hear who?"

"Join us next week as the teams face off in a cooking challenge you won't want to miss! Remember, it's not fast food, it's fabulous food!" With Bobbi's wave, our taping comes to a close. As soon as "Cut!" is yelled, Bobbi leaves and Sloane takes her place at the microphone.

"You all did an amazing job. We have two days off from filming. Get some rest, explore Clementine and the surrounding areas, or set up your trucks and get some business done. The choice is yours."

Spinning around, I glare at Rylie. "Who were you talking about? And why did you pinch me?" I ask, keeping my voice low.

"Willa," she whispers, looking past me.

"What about Willa?" I turn.

"No!" She grabs my shoulder. "She was sitting in front of me, and, after the Katapangs were eliminated, I overheard her say to Bria, 'One less team to stand in my way.'"

I spot Sloane, who appears to be getting ready to leave.

"What do you think Willa meant?" Rylie asks. "Should we worry about her?"

"We should always worry about Willa," I say while keeping an eye on Sloane. "She's a loose cannon, and I don't trust her. Never have. After Benji died, we all heard her say that winning requires doing whatever it takes. Maybe that's what all this is. Willa doing whatever it takes for *her* truck to win. Add what you heard to the Kluckin' Clues list. I gotta catch Sloane." I find my way to Sloane and Sergio through the crowd. "Sloane!" I wave to catch her eye. "Do you have a minute?" I ask, joining them. "In private?" My eyes wander to Sergio.

"Sure." She glances at her watch. "But I don't have much time."

"I'll be quick," I say, stepping to the side, waiting for her to follow.

Right as I'm about to inquire about what's happened with Benji's note, a voice I vaguely recognize grabs my attention from behind. "Ms. Lloyd?"

"Yes?" I answer, slowly turning around. "Can I help you?"

"I'm going to need you to come with me to the station. I have additional questions for you about the murder of Benji Mayhew."

Chapter Eight

"You want to talk to me about Benji's mur . . . murder?" The word clumsily falls out of my mouth.

"Yes," answers the familiar deep voice as the tall figure stops incredibly close to me.

My eyes sweep over the man standing before me. Déjà vu. I remember those strong shoulders and the strawberry-blond hair forming a slight widow's peak. But it's those eyes I can't forget. Deep ocean blue I could drown in. Only this time, they're not clear and inviting. Instead, they look like storm clouds with swirling blue bits trapped inside.

This can't be happening.

Again.

"You!" I say and point.

"Detective Kane." Officer—correction—*Detective* Pretty Boy pushes his jacket to the side, brandishing a shiny gold badge resting on the side of his belt next to a firearm.

"I don't understand. I've already spoken with Detective Hamstead."

"That's my partner." He drops his jacket back down. "And we appreciate the time you took last week to answer his questions. However, the police chief received an anonymous tip that leads us to believe you may have more information to share." Sloane scurries away, leaving me alone with *him*.

He wants to speak with me further about the *murder* of Benji Mayhew. My intuition was spot-on. According to my mom, women should always trust their gut. She always says, "The stomach is a reliable compass, unlike the treacherous heart." My stomach's compass pointed due north. Or in this instance, due murder.

My lips part to speak, but no words form as I struggle to form a sentence. It's incredibly difficult with those eyes penetrating my thoughts.

"What's going on here?" Seth demands, coming to stand next to me.

While keeping his eyes on me, he again slides his jacket to the side, identifying himself. "I'm Detective Kane."

"I remember you," Seth says.

"I need to speak with Ms. Lloyd."

"What is this regarding?" Seth asks, slipping into lawyer mode.

Detective Kane shifts his gaze from me to my brother. "We have a few more questions regarding her relationship with Benji Mayhew."

"Relationship!" I shriek as Seth shoves me behind him.

"And you believe my client has information you need?" Seth asks, attempting to take over the conversation.

"We do." Detective Kane looks to me, and my brother becomes invisible as those stormy eyes meet mine. "If you would please come with me, Ms. Lloyd."

"What more could I know?" I give a hollow laugh. "Benji and I had minimal interaction. Besides, the production staff told everyone during taping that he'd died of a heart attack." *Not that I believe that's what really happened for one second.* "If Benji was killed, why is everyone on set being told differently?"

Folding his arms over his chest, the detective shifts on his feet. "We've been talking with some of your fellow contestants. It sounded like the two of you had more than minimal interaction."

He completely ignored everything else I said.

My mind races back to the last time I spoke with Benji. It was right before the results of the first challenge. He wasn't pleased when I knocked on his truck, wanting to know who he was talking to. He stressed it was in my best interest to steer clear of him.

Oh god, I asked him if it would kill *him to be nice. This doesn't look good . . .*

"Plus," the detective continues, "let's not forget you assaulted his truck." He offers me a pitiful smirk. "I'm confident you have more to share."

Of course Detective Pretty Boy has a memory like an elephant.

"The police dropped those charges," Seth reminds him. "Beth has no record or prior histories other than this one encounter you speak of."

My lawyer brother is pushing full steam ahead.

"We still need to have an official chat," Detective Kane tells him. "You can meet your sister at the station." He motions toward his unmarked car.

"Are you arresting my client on charges of suspicion?" Seth's voice rises an octave as he steps further in front of me.

"Not at all." The detective strides closer, coming toe to toe with my twin as they size each other up. "We're just going to sort out a few things." Our eyes meet again, and I feel trapped. "Unless you have something to hide."

"My client already gave a statement," Seth says. "If it's truly just a few questions, why can't we do it here?"

"It's just a formality. It won't take long, and your client is free to leave at any time."

I'm acutely aware of the cluster of people gathering nearby, eager to learn what's going on and spread their own rumors about me. This needs to end now. As I grab my brother's arm, I sense a slight tremble. Not from nerves. Anger is emanating from him in waves. The last time I saw Seth like this was when he confronted my ex-boyfriend Brad about how he broke up with me.

"Seth," I whisper. "I have nothing to hide. It's best to wrap this up as quickly as possible."

The detective offers me a satisfied smirk as he tilts his head in my direction. "It's just a few questions. We'll have everything wrapped up in a jiffy."

"I need a moment to speak with my client. Alone." Seth pulls me aside. "I'll have Rylie take the truck back to Mom and Dad's. I'll get my car and meet you at the station." Grabbing my shoulders, Seth looks me in the eye. It's obvious he's struggling to find the words. "You have the right to remain silent. Anything you say can and will be used against you in a court of law."

"Are you reading me my Miranda rights?"

"Do not answer any questions until I'm with you. Do you understand?" Seth's grip on my shoulders tightens. He hugs me, and I give a weak nod. "Let me handle this, Beth. Just please don't say anything stupid or incriminating."

Detective Pretty Boy approaches, and I step back, forcing a brittle smile. "See you soon, Mr. Lloyd," the detective says before escorting me to his car.

Once again, I find myself sitting in the back seat of a police cruiser.

As I wait in the interrogation room for Detective Pretty Boy to come back, I squirm in the cold metal chair, trying to get comfortable. Glancing around, I spot a camera in the upper right corner with a blinking red light. The urge to stick out my tongue arises, but I fight it.

Compared to my previous holding cell, this room is slightly better. Unlike last time, I'm not dressed like a giant chicken. If I were, I could bury my head and hide until this nightmare is over. At least Detective Pretty Boy gave me a cup of coffee before leaving.

Sniffing the paper cup, I bring the lukewarm liquid to my lips and take a sip. Wincing, I wish I hadn't. Whatever rubbish this is, it's not coffee. It tastes more like dirty dishwater. Nudging the cup away, I shake my head in disgust. It's for the best because I need to pee, and there's no restroom around.

The door swings open, and in steps Detective Pretty Boy with a determined expression. "Thank you for waiting."

"Not like I had a choice," I mutter under my breath while trying to get comfortable in this terrible seat.

He arches an eyebrow, studying me for a long moment before pulling out the chair across from me. "I know this has been a long day for you. I'm sure you'd like to be done as quickly as possible."

Oh yeah, he sounds sympathetic.

"If I'm not mistaken," he says, "I'm pretty sure I told you I didn't want to see you around here again."

"Maybe you shouldn't have brought me here then." Quickly, I clamp my hand over my big mouth.

After taking out a notepad and ballpoint pen from his suit jacket, he scribbles on his pad, his pen making soft scratching sounds against the paper. I assume it's something about me and my smart mouth. When he looks up, his expression is unyielding. "Would you mind telling me how you felt about Mr. Mayhew?"

"Do I need my lawyer?"

"Do you think you need your lawyer?"

Looking around the space, I sarcastically say, "Does this room have an echo or something?"

His intense gaze narrows, a sign that I've crossed a line.

"Sorry," I say half-heartedly. "I think Seth should be in here with me."

"You're well within your rights to have a lawyer present, but you're not under arrest. As you've stated several times, you did nothing wrong."

"I haven't!"

"Then why delay our chat and wait for him?" he asks in a calm yet authoritative tone. He must read the skepticism on my face because he shrugs. "The sooner we finish these questions, the sooner you're free to go."

If I'm not in custody, there's no reason to wait. So, I answer. "Benji may have been an entitled jacka . . . um, I mean jerk, but I didn't kill him. And I didn't wish for any harm to come to him, if that's what you're implying."

Boy, I need to think before I speak.

The detective absentmindedly twists his pen between his fingers. "I wasn't implying anything. However, since you mentioned it, are you absolutely certain that's how you felt?"

"Of course." I'm having a hard time keeping the shock out of my voice over his question.

The detective's eyes bore into me while his fingers tap on the cold metal table. "I'll repeat my question. Are you sure that's how you felt?"

"Why are you asking?" I refrain from squirming in my seat.

Resting his elbows on the table, he leans forward and clasps his hands together. "I arrested you for attacking his truck." After a beat of silence, he says, "Remember?"

"That was . . ."

"You were dressed as a giant chicken."

Of course he mentions that detail.

"Plus . . ." The word lingers, intensifying the already mounting tension within me.

Never one to do well with too much uncomfortable silence, I prod him. "Plus, what?"

He reaches for his notepad and thumbs through a few pages. "Ah, yes, here it is. You wished to 'cut off his head.'"

Shutting my eyes, I exhale through my nostrils. As Seth predicted, the day has arrived where my stupid mouth has gotten me into trouble.

"Ms. Lloyd."

At the sound of my name, I open my eyes. "Is it safe to assume we're all guilty of saying things we don't mean? That we're just angry at that moment?"

"Were you angry with Mr. Mayhew?"

"Did you ever meet the man?" I snap.

Darn my stupid mouth.

"I did. Mr. Mayhew could be quite . . . disagreeable."

I watch as the detective settles further into his chair, getting comfortable. "What additional questions do you have for me?" I ask.

"An anonymous tip suggests you and Mr. Mayhew were more than mere acquaintences."

"Who said that?"

Detective Kane raises a questioning eyebrow. "You are familiar with the term 'anonymous tip,' right?"

"I feel like that's a rhetorical question."

"It was." After a beat of silence, he says, "We don't know who made the call. Even if we did, I wouldn't tell you."

"What is the point of all this?"

Detective Kane ignores me, reaching into his pocket and pulling out his phone. "I looked you up." He taps on the screen a few times. "You have quite the online following. Cute website too."

"Thank you."

"Your aunt, Dorothy Hendrix—"

"Aunt Dolly," I correct.

He nods. "Although I'm new to Clementine, the online information I found suggests that your Aunt Dolly was a shrewd businesswoman. Many newspaper articles in the Bay Area highlighted Kluckin' Good, calling her truck the 'it' place for wings."

"She was a very savvy small business owner." There's a hint of pride in my voice. "She dedicated herself to building her business and cultivating strong relationships with her customers. She wanted her wings to be known as the best wings in the Bay Area, and they were. My goal is to emulate her."

He puts his phone face down in front of him and looks at me. "Did you ever work with your aunt before inheriting her business?"

"Of course. It's where I learned to cook."

"And do you continue to operate the truck in the same places she did?"

"Yes," I answer, wondering why we're discussing my late aunt. "She built up a loyal customer base in multiple locations spanning from Clementine to San Francisco. It's logical for me to continue operating in those same places."

Where is he going with this?

"Hmm," he says, then nods. "Would it be safe to assume you knew other food trucks she worked alongside?"

I nod. "Sure, I know some of the other foodies around here."

"So that would mean you and Mr. Mayhew operated in the same circles and locations." Flipping his phone over, he spins it around to show me. Someone shared a photo online a few months ago of a half-eaten hot dog from Benji's truck at the Clementine Farmers Market. My bright-yellow truck and Rylie's chicken suit are clearly visible in the background.

I avert my eyes as he takes his phone back. "It's interesting how you conveniently neglected to mention all of that in your initial statement. Why would you not tell us that you were well acquainted with him?"

"I . . . well . . ." I stammer searching for the right words. "I knew Benji, but I didn't *know* him."

The detective jots down several things in his tiny notepad. "Could you elaborate?"

"All right, look." Leaning forward, I clasp my hands on the table. "Yes, I knew Benji for a while. Back when my aunt was alive, I would see him around. I tried with Benji. Honest to god, I did. But he wouldn't have it."

"What do you mean?"

"I'm not sure how familiar you are with food truck culture."

"Not very," he admits.

"Starting with the Chuckwagon, America became the food truck nation. The popularity of food trucks in the Bay Area is off the charts, with festivals and events dedicated to them." As I talk, my hands make exaggerated gestures. "You saw the articles. Aunt Dolly's truck was popular.

"Benji, along with several other people, resented me for taking over her business. They'd been in the trenches. I hadn't. According to my aunt's lawyer, Benji was one of the many who tried to buy her out while she was alive. But she had other plans for her truck. Plans that involved Seth and me becoming the new owners, on the condition that one of us completed a degree in business management—"

"But it's only you who operates the truck? Is that correct?" Detective Kane interrupts me.

I give a small nod. "When we found out about the inheritance, Seth was already on the path to becoming a lawyer. My role includes managing the daily aspects of the business while Seth serves as a silent partner. That was a topic Benji and I often disagreed about."

Detective Pretty Boy tilts his head over my comment but doesn't interrupt.

"I tried not to cross paths with him, but every time I did, it reminded me how old-school Benji was," I continue. "He held the sexist belief that women can't run a business. His favorite saying was that if women were in the kitchen, it better be at home. It was something he said to me and my aunt more than once. I know that cooking is a male-dominated business, but I never expected the amount of disdain directed at me. Gender is not a factor in owning and operating a successful business. Something I kept emphasizing to him, but Benji was petty. He took my aunt's decision to leave the business to me as a personal insult. He never forgave her, or me."

Silence fills the interrogation room, making it uncomfortable. The whole time, he stares at me with his stormy gray-blue eyes. When the pressure becomes overwhelming, he breaks the silence.

"Someone overheard you and Mr. Mayhew have an unpleasant exchange, and video footage from the CCTV cameras shows the two of you engaged in a conversation. In fact, you are the last person seen having any interaction with him on the day he died."

Chapter Nine

The CCTV cameras? Imogen said the refreshment tent blocked those cameras. She also said the cameras were on the fritz.

"What do you have to say about that, Ms. Lloyd?"

Oh my god! The police suspect me. They think I played a role in Benji's death.

Benji was killed before the current setup, when the CCTV cameras had an unobstructed view of the lot.

Where I would have been seen talking to him! Of course they would work and I'd be on camera arguing with him right before he died. It's no wonder the police suspect me. How could Imogen have been so wrong about the cameras?

My chest thumps, and bile rises in my throat. I swallow it down.

Reaching for the now icy black coffee, I finish the remains. Despite the challenge of swallowing the unpleasant taste, I'm grateful to have a task to focus on, even if it's just for a second.

"Ms. Lloyd, I believe I asked you a question."

My hands tremble slightly as I shift uncomfortably in my chair. "I think I want my lawyer."

"Are you sure that's what you want?" he asks, his unblinking eyes fixed on mine.

"Yes." I swallow hard.

He considers me for a moment before pushing away from the table. The only sound in the room is his chair scraping against the floor. Once he's gone, I take deep breaths to regain control of my rapidly increasing blood pressure.

How can the police believe I had something to do with Benji's death? That I murdered him? I mean, sure, we were the furthest thing from friends, but I didn't kill him!

Once again, the door cracks open and in slips the detective.

"Where's my brother?" I ask.

"He's coming. I had someone fetch him for me."

I snap under the pressure of this room. "There was shouting coming from inside his truck." My voice is scratchy, and my tongue feels heavy, making it hard to swallow. "I went to see what was happening. It sounded like Benji was arguing with someone. Your partner knows everything I just told you."

"No one else around his truck is visible on the cameras. Only you."

"I . . . that's . . . that can't be right. I know what I heard. He was yelling at someone."

"Perhaps he was on the phone."

A thought occurs to me. "His truck is like mine. There's a back door that leads into my truck's kitchen, and Benji's is the same way. If a person had been inside his truck, they could have used that method of entry. Is it possible you couldn't see the back of his truck on the CCTV footage?"

"Ms. Lloyd—"

I slam my hands down on the tabletop, pushing myself out of my seat. "This is ridiculous! Do you honestly believe I had something to do with whatever happened to Benji? Why would I purposely do something to him on a studio lot filled with cameras?" Realizing my actions and tone could be construed as aggressive, I quickly sit back down and fold my hands together. "I'm sorry. It's just, you know. Upsetting."

"I'm just following the breadcrumbs. Or should I say . . . the feathers?"

He follows this statement with an even more intense stare. His lip may have twitched. From annoyance? Or is he holding in laughter? I can't be sure. As the silence thickens, I again battle against the urge to squirm in my seat. I'm at my breaking point when—

Knock, knock.

Relief washes over me as Seth shatters the tension upon entering the room. He immediately steps to where I'm sitting. Standing behind me, he places his hands on my shoulders. "You have no right to be questioning my client without me present."

I have never loved my twin more than I do right now.

"Ah, Mr. Lloyd. Kind of you to join us." The detective grins at my brother. "Just so you are aware, your client spoke freely of her own volition."

My jaw drops. "But I asked you for a lawyer!"

"Correction, Ms. Lloyd. You asked if you *needed* a lawyer."

"And you said no."

"I never said 'no.'"

"You talked me out of it!"

"I said you're not under arrest. You were the one who started talking after that."

"I . . . that's . . ." I glance at my brother for answers. "Seth, can he do that? Does that even count? That's not allowed, right?"

"Oh, it's allowed." The detective chuckles deeply.

"You tricked me!"

Detective Pretty Boy leans forward, offering me a cocky grin.

"I hate you." I spit the words at him.

"You're not the first person to say that to me in this room."

Pinching the bridge of his nose, Seth exhales deeply. "Bethany, I told you not to answer questions without me."

"He tricked me!"

"It doesn't matter," Seth says with a sigh. "If you never said the words 'I want my lawyer,' or 'I won't speak without my lawyer present,' then yeah, Beth, it counts. You spoke to him without me present, and that counts."

I protest, but he holds up his hand to stop me as he addresses the detective. "I'm here, and from now on, you are not to speak to my client unless I'm present. Is that clear, Detective?"

"Crystal."

"Unless there is something you can hold her on, we're leaving." Seth motions for me to stand and follow. I rise, but the detective signals for me to take a seat.

"Ms. Lloyd is not being charged with anything as of this moment."

Why do I feel like he's trying to lull me into a false sense of security?

"We believe Mr. Mayhew died by foul play. We're investigating everyone who spent time with him."

Having Seth beside me allows me to relax enough that hearing the words "foul play" reminds me of a joke our father once told us. *"What do you call a rendition of* Death of a Salesman *performed by chickens? A fowl play."* I smile at the memory.

"Do you realize the gravity of this situation, Ms. Lloyd?" The sharp tone shatters my memory.

"Bethany." My brother says my name through gritted teeth. "This is no time to be laughing."

"Oh no." I try to recover as I realize they've misinterpreted my smile. "I'm sorry. I was thinking about a joke our father told us when we were kids about chickens performing a play. You know, a 'fowl play.' Or in this case, I guess we could say it's 'a murder most fowl.'"

My uncomfortable laughter fills the room.

"I advise you to stop talking," Seth growls.

With a click of his pen, the detective jots something down on his notepad.

"Are you writing down 'a murder most fowl'?" I ask, leaning forward.

"Thank you for updating us on the status of the investigation, Detective Kane," my brother coolly says. "Again, unless there is something you can hold Beth on, we're leaving." Pulling out a glossy black-and-gold business card from the firm where he has an internship, he slides it across the desk. "If you have anything else to discuss with my client, you can reach me at this number to set up an appointment."

The detective's gaze moves from my brother to the card, then to me. "Thank you for your time, Ms. Lloyd. I'll be in touch."

He smiles, and I stare back at him. The clouds in his eyes clear, leaving behind only a serene ocean blue. As I stare at Detective Pretty Boy, my lips part, and I'm speaking before I can stop myself.

"You should be looking for whoever Benji was yelling at inside his truck, not me. Or one of the other teams competing in the show. Or maybe ask Sloane Owsinski about that note I found that Benji dropped."

This catches the attention of Detective Pretty Boy. "What note?"

Frustrated, I throw my arms in the air. "I told the other detective about all of this! Benji dropped a note that said, 'Back off unless you want to end up like your steamed buns.' I gave it to Sloane, who said she would look into it and see if it tied back to the show. Even she agreed it seemed eerie and threatening. Then later, I overheard Benji yelling at someone. That's what I was talking to him about on the CCTV footage."

"Bethany." Seth locks eyes with me. "Detective Kane can schedule an appointment if he wants to speak with you more."

"But you didn't see anyone in the truck with him?" Detective Kane ignores my brother and scribbles on his pad. "Can you provide any details about who this mystery person is he was yelling at?"

"Again, I told all of this to the other cop." I sigh, realizing I was right. Detective Hamstead didn't take me seriously that day. "No, I didn't see anyone. It's not like Benji invited me inside. All I heard was Benji yell, 'I caught you red-handed,' and 'You won't get away with this!' When I asked who he was talking to, he told me to get lost, then slammed the door."

"And who are these other teams you're referring to?" Detective Kane asks.

Seth grumbles about not giving me permission to speak, but I don't care. It's not his reputation on the line.

"Lumpia-Licious. The Katapangs have a habit of lurking in places they don't belong. According to rumors on set, during the first challenge, Benji found one of the sisters lurking around his truck, which made him upset. Not to mention they sell steamed buns."

"So?" Detective Kane prompts, his expression unreadable.

"Benji's note was about steamed buns, and they sell pork dumplings," I explain, the pieces clicking into place. "It's odd—he writes that note, and next thing you know, he's dead. It's not a stretch to connect their truck with the note."

"Or his truck," Detective Kane counters, leaning back. "Hot dog vendors steam buns all the time. Who else do you have?"

"Nacho Momma's Tacos. Willa Garza owns it."

"We spoke with Ms. Garza. She was unfamiliar with Benji before filming the show."

"She's lying! Willa worked with Benji on his truck. I can't believe she would deny knowing Benji."

"We need to go," Seth says. "The detective can schedule a meeting to continue our discussion."

I mirror my brother's tone. "This is my name at stake, not yours." I look back at the detective. "When I was in business school, I learned Willa worked with Benji for a brief stint, but things turned sour between them when she quit. She opened her own food truck, and it was a blatant copy of Benji's business."

Detective Kane furrows his brow, processing the information. "You believe there was bad blood between them?"

"If you have anything further to discuss, call my number to set up an appointment," Seth tells the detective. "We're leaving. Now."

My brother grips my arm, pulling me out of the room, but I stop short. "Believe me, Benji had a talent for holding grudges," I say to Detective Kane. "Benji was bitter toward Willa for appropriating his idea. Yes, things went south between them. He threatened to sue and had her blacklisted from events. A grudge left unchecked can become a dangerous thing."

Chapter Ten

Two days have passed since my interrogation with Detective Pretty Boy. Seth asked me not to make a habit of getting arrested. But based on what's been happening recently, it seems like I can't keep that promise.

As Rylie and I go through the motions of our daily routine on the truck, my mind replays on a loop all that's happened this week. Having a couple of days off from filming is a good thing. After everything that's happened, I need these days to get my blood pressure under control.

People are eagerly waiting in a long line to order, enticed by the aroma of sizzling chicken wings fresh from the fryer and a tantalizing blend of spices. Parked in our usual midweek spot, our cheerful yellow food truck is positioned in front of the stately facade of City Hall. I'm currently feeling envious of the happiness my chicken logo is exhibiting.

Inside our truck, the scent of sizzling chicken wafts through the air as Rylie and I are busy serving hungry customers. Ever since the first episode of *The Food Truck Showdown* aired, our customer base has exploded. Before filming began, our team agreed not to watch the show until we finished recording. We were concerned about our behavior being influenced by the way we were portrayed. Our focus should be cooking and the competition, not worrying about anything else.

Two older women approach the window. Both have wide grins. “You’re that truck from the show, aren’t you?” one of them asks.

“If you mean that show,” Rylie says, gesturing to the life-size cutout she had made of Bobbi Taylor to advertise our participation in the competition, “then yes, that’s us.”

“I knew it!” the first woman says. “I checked your social media page to see where you would be parked today. Cathy, didn’t I say it was worth the drive for us to come over here?”

“You did, Helen,” the second woman replies.

“Where are you from?” I ask the ladies. “Are you visiting the Bay Area?”

“We’re out by Aptos,” the first woman, Helen, replies.

“You drove for almost an hour and a half just for our truck?” The shock is obvious in my voice. We are a fan favorite!

“It’s no big deal,” says Cathy. “We’re retired and have little to do these days.”

“Plus, we haven’t made a trip into the city in ages,” Helen adds. “We’re going to stop and have a drink in Oakland on the way back. Did you know that Jack London used to write at Heinold’s First and Last Chance Saloon?”

“Mm-hmm,” I say with a nod. “It’s a National Literary Landmark.”

“Your wings looked mouthwatering on the screen,” Helen says. “We’ll take two baskets of your best sellers, and those fries you made in the last challenge.”

“Sure thing,” I say as Rylie begins preparing an order for them. “Anything else?”

The two women share a mischievous grin. “Well, since you asked,” Helen says.

"Spill the beans, darling!" Cathy demands. "We want the juicy details, the backstage drama, all the good stuff!"

"Sorry," I say. "The producers won't take kindly to me sharing insider secrets."

"We're sworn to secrecy," Rylie says, passing them each a basket of Plucked and Truffled Fries, along with a basket of the Kluckin' Greek and Klucked in the Bayou. "But I can promise you that this season has been a wild ride."

That's one way to put it.

"What happened to the hot dog truck? What was his name?" Helen asks Cathy.

"Benji Marley?" Helen says.

"No, you're thinking of the singer, Bob Mayhew."

Well, they each got the name half right.

"Do you mean Benji Mayhew?" I ask.

"Yes! That's him," Helen says. "Bobbi's announcement about him passing away from a heart attack was very heartbreaking."

"They showed that?" I'm shocked the producers included the part of Bobbi addressing his death with the contestants. What else have they added?

"Yeah." Helen nods. "Aren't you watching the show?"

"Our team decided to wait until the season ended or we got eliminated," I explain. "We didn't want our performance to be affected by the show."

Like worrying about how I look or how I'm portrayed when I have zero control over how I'm edited.

"I guess that makes sense," Helen says. "Can you tell us what happened to him? Was it sudden?"

Rylie and I look at each other. "Honestly . . ." I start.

"We don't know what happened," Rylie finishes.

"The producers haven't told us anything more than what you heard on TV," I tell the women.

Helen and Cathy give us a skeptical look. "That's strange. You were costars, after all."

"I don't know that I would call us costars," I mumble. "Like Rylie said, there hasn't been much talk about it. It's terrible he passed away, but I don't have anything else I can share."

Or will share. There's an ongoing investigation, and I'm in the middle of it.

But they're right. It is strange that the network isn't providing any details about what happened. They're telling us—and the viewers—that Benji died of a heart attack. Clearly, that's a lie. The police wouldn't be calling this a homicide for no reason, right?

Cathy gives us another skeptical look while handing over a credit card. "There must be something you can share about the show. A sneak peek, perhaps?"

"Who's the toughest competitor?" Helen asks. "Are there any alliances or behind-the-scenes romances?" Her silver eyebrows give me a playful wiggle.

"Yeah!" Cathy nods at her friend. "What about the youngest Dough Brother boy? He's cute. Do you like him?"

I can feel my face getting hot with embarrassment. My cheeks must be turning bright red.

"There's nothing between me and Beckett," I tell them while returning their card after processing their orders.

"Well, that's a shame," Helen remarks.

"Yeah," Cathy says. "Our church bingo was hoping the two of you would get together."

"What about you and her brother?" Helen points at Rylie.

"Is he here?" Cathy strains to see inside the truck.

"Seth's on his way," I say.

"So what's going on between you two?" Helen asks Rylie.

"Wh . . . what?" Rylie stammers. "I'm not sure what you mean."

"Oh, come now," Cathy says, grabbing a fry. "You don't mean to tell me there's nothing between the two of you either?"

"Don't know what to tell you," I say to the nosy women. "There's nothing romantic happening on set that I'm aware of. Isn't that right, Rylie?" I look at my best friend.

Rylie gives a high-pitched laugh. My eyes turn to slits as I examine her.

"She's right. There's nothing going on with us. Well, at least nothing that's worth talking about," Rylie tells them. "We're friends. The three of us grew up together. But Seth and me?" Rylie lets out another laugh, this one strangled. "We're *good* friends, that's all. Have been for years. Our families were even next-door neighbors for quite a while. But enough about the show, ladies. How do you like our food?"

Why is she rambling?

"Humph," the women say at the same time.

"Well, your food is . . . how do the youngsters phrase it?" Cathy asks. "The bomb?"

"I believe it's '*Da* Bomb,'" her friend corrects her.

"Well, now, that doesn't make sense." Cathy shakes her head, sampling more of our food. "There's no such word as 'Da.'"

"I don't know what to tell you, Cathy," Helen says. "Kids these days speak a language that doesn't make sense."

These two women are characters. "Don't they remind you of Loretta and Ella Mae?" I whisper to Rylie, who nods in agreement.

Realizing they won't get any more information out of us, they smile and say goodbye.

"At least these wings were worth our butts going numb on the drive up here," I overhear one of them say as they walk away.

"That's the third customer today who told us they stopped by because of the show," Rylie says while grabbing a rag to clean the serving counter.

"I know." I smile. "It's great how much business has picked up."

I begin making another batch of mac-and-cheese poppers when I hear Rylie ask a customer, "What can I get you?"

"Tell me, what makes your wings and sliders so special?"

That voice!

"Detective," Rylie says. "How nice of you to stop by. What makes us so special is the secret sauce. Our homemade concoctions set us apart. Tangy, sweet, spicy—you name it, we've got it. Our customers can't get enough."

How is she so calm while engaging with him?

"Secret sauce, you say? Whaddya say, Drew? Should we try it?"

Not him too.

"Sure," the first voice says. "I can always eat."

"It's such a delightful surprise to see *both* of you at our truck today," Rylie says. "Is there something we can help you with?" She glances in my direction.

"Just curious about your daily specials," Detective Hamstead says.

Rylie points to the chalkboard menu outside the truck. "Have a look. We've got a wide range of flavors. Let me know if anything catches your eye."

Listening to the men responsible for my stress and anxiety, I accidentally spill a cup of breadcrumbs on myself and the prep counter. Walking toward the window, I brush the mess off my shirt and lean out, ignoring what my customers must think.

"Is there something I can help you with, Detective Kane?" I try to keep my tone modulated, but it's harder than expected once I see him. "Are you here to lob more false accusations at me?" The words come out rough and accusatory, but I don't care.

"I lobbed nothing at you," he says. "I merely asked questions."

Rylie's attention shifts uncomfortably between us.

"Wow, you are something," I say, crossing my arms.

"Something special, I hope." He winks at me.

The man has the audacity to smile at me with those charming dimples of his!

Despite my best efforts, I can't hide my feelings, and I scowl. "What can I do for you, Detectives?"

Now he's not just smiling but also chuckling. *If I weren't under suspicion of murder, I would give him a piece of my mind.*

"That was called 'doing my job.' It's nothing personal."

"It sure felt personal," I say.

"Oh, trust me. You'll know when I get personal."

"Maybe you should step outside," Rylie suggests to me, as our line of customers grumble impatiently. "I'll cover the truck."

Looking between Detective Kane and Detective Hamstead, I say, "It's fine. I don't need to go anywhere. I'm sure they were just leaving."

"We just need a moment of your time. Again." With one swift move, Detective Kane reveals a badge, instantly capturing everyone's attention and silencing their protests. "I appreciate the patience, everyone."

Over the past two days, I've been doing some investigating of my own into Detective Kane. His sharp wit and investigative skills have made him a well-known figure in town, despite being new to the area. The crowd's grumbles turn into hushed whispers of curiosity, and likely rumors too, as they gawk at my truck.

Yesterday, I told Rylie that the officer who arrested me a few weeks ago and the detective at the studio lot are the same person. "Officer Pretty Boy looks better than I remember," she whispers.

A deep and pleasing sound emanates from outside the truck. "What is wrong with you?" I ask her. Rylie gives me an apologetic look, while Detective Kane and his partner continue to laugh.

Listening to him causes a warm shiver to run down my spine. *My blood pressure must be spiking again. Why else would I feel tingles?*

"It's Detective," he corrects her while casually leaning against my truck. "Detective Drew Kane. And this is my partner, Jerry Hamstead."

"He also goes by Officer Pretty Boy," his partner adds.

"I'm still new to the department and didn't have a nickname." Detective Kane says. "That all changed when I brought you down to the station dressed as a giant chicken and you called me that."

There's no malice in his words. If anything, he seems to find the entire situation rather comical.

"You're welcome," I say.

"This seems like a private matter. Maybe I should go." Rylie looks between the three of us.

"The detectives won't be staying." *At least I hope they won't be.* "Anything they have to say to me they can say to you."

"She's right. We won't be here long," he says with a dimpled smile. His annoying, albeit good-looking, face is getting on my nerves.

The customers standing in line resume grumbling, causing Detective Kane to turn around and flash his badge again. "Sorry, everyone, the truck is closed. Police business. You can come back in ten minutes."

"Are you serious?" I shout as I watch my lunch rush of patrons walk away. "There were fifteen people in line! Do you know how much you just cost me?"

"If they're hungry, they'll come back," Detective Hamstead says.

"I need to make a call." Rylie mutters something in Portuguese and bolts from the truck.

"Rylie!" I call out, but she's already gone.

"Now that we don't have any distractions, we can talk," Detective Kane says.

"Make it quick, Detective," I say irritably. "I've got bills to pay, and talking with you is cutting into my lunch rush. Is there a reason you're here?"

"Can't a man have a craving for some wings and fries?" he asks.

"Can you get to the point already?" I'm frustrated by how much money this conversation is costing me.

As Detective Kane moves away from the truck, he flicks his tongue out to moisten his lips. "I wanted to discuss—"

"Not another word!" The back door of my truck slams shut while a voice yells in agitation. "Detective," Seth says, appearing next to me, "I explicitly stated that my client is off-limits unless I'm present."

My brother looms over me as I look up. His eyes burn with intense anger as he glares at the men outside the truck. If this is his lawyer face, I wouldn't want to be in court against him.

"What are you doing here?" I ask.

"Rylie called. I was nearby, so I made a quick detour. You know not to discuss things without me." Then, with steely eyes, Seth looks back at the officers. "Are you harassing my client?"

In a placating gesture, Detective Kane holds up his palms. "Relax, Counselor. Or should I say, Mr. Lloyd?" His eyes sparkle, almost as if he's enjoying this game with Seth. "I checked into you. It seems you've yet to pass the bar exam."

Taking a deep breath, my twin turns to look at me.

"Seth," I warn.

"You're right. I haven't passed yet," Seth admits with a hint of cockiness. "But, had you completed your homework, you would know that the California Supreme Court has sanctioned a temporary lawyer's licensing program for law school graduates."

"Meaning?" Detective Hamstead asks.

"Meaning," Seth says in a haughty voice, "as long as applicants have an offer of employment, which I *do*, they're considered provisional lawyers. I have the mandatory mentor training and guiding me. In December, the provision will no longer be in effect. By then, my only requirement is passing the bar. Which I *will* do."

Seth looks like a smug poker player who knows he's about to win a big hand. "Under California law, I may act on my sister's behalf." *BAM!* Seth plays his trump card and, based on Detective Kane's expression, just won the game.

"Remind me never to underestimate you, Counselor," he says.

Seth's anger dissipates as he cracks his neck from side to side. "What can we do for you, Detective Kane?"

"My partner and I stopped by to inform your sister that she's no longer a person of interest in the investigation of Benji Mayhew."

"I appreciate the information, but why?" I ask. This feels like a joke and I'm the punchline.

"We're following new forensic evidence," he says.

"Your hair don't match the profile—"

"Jerry," Detective Kane cuts his partner off.

"Can you clarify what you mean?" Seth asks.

"Yeah, how does that rule me out as a suspect?"

"Person of interest," Detective Kane corrects.

"What's the difference?"

"The difference," Seth answers, "is a person of interest is someone who the police believe has information that can help further their investigation, whereas a suspect is a specific person who authorities believe may have committed the crime."

Detective Kane taps his nose. "Also," he adds, "a person of interest may be someone who can provide information that leads to a suspect or turn into a suspect themselves."

"And why do I no longer fit the bill?" It annoys me to have to ask, but I need to know.

"Whoever did this to Benji used—"

"Jerry!" Detective Kane gives his partner a withering look.

"Despite your history and having the last known interaction with the deceased, evidence has us looking elsewhere."

"That's not an answer. I could've killed him for all you know."

"Bethany!" Seth yells, and Detective Hamstead laughs.

"Nah," Detective Kane says with a faint smirk that feels annoyingly self-assured.

I narrow my eyes at him. "It's been well established I didn't like the guy. How can you be so certain I didn't do it?"

"Bethany," Seth growls. "Shut up!"

Detective Kane tilts his head, studying me like he's trying to decide whether I'm testing him or just being reckless. "You're not the type," he finally says.

"Oh, really? And what exactly is my 'type,' Detective?"

His grin widens, slow and infuriating. "The type who talks too much to pull off murder."

I blink, caught somewhere between outrage and a begrudging urge to laugh. "You don't know me."

"No, but I'm getting a pretty good idea."

I can't stand him, his comments, or those infuriating dimples.

"Bethany Anne Lloyd." Despite his efforts to remain professional, Seth's frustration with me is obvious. "Would you shut up? He's saying you're innocent."

"Guys?" Turning around, I see Rylie at the back of the truck. "The lunch line is forming again." She walks up to the order window. "Detectives, are you still interested in something? Perhaps to go?"

Detective Kane turns and gives a nod to the customers who are standing a distance behind him. "Sure, we'll take anything you have. Thank you," he says to Rylie.

"Meu Deus!" Rylie touches her temple. "Beth, I think you should get the food."

I grumble as I move out of the way and box up two orders of Korean BBQ beef sliders from the hot holders. On the side, I add the poutine gravy, with a large order of Plucked and Truffled Fries. After securing the lid, I hand Detective Kane their order through the serving window.

"Thank you." As he grabs the box, his fingers brush mine, and I jump back.

"What's wrong with you?" Seth stares at me.

"Static electricity," I say, rubbing my hand. Detective Kane looks at his hand, then raises a questioning eyebrow at me.

I have a bad habit of shuffling my feet when I walk. There's no other reason to feel a spark when I touch a person's hand.

Except there's no carpet in here.

"By the way, what's wrong with my hair?" I touch the back of my baseball cap and feel my small ponytail stick out.

"Nothing," he says as he passes a box to his partner.

"We found the victim holding several strands of dark, medium-length hair, not strawberry-blond," Detective Hamstead shares while staring longingly at his food.

"You're killing me right now, Jerry," Detective Kane says. "Shove something in your pie hole and shut up, will you?"

Detective Hamstead gives his partner a blank stare before devouring a slider in one large bite.

"Benji had a severely receding hairline," Seth recalls, gazing into the distance. "So, the hair wasn't his. Since Benji ran his truck alone, it's reasonable to assume that the hair you found belongs to the killer."

I gasp and point at Rylie. "You have dark, medium-length hair!"

"It wasn't me!" Her hand flies to her hair in a hurry.

"It's the most common color," Seth says. "Relax."

Detective Kane samples a few fries, humming in satisfaction. "Don't worry, Ms. Cortes, you've already been ruled out."

"You investigated me?" She clutches the front of her neck. "I feel violated."

"Just doing my job." He stuffs a few more fries into his mouth.

"Is there anything else we can do for you, Detective Kane?" My fingers are still tingling.

"Keep your ear to the ground and tell me if you hear anything while filming." Taking a bite of one of his sliders, he lets out a moan. "Delicious."

We take pride in our food, but hearing appreciation is always welcome.

"What kind of stuff?" Rylie asks him.

"Anything suspicious," he says. "You never know what you might come across."

"The Jaxsons received a creepy note," Rylie informs the detectives.

"What kind of note?" Detective Kane asks.

"It said 'Piss off,'" I say. "When Dane lifted a lid on a pot, he said someone had poured sour lemonade in it. The resemblance to the first note was uncanny. You should talk to Imogen. She's the one who has it."

"This whole note business sounds like a juvenile prank, if you ask me," Detective Hamstead says.

And he's the reason I'm not ready to share my Kluckin' Clues list with the cops just yet.

"Sure," I tell Detective Kane. "If I come across something, I'll let you know."

"Is there cause for worry about staying on the show?" Rylie asks.

Before responding, Detective Kane exchanges a glance with his partner. "I can't make that decision for you. Just be smart. Keep your feathers up." Shifting his food container, he pulls out a card from his pocket and places it on the serving window ledge. "Here's my number. Call anytime."

"Will do," I say in a neutral tone.

Detective Kane gives me another wink and walks away with his partner.

"Hey!" I hang my head out the serving window and call after him. "You forgot to pay!"

"Put it on my tab!"

The nerve!

Chapter Eleven

With my hair brushed until it shines, mascara applied, and my lips tinted to their everyday soft pink-beige shade, I take one last look in Rylie's compact mirror and feel ready to face whatever awaits me for a day of filming.

Or so I thought.

I'm immediately bombarded by my fellow competitors just a few feet from my truck. "What happened to you the other day?" asks Sofia.

"Did the police really arrest you?" Marco asks.

"Did you and that there Benji fella have a lover's spat?" asks Loretta. "Is that why you killed him?"

"Loretta!" Ella Mae slaps her partner's arm. "What in tarnation is wrong with you? You don't ask people that."

Loretta ignores Ella Mae's scolding and waves her away. "You were too good for him, anyway. You're as pretty as a mess of fried catfish."

Is that a compliment?

"You're not answering us," Ness says. "Are we to assume you're a lover scorned? Were the two of you involved in a tawdry affair? Did he leave you for someone else? Someone younger?"

Ness's comments and everyone else's questions cause me to choke on my saliva.

"What?" she asks. "I've seen stranger things happen."

"Just tell us," Dane says. "We know Benji didn't die of a heart attack." He looks around, then whispers, "Why'd you do it?"

"We don't know that!" Marco says. "This whole thing could be a big misunderstanding."

"There's no misunderstanding that Benji's dead," Ness says. "The question is, why?"

"No," Dane says. "The question is, *how*?"

"The why and the how go together," Ness replies. "*Why* is Benji dead, and *how* did he die?"

She's right. Why is Benji dead? How did it happen? Who did he piss off? And why is Marco unwilling to believe that he was killed?

"Tell us, Beth." Ness stares at me. "*Why* did you do it?"

"I didn't do anything."

"*How* did you do it?" Dane asks.

"I'm not involved with this!"

"*Mãe de Deus.*" Rylie shakes her head. "What's wrong with you people? Beth is innocent! Do you have nothing better to do than gossip?"

"It's fine, Rylie." I try to ignore the comments buzzing around like annoying flies, but it seems everyone has formed their own opinion already. "No, everyone, I'm not a lover scorned. Benji and I were the furthest possible thing from lovers." Pausing, I cover my mouth with my hand at the word "lovers," trying to hold back the urge to vomit. When I'm sure I'm fine, I continue. "I didn't do anything to harm Benji." This conversation is so eye roll–inducing. "The police just had a few questions, that's all."

"About what?" asks Sofia. "I spoke with, oh, what's his name?" She snaps her fingers. "Matteo? No, no, Diego? The guy with glasses who helps Imogen."

"Do you mean Sergio?" I ask.

"Yes! That's him. He told me it was a heart attack that killed Benji. The same thing that Bobbi Taylor told us."

"That would make sense," Ben Quill says. "When I was at the police station yesterday to give a formal statement, I overheard someone talking about a heart attack on my way out of the building."

"Did someone at the station specifically tell you Benji died of a heart attack?" Rylie asks him.

"Well, no," he admits. "But it must be what killed him. Why else would the network keep the show going? Besides, why would there be talk of a heart attack at the police station?"

"It sounds to me like you're assuming," Seth says. "There are countless explanations for why you heard the term 'heart attack'. It's possible that an officer experienced one recently. Perhaps you caught just a snippet of a conversation warning someone about their eating habits. Or, someone was having a phone conversation with their doctor, discussing symptoms to keep an eye out for."

"I mean . . . well . . ." Ben stammers. "I guess all of that's true. But it's the only logical conclusion for Benji's death. Otherwise we would've all gone home by now."

He's right. We should've gone home. It wasn't a heart attack that killed Benji. Something bigger is at play. They wouldn't continue the show if we were in danger. Right?

"What about when you spoke to the police, Beth?" Ben looks at me. "Did they tell you how he died?"

"Nope." A reddish-blond lock tumbles over my eyebrow, and I push it back. These food truck owners may not be familiar with me, but I know for a fact that they love to gossip. There's no way I'm adding anything to their theories.

"If it's a heart attack, why did the police talk to you?" Sofia asks Ben. "That's *if* a heart attack is the true cause of death. Seems to me like this would be open and shut if it were a heart attack."

"Why is everyone so determined to blow this out of proportion?" Marco asks his wife.

"Are you afraid?" Sofia asks.

"Yes, I'm afraid!" Marco makes a cross over his chest. "I'm worried about *la mia famiglia.* But there's too much at stake for us financially. We need to see this through." Pinching his fingers and thumb together, he shakes a hand in front of his face.

"Marco thinks someone broke into our truck and stole ingredients." Sofia nibbles on her lower lip. "It's happened twice."

"It's been three times!" Marco shouts. "Don't forget our pasta noodles were dumped on the floor." In Italian, Marco mumbles a string of words. "Something is going on. We're getting a camera for the truck today," he says while jabbing a finger into his palm. "I found a shop downtown that can install a new system. It's pricey, but it's worth it. If there aren't cameras on this lot to protect our property, then we'll do it ourselves!"

"What do you mean?" Sofia has switched from chewing her lip to wringing her fingers.

"I told Imogen what happened and demanded she check the cameras," Marco explains. "But she said there wasn't anything she could do because filming of trucks doesn't happen unless a challenge is underway."

How convenient. Another truck is sabotaged, and there's no evidence.

"Let's add this to our Kluckin' Clues list," Rylie suggests as she takes out her phone to type.

"If you're worried, why do you stay?" I ask Marco.

"If we lived closer, I would leave." Marco says.

"I understand," Ben says to Marco. "Like you, I also have a wife and children. The officer wanted to know if I saw anything dodgy happening when we were selling at the pier," he says to the group. "Apparently there were some issues down there the day of filming."

"What issues? What did you tell them?" Sofia is leaning in, eager to hear every word.

"The details were vague, but there were complaints about people trespassing in trucks." Ben leans forward a little, using a parking cone for support. "My brothers and I were more focused on selling and keeping up with the crowd to notice anything else."

"Was it Detective Kane you spoke with?" I ask Ben.

He points at me and nods. "Straight shooter, he tells it like it is."

"What did the police ask you, Beth?" Sofia is sweet in a motherly way. But boy, is she nosy.

Seth briefly makes eye contact with me. Our twin connection does the talking for us.

Don't be stupid, Beth.

I'm not.

Don't say anything.

I won't.

I casually shrug at the group. "Same as Ben. They just wanted to see if I'd noticed anything else. Nothing gossip-worthy, I'm afraid."

"That's not what I heard," says Willa Garza as she struts over to join the conversation, her daughter, Bria, in tow. "You were the last person to talk with Benji before he died. The two of you got into an argument and exchanged threats. I'll bet that's the real reason the police took you in."

"Mierda," Rylie swears under her breath. "What do you know, Willa? You weren't even around when Beth and Benji chatted."

"Chatted?" Willa gives a scornful laugh. "Is that what you're calling it?" Then she turns her vulture eyes on me. "It's a small lot, Beth. Word gets around."

Rylie is right. Willa wasn't around while I talked to Benji. She might have been hiding around his truck, similar to the Katapang sisters. Perhaps the Katapang sisters were the source of Willa's information. Benji wasn't quiet when he told me to get lost. But Willa and Benji had a less than pleasant history. Could she have been the person he was yelling at?

Was she in the truck with him?

Was she the anonymous tipster?

"You don't seem to be broken up over his death," I accuse her, fishing for answers. Or clues. "But then again, why would you? You don't like anyone."

She looks directly at me, her dark brows forming a thin, arched line. "At least I never beat up his truck." Flipping her dark-brown ponytail, she looks away from me.

Dark brown . . .

"No, you just ripped it off," I say sarcastically.

Someone makes an "ooooh" sound.

"Perhaps Benji was still upset after all this time, and he provoked you. Did you attack him, Willa?" My question elicits gasps and muttering in Italian from Marco.

This probably isn't what Detective Kane meant when he said to "keep my ear to the ground," but I can't pass up this opportunity.

I scrutinize her face, looking for any sign of a tell. She's like a stone wall, showing no emotion. Her face serves as a flawless representation of the advantages of Botox.

Keep a straight face with the help of Botox.

And avoid revealing your possible involvement in murder.

"You know what Benji was like," Willa says. "He held grudges."

Not the confession I was hoping for.

"Well, it's not like I'd blame Beth if she hauled off on him." Loretta throws her two cents into the conversation. "I only talked with him twice, and that was two times too many. That man acted like the sun came up just to hear him crow."

"Loretta," Ella Mae warns.

"Beth, you're as hot as a two-dollar pistol and prettier than a speckled pup in a wagon. You did what you had to."

Loretta's comments again leave me questioning whether I should be offended.

"I haven't done anything," I remind the crowd.

"Mom, we should go." Bria tugs at her mother's arm. "Let's not start anything again."

Again? What does she mean by that?

I observe closely as Bria talks with her mother. They share the same luscious, dark waves and are both taller than the average woman.

Clapping her hands, Imogen walks up with Sloane, dispelling the tension, and addresses everyone. "All right, I know things are a little tense, but we can't afford anymore setbacks. Disagreeing is fine, but it can't slow down filming." Imogen's focus is on Willa and me. "It's important to keep personal issues off the set and focus on work."

"Beth started—"

"I don't care who started things." Imogen reprimands Willa like a child. "We are all adults, and I expect you to act like it. The network won't think twice about canceling another underperforming show, which is what we will be if you don't keep your personal issues in check. Save the drama for when the cameras are rolling. Now then"—Imogen looks at everyone—"please follow me to the stage to start your next challenge."

"Hang on." I stop Imogen and Sloane. "Can I talk to you?" I lower my voice. "It's about the notes going around—"

"Later!" Imogen cuts me off. "The clock is ticking, which means we're losing money."

She and Sloane walk away before I have time to finish my sentence. "I'm never gonna get to ask her about that note from the grocery store," I say, venting my frustration to Rylie.

"You will." She pats my shoulder. "Let's go before we get yelled at."

The cool autumn breeze picks up, causing a shiver to run down my spine. "I'll catch up with you," I tell her. "I need to grab a sweater. Save a sprinkled doughnut for me."

On my way back to the truck, I spot a folded paper taped to the front door. Peeling it off, then unfolding it, I read what the bold, clunky letters spell out.

Keep snooping, and you'll be cooked before the next elimination round. I read the note again and again, trying to make sense of it. I stop a showrunner looking at a folder. "Did you see anyone near my truck?"

The guy shakes his head. "I just got here, sorry." He goes back to his folder and walks away.

Leaving my sweater behind, I tuck the paper into my jeans pocket. According to Imogen, the cameras on the lot aren't filming anything unless they're actively shooting. Looking toward the warehouse, I confirm the production trailer and refreshment tent are blocking my view. Looks like the CCTV caught nothing, if they're even working. I glance around the parking lot to see if anybody's watching me. The only thing I see is Hoot Jackman, perched in his nest on the edge of the warehouse building, staring right at me. I wave at him, and he turns his head. I sigh. I was hoping we'd be a dynamic duo. Without wasting a moment, I hastily rejoin the group.

"Where's your sweater?" Seth whispers as I plunk down next to him. "Rylie said you were grabbing a sweater."

"Listen up, everyone!" Imogen adjusts her glasses, calling out to the contestants. "We'll record pre-competition interviews before starting the challenge. Follow me to the greenroom in the warehouse building." Using her clipboard, she signals for us to follow.

"Where's my doughnut?" I hold out my hand to Rylie.

"Sorry, *irmã,* you took too long. I got hungry." She licks a sprinkle from her upper lip, completely unapologetic.

"Where's your sweater?" Seth asks again.

"What?!" I let out a piercing squeal. "You ate my doughnut!" I've been accused of being Benji's lover—*ick, gag, shudder*—and of killing him, and I just received a threatening note. I'm hangry, and no one, including Rylie, can eat my doughnut.

"Sorry, *irmã.*"

I lean over Seth and poke a finger at her to make my point. "You are no sister of mine."

"Here," a man's voice says. I look up to see Beckett extending one of the wrapped items he's holding. "It's not a doughnut, but it's worth a try."

I blink a few times and stare. Beckett Quill, the youngest of the Dough Brothers, hardly talks, especially to me. He goes to great lengths to avoid unnecessary conversations with people. When I don't reply, he sits next to me and puts the item in my hand.

"Thanks." I look at the warm, cinnamon-scented bundle. As I unfold the foil, I gasp. "Is this what I think it is?" I bring the pastry to my mouth and take a bite. "Oh my gawd, ghffuh mmnet."

"What?" Beckett looks disturbed as he watches me moan and chew. Has he never seen a foodgasm before?

"Allow me. I'm fluent in Bethenese," offers Seth. "She said, 'Oh my god, give me a minute.'"

I nod emphatically while the cinnamon sugar heaven explodes in my mouth. These round sugary delights were a hit during the first challenge, and people couldn't stop talking about them. I was hoping to get my hands on one, but Ben told me they sold out.

"Oh my god, Beckett!" The loudness of my squeal would hurt even a dog. "This is amazing!" I stuff another chunk into my mouth, like a squirrel gathering nuts for winter.

"Elephant ears are one of our biggest sellers."

Seth swoops in like a bird of prey, snatching the last bite of the sugary sweet bread. Hangry Beth is still in charge of me, so he's lucky there are people and cameras around.

"Oh wow." Seth's eyes double. "This is amazing. Man, everybody better watch out for you guys," Seth says, smacking his lips.

Beckett gives Seth a two-finger salute and leaves to find his brothers, while Seth eagerly licks his lips, trying to get the last of the sugar granules.

"Speaking of watching out"—I fish the note out of my pocket and hand it to my brother—"here."

He scans the paper before flipping it over to examine the back. "That's it? Nothing else?"

"Nope, just that," I say, sucking the last of the cinnamon sugar from my fingertips.

"Did you tell Imogen?" he asks. "Maybe she can check if a camera caught something."

"Imogen told us that unless we're actively filming, cameras aren't recording. Someone left the note before the show started."

"I still think she should know about this." Seth shakes the paper. "Someone is trying to send a message."

"I'm aware. If I find her, I'll tell her," I say, more to pacify him than anything.

"What's on the paper?" Rylie asks, looking over Seth's shoulder.

"Looks like a threat to me," Ben remarks, joining us from behind.

"What's the point of these notes? Who would target *our* food truck? We've done nothing."

"Well, you won the last challenge," Ben says. "When Dane and Ness won, someone took a leak in their pots. Maybe this is the same."

"They didn't win," I correct him. "Benji was the winner, but he . . . you know . . ." I motion with my hand.

"Died," Rylie supplies.

"Yeah . . ." I say, while chewing on my thumbnail.

"So really, it's not that far of a leap to think we're being targeted because we won," Rylie suggests.

Did someone know Benji was going to win, and he was killed because of it?

"Surely, someone wouldn't be taking this competition so far as to try to . . . you know . . ." I drag my finger across my throat.

"You're a true-crime enthusiast but have difficulty saying the word 'murder'?" Seth is totally judging me right now.

"I want to point out that those documentaries are quite relaxing," I say.

"As expected from a genuine weirdo," Seth comments.

"Guys," Rylie interjects. "Can we focus on the note?"

"Do you think the threatening notes are connected to the missing ingredients?" asks Beckett.

All of us look at him. "I may be quiet, but I listen. Almost everyone has had something go missing or received a threatening note."

"Could Beckett be on to something? Are the two things linked?" Rylie asks.

"I wonder," I say to her. "Perhaps it's a game of cat-and-mouse."

"But who's the cat?" my brother asks.

"I think it could be someone here," I answer, looking around at the group.

"Beth, it's clearly someone here," Seth scoffs.

"Stop being a jerk face." I shove my brother's shoulder. "What is the one thing that all seasons of this show have in common, Rylie?"

"Someone leaving in tears?" she guesses.

"We already had that when Lila Katapang broke down crying after their elimination," Ben says.

"Well, yes, someone always cries at some point," I say. "But there's always drama. Equipment breaking down. Or tension between the contestants." Before advancing with my theory, I take a moment to think. "The show always has viewers glued to the screen each week to see what happens next."

"What's your point?" Ben asks.

"It's television," Seth says, seeing where I'm going. "Anything is possible on reality TV. If there isn't enough drama, they'll create it. I've seen cases like this at work. A reality TV client will want to take legal action for their portrayal in a show. Unfortunately, people often overlook the fine print in their contracts that allows a network to depict them in any manner they choose."

Media law was Seth's focus in school. He knows what he's talking about.

"If that's true, a production member could be the one pulling the strings," Ella Mae speculates as she and Loretta become a part of our group.

Seth rubs his chin. “Manipulating content for better ratings is not uncommon in the TV industry. Contestants sabotaging each other is also not an uncommon occurrence.”

Whatever is going on here is beyond sabotage.

“This might be the type of thing Detective Pretty Boy would want you to tell him,” Rylie points out.

“I will,” I say. “Once I’ve done some more investigating.”

“Why wait?” Ella Mae asks me.

“Detective Hamstead didn’t give any importance to what I overheard in Benji’s truck,” I tell her. “When Rylie mentioned the note that the Jaxsons received, he dismissed it as a juvenile prank. I need concrete evidence that can’t be refuted. My gut is is telling me that everything is connected.”

“Are you sure your gut isn’t just reacting to that elephant ear you just housed?” Seth asks.

Ignoring him, I gesture toward the paper that Seth is still clutching. “We need to find out for sure who’s behind that note.”

Before Seth can weigh in, Sergio calls out to us. “Team Kluckin’ Good! We’re ready for you in the greenroom.”

Chapter Twelve

"These stupid interviews are the worst," I mutter as I storm out of the greenroom.

With a soft laugh, Seth reflects, "It's not that bad."

I take a generous sip of water to wash away the taste of vomit in my mouth. "You weren't the person dry heaving on camera." Swallowing after swishing the water around, I take another gulp. "Do you think they'll keep the footage?"

"Of course they will. That was comedic gold!" Seth laughs again.

"I'm gonna be sick!" I groan as I take another swig from my bottle.

I knew there would be some things I wouldn't like about being on the show. The editors could depict you as the villain or the hero. Okay, fine. But I never expected to be mistaken for a couple instead of twins. When the interviewer asked how I enjoyed working with my "significant other," I again had to stop myself from vomiting. I avoided puking everywhere, but the retching sounds I made were beyond my control. First, people thought I dated Benji, now this?

"It was just an intern covering. The kid confused us with Dane and Ness." Seth tries to get me to lighten up.

"The thought of you, my twin, as my life partner—*gag*—I'm gonna be sick." Taking a seat on a bench, I tuck my head between my knees.

"I hate to break it to you," Seth says, "but we are life partners."

"Not in the traditional sense!" I shout, taking deep breaths like I'm in labor.

"Beth," Loretta calls as she and Ella Mae walk over. "What's got your goat?"

Seth waves off her concern. "She's being overdramatic about our interview."

"Overdramatic?" I shout, while keeping my head buried between my knees.

"Ignore her," Seth says. "What can we do for you ladies?"

"I heard 'bout that note you found," Ella Mae drawls, her tone casual. "You gone and talked to Imogen or Sloane 'bout it yet?"

"I haven't," I admit.

"I reckon you should," she suggests.

"I intend to, but I'm still talking with a few of the others to determine if there's a pattern emerging. Then, I'll go to Imogen, and hopefully she'll take me seriously."

"Don't be so quick to butter your biscuit," Loretta drawls. "I've already tried talkin' with Imogen. That conversation was as worthless as gum on a boot heel!"

Without waiting for a response, Loretta launches into a long story about someone taking their biscuit dough, leaving them without biscuits to accompany their chicken and dumplings. "Them judges blamed us for not havin' what we needed. That's cattywampus, I'll tell you what!"

Loretta fixes her wide-brimmed hat, which is decorated with a bright feather, then exchanges a glance with Ella Mae. "Quit being ugly, Loretta," Ella Mae tells her. "Ignore her. She's just worn slap out."

Loretta gives Ella Mae a look that speaks volumes. "If it weren't for the Katapangs being eliminated for their bitter radicchio, we would've been sent home packin'."

"I've had it up to here"—Ella Mae gestures with her hand—"with you and that biscuit dough. I don't want to hear it anymore. It doesn't amount to a hill of beans." She shakes her head, her silver curls bouncing.

Loretta shifts her attention back to Rylie, who is jotting down notes. "I tried talkin' with Imogen about the stolen dough. She ignored me, so I decided to mention it during our interview. The producers threw a hissy fit when I tried s'plaining that perhaps the same individual who ruined Dane and Ness's pots and pans could be responsible for takin' our ingredients. But, good gravy, you would have thought I said 'son of a biscuit eater' on live TV." Her Southern twang really comes out when she's worked up. "I cain't stand all this nonsense. This show is gonna make me lose my religion. I'm ready to just quit this whole thing."

Loretta's feelings are valid. The purpose of the show is to offer contestants a food truck culinary adventure. The stress we experience should stem from the challenges we face and striving to reach our full potential. Not because we're always on edge, worried about being the next target.

"That's everyone," Rylie says after we finished talking with our fellow contestants.

Seth stands nearby, snacking on a pack of peanut butter crackers he swiped from my bag. Despite teasing me about my snack-carrying habit, he's always the first to ask for food. I look at the shared note on my phone. "Our Kluckin' Clues list indicates that something eerie or threatening has happened to every team since the show began. All except Willa Garza. What are the odds of that?"

Seth steps closer, popping another cracker into his mouth as he peers over my shoulder at the screen. "That is weird. Why would she be the only one left out?"

Just then, Willa walks by with her eyes glued to her phone. It's almost as if the mere mention of her name summoned her. I need to see if I can glean any info. Maybe she has been targeted and we just don't know. Plastering on a smile, I call to her. "Hey, Willa."

She shows no interest in looking up from her screen. "Beth." The way she says my name oozes with hostility.

I force myself to stay calm. "Willa, I have no desire to argue with you. I'm just being polite, nothing more."

"Of course you are, Little Miss Goody Two-Shoes. But I'm not looking for friendship or polite conversations."

I cross my arms. "Congrats for being the reality show contestant who's not here to make friends. How original."

She glares at me before shooing me with her hand and returning to her phone.

I clench my jaw, my patience wearing thin. "Is there a reason you're being so hostile, Willa?"

With a dark chuckle, Willa looks up, and her eyes glint in satisfaction for getting to me. She leans in closer, her voice barely above a whisper. "Let's just say I've had an interesting phone call recently with people who have a keen interest in what goes on behind the scenes of the show."

My breath catches in my throat as I watch Willa straighten and the puzzle pieces align. "It was because of *you* that the police appeared on set and brought me to the station." I take a moment to stare into her icy brown eyes. "You're the anonymous tipster!"

Her smirk turns into a knowing smile. "I never said that, did I? But then again, who's saying what I do in my free time?" She takes a few steps away, then pauses, looking back over at me. "Anonymous implies that you will never find out."

My heart races as I clench my fists tightly. "I can't believe you did this, Willa!" I take a step toward her, but Seth's hand grips my wrist, pulling me back.

"Let it go," Seth whispers. "She's not worth it."

"Do you realize what you could have done?" I ask her, ignoring Seth's advice.

Willa shrugs. "It's a dog-eat-dog world in this business. I don't regret a thing."

Anger and tension fill the air as Willa returns to her phone and heads to the warehouse. While I'd love to get revenge on her, I won't degrade myself. What's important to me is clearing my name, not resorting to her questionable methods.

"Mulher horrível, horrível." Rylie lets loose a string of words I don't know and am not sure I want to know. "She's an awful, horrible person." Shaking her head, she attempts to calm herself. "Remember what I heard her say to her daughter, Bria, after the Katapangs were eliminated? 'One less team to stand in my way.'"

"What are you going to do with that information?" Rylie asks while we head to the truck. "Do you want to go to Imogen with this?"

"No. I feel like we've been getting the blow off from her and the rest of production. Even Loretta got the same treatment. I find it hard to believe that there are no cameras recording what's going on. We're on a production lot, for goodness' sake!" Pausing outside my truck's door, I think for a moment. "But I do know someone we should talk to."

Chapter Thirteen

"Kane here." He picks up on the second ring.

I wish I had thought this through better before calling.

"Hello?"

I'm wheezing like my parents' old Boston terrier, Winnie, who's a little too heavy and pants after jumping on the couch.

"Is someone there?"

Terrific. He sounds annoyed, while I'm on the other end of the line panting like a weird stalker. *Say something, Beth. Stop acting like a freak!*

"Hiya," I say, slapping myself on the forehead. What am I, a ninja?

"Who is this?" His voice, deep and gruff, travels through the line, causing a weird sensation to run down my spine.

Why am I nervous? It's not like I like the guy. Sure, he has captivating eyes, and I'm positive his strong arms would be perfect for hugging or cuddling. But he also questioned me like I was a criminal. Sorry, bud, the purpose of this call is strictly business.

Then why am I still not speaking, and why is my heart racing?

"Look, if this is some kind of—"

"It's Bethany. Bethany Lloyd."

"Beth?" He pronounces my name like it's a mystery.

"Yep, that's me, Beth, Beth Lloyd. You remember, the individual you apprehended who was dressed as a large chicken and who you believed was responsible for Benji's death? Ha-ha!" Can this get any more awkward?

His laugh, raspy and deep, echoes through the line. "I know who you are. You don't have to remind me."

"Er, yeah, of course."

I swear, I'm better at phone calls than this.

His deep laughter echoes again. "I've been hoping you might call me."

"You were?" *What does that mean? Has he been wondering if my soft arms would make for great hugs too?*

"Yes." He coughs to clear his throat. "Have you heard anything while on set?"

Right, keeping my ears open. I don't know why I thought it was something else.

"So what's up?"

"Up?"

"You called me," he says.

He caught me off guard by answering the phone so quickly. My intention was to leave a voicemail, not speak with him.

"Beth? Are you still there?"

Get it together, chicken girl!

I clear my throat. "Yes, the reason I'm calling is to share some things happening on set. There's been a string of threats and stolen items. Since Benji was murdered, I've wondered if it might be relevant to your case." I don't know if it's true, but it won't do any harm to tell him. Besides, he might share information with me as well. It's worth a shot.

The line fills with sounds of muffled voices and clicking keys. "Interesting" is his only response.

"Would you like to hear what I've found? I've compiled a list detailing everything."

"No."

"No?" *Am I seriously getting the brush off again?*

"I'd rather talk in person. Why don't you come down to the station, and we can—"

"No! I don't want to come to the station. I've visited that place more than enough times, thank you."

"Okayyy. Since you don't want to come to the station, let's meet at the Tipsy Cow. Would one hour work?"

"The Tipsy Cow?"

The Tipsy Cow is a brew house that's a frequent spot for officers. But it's not a police hangout. The bar attracts people of all backgrounds. It's known for its live music on the weekends, karaoke night, and an overwhelming number of pool and air hockey tables.

It's also a place I vowed never to visit again.

"Does that work for you?" he asks, waiting for an answer.

"See you in an hour."

Pushing through the saloon style swing doors of the Tipsy Cow, my eyes wander around, past the giant red cow statue in the middle where people are taking selfies. Everything looks unchanged. A flood of memories rushes in, some good and one very terrible. I haven't been here since my group date with Brad over two years ago.

It was karaoke Thursday, one of the busiest nights of their week. Brad had taken the stage for his solo and said he had a message for a special person in the audience. He extended his hand, and I stood up as he called for Tiffany. His *step-cousin.*

As Tiffany joined him at the mic, I stood frozen in shock. We had been in a relationship for more than a year, and I thought we were heading toward the next stage. I didn't realize I wouldn't be included in that next stage. In front of the packed house, he bared his feelings to her. Following my humiliation, they left together without even acknowledging me. I should've known something was wrong when they performed *Secret Love Song* as a duet.

A heavy hand on my shoulder startles me. "There you are."

Turning my head, I see Detective Kane smiling at me. "Here I am," I say.

"I had my doubts you would make it. You didn't seem completely comfortable meeting here."

Unsure how to respond, I nod.

My mind is overflowing with too many thoughts going in different directions. The one feeling that stands out the most is his hand on my shoulder.

"Grab a pint." He leans in and calls out to the bartender, "Put her on my tab."

Hearing his offer, I shake my head. "Oh, no."

"I insist." His palm presses into my shoulder, and I shift my gaze to his hand. He steps back as he lets go. "The department is buying. Plus, Jerry and I are off the clock. Get yourself a pint and meet us outside in the Beer Garden. This place is too loud!" he yells above the music.

Detective Kane walks away without waiting for a reply. If the department is footing the bill, I might as well accept.

"I'll take a whiskey sour with rye," I tell the bartender. "You know what? Since he's buying, make it a double."

"Yes, ma'am. Anything else?"

"A pretzel with pub sauce and an order of garlic fries. Heavy on the garlic." Since he won't pay for the food he takes from my truck, this is the least he can do.

Standing at the bar, I anxiously tap my fingers on the stone top, waiting for my order. The Kluckin' Clues list in my purse feels as heavy as a stone against my side. Every item on it serves as evidence of the contestants' sabotage. Inhaling deeply, I brace myself for the impending conversation, fully aware that Detective Hamstead will probably be skeptical. My gut is telling me that there's a connection between what's happening on set and Benji, and I need to speak up.

However, I momentarily push those thoughts aside as I turn around. Smiling at the room, I lean my back against the countertop. The Tipsy Cow has always had a special place in my heart with its easygoing ambiance and the way strangers connect like lifelong buddies. For months, Seth has been telling me I need to get over Brad and come back here. A humiliating breakup shouldn't ruin the love I have for this place. He's right. It's about time I reclaim it and put an end to Brad's haunting memories. Does it matter that he ended things with me for his step-cousin and left me with a $200 bill to pay? He'll make ugly babies with his cousin anyway. I spin back around when I hear my name being shouted from the bar and grab my order. With my tray in hand, I make my way outside.

Stepping into the Tipsy Cow Beer Garden is like entering a fairy tale. The garden's path, with its flagstone pavers twisting and turning through the dirt, has a harmonious blend of nature and design. The design includes twinkling lights on the trees and seating options such as tables, benches, and Adirondack chairs.

"Over here!" Detective Kane pushes himself away from his table. "I was going to send out a search party to find you." He walks over and grabs the food tray I'm holding.

Detective Kane points for me to take a seat across from his partner. "You remember Jerry, don't you?"

I nod stiffly at the big man in front of me. "Sorry it took so long." Extending the basket, I offer Detective Hamstead some garlic fries.

He grabs a handful. "I like her," he says while eagerly munching. "Mmm, garlicky."

Detective Hamstead seems to be a bit more friendly than the first time we met. But they were called to investigate a suspicious death. I can see how that would make someone grumpy.

"Detective Kane said the department was buying, so I thought I'd grab a light snack for us to share."

Detective Hamstead gives his partner a cockeyed grin. "I assumed she'd call you Officer Pretty Boy." His bearlike paw lands heavily on his partner's shoulder as he gives a bellowing laugh.

Definitely more relaxed than our other encounters, for sure.

"Have I thanked you for that nickname?" Detective Kane says to me.

"My pleasure. But since I learned you're a detective, Rylie and I call you Detective Pretty Boy now."

"Yeah, but Officer Pretty Boy sounds better than Detective Pretty Boy, don't you think?" Hamstead laughs.

"Do I need to be worried that you and Rylie are talking about me when I'm not around?" Detective Kane raises his eyebrows at me.

My neck flushes, and I grab my drink. *Me and my big mouth.*

"I thought you were getting a pint?" The detective watches me as I consume half of my whiskey sour.

"I prefer whiskey." I take another sip. "Not beer."

"Behaves like a crazed chicken while munching on garlic fries, pretzels, and whiskey." Hamstead whistles under his breath. "You better marry her before someone else does."

"Jerry!"

"Not interested." I gulp down more whiskey, pretending not to notice the death stare Detective Kane is giving his partner.

"You had something you wanted to share with us?" Detective Kane tugs at his collar. Glad to know we're both feeling the warmth of this uncomfortable conversation.

I take out a printed copy of the Kluckin' Clues list from my purse and pass it across the table.

While licking pub sauce from his fingers, Detective Hamstead picks up the paper. "What's this?"

"I've been keeping track of all the suspicious things happening since the start of the show," I explain. "My list includes everything from sabotaging food trucks to threatening notes."

"Is this everyone from the show?" he asks, passing the paper to his partner.

"From this season, yes. One team remains unscathed, headed by Willa Garza. She owns Nacho Momma's Tacos."

Detective Hamstead breaks off a chunk of pretzel, showing little interest in my list, but his partner studies the paper while taking sips from his beer. "Someone sent a threatening note to your team. Do you still have a copy of it?"

Reaching into my purse, I pull out the folded slip of paper and hand it to him.

"'Keep snooping, and you'll be cooked before the next elimination round,'" Detective Kane reads aloud. "And you took this as a threat?" he asks, handing the note to his partner.

I give a firm nod. "After my victory in the second challenge, I found that on my truck. But remember, I'm not the only one." Grabbing my phone, I scroll through my photos to show them a picture of Ben's note warning him he could end up deep fried like his doughnuts.

"May I?" Detective Kane takes my phone and sends himself the picture. "Did you share this note with any of the workers on the show?"

"I didn't."

This seems to pique his interest. "Why not?"

Using a garlic fry, I scoop up some of the dipping sauce. Multiple times, Rylie has asked me this same question. While chewing on the fry, I voice my concern. "I've attempted multiple times to discuss these notes with Imogen and Sloane, but they continue to dismiss me. These notes have been going on since the first day. It doesn't feel like the production crew is taking us or the situation on set seriously."

Detective Hamstead dips a piece of soft pretzel into the housemade beer cheese sauce. "Why is that?" he asks before popping the pretzel into his mouth. That is interesting coming from him, who also hasn't taken me seriously.

"Several contestants have voiced grievances, but nothing is being done despite promises to investigate," I say. "But I'm not sure how they'll investigate anything. Those old cameras are unreliable at best."

"What are you talking about?" Detective Hamstead asks before taking a swig of his beer.

"The CCTV cameras. They're old and always on the fritz. Even with several visits from a Wiz Tech technician, it's still a fifty-fifty chance that the cameras will capture anything."

He rests his pub glass on the table. "What about the new—"

"You've got my attention, Beth," Detective Kane says, cutting his partner off.

What was Detective Hamstead about to ask me?

Could there be new cameras on the lot, and he was on the verge of asking me about them? It's always struck me as strange that a lot this size would be equipped with only two cameras—

"Who do you believe is behind the threats?" My mental line of questioning is interrupted by Detective Kane. "I agree it's strange, but why do you think it's connected to Benji? Not saying that it isn't . . ."

"I'm not sure," I tell him.

Resting his elbows on the table, he stares at me. "I don't believe you."

"You think I'm lying?"

He shakes his head. "No, but I think you're reluctant to share your theory."

While tracing the rim of my glass with my middle finger, I consider his questions. "It's just a hunch, but you said you believed Benji was a victim of foul play. If that's the case, can we really dismiss these notes as childish pranks? Maybe Willa is involved somehow."

"First," Detective Kane says, "there is no 'we'." He gestures between us. "And you're bringing up Willa again?"

"Correction," I say, holding up a finger. "You asked me to keep my ear to the ground. That makes us a 'we.'" I gesture between us like he did. "And isn't it obvious? She hasn't had anything happen to her. If it walks like a duck and acts like a duck, that duck is a duck."

After a moment, Detective Kane says, "It seems plausible . . ."

"I'm sensing a 'but' . . ." I say.

"But appearances aren't always what they seem," Detective Kane says cryptically. "Think about everything for a moment. I'll wait."

While mentally reviewing the show's events, I feel his intense gaze on me. "If it were Willa," I say, testing my theory, "then she made a foolish move . . ."

"Go on," he encourages.

"Because excluding herself would only put her more in the spotlight," I say, realization dawning. Willa isn't careless. She calculates every move she makes, including the intentional disclosure of her role as the anonymous tipster. She knew that revelation would rattle me and shift my attention, even if only briefly. "The natural assumption would be that she is the culprit. So . . . it's probably not Willa."

"Very astute observation, Watson," Detective Kane says with a wink.

"Thank you, Holmes." I wink back.

"Here." Detective Hamstead's brows furrow as he hands me a napkin. "It looks like there might be something in your eye."

Apparently, winking is not my forte.

As I take the napkin and pretend to wipe my eye, Detective Pretty Boy leans back in his chair with a smirk. "The person behind the threats and sabotage is clever."

Crumpling the napkin, I toss it on the table. "They're targeting only a few teams at a time."

"Attacking everyone at once would be too obvious," Detective Kane agrees.

Leaning forward, I fold my arms on the table and lower my voice. "What if Benji discovered what was happening with the contestant sabotage and planned to do something about it?"

"Let me get this straight. You think Benji was murdered because he found out someone was going to steal his buns?" Hamstead bursts out laughing.

"There's fifty thousand dollars on the line. I'm sure people have killed for less," I reply with more confidence than I feel.

Detective Kane casts a sideways glance at his partner. "It's obvious there's something going on. We appreciate you sharing this with us, Beth."

"Did you talk with the Katapang sisters? Or Willa Garza?" I ask. "What about the yelling I heard inside Benji's truck? Did you find out anything?"

"I have taken everything you've shared with me seriously and we're looking into things," Detective Kane says in his not-so-subtle way of telling me to butt out.

"The Katapang sisters are a group of meddling gossipers. Let's hope they learned to stay away from people's trucks," says Detective Hamstead.

"Jerry, enough," Detective Kane says.

"You take things too seriously, Drew," he says. "Her learning the truth about the Katapangs won't affect our investigation. Besides, maybe she'll learn to keep her truck locked."

"My truck?" I look at Detective Hamstead for answers. "What about my truck?"

"Lila admitted to searching through multiple trucks, including yours," Detective Hamstead reveals before finishing the remains of his beer.

My eyes widen slightly. "That's unsettling. Why would they do that?"

Using the back of his hand, he removes the beer residue from his upper lip. "Lila claims that someone suggested it would be a good way for them to learn what the other teams were preparing."

"To get the upper hand by seeing what seasonings I used." Then it hits me. "They were in Benji's truck for the same reason, weren't they? Was that who Benji was yelling at?"

Detective Kane holds up a hand to silence his partner. "Enough with the questions. But you should keep your vehicle locked."

Leaning forward, I whisper-shout, "They killed Benji, didn't they?!"

"You really are a crazy chicken," Detective Kane says.

"They did it!" With a triumphant gesture, I slap my hands on the table. "They all had long brown hair and were in his truck the day he died. Case closed." Leaning back, I fold my arms and give the detectives a grin.

"Not by a long shot," Detective Kane says.

"How can you be so sure?" I ask, refusing to give up.

"I don't just wear this suit and badge to look good," Detective Kane explains with annoyance. "It's my job to ask questions and find the answers."

"They have an alibi," his partner tells me. "During the time frame Benji was killed, Sloane Owsinski was discussing their video diaries with them."

Well, there goes my theory.

"What about Willa?" I ask. "She remains unaffected while the rest of us suffer. When talking to her, she is evasive and redirects focus."

"Thanks for meeting with us, Beth," Detective Kane replies.

"She also has long dark hair," I remind them.

"As do several people who were on set at the time of his death," Detective Kane reminds me. "We appreciate your time."

I know a brush-off when I feel one.

"I think you should deputize me and let me help," I suggest. "That's a real thing, right? I've seen it in the movies."

"No chance," Detective Kane firmly states. "I'm not interested in having an amateur play detective."

I scoff. "I'm an independent woman and can do what I please."

"Not if that independence leads you into an active investigation," he tells me.

He finishes his beer and says nothing more. Knowing the conversation has ended, I toss back my whiskey sour and stand.

"Good day, sirs."

Detective Kane leans forward, snatching my wrist before I can leave the table. "Be careful not to poke your nose where it doesn't belong." My protest dies in my throat when he gives me a frosty stare. "Don't play innocent with me. We both know that you'll walk out of here and keep investigating."

Pulling my arm away, I touch my palm to where his hand was. "Hypothetically, let's say I continued poking my nose where it doesn't belong. What do you think I should do?"

Detective Kane shifts back into his seat. His tall and sturdy build commands power even in this relaxed setting. His shirt grabs my attention as it stretches taut around his shoulders. *Did he pick that shirt on purpose?* He must know the thin fabric clings to his body, showing off his muscles underneath. I wish I hadn't finished my drink so fast.

I could use a beer dog right now.

"Call me," he says, interrupting my treacherous thought, "If you find something. *Do not* attempt to solve it by yourself. Leave it to the police. It's safer that way."

Without a word, I leave the table. Five steps later, I crash into someone and get soaked in cold liquid.

"Oh my goodness, I'm so sorry!" I barely have time to react before a hand pats the front of my chest with a wad of napkins. "Don't worry, everything is fine."

I brush away the hand that feels like it's trying to get to second base. "I got it, thanks." A familiar green hairstyle catches my eye. "Imogen?"

Her eyes widen in surprise as she realizes it's me. As the bright golden liquid trickles down my shirt, she gasps and freezes. "Beth! I'm sorry." She takes another bundle of napkins from Sergio and continues to pat down my front.

"It's fine, Imogen. These things happen to me all the time." It's sad to say, but they do.

"I didn't even see you. I was walking and talking with Sergio when Sloane unexpectedly slammed into me from behind, making me spill my beer."

"Oh! Where is Sloane? I've been needing to speak with her."

Imogen looks around. "Where did she go?"

Hmm, where indeed?

Chapter Fourteen

"Wait, wait, wait." Rylie shoves her hands between us, making the universal sign for time out. "You said *what*?"

Gobbling down the rest of my turkey panini, I shoot her a look. "You gnow whatf I saifd," I tell her, not caring that I'm speaking with a mouth full of food.

"I just want to hear it again. Especially the part about you not knowing how to wink." Rylie leans back in her chair, her chocolate-brown eyes wide with shock. "How can someone be incapable of winking?" To emphasize her point, she gives an exaggerated wink.

I flash her a wide, toothy grin, which I'm pretty sure has some lunch remnants in it. "Because I'm special, that's how."

"Don't look at me like that." My friend pouts across the table at me. "And please, would you stop smiling? I love you, but it's creepy and not flattering. Your spinach is showing." Rylie points at her front teeth to show me where.

With an eye roll, I chew my food and finish my iced tea to wash it down.

Lunch with Rylie didn't help my mood, even though I was hoping it would. I know what I have to do next, but I still have a ball of nerves bouncing around in the pit of my stomach. "I should have ordered a second panini."

"No, you shouldn't have. You only eat that much when you're stressed. You'll end up with a stomachache and complain all day if you eat too much."

She's not wrong; I'm a stress eater and a stress baker. I can't help it. It's what I do.

"All right, *feminina,* what's the plan? You still wanna snoop around?"

Shoveling a handful of chips into my mouth, I nod.

"And you wanna do this, even though Detective Pretty Boy told you not to?"

"He just suggested I keep my nose to myself." *More or less.* "Besides, this is our truck we're talking about here!" I jab a finger into my palm for emphasis. "If the Katapangs were inside our truck without permission, who else went inside? Now that I know Imogen was lying and there *is* likely a working camera somewhere on the lot, we have a right to review the footage and ensure our personal property is safe. Even with the cameras malfunctioning and only partial recordings, we can still try to piece together the situation."

"You don't have to convince me. I'm already on board. I'm double-checking if *you're* okay with this, as it might require lying."

"I can lie as well as anyone else."

"You're stretching the truth already if you believe that."

"You don't know what you're talking about."

"Your voice takes on a helium-filled balloon quality when you lie." Rylie gets up and throws the trash from our lunch into the garbage cans. "*Vamos!* Snooping waits for no one."

God, I love Rylie. She's the friend who will help hide the body first and ask questions later. Metaphorically, of course. All things considered.

"Shall I drive while you finish working on that brownie you just pulled from your purse?"

Standing up from the table, I swallow the remaining food in my mouth. "Don't food shame me. But yes, you can drive."

It's Sunday afternoon, and I don't know if anyone will even be at the lot. We hope someone from production is working a weekend shift. Rylie pulls up to the gate where the security guard is standing and rolls down her window.

"*Buenas tardes.*" Rylie tilts her head and flashes a megawatt smile. "*¿Cómo estás, Héctor?*"

Leaning over the center console, I whisper. "Since when do you speak Spanish?"

With a smile still on her face, Rylie shoves me back to the passenger side of her jeep.

"*Bien. Buenas tardes,*" Héctor's kind voice reaches me from the other side of the car. "What can I help the two of you with?"

"Oh, you know." Rylie reaches out the window, brushing her fingertips along the top of his hand. "A little of this, a little of that."

Héctor's Adam's apple bobs as Rylie smiles at him. This is why I had her drive, not because I needed to stuff my face with more brownies. Well, that was part of it, but not the sole reason. Rylie is irresistible. With a smile or a flutter of her naturally long eyelashes, she can get anything she wants. But I can't even wink without people thinking I have something in my eye.

Clearing his throat, Héctor finds his voice again. "There's no filming today. Everything is already finished with the contestants for the weekend. Is there something I can help you with?"

"We need to speak with Imogen."

"Oh, she's not here." Héctor shakes his head. "I'm sorry, but you will have to—"

"*Oh não,*" she says while touching her temple and shaking her head. "No, it's urgent. She said either she or her assistant would be here to help us regarding filming issues." Rylie speaks a mile a minute, and poor Héctor looks unsure of what to do.

"Hold on," he says, holding up his palms to stop her from speed talking. "Imogen isn't here, but Sergio is. Maybe he can help." He steps back, opens the gate, and makes a sweeping gesture for us to drive through.

"*Gracias*, Héctor." Rylie waves at him as she drives through as quickly as possible without raising suspicion.

"I don't know how you do it," I say as she parks her white jeep and I unbuckle from my seat. "When did you become fluent in Spanish?"

"I'm hardly fluent," she laughs. "Portuguese and Spanish are similar. If you can speak one, you can manage with the other. As far as winking is concerned, it's all in the eyes," she says, giving me another exaggerated wink. "Before we go in . . ." She stops me from opening the door. "Don't worry about lying. I'll do it for you. Just speak normally."

"Rude! I can lie just fine!"

"Says the woman who just squeaked."

Exiting the jeep, I inadvertently slam the door. *I'll die before admitting I just squeaked a little.*

Maybe it's a good thing that it's Sergio here instead of Imogen. He's not been dealing with the contestants as much as she has, and it feels like we can more easily convince him to allow us to review the CCTV footage. Rylie is my backup plan, in case he doesn't agree. Thankfully, her persuasion skills are much stronger than her cooking skills. She can get almost anyone to do what she wants. And I don't know what she's talking about. I don't sound like I've inhaled helium when I lie.

Rylie opens the production trailer door leading to a bunch of cubicles. The only sound is a quiet conversation at the back. Straining to listen, I take a few tentative steps forward to hear better.

"This is too much. I've had enough," whispers a voice I can barely make out.

"You've said this before. Maybe you just need a break," another voice whispers.

The first voice murmurs back, "It's been going on for too long. What I need is a permanent break. I'm done. With everything."

Creeping forward to hear more, my foot bumps into a desk corner, causing a travel mug to fall and crash. I wince and pause mid-tiptoe. Rylie rolls her eyes, clearly unimpressed with my attempts at remaining undetected.

The trailer's back door opens and slams shut.

"Who's there?" a male voice calls out from behind a low partition.

"Just Beth," I reply. Popping up, I smooth my hands down the front of my shirt. "I came to speak with Imogen."

Like a meerkat at the zoo, Imogen Comestible's personal assistant, Sergio Romare, also pops up from behind a low wall at the back of the trailer. His appearance is more rodent-like than that of a cute meerkat. He's staring at me with his small brown eyes through wire-rimmed glasses too large for his face. His thin lips highlight his large teeth, and his skittish, cagey demeanor matches his mousey appearance as he looks around nervously.

"Sorry to catch you off guard, but I was looking for Imogen," I say again as I walk toward him.

Sergio nods, causing his slicked-back hair to bob over his glasses. "She's not here."

"Oh, that's all right." I wave away his comment. "Maybe you can help me. It's about the sabotage taking place on the lot."

"I've heard contestants complaining about it." He pushes the hair back from his face. "But I don't think 'sabotage' is the right word."

"What word would you use when someone maliciously tampers with ingredients? Or leaves threatening notes?" I ask.

I smile at Sergio as he eyes me warily. I don't want to scare the rodent away, but I also won't back down from this. Finally, he asks, "What can I help you with?"

"You can help me by letting me review footage from the studio lot," I say.

"Excuse me?" My directness catches him off guard. "You're a contestant. Why would you think you could view any prerecorded footage?"

"You're right. I am a contestant." I look at Rylie before continuing. "A contestant who thought it was safe to park my truck here. Security is supposed to be protecting our property. Only, it's come to my attention that someone has been inside my truck."

"Do you have proof of this?" He fiddles with his glasses. "Because if you do, then you should take this up with the police."

"Brilliant suggestion. I already did!" I give him a broad smile. "Would you like to know what I also learned after talking with my lawyer?"

I called Seth to discuss hypothetically what happens if an accident occurs on private property. *What's the point in having a lawyer for a brother if you don't use him?*

Sergio noticeably swallows. "I'm listening."

"Someone broke into my truck on this property. I was told it's safe to park my *business* here. Because that's what my food truck is, my business. I was deceived into believing it would be safe—"

"No one deceived you," Sergio interrupts me.

"Let the woman speak," Rylie chastises him.

"Thank you," I say with a nod to my partner in crime. "My truck's damages can cause liability for both the property owner and the network, especially since I was deceived by the false sense of security being promoted."

I may not be the best liar, but I can certainly spin information to benefit me.

"What are you implying?" Sergio asks.

"I'm not implying anything," I say. "Either let me watch filmed or CCTV footage from this lot to see who broke into my truck, or I'll sue the network. I imagine it won't look good for any of you to be working on a show that gets sued." My voice squeaks, and I quickly clear my throat.

"You don't want to do that." Sergio grinds his teeth, making him look even more rodent-like.

"You're right. I don't." *I don't even know if I can*. "But I will do whatever is necessary to keep my personal property safe." I offer him a sympathetic smile. "I understand there have been unexpected issues, and the network can't afford any more costs this season. All I'm asking is to look at a few rolls of footage. Is that too much to ask?"

Rylie slides next to him and says, "As a busy assistant, your time is valuable. Everyone knows that."

"That's true." The rodent fiddles with his glasses. "Sometimes it feels like I'm doing the job of two people."

"Of course," Rylie says sympathetically, touching his forearm. "Everyone sees you running around here doing all the work and receiving no credit."

"I'm not in it for the glory," he admits, blushing.

Rylie strokes his ego. "No, of course not. But imagine being the person who singlehandedly saves the network from a lawsuit, all by simply letting us look at a few rolls of footage."

"Hang on," he says, shaking his head to gather his thoughts. "I've already checked the available CCTV camera footage and found nothing."

I tag myself back into the conversation. "You know what they say about fresh eyes."

"No, what?" Sergio asks.

"Er . . ."

Rylie facepalms in response to my clever reply.

"Fresh eyes are better than old ones?" I guess.

Smooth, Rylie mouths at me.

"Consider this," Rylie says, taking back the conversation. "If we find the person responsible, not only will you receive the credit, but you can film the confrontation."

"Why would I want that?" he asks.

"Drama," she says, as if it's the solution to everything. "Believe it or not, my girl here can get pretty *dramatic*," Rylie says, motioning toward me.

What is she getting at?

"She stabbed me once when I tried to take an egg roll off her plate. Imagine how she would react to the person who broke into her truck and left a threatening note."

"I didn't stab you!" I can't believe she's bringing that up.

"What do you call this?" With a flick of her wrist, Rylie shows me the back of her hand. "Let's settle this: Did you or did you not jam your plastic fork into the back of my hand at the Fourth of July weekend picnic?"

"Trying to take food from my plate was your mistake," I tell her.

"You shouldn't have been hoarding egg rolls."

"I wasn't hoarding!"

"You had six!"

Sergio looks like he's watching a tennis match as we shout at each other.

"Brad had just dumped me for his cousin. You know I'm a stress eater."

"His cousin?" Sergio seems horrified.

"*Step*-cousin," I amend.

"Is that better?" he remarks.

"It's a little better," I say.

"See what I mean?" Rylie holds out her hand in triumph.

"What is that supposed to mean?"

"Ladies." Sergio runs a hand over his face, then fiddles with his glasses again. Either something we said clicked with him or he's fed up with us, because he walks out of the trailer.

We chase after him as he heads to the warehouse. He opens the door, and we step into the dimly lit building. Aged wood and dust mix in the air, creating an eerie atmosphere that gives me goose bumps. As he keeps walking, we stay close behind him until we reach a cramped room slightly larger than a walk-in closet. At the center is a desk with a single chair, and against one wall are a TV and a few cabinets.

"Stay here," he instructs before leaving.

Once again, the ball of anxiety in my stomach bounces. I'm certain the person responsible for everything happening must be a fellow competitor. It's the only logical conclusion. We have the freedom to move around the lot, frequently going in and out of our trucks. During interviews and before and after challenges, we leave our empty trucks parked on the studio lot. At least twice, I've noticed the Dough Brothers leaving their sliding door open while conducting post-competition interviews. Any contestant could easily leave a threatening note or quietly steal something important from a truck. If Imogen would stop ignoring me, I wouldn't need to handle things myself.

Sloane hasn't been much better. If you can even find her, that is. She's always busy with errands for Bobbi. Speaking of Bobbi, do I talk with her about this? Or should I find out who the head network producers are and go to them? Sloane told me she would look into things. Did she already talk to them? It's possible she's been avoiding me because she hasn't found any answers yet. But if that's the case, why not just tell me?

Sergio returns holding a laptop and sets it on the desk. On the front casing is a worn red sticker of the Cooking Channel logo. "You can't watch everything, because we're still editing and piecing stuff together. When is the day you believe someone broke into your truck?"

"The second challenge." I unintentionally emit a soft squeal and hastily follow it with a cough as I look at Rylie for help.

"Don't mind her. She just swallowed some air wrong." Rylie looks at me with an 'I told you so' expression.

To be honest, I'm not worried about the Katapangs being inside my truck. I care more about uncovering the culprit leaving the threatening notes. Hopefully, the video footage will give us something to work with.

"That was right around the time when Dane and Ness had their cookware vandalized," Sergio says while holding the laptop, looking at the screen. "I think that's the catalyst for everything." He sets the laptop on the desk and shields the screen to keep me from viewing the files he's clicking on. "Don't tell anyone what I'm about to let you watch."

"Thank you, Sergio. We won't," I reassure him.

"The film crew doesn't record unless we're shooting footage for the show," Sergio explains while clicking the mouse. "But the CCTVs are supposed to run 24/7. The tent and trailer do block the trucks, but there's limited coverage of the area directly around them."

"And the CCTVs cover my truck?" I ask.

"They should," he says. "At least a partial view. Assuming they were working that day." Sergio clicks on a folder but moves to the right when I try to read the name. "There's also a third camera in the concealed cell tower behind the warehouse that gives more of a bird's-eye view."

Aha! A third camera! As I suspected.

He narrows his eyes at the screen as he types. "It's common for buildings, such as this one, situated on expansive lots to be equipped with numerous cameras."

"This is great news! Then my truck should be fully visible. Particularly if there might be additional cameras present." Things are looking up.

"Doubtful," Sergio says. "Although it's typical for buildings to have multiple cameras, the cameras in this old place haven't been maintained." Sergio diverts his attention from the laptop to look at me. "For weeks, James from Wiz Tech has been attempting to make the security system fully functional. He's done everything he can, but it seems there's nothing more to be done. Even with multiple cameras around the building, there's a fifty-fifty chance that your truck was recorded that day."

How convenient . . .

"When did that start?" Rylie asks him. "Being on the fritz, I mean."

"It's been that way the entire time the production has been on the lot, as far as I know," he says. "We got this place for a bargain. When the network is literally saving thousands of dollars, outdated equipment doesn't matter."

"That's more than outdated," I say. "While I'm all for saving and budgeting, I think it's irresponsible to rent a facility with faulty equipment."

"Good thing you aren't the one in charge of those decisions, then."

"Wouldn't that be something important, though, to have up and running?" Rylie asks. "A security camera not working after someone died here is kind of a big deal."

"I guess." He scratches his jaw. "That's above my pay grade. You can contact IT and see what they say."

"How did you get these files?" I ask him.

Sergio shifts his gaze from the screen and asks, "What do you mean?"

"I suggested to Imogen that we look at the CCTV footage after the incident with Dane and Ness," I explain. "Since the network was renting the location for the shoot, she mentioned the files had to be obtained from the property owner."

Sergio stands up, crossing his arms defensively. "Why are you two asking so many questions?"

I mimic his stance. "Why are you avoiding answering them?"

"She had me request access to the CCTV footage because it gets overwritten after two weeks. If you'd like, I can explain the process of formally requesting access or let you watch the footage. Pick!"

I motion with my hand for him to press Play. Sergio stoops back over the laptop, clicks on a file, then stands up. Grainy gray-and-white footage of Sergio and Imogen talking outside the warehouse plays in fast-forward mode.

"What's that about?" I ask him.

"That was the day I was supposed to deliver the cookware to the Jaxsons," he tells me.

"Supposed to?" I ask, while staring at the screen. "Imogen said you delivered it."

"I was about to, but Sloane offered to instead."

"Why would she do that?" Rylie asks.

"She's helpful by nature," Sergio says. "She knew I was behind schedule. I was helping Bert with contracts for a different project. I didn't want to be ungrateful by asking Sloane questions."

Were her intentions solely to be helpful?

A buzzing noise fills the tiny room. "Hold on." He pulls out his phone from his pocket and checks the screen. "Look at the files I just pulled up. I'll be back in five minutes. Stay here." He answers his phone while walking out of the room, closing the door behind him.

"We don't have much time," Rylie says, surveying the cramped area. "I'll snoop around and see if I find anything while you watch the recordings."

Backing up the footage Sergio skipped past, I watch everything on fast-forward. "What are you looking for?" I ask her.

"I don't know," Rylie says while opening a cabinet. "Maybe a possible murder weapon. Or a hidden stash of chocolate. Both are acceptable options." After closing the cabinet door, she opens another one. "Bingo!"

"Did you find a weapon?" I turn to see what she has.

"Better!" Closing the door, she spins around, smiling. "Dark chocolate hazelnut." She unwraps the bar and comes over to join me at the laptop.

"Do you have any idea how old that might be?" I scrunch my nose when she offers me a piece.

"Chocolate's chocolate." She pops a chunk in her mouth. "Do you think the Katapangs are involved with things?"

"Well, I mean, they have dark-brown hair," I say, my eyes returning to the screen. "But the detectives seem pretty certain they didn't have anything to do with Benji."

"How so?"

"They had an alibi with Sloane." I relay what I know while monitoring the screen. "But now I'm wondering if Sloane is somehow wrapped up in all of this."

"Why? I thought you said she was going to look into things?"

"She did say that, but she's been avoiding me. If there's nothing to share, I get it. Why not just tell me instead?"

"That doesn't mean she's the culprit."

I shoot her a quick look, then return to the footage. The camera malfunction is evident as static fills the screen.

"Let's make sure we consider all angles before deciding she's guilty." She pops another piece of chocolate into her mouth. "Lack of discussion doesn't equal guilt."

"I know that." She's right, and I hate to admit that I've even been considering Sloane, especially when she's been so nice. "That's why I'm in here trying to cover all possible angles, because I believe the notes, the sabotage, and Benji's death are related."

"I don't mean to be harsh, but why do you care so much? Let the police handle it," Rylie says. "It's not like you liked Benji."

"Just because I didn't like him doesn't mean I wanted him dead." I click on another folder. "Aside from that, I was interrogated and ignored by the police when I brought up legitimate concerns. Some contestants think I'm involved. It's personal for me now."

Each new video I scroll through ends up being another dead end. Either it's full of static and fuzzy, or it didn't capture anything important. Just when I think there's nothing useful in this footage and I'm about to click out, movement in the corner catches my eye: a shadowy figure lingering behind one of the food trucks. "Rylie, check this out!" I freeze the frame.

"Try to zoom in," she says, leaning over me. "It's too far away. We need a clearer view."

As I'm about to do what she asks, the lights in the room suddenly flicker, and our tiny room plunges into darkness.

"AAAAAH!"

"AAAAAH!"

Rylie and I clutch on to each other tightly. "What just happened?" I ask, not ready to let go of her.

"Por que você está me perguntando?"

"In English!"

"Don't yell at me!" she whisper-yells back. "I don't know what happened. Your guess is as good as mine."

"It seems too coincidental to be a mere electrical issue." Slowly, I loosen my death grip on her.

"*Sim,* time to get out of here."

With a forceful slam, I close and leave the laptop, and we swiftly exit the pitch-black room. Following the soft yellow glow of the emergency lights, we use the flashlights on our phones to navigate the hallway. Despite taking a few wrong turns, we make it outside.

Sergio marches toward us with an angry expression. Who knew a mouse sporting oversized glasses could be so intimidating? "What's happening?" he demands. "Have you seen Bert?"

"Bert?" *I still haven't met the mysterious Bert.* "We came looking for help. Do you know what happened? And who is Bert? I've heard the name a few times. Does he have something to do with the lights going out?"

"That's what I plan to find out." Mumbling, Sergio heads back inside the warehouse.

"Who's Bert?" I call out as he storms inside the building.

Deciding it's best to stick close, we follow him, although as we head back into the darkness, it soon becomes clear that maybe it would've been better had Rylie and I stayed outside. He walks us through many doors, finally stopping in front of a panel.

Handing over his phone with the flashlight shining, he barks, "Hold this." Within a few seconds, the lights sputter back to life. Sergio curses as he turns to me. "Someone tripped the circuit breaker."

"On purpose, no doubt." I say what we're all thinking.

He grunts at me. "We're done here." He storms back toward the small warehouse office in a fit of anger.

"The door is shut," I announce as we get to the small closet-sized storage room.

"So?" He says the word like I'm an idiot for stating the obvious.

"We left it open," Rylie tells him.

We exchange a quick glance before Sergio twists the knob. The moment he steps in, I notice the empty desk.

"The laptop," I whisper. "It's gone."

"If the laptop is gone . . ." Sergio trails off, his eyes darting around the tiny space as he swears again. "Then so are the files."

His words knock the wind out of me like a punch to the gut. That means one of two things: either this Bert person who Sergio was looking for took the laptop, or the culprit is here.

Or Bert is *the culprit.*

Detective Kane might believe me if I told him.

But he also told me to stay out of things.

Either way, more than just evidence of sabotage is on those files, and someone stole them before I could unravel the truth.

Chapter Fifteen

"The two of you did what?!"

Do you remember those cartoons from your childhood where steam would come out of characters' ears when they got angry? Right now, Seth looks like that. If literal steam could escape from his head, that's what would happen.

His brows tighten, and he squints at me, expecting a reply.

"If I want to investigate things relating to *my* business, I can," I say. "With physical evidence, the police cannot dismiss my claims. I'm on to something, Seth, I know it." I walk past him into my small kitchen.

"Detective Kane can handle things," he says, following me. "It's his job, not yours. Why are you so insistent on pursuing this?"

"I know he can," I admit. "But it's my reputation associated with everything. And stop snorting like a wild boar."

Returning to the oven, I take out the snickerdoodle cookies I've been baking to cope with my stress. A pound of butter and who knows how much sugar later, my racing thoughts have subsided. The scent of sweet cinnamon sugar fills my apartment, reminding me of childhood memories with our Aunt Dolly. Oh, how I miss her.

Seth's sudden arrival shattered the calmness as he banged on my front door like a lunatic. Later, I'll have to send a message to Rylie and a big ol' thank you to her for being a narc.

I notice my brother rolling his shoulders twice as I place a tray of cookies next to him to cool. After a few deep breaths, he gains control over his emotions. But judging by the way he aggressively bites into the snickerdoodle, he's struggling to maintain his composure.

"How much did Rylie tell you?" I ask, picking up a cookie to nibble on.

"What makes you think it was her?"

"Who else was it? I certainly wasn't going to tell you."

"It was Kane," he says, taking another cookie and devouring it.

"Detective Kane?"

How would he know? Does he have a tail on me like they do in the movies?

"Do you know any other guys named Kane?"

I glare at my brother while slowly chewing. The sugariness of this cookie is the only thing stopping me from snapping. After an uncomfortable minute of my glaring and chewing, and a bead of sweat forming on Seth's brow, he finally blurts, "Fine! Rylie told me about the warehouse."

I give a satisfied nod, having successfully broken Seth, and swallow the cookie.

"But I did talk to Kane also."

"What did he say?"

"That you two shared drinks yesterday, and he was worried that you might start poking around and get into trouble."

He waits for my reply, which I withhold.

"You went to the Tipsy Cow?" The way he asks feels like an accusation.

"You make it sound like I was on a date with the man."

"Were you?"

I bristle over his tone. "It's none of your business! But what if I were?"

I wasn't, but I'm curious to see what he would say.

Raking a hand through his wavy brown hair, Seth sighs. "This is the same detective who questioned you for murder, in case you forgot."

"Everyone is entitled to wrong assumptions now and again."

"Jeez, Beth, you sure know how to pick 'em."

"I resent that. It was not a date. Far from it. His partner was there and ate all my fries. After that, I had a drink spilled on me."

"This sounds exactly like one of your usual dates."

My mouth falls open. "Rude!" In a typical sibling move, I grab a pinch of flour and flick it into his face.

He blinks at me, and I feel a sense of impending doom. He's wearing a black button-down shirt. To be specific, it's one of his *date* shirts, which is now dusted in flour. To my surprise, he laughs as he brushes it off.

"Playing spy games while sneaking around the warehouse was dangerous." Although Seth is more lighthearted, he hasn't ended the conversation. "You could have gotten yourselves into some serious trouble."

"Thanks for the reminder. Here's a reminder for you: I'm a grown woman who doesn't need a babysitter."

"No, you don't." Snatching a hand towel from the counter, he rubs at more of the flour on his shirt. "You just need a chauffeur every other week because your car is always in the shop. Or you need to be bailed out of jail while dressed as a chicken."

"One time! I get arrested one time as a giant chicken and you never let me live it down." My arms flail angrily as I storm into my bedroom, Seth trailing me. Riffling through my drawers, I find a shirt he left last time he was over. "Here." I chuck it at him. "The more you try to wipe away the flour, the worse it gets. And for the record, my car is working fine. The check engine light has been on since I purchased it."

"I'm serious, Beth," he continues as he peels off his flour-covered shirt and slips on a clean red polo. "You didn't tell anyone what the two of you were doing. What if something nefarious was happening when you showed up?" Seth tosses his dirty shirt into my hamper.

So that's why I keep finding his clothes here. He's been tricking me into doing his laundry.

"And that car of yours is going to break down on you. It's a lemon."

"Her name is Audrey, and she's a lady." I refuse to allow him to defame my car. "As far as letting you know my plans, I'll keep you posted next time."

"Before you do something stupid," he warns.

"Our definitions of stupid differ."

Digging the heel of his palms into his eyes, he lets out another sigh and plops onto my bed. "Did you find anything useful at least?"

"Sergio set us up with CCTV footage from around the time the Katapangs might have broken into our truck. But the quality wasn't great."

"The Katapangs were in our truck?" Seth looks at me, confused.

"I found out about it from the detectives at the Tipsy Cow. It seems the Katapangs were secretly entering all the trucks. Someone allegedly suggested they should find out the other teams' secret ingredients."

"And they understood that to mean they should break into other people's trucks?" Seth asks.

"They must have thought it would give them the upper hand," I say, not sure what those sisters were thinking. "Their efforts backfired, though."

"That's what they get for spending more time snooping than cooking," he says. "I thought Imogen said the refreshment tent blocked those cameras. And that the files were the property of the owner of the site."

"Sergio told me he got the footage."

"Did he say how?"

"I asked, and he said I can either learn the details of how he got the surveillance footage or watch it."

"And you picked watching?"

"I am not concerned with how the sausage is made, as long as I have it," I respond. "Sergio also said there's a third CCTV camera that gives a bird's-eye view, but it also is on the fritz. He claims it's been that way all along, as far as he knows. He mentioned that there might be additional cameras on the premises, but they're likely in the same state as the others."

"How convenient." Seth collapses onto my comforter, his hands clasped behind his head, and looks up at my ceiling. "Keep going. Tell me what else you learned. Did he provide any information on where these additional cameras could be? Would the refreshment tent and production trailer partially block them too?"

"He didn't. I'm not sure he even knows. I looked it up. The lot the network is renting is older. So most likely their CCTVs are about two decades out of date. Hence why it's monochrome, grainy gray-and-white footage instead of color. The other issue with CCTVs is footage gets overwritten after a period of time. They not only lack a wide range of focus but also are usually neglected for maintenance, which I'm assuming is the case here. If there are other cameras like Sergio assumes, they could have valuable footage. There's a chance they're also neglected."

"Other than a history lesson on closed-circuit cameras, did you learn anything else?"

"I didn't have much time to go through the files, and most of them were either filled with static or had a blank image. However, the cameras partially captured a truck in their view. The truck was backed in, making it impossible to identify the specific one, as I could only see the tail end."

"What did you see?" Seth's voice carries an edge.

"A shadowy figure lingering around the side. Between the poor-quality footage of only the rear end of a truck, the individual was barely visible."

"Beth, I'm not liking what I'm hearing," Seth says while staring at the ceiling.

"If you didn't like that, then you'll hate what's coming up next. The laptop we were using to view the footage was stolen after someone tripped the circuit breaker."

Seth sits up and curses. "The situation is escalating, and it's endangering you and Rylie. Why even stay on the show at this point? The wise choice is to get out and cut your losses while you still can."

I look at my twin in shock. "Do you even know me?" I ask, wondering what he's thinking, telling me to drop out. "My reputation is now connected to Benji's murder and this show. The police interrogated me and have dismissed my legitimate concerns. I'm going to see this through and clear my name."

"Even if your name is tarnished, does it matter? Your well-being matters more than what other people think of you."

"If you were a woman working in a male-dominated profession, you'd realize how much harder it is for us to earn our reputations."

My twin gives me a look as if I'd just slapped him. He doesn't understand the struggle women go through to establish themselves in a male-dominated world. Seth is someone who treats everyone with respect regardless of their gender, which, sadly, is not common among most people.

"You're right," Seth says, standing up from my bed. "Women have to work twice as hard as men, both professionally and domestically. However, we're not discussing those other women. It's you we're discussing. My twin." He strides toward me and firmly grabs my shoulders. "If something happened to you, what would I do? Protecting you is my responsibility."

"We're not kids anymore, Seth. You don't need to protect me."

"Then what do you want me to do?" Letting go, he steps back.

"Talk things out with me and support my choices, even if you don't agree with them. Because I'm not dropping this."

"You know I almost never agree with your choices. But I will always support you." He sits back down on my bed, then huffs and runs a hand through his hair. "The staff has complete freedom to come and go as they please. Tripping the circuit breaker and taking the laptop was possible for anyone who was working on Sunday. All the trucks are accessible to them, making it easy to slip in unnoticed."

"But why?" I ask, chewing on my thumbnail. Then I remember what Sergio had said. How the network got this place for a bargain and outdated equipment doesn't matter to them. "What do you think Imogen meant by the network not being able to afford any more costs?"

"That could mean anything." Seth scratches his chin in thought. "Filming on the road has no doubt caused production costs to skyrocket."

"For this season, wouldn't it lower the cost to stay put?" As I ask, I take a sip from my water tumbler on the nightstand. "Staying local must be cheaper than traveling across the West Coast desert."

"It may be cheaper, but filming a reality show can still cost anywhere between $100,000 to more than $500,000 per episode."

Water sprays out of my mouth. "American dollars?"

"A show like *The Food Truck Showdown* that has a prime-time slot on the Cooking Channel is going to be on the higher end of the estimate. Any unexpected delay during filming can cause a massive ripple effect on budgeting. In order to maximize their own profits, they need to reduce expenses. This is likely another reason the network leased a dilapidated facility with subpar equipment."

Sergio did say the network is literally saving thousands of dollars by renting this place.

I sit next to my brother on the bed. "And they're only paying us $50,000 if we win?"

"Welcome to showbiz. Plus, they have a celebrity chef as this season's host. Bobbi's salary alone will cost them a hefty chunk of change." Seth flicks his wrist, checking the time. "I've gotta go. I'm gonna be late."

"Oh, that's right. You showed up here wearing your *date* shirt. Who's the lucky girl? Or hand puppet?"

"Hand puppet?" he says with a laugh.

"I don't judge how people identify. According to the back of the lasagna box, I'm apparently a family of four."

"I'm not going out with a hand puppet." Standing up from my bed, he tousles my hair like he did when we were kids. "Don't do anything stupid tonight, like breaking and entering."

"No promises." I cast a quick glance at him, admiring the meticulous styling of his outfit. "Where are you going? Who are you seeing?" I follow him from my room into the living room.

Taking one last cookie, he says, "Good night, Beth." Then he leaves.

Seth's theory holds weight—a crew member has the most convenient access to the trucks. The missing laptop comes to mind, and I realize how perfectly everything connects. The saboteur who turned off the lights likely stole the laptop. But is it possible one person could have done that themselves? I didn't pay attention to how close the control panel was to the closet-sized office we were in. Is it possible for a single person to trip the circuit breaker and steal the laptop in the given time frame, or would that have to be a two-person job? Could the culprit have had a partner in crime?

Besides Héctor and Sergio, who else was on the lot with us? None of the other parked cars were familiar to me. Let's not forget about the mysterious Bert. What is his role on the show? There's no doubt in my mind: This is an inside job. But this leads me right back to Benji. Why was he killed?

"I have a feeling the answers we need are at the warehouse," I mention to Rylie as we tidy up after work. "We can head there once we drop the truck off at my parents' house. It's Monday, so there should be people working to finish the edits for this week's episode so it can air on Wednesday. I think we can persuade Sergio to let us continue reviewing the footage."

"But the laptop is gone."

"There has to be another set of files, right? Those couldn't be the only ones."

"I would hope not. I agree that there's more to uncover, but I can't come. I have plans," Rylie says while wiping down the stainless-steel counter.

"With who? I'm your only friend."

"Don't worry about it." She sprays some disinfectant and wipes some more. "Look, if you want someone to go with you, call Detective Pretty Boy."

"Why would I do that?"

"You like him," she says while scrubbing at a spot that's been there since my Aunt Dolly had the truck.

"No, I don't," I say in a high-pitched voice, coughing to hide it.

Rylie stops cleaning and looks at me with a huge grin on her face. "I knew it!" She points at me. "You do like him!"

"I don't even know him!"

"Mm-hmm," she replies while she collects her things and gets out of the truck.

I start the truck. "I just wanted a fun bonding moment, but forget it. You're *too busy* for me."

"*Você é ridículo.* I'm not *too busy* for you. I'm just busy right now. Call Detective Pretty Boy."

"I don't need a babysitter, and I definitely don't need Detective Pretty Boy. He'll make me do things like follow protocol." Keeping my foot on the brake, I put the truck in gear.

"That's not always a bad thing!" Rylie shouts above the noise of the truck's engine. "A touch of protocol might be good for you!"

As I drive through the peaceful, tree-lined neighborhood, I'm welcomed by the familiar sight of my parents' charming yellow house, complete with a craftsman-style front porch. The wide and well-maintained driveway next to their house provides ample room to park my truck with ease. Pulling into the driveway, I roll down my window and wave to my father, who's raking leaves from the park strip.

"You're getting a bit too close to your mother's hydrangeas," my dad warns. The sound of leaves crunching under his feet tells me he's walking over. "Could you back up and straighten out? If you run them over, I'll never hear the end of it."

"Why does it matter if I run them over?" I shift the truck into park and turn off the engine. "They're already dead."

"The bush still has three green leaves."

Leaning over the steering wheel, I see her brown hydrangeas through the windshield. "The plants are beyond saving. Not even Jesus could revive them."

"I know," he says with a sigh. "But you know what your mother is like. Moving the truck will make things much easier for me, so please do it."

Restarting the truck, I do as he requests. "Better?" I ask before I get out.

"Much! Thanks, kiddo." He places the rake against the fence. "Any leftovers?" He quickly glances behind him, then back at me. "Your mom is cooking tonight."

"Say no more." Exiting the truck, I give my dad two boxes of leftover wings and fries.

Giving me a quick kiss on the head, he takes his food inside. My mom is amazing, but cooking is not her strong suit. Unlike her sister, my Aunt Dolly, who was a fantastic cook, my mom, well, she tries her best.

I glance at my watch. It's almost three thirty in the afternoon. I don't want to miss Sergio, and I'll have a better chance if I talk to him now while everything is still fresh from yesterday regarding the video files. I get in my Volkswagen Rabbit and drive straight to the studio lot.

Rolling down my window, I see Héctor standing outside as I pull up to the gate. "Hello, Héctor," I say with a smile, praying he won't question why I'm back again.

He walks up to my car and says, "There's still no filming today, Ms. Lloyd."

"I know."

"Are you here to see Imogen again?" Héctor asks.

"I'm looking for Sergio this time. Is he here?"

Looking over his shoulder, he nods. "There are still a few cars here. Try the trailer."

Placing an earbud in his ear, he walks over to his seat.

"Hey!" I call out to him. "Quick question for you."

"Yeah?" Removing the earbud, he walks back over to my car.

"Did anyone else come by yesterday when Rylie and I were here? Maybe another contestant?"

It seems like he has no clue what I'm talking about.

"What about Bert?" I ask instead. "Was he here?"

"This place is always bustling with cars coming and going. I don't get paid enough to remember every face I see."

"I see." I give him a tight-lipped smile. "Thanks for your time."

"Have a great day!" Returning to his chair, he adjusts the earbud and pulls out his phone.

They aren't exactly running the tightest ship around here, with broken cameras and distracted guards. It's no wonder there's been so much crime. No one here cares enough to stop it.

As I drive through the gate, I can't help wondering how the show would look if we had hit the road as originally planned. Pulling into the parking spot next to the producers' trailer, I'm ready to find Sergio and wrap up this video file business. I take a deep breath. Climbing the three steps, I open the door to the trailer.

"Hello?" I call out, stepping inside, but no one answers.

Sergio might be in the warehouse. If nothing else, I could ask Sloane or Imogen about his whereabouts. Before heading back outside, I take one more glance around the trailer. Closing the door, I cross the parking lot to the warehouse.

"Hello, Hoot Jackman," I say as I wave up at the northern hawk-owl. *"Hoot, hoot!"* Hoot Jackman looks away. "Rude," I tsk before making my way into the warehouse.

I wander around the building in search of someone to assist me, but the place is silent. Too silent. All the office doors are open, with the lights off. As I walk down the hall, I search for help and eventually find a closed door with light seeping out from underneath.

"Aha, they must be in here," I murmur to myself and try the handle. The door creaks open a crack, then abruptly stops, as though it's snagged on something. "Hello?" I knock on the door. There's a slight shuffling sound, then complete silence follows. "Sergio? Imogen?" I bang on the door again. Using my shoulder, I successfully force it open.

In horror, I instinctively cover my mouth, regretting opening the door. I was right about one thing. Imogen is here, but she's not alone. She's lying on the floor next to Sloane, who's motionless in a pool of blood.

Chapter Sixteen

My palms are sweaty and my stomach feels queasy. Gasping for air, each breath becomes a struggle. *Is this what hyperventilating feels like?* A sweet, metallic scent fills the room, and I want to vomit. Panic wraps around me, gripping tightly like a vise. Seth was right. I should have told him what I was planning.

Pressing my clammy palms against my pants leg, I try to speak. But when I see the puddle of red liquid pooling on the ground around Sloane's body, a terrified, bloodcurdling scream releases instead. Even though I take deep breaths, my mind is still screaming at me, *You shouldn't be here!*

Bursting into the hallway, I cry for help. After yelling multiple times, I step back into the room and assess the situation. Imogen Comestible is on the ground near Sloane Owsinski. Her once bright-green hair is now smeared crimson. Shifting my attention to Sloane, her head is lolled to the side. Her brown hair is matted and stained red, and her temple has an angry purple bruise.

A wheezing sound, barely audible, shatters the silence. Looking at Imogen, I see her chest rise, ever so slightly. I think. Even in this dire situation, there's a glimmer of hope. Rushing to her, I touch my fingers to the side of her neck and find a faint pulse. Yanking my phone out of my pocket, I scream for help once more.

"Nine-one-one, state your emergency."

"I need an ambulance right away." Panic fills my voice. "A woman is dead, and another woman is injured but alive. Barely. Her breathing is very shallow."

In a calm voice, the dispatcher asks, "Where are you?"

I stay on the line with the dispatcher, following her instructions as I give the address of the lot. My stomach churns as I look at the blood snaking around the room. I don't want to think about what happened here or the monster responsible for this. While Sloane is beyond my help, I can do something for Imogen.

Detective Kane and Detective Hamstead are the first to arrive at the scene. Following them are two sets of paramedics, each carrying a stretcher. Despite the chaos surrounding me, I'm unable to process what's happening. My right hand clasps Imogen's while my left hand strokes her reddish-green hair.

"Ma'am," a voice says. "We need you to step aside."

I can't move. Instead, I straighten Imogen's glasses and resume petting her hair, whispering that everything will be okay.

"Beth." Two hands grip my shoulders, pulling me away from Imogen. "Let the medics do their job, please."

Detective Kane takes me out of the room and sits me down in a chair. At some point, someone, I don't know who, wraps a blanket around my shoulders.

"Here, drink this. It'll help." He presses a paper cup into my hands.

When I look down, I see green tea swirling in the cup. My stomach churns as I think of Imogen's mohawk and immediately shake my head, handing it back. "Thank you, but no. I can't."

"Can you tell me why you're here? According to the security guard, there's no filming today." Detective Kane speaks in a calm, patient voice.

"I was looking for Sergio," I explain.

"Why?"

"I didn't finish watching the CCTV footage of my truck yesterday. I planned to do it today."

His brows furrow in confusion. "What happened yesterday?" He kneels in front of me and locks eyes with me. "Why were you looking at footage from the show?"

I tell him everything.

Scrubbing his face with his hand, Detective Kane rocks back on his heels. A muscle twitches along his jaw as a storm brews in his eyes. "I thought I told you to let the police do the investigating."

"I was being careful."

He's biting down on his teeth so hard that it's making me anxious. "You could've gotten hurt, or worse. And then what? Would I be looking into your murder too?"

"That's harsh," I whisper.

"Well, maybe harsh is what you need. I don't want to see something happen to you. Why would you even think it would be all right to look at video footage?"

"I was worried about my truck. Detective Hamstead told me the Katapangs broke into it—"

"You're blaming Jerry for your reckless actions?" Detective Kane roars.

"Would you stop shouting at me?" I raise my voice to speak over him. "I'm not putting the blame on anyone. I have a right to know what's happening, since my business is involved with the show."

Detective Kane pinches the bridge of his nose and shuts his eyes. "I told your brother to watch you."

"You did what?"

Just as he's about to reply, Seth yells my name. "Beth! Where are you, Beth?" As I turn to the sound of his voice, he pushes past an officer and runs toward me. "Are you okay?" He hugs me so tight that my vision blurs. "I got a call that something happened."

"I'm fine."

"This time," Detective Kane mutters under his breath.

The blanket slips off my shoulders as I stand up and face him. "Why are you so mad at me?"

"Because you don't seem to understand that your behavior is reckless. This isn't a movie. You will get hurt. I've seen too many bad things happen to good people. I don't want even a fraction of that to happen to you."

Wrapping his arms around my shoulders, Seth says, "And nothing will."

Out of nowhere, I feel completely drained. "I want to go home."

"I'll set up a patrol to drive by your place," Detective Kane says as he pulls out his phone and starts tapping away.

"No need. You're staying with me, Beth." Seth leaves little room for argument. I'm too exhausted to say anything. Besides, I don't need two men yelling at me at once.

"Even so, we'll still be monitoring her place," Detective Kane informs us before heading back to the room where I discovered Sloane and Imogen.

"C'mon." Seth directs me toward the exit. "I already called Dad. He's picking up your car, and we can get it later. You're coming home with me, end of story.

"Sergio just called," Seth informs me, setting his phone down. "He said they want all contestants to return tomorrow morning at seven to discuss the show."

Sitting on the edge of Seth's bed, I say, "Okay," while staring into space.

"Also, Mom texted me. Again," he says, drying his wet hair with a towel. "If you don't call her, she's coming over."

It's been two days since I stumbled upon Imogen and Sloane in the warehouse. Our mother wasted no time calling me after my discovery made headlines on the evening news.

"She's worried about you," he tells me. "Call her, if for no other reason than Dad. He's probably losing his mind with all her worrying."

"I know." Seth has done a great job of running interference with our mom. But it's time for me to face the music. "I'll go call her." Getting up from his bed, I walk into the kitchen to make a cup of coffee.

My mom answers the phone on the first ring. "Bethany!" Her loud screech makes me move the phone away from my ear. "Oh, thank the heavens! Henry, it's Bethany!" she yells to my dad. "You're on speaker phone. Where have you been? Say hello to your father. Are you all right? Why haven't you called? Are you eating? How come you aren't answering me?"

"Let the girl talk, Louise," my father says.

"Hello, Dad," I say as I put a coffee pod into Seth's off-brand coffee maker. "Mom, you know I'm staying with Seth. I'm fine. I haven't called because I needed time to process what happened."

"Finding a dead body doesn't mean you can ignore me," my mother chastises me.

"It was two bodies," I correct her as the brown liquid fills a cup labeled "World's Okayest Brother."

"I'm sorry," she says with a sigh. "This must be difficult for you."

"I've had better weeks," I admit, removing the cup of steaming coffee from the drip tray.

"But that still doesn't excuse you for ignoring me," she says.

As I sip the hot beverage, I wince and set it down. "I'm sorry. The next time I find a dead body, you'll be the first person I call."

"I don't appreciate the dark humor, but I'm holding you to that," she says in her no-argument tone while my dad laughs.

My mother has a knack for making things in my life all about her.

"What's happening with the show? You're quitting, right?" From the start, she didn't like the idea of me being on TV. It was fine for her that Seth be on TV, but not me. "I said it wasn't a good idea to sign up. Didn't I tell her, Henry, that she shouldn't do this?" My poor father is likely being held hostage while she talks to me. "I told you all those chicken fetish people would find you."

"There aren't any chicken fetish people approaching me, Mom."

"That you know of," my dad says with a laugh. "Have you had anyone ask to check your eggs? Or maybe ask that you pluck their feathers?"

"Henry!" I can picture my mom's shocked expression now.

"The show halted production immediately," I tell them. "Honestly, I'm a little indecisive about what I want or how I feel right now. All I know is I have to get away from Seth." I quickly clamp a hand over my mouth, realizing what I said out loud.

Maybe she didn't hear me?

"You could always come home," she suggests.

No such luck.

"It's fine, Mom—"

"Your room is just how you left it," she says, completely ignoring me.

These have been the two longest days of my life. Seth has been so overbearing, but the thought of returning home is unacceptable.

"I appreciate your concern—"

"She doesn't want to come home, Louise," my dad cuts me off. "She just moved out a few months ago, and I've already turned her bedroom into my music room. I'm sorry, Beth, but you can't come home."

"She needs to, Henry. Seth told me she hasn't been showering."

"Well, then that should keep the chicken freaks away from her," my dad says with a snort.

"Seth's exaggerating!" I raise my voice to be heard over them. *Of course Seth would tattle on me.* "I'm showering, but I refuse to do so with the bathroom door open. That's why Seth is upset."

"He has legitimate concerns," my mom defends him.

"He thinks someone is going to break in and go all Norman Bates on me," I say. "That is not a legitimate concern."

"He's right, you know," she says. She's always defending him. "Someone could break in and try to attack you."

"Seth lives on the second floor, and his bathroom has no windows. If someone breaks in from outside while I'm showering, they've earned the right to kill me."

"You have a twisted sense of humor," she says in disgust.

I guess my comment didn't amuse her.

"Look, Mom, I—" The sound of the front door creaking open makes my spine stiffen. I left Seth in his room to get dressed after showering, so I know it's not him. "I gotta go," I whisper into my phone before ending the call.

The last two days have put me on edge, so I grab the closest item within reach—a bread knife. The sound of the front door slamming shut startles me, causing me to spin around in the kitchen while screaming and clutching the bread knife to my chest.

"*Oh meu Deus,* put that thing down!" Rylie scolds as she shuffles toward me, balancing a box of doughnuts on a tray of coffees. "What has gotten into you?"

"I just got off the phone with my parents," I say, setting down the bread knife. "And I can't take Seth anymore. He made me watch *Conspiracy Theory* last night."

"The Liam Neeson movie? Oh, he's hot for an old guy. He can rescue me from Paris anytime." Rylie smirks, thinking about her cinema crush.

"He is, but it wasn't one of his movies. This was from the nineties, starring Mel Gibson. Just like in the movie, Seth put a beer bottle on the front doorknob to alert us to an intruder in the middle of the night, but he'd taken it off by the time I got up this morning. How did you get in, by the way?"

"He just cares," she says, motioning toward the box of doughnuts, ignoring my question. "Besides, there are worse people you could be stuck with than Seth."

"Ha!" Grabbing the doughnuts, I snort. "You've never lived with the man. You think his place is usually this clean?" Slowly spinning around the room, I fan out my free arm. "If it weren't for me, you would be wading through dirty laundry right now."

I think the actual reason Seth insisted I stay with him was so he could get free house cleaning. He knows I can't stand a cluttered space.

With a tie hanging loosely around his neck, Seth walks out of his room barefoot and takes the pink box from me. "She's right. You could be stuck with worse people. Like Mom."

Walking past me, Rylie puts the coffee tray down on the counter and takes out three plates from above Seth's microwave. "The place looks good."

"It didn't look bad before," he says, flicking open the lid.

"Speaking of Mom"—I give him my best death stare as I grab a doughnut from the box—"why are you tattling on me?"

"I don't know what you're talking about." He reaches for a coffee, then pauses, looking at the cups.

"Take the left one," Rylie says. "Two creams, no sugar."

Seth nods at her, then picks up the cup she mentioned.

She knows how he takes his coffee?

"I didn't know you were coming." I take a plate from Rylie. "Don't get me wrong. I'm not complaining."

Shaking a sugar packet, she looks at my brother. "I told Seth I'd be stopping by to check on you this morning."

Midway through eating an old-fashioned doughnut, I pause. "Seth knew, but I didn't?" I look at my twin.

He coughs, and coffee dribbles down his chin. Setting down the cup, he reaches for a napkin. "I was talking to her last night about the truck. When she asked about you, I suggested she come over."

"You talked with her about my truck?"

"It's our truck," he reminds me.

Ignoring his remark, I give Seth a suspicious look and finish chewing my doughnut. "Let me get this straight." I wipe my hands on a napkin. "You left the front door unlocked because you knew she was coming over?"

Tying his black and silver striped tie, he says. "Yeah, you were showering, and I was getting ready for work."

"I didn't shower this morning," I say, narrowing my eyes. "You did."

He never leaves the front door unlocked.

Dramatically, Seth uses the back of his hand to wipe his forehead. "Well, that's good because I didn't want to say anything, but you could use one. I assumed you ran out of deodorant."

Before I can push the topic further, my phone vibrates across the counter, disrupting the conversation.

"Do you plan on answering that?" Seth asks, smoothing a hand over his tie before shoving an entire doughnut into his mouth.

"As long as it's not Mom calling me back." Seeing that it's not, I tap on the screen. "Hello?"

"Beth, it's Detective Kane. You remember, the officer who arrested you when you were dressed like a chicken and questioned you in the murder of Benji Mayhew?"

My face breaks into a grin. "I remember.'"

Seth gives me a strange look as I grin wider when I hear Detective Kane's deep, throaty laugh on the other end. "What can I help you with?" I ask.

Who is it? Seth mouths.

Switching the phone to my other side, I swat Seth away. Leaving the kitchen, I plop myself onto his ugly couch.

"Nothing," he says. "I was just calling to see how you're doing since everything happened."

"You mean since I found two women tied up? One dead and the other almost dead?"

"Yeah." Detective Kane lets out a sigh. "I wanted to call sooner, but I've—"

"You don't owe me anything," I say, cutting him off. "Can you tell me how Imogen is?"

"She's stable, but still unconscious. She received a hard blow to the back of her head."

I fidget with the blanket on Seth's ugly plaid couch. "Any idea when she'll wake up?"

"Sadly, no."

"Well, thanks for calling, Detective."

"Do you need anything?" he asks before I hang up.

While my brother hovers like a mother hen, I contemplate his question. "Actually, yes."

"Name it."

Putting my phone on speaker, I share my comment with everyone in the room. "My brother has become extremely protective of me. I've not been allowed to leave his apartment."

"That's not true!" Seth snaps at me. "I took you out for a walk yesterday."

"Thank you for treating me like a pampered pooch you took to the park for some fresh air."

Detective Kane chuckles. "I'm not sure how I can help you with that, Beth."

"I need you to tell my brother I can go home."

There's stuttering coming from the other end of the line. He doesn't seem to want to take sides in our sibling squabble.

"Look," I say. My twin and I lock eyes. "You have two options: tell Seth to release me or apprehend me for attempted manslaughter. I'll end up killing him if I'm forced to stay here any longer."

"It's fratricide, not manslaughter," Detective Kane corrects me.

"Not helping!" Seth yells at the phone.

"I don't want to get involved in whatever is happening between you two. But I feel it's safe for you to return home," the detective says. "There has been no activity at your apartment, and I'll have a squad car drive by your place for a couple of days longer, plus a plainclothes officer outside."

Seth grumbles something inaudible while I hastily get up from the couch to pack my things. "Thanks, Detective. I owe you!"

People say the fastest land animal is a toddler whose mother just asked what he has in his mouth. I wouldn't know. I don't have kids. But I'm certain the exhilaration I feel while running around my apartment is like what a toddler feels when their mother chases after them, shouting, "Come back here!"

Stepping into my apartment and crying tears of joy was something I never expected. But that's what happens. As soon as I lock my front door, fat tears start rolling down my cheeks. There's nothing special about my tiny apartment. It's small, and you can see from one end to the other without moving an inch. It's not as cramped as a New York shoebox, but it's still tiny, with an even smaller galley kitchen. There's nothing fresh or modern. I'm sure I have asbestos in my ceiling, but I don't care. Although it's small, the place is clean, organized, quiet, and has a surprisingly large tub.

But mostly, it's Seth-free.

I love my twin. He's my other half. But I can't seem to stress this enough. I *hate* living with him and that ugly plaid couch our father gave him. Anyone would run for the hills after two days of listening to Seth belch and scratch himself. One night, I thought he had rats inside the walls. Nope, it was Seth, claiming he had an itch. Well, I'm sorry, but if your skin is that dry, you need to see a dermatologist.

Tossing my duffel bag next to my oversized gray love seat, I sink into the cushions, enjoying the peacefulness of my home. As soon as I close my eyes, someone knocks on my front door.

"Seriously?" Frustrated by my life's irony, I get up from the couch.

"What's wrong with you?" Seth barges into my apartment as soon as I open the door, shoving me aside. What little free space I have is being taken up by his brooding attitude.

"Are you kidding me?" I glare at my brother and point to my front door. "GET OUT!"

"Are you kidding me?" he says with just as much attitude. "I could have been a killer, and you just opened up your house to him?"

"That's sexist of you. Women are just as capable of being murderers, It's not exclusive to one gender."

Seth pinches the bridge of his nose. "I don't have time for you and your feminist comments right now."

"Let me help you since you're so busy." Marching toward him, I push his shoulder.

My stupid boulder of a brother doesn't so much as budge. Despite my pushing, pulling, and poking, nothing happens. He just folds his arms, waiting me out.

"Are you done yet?" he finally asks.

Collapsing onto my love seat, defeated, I whine, "Why can't you leave me alone?"

"Do you think I'd be okay with you leaving just because a cop said so?" There's a mix of concern and annoyance in his words.

Grabbing his hand, I tug him over. "I know you love me, but I'm asking you to love me less."

"I just worry."

"Worry less." I smile at my teddy bear of a twin. "Now, as the older sister, I'm ordering you to get out!"

"You live on the first floor, so I want you to call me for anything, no matter the time. Even if it's only a cat howling outside."

Standing up from the couch, I tug him toward the exit. "Will do!"

"And we're riding to the lot together tomorrow to meet about the show. I'm picking you up. That's all there is to it."

Pressing both my hands flat against his back, I push him forward. "Sounds great. Bring me an onion bagel."

Bracing his hands on either side of the doorframe, Seth glances back at me. "Beth, I'm legally seven years older than you."

"GET OUT!" I slam the door closed.

"Lock the deadbolt!" he shouts from the other side.

"Go away!"

Chapter Seventeen

"The driveway looks smaller than I recall," Seth complains, turning into the studio lot.

"I don't know why you insisted on driving when we're running late," I say, watching as he narrowly avoids the orange cones. "You should've let me or Rylie drive, since we have more experience."

"Just because I don't drive this beast of a truck every day doesn't mean I'm incapable of doing so." Gritting his teeth, Seth attempts to steer the oversized vehicle into the tightest spot. "And we're late because I stopped for your stupid onion bagel."

"*Oh meu Deus*, this is going to be tight." Rylie, who is riding shotgun, nervously checks the side mirrors. "Watch out for that lamppost on the right!" Seth jerks the wheel to the left just in time, barely avoiding a catastrophic collision.

"Just a little to the left, Seth. No, not that much!" My scream echoes as he comes close to hitting Porked 'n' Rubbed's side mirror.

"Okay, okay, stop," Seth huffs, maneuvering the food truck. I'm sure he feels the weight of everyone's eyes on him. The other food truck owners are watching, some amused, others worried. "I can do this."

After what seems like an eternity, Seth aligns the truck somewhat evenly within the spot. He lets out a sigh of relief, wiping the sweat off his brow.

"Umm . . ." Rylie points to the side mirror.

"Oh, come on!" Seth groans, realizing the new dilemma. The truck's rear end is sticking out into the narrow aisle, hindering the other food trucks when it's time to leave.

"Can one of us park the truck, please?" I ask my brother. "I can't afford a repair bill right now, and we need to hurry if we want to hear the announcement."

"Fine," Seth says, switching seats with Rylie.

Reversing and changing gears, she maneuvers the truck into a better position. "You just need more practice," Rylie says, patting Seth on the back.

We're the last team to arrive, and I'm assuming everyone knows by now that I found Imogen and Sloane. I got a couple of texts from my fellow contestants checking on me. Even Bobbi Taylor messaged me and said she was thinking of me and couldn't imagine what I was going through after witnessing such a gruesome sight.

As we take our seats in front of the stage, Bobbi is already standing before the group. She looks around, clearing her throat and appearing a little out of sorts. The action highlights the absence of Imogen and Sloane.

"With a heavy heart, I must inform you, we have lost two members of our television family."

Bobbi must realize how her words sound because she corrects her comment. "I didn't mean to phrase it like that. We lost an excellent and talented member of our team. Sloane Owsinski has passed away. Imogen Comestible is alive but in a coma. Her condition remains unchanged." Bobbi bows her head in silence, giving us a moment for her words to sink in.

"Will there be any services for Ms. Owsinski?" Ness Jaxson asks.

"There will, but it's a private ceremony. The families of Sloane and Imogen are asking for privacy during this difficult period," Bobbi answers. "I'm sure that the Clementine Police Department will do everything in their power to bring justice to Imogen and Sloane." Bobbi visibly swallows a lump in her throat. "For years, Sloane and I were colleagues. Initially, we vlogged about cooking together until I got a minor role on a test kitchen show. With Sloane by my side, I continued auditioning for cooking shows. She started as my personal assistant but climbed the cooking ladder with me to become a producer. But she was much more than that. She was a dear friend. Trust me, I get it—it's difficult for any of you to be here. The best way to honor them is to keep doing what they loved—working on this show. In that spirit, the season will continue as planned—"

"But there's a killer among us!" Marco shouts.

Everyone looks around at one another as possible suspects.

Despite the sudden outburst, Bobbi remains composed. "I understand if anyone wants to leave before filming is over. Sergio Romare is now in charge of the daily operations, and you can speak with him about leaving."

Stepping forward, Sergio offers a solemn wave to everyone before stepping back.

"Correct me if I'm wrong," I whisper to Rylie. "Has Sergio taken Imogen's place?"

She nods while we exchange a look.

How convenient for him.

My hand shoots up in the air. "I have a question!"

Bobbi signals to me. "Yes, Beth."

"The tally of attacks is now at three, with two individuals having lost their lives. What is the network planning to do to make sure we're safe?"

The group agrees and some respond by saying "That's a good question."

"I agree with Beth!" Marco stands up. "Completing this show is important to me. However, my family's safety takes precedence."

Bobbi raises her hands to the restless crowd. "First, let's be clear. Benji's life being cut short is tragic, but let's not call what happened *three* attacks. Benji suffered a heart attack and died."

Why does the network keep claiming it was a heart attack? Detective Kane, although not disclosing much, confirmed they were looking into things surrounding Benji. Detective Hamstead essentially gave away the information by stating that Benji was killed. Why are there two different stories about what happened? Does the network have something they're trying to hide? Or is it possible that they truly have no knowledge of what's going on and think that Benji passed away from a heart attack?

"People have died here!" Marco shouts.

"And it's tragic, I agree," Bobbi says.

"Our aunt died of a heart attack," I add. "The police didn't give us the same scrutiny as they have with Benji. It seems like there's something else going on."

"Second," Bobbi says, ignoring my comments, "nothing is more important than the safety of you contestants. Additional security officers have been arranged by the network to patrol the grounds. Security will be present with us during filming on location. As we speak, local law enforcement is working tirelessly behind the scenes to solve what is happening. You can trust me to take action if there's a direct threat to anyone." Bobbi places a hand over her chest. "If I thought any of us were at risk, I wouldn't be standing here. Please consider staying with us until the end of this competition. If you won't do it for yourselves, do it for Imogen and Sloane. It would be a shame if all their hard work on this show was for nothing."

"I have a few questions." Ness Jaxson raises her hand. "If we stay, what happens with filming? What incentives are being provided for us to continue? It's clear that the network's success depends on one of their top-performing programs continuing; otherwise, this season would have been scrapped."

Excellent questions.

"I spent much of yesterday discussing this with the executive producers on how the rest of the season will proceed," Bobbi says. "What has happened on set is beyond words, and grief counselors are available. If you're interested in exploring this option, Sergio can offer guidance." Once again, Sergio gives a pitiful wave to the anxious group of contestants. "The network does not believe that the incidents are connected. The tragic events that have occurred appear to be unforeseen and unrelated. However, they acknowledge the existence of valid safety concerns and are doubling the prize money for the winning team from $50,000 to $100,000."

Gasps and hushed whispers fill the area in response to this surprising announcement.

"For anyone who remains for the rest of the season, the next episode will resume Saturday afternoon," Bobbi says. "We intend to wrap up filming on schedule. I hope to see you here." She leaves the stage and heads toward the production trailer.

Without a word, everyone gets up and heads back to their trucks. "I feel guilty ever thinking Sloane had anything to do with things."

"How do you feel about continuing to compete?" Rylie asks. "And what about our Kluckin' Clues list?"

"Clearing my name is still a priority, but I refuse to be reckless and endanger our lives."

"What are you saying?" Seth asks. "Are you finally going to listen to me and let the police handle this?"

Before I can answer, Sergio calls my name, jogging over to us. "Beth, do you mind coming with me? Bobbi has asked to speak with you in her office."

Several of my fellow contestants exchange looks.

Bobbi wants to speak to me*?*

I don't know why Bobbi wants to talk to me, but I have a strange sensation in my stomach. It's possible she wants to remind me to keep quiet about anything I witnessed during my confessionals. Is it also possible she learned of my viewing surveillance footage and now somehow holds me responsible for what happened to Imogen and Sloane?

"Okay," I say as Rylie moves close to me in a sign of solidarity.

"Bobbi wants only Beth," Sergio remarks as Seth flanks my other side.

"Too bad," my brother says, crossing his arms. "I'm half owner. Whatever she wants to discuss with Beth, she also discusses with me."

"Anywhere they go, I go," Rylie adds.

Sucking his bottom lip through his rodent-like teeth, Sergio nods.

"Did you color your hair?" I ask as he leads us through the maze of pop-up tents. "It doesn't look as dark as it used to."

"Or as long," Rylie adds, as I make a mental note of his new color.

"Just a trim and I frosted the tips." He smooths a hand over his hair. "I wanted to freshen up my look. Why? Does it not look good?"

"It's fine, if you're going for that early-2000s look." Rylie snickers.

"The lady at the shop told me it was in style," he says, walking up the steps to the white production trailer.

"Yeah, back when Justin and Britney wore matching denim," Rylie says to me under her breath.

"Here we are," Sergio announces. With a firm knock, he opens the door to Bobbi's private office.

He hangs back as we step inside and wait for Bobbi to finish up. "Thank you, Sergio, that will be all," she says, without looking up from her desk.

"Just let me know if you need anything. I'll be right outside." He leaves but neglects to shut the door completely.

The interior of her office is cozy, as cozy as a temporary office trailer can be.

Bobbi momentarily pauses her focus on the papers and looks up. "Seth, Rylie? I'm sorry, I didn't ask for anyone other than Beth."

"Seth is half owner," I remind her. "And Rylie is my assistant. Whatever you want to say to me about the show involves them."

There's no chance Seth will allow me to go anywhere on this lot without him anyway.

She lets out an annoyed huff and motions for us to take the seats on the opposite side of her desk. Seth stands behind Rylie and me, acting as our personal bodyguard. There's a long pause before Bobbi finally speaks. "I want your help."

"With what?" I ask, unsure of where this conversation is about to lead.

"I need someone with eyes and ears I can trust."

"Do you not trust your own team members?" I ask.

"Trust is a fragile thing. I need someone who can slip between both the staff and contestants, someone who won't raise suspicion when they're in areas where it would seem strange for a production member to be listening."

"I'm having a hard time following what you're implying," I say.

Bobbi gives me a look like I'm not keeping up. "Something is going on here. My belief is that there might be others who know how deep everything goes. And I want you, Beth, to find out."

"I was actually considering leaving," I tell her. "The situation is becoming too dangerous to stay on the show."

"So, what? You're just going to walk away?" Bobbi asks, irritated by my confession. "I'll be honest, Beth. I thought you were braver than that."

"With all due respect," Seth says, speaking in his lawyer voice, "what you're asking for is a job for the police. We came here to win a competition. Not play detectives."

"What if we had an understanding?" Bobbi proposes. "Would that keep you here?"

"What are you suggesting?" I ask her.

Bobbi looks at each of us for a long moment. "If you do this for me, I will make sure that Kluckin' Good wins the competition."

My mouth hangs open. I must be hearing things. *She can't be serious.*

"I realize you may feel my offer is unfair." It's like she can read my thoughts. "But isn't the fairest thing to seek justice for Sloane and Imogen?"

"That's a job for the police," Seth says again in a firm voice.

"And while I agree, I do question how fast they'll be able to find who's responsible."

"These things do take time," Seth tells her.

"My television family has suffered attacks. There's a monster on the loose, Mr. Lloyd. How much time will they take?"

"Can you even do what you're suggesting? Rig the competition in exchange for my spying?" I ask, still mulling over everything in my head. "That doesn't seem ethical."

"I consider it sleuthing, not spying. Besides, who do you think selects the judges and scores the contestants?" Bobbi leans back in her chair and points at herself. "Another team was already set to win this season, but sometimes we have to change course mid-season, and your truck is well-loved by our viewers. Especially with Rylie as your mascot," she notes. "Your truck has consistently been trending on all major social media platforms this season. Swapping the two teams would be a simple task."

I draw in a sharp, audible breath. "The show is rigged?" I don't believe my ears. "How is this fair?"

"More importantly, who was the other team?" Rylie asks.

"Rylie!" My eyes widen. "How can you be concerned about that after discovering the show is rigged?"

"I'm not saying it's fair. I just want to know who we beat out," Rylie says. "If the other team was Chowder Bowl on the Roll, I would strongly object. Their combined personalities are comparable to that of a goldfish."

Seth chuckles before quickly coughing to hide it.

"It was Porked 'n' Rubbed," Bobbi states matter-of-factly.

"Ooh, they're good!" Rylie nods in approval. "Loretta and Ella Mae are a hoot! I'd vote for them if we weren't competing."

"You're not helping matters, Rylie." My attention returns to Bobbi. "How is this fair?" This revelation raises so many questions for me now. "People join with the hope of a fair chance to win."

"And when the season starts, everyone is on equal footing. But this is reality TV. Your brother is a media lawyer. I'm sure he can explain to you just how 'real' reality shows are."

"It's unethical!" I say.

"Bobbi's right," Seth says. "Reality shows are only 'real' in the sense that they're constructed from unscripted footage."

"'Unscripted' does not mean 'unwritten,'" Bobbi adds. "Strategic editing and predetermined constraints are used to shape the action, add flavor, and subvert expectations. The end credits include writers."

"What she's offering is not uncommon in the industry," Seth remarks.

"And you're okay with this?" I ask my brother. "It's unfair to all the contestants!"

"I wouldn't say I'm fine with it," Seth admits, shrugging a shoulder, "but that's just how things are."

"Imogen and Sloane were wonderful to me. I'm not sure I'll find someone even half as good as them," Bobbi says, her voice trailing off. "It's my duty to put things to rest with them."

"I don't know . . ."

"If we agree to this, we need everything in writing," Rylie states, taking over the conversation. "Including a misconduct clause freeing us of anything considered questionable."

"Done." There's no hesitation in Bobbi's reply. "I will see that all the legal papers are in order."

"Any attempts to include anything suspicious in the documents will not go unnoticed by Seth," Rylie tells her.

"You have my word," she says. "Do we have a deal, then?" Bobbi looks expectantly at me.

I don't know what to make of all this.

But . . .

This is my best shot at uncovering everything.

"I'll need access everywhere," I say. "Including all the footage—CCTVs, the video diaries, and confessionals."

Rylie shakes her head. "The files are missing. Remember?"

"You mean the files that you already viewed?" Bobbi asks with a smirk.

"How did you—"

"I know everything that happens on my shows," Bobbi says.

Well, that's unsettling.

"Don't worry. There are extra copies."

"Sergio only showed us one set," I say, seeing no reason to pretend. "I'll need all the footage. Not just what he feels like sharing."

"Done," she says without hesitation. "I need this resolved quickly and quietly. I have a career to maintain. The network will not continue to work with me if contestants are afraid for their lives."

"Why us?" I'm still on the fence about her offer.

Bobbi lets out a sigh, her gaze fixed on a framed photo of her and Sloane. They appear much younger. "This isn't just any case, Beth. I loved Sloane. We've been together since the beginning of my food career. What happened to her is personal. Women have to work tirelessly to build and maintain our reputations. One action can undo all our hard work. Something like this can destroy my reputation. Please, don't let this be what unravels years of my hard work."

I don't say anything, but she's right. I know what she means about having to prove ourselves when others don't.

"Then there's also the fact that you've already been investigating by yourself. Why else would you have gone to Sergio asking to watch video recordings? Or take notes while talking to your fellow contestants?" Bobbi holds my stare as she gives me a pointed look.

"I'm not sure what to say," I answer honestly.

How did she know I was taking notes?

Oh right, she knows everything happening on her shows.

"Wait to answer until you see this," she requests, swiveling in her chair she opens a desk drawer. She turns around and slides an unmarked, somewhat thick manila folder across the desk. My eyes dart toward the folder, then back to her. "Inside is the medical report on Sloane Owsinski."

Rylie has no reservations. She takes the folder and starts looking through the documents inside. Where did Bobbi get this from? Is this a privilege that only celebrities enjoy? Are people willing to do anything for a shot at being on her show?

The blood and violence in the pages doesn't faze Rylie as she flips through them. "Hmm . . ."

"What?" Seth inquires while peering over her to read the page.

"The report states that a blunt object killed Sloane," Rylie says. "A blow across the back of Sloane's skull was delivered by her attacker. Blood patterns suggest that Sloane Owsinski was attacked with extreme force." Rylie looks up from the papers. "That sounds awful."

"It was," I shudder.

As I close my eyes, the memory of finding Sloane in a pool of blood on the cold concrete floor comes rushing back. Whoever did this was angry. But why?

"So, you see," Bobbi says, looking at us, "it's my duty to tie up all loose ends for Sloane." She takes the file from Rylie and slips it into her desk. "The papers will be drawn up and notarized to ensure that Kluckin' Good is declared the winner of this season. In exchange, I'm assigning you to investigate this for me. I need everything handled. Quietly."

Six eyes are staring at me, waiting for an answer. "But can't there still be a way for us to compete fairly?" I ask. "I joined this show with the intention of playing fair, not cheating. This won't establish our truck as the top team. Your arrangement simply implies a mutual exchange of favors."

"Isn't uncovering the truth more crucial than identifying the top-performing team?" Bobbi pointedly asks.

This doesn't sit well with me. But she's right. Someone needs to stop the person responsible. My brother and I share a look.

But does that person need to be you? his eyes plead with me.

Who else? I respond.

The police!

Pushing away the seed of doubt, I extend my hand to Bobbi.

I know this agreement is wrong, but winning will enable me to donate money to The Heart Foundation in Aunt Dolly's memory and in honor of others who died too young from heart disease.

"Thank you, Beth," Bobbi says, ushering us out of her office. She approaches Sergio's desk, where he's staring at us. "Sergio, please hold all my calls, as I have some paperwork to take care of."

Sergio's slicked back hair bounces as he nods. He keeps his eyes on Bobbi until she disappears, then he turns his gaze toward me. "How was your meeting?" He sucks the front of his rodent-like teeth.

As I stare at him, a feeling of distrust sinks deep into my gut. "Educational," is all I reply. "Have a good day, Sergio." His gaze feels like a heavy weight on my back as we walk away.

For some reason, my thoughts return to the threatening note we received, warning us about snooping. Pausing at the trailer door, I glance over my shoulder and find his eyes still fixed on me. Like an unwelcome shadow refusing to dissipate. The way he's staring unnerves me, as if he's hiding secrets I shouldn't know.

Each second spent under his scrutiny only deepens my resolve to keep my guard up. Without glancing back, I quickly head to the truck with Seth and Rylie in tow.

Only Héctor is at the gate, now that the other participants have departed. As Seth opens the truck door, a folded paper drifts to the ground. Picking it up, he unfolds the note.

"Someone else seems to know what we've been asked to do." He hands me the slip of paper.

I read it aloud for Rylie to hear. "'Stay away from Imogen, Sloane, and Bobbi unless you want your feathers plucked.'"

Chapter Eighteen

"You know what would be great?" Seth says as he comes through the back door of the truck. "If you would keep this door locked."

"Why are you here?" I ask.

"Is there any coffee left over?" He looks miserable as he rubs his temples.

"You seem a little irritable," I say, reaching for a cup.

"I got it," Rylie says, already preparing a coffee for Seth. *Two creams, no sugar*. She hands him the cup.

While Rylie resumes cleaning the counter, I turn to Seth. "Aren't you supposed to be at work?"

Using two fingers, he loosens his tie and takes a sip of coffee. "What do you mean what am I doing here? I'm working with you and Rylie, remember?"

"Only when we're filming the show, which is tomorrow, not today," I remind him. "Besides, our shift is almost over."

"You know, Beth, it sounds like you don't want me here," Seth says as he takes another gulp of coffee.

"I want you to stay," Rylie says as she moves on to washing a mixing bowl.

"You do?" Seth and I say in twin unison.

"We can always use free help to clean." She winks at Seth.

She makes it look so natural. I need to ask her for lessons.

Leaning against the prep counter, I stare at my brother. His face is ashen, and his hair is tousled. He didn't even bother to shave. "What's up with you? Why aren't you at work?"

Pounding back the rest of the coffee, he ignores me and pours himself another cup.

"Earth to Seth." I poke his side.

"I was only there for half a day," he says, making no sense as he rubs his temples again.

"I don't suspect you're trying out a new look here." I gesture to his face. "Did something happen with a case at work?"

He mutters, "Or something," then falls in line beside Rylie to help clean up. I decide to drop it for now and continue cleaning up.

Picking up a bottle of glass cleaner, I spray the windows near the serving counter. Nothing is more off-putting than an order window with smudgy fingerprints all over it. I'm trying my best to ignore the tension hanging in the air between us. Seth is stacking dishes with excessive force and has become uncharacteristically silent.

"Is your attitude related to Bobbi's offer?" I ask, unable to tolerate his brooding attitude any longer.

Seth pauses, setting down the dish he's holding, and locks eyes with me. "No, my attitude isn't about Bobbi. But since you've mentioned it, let's talk."

"*Deus me dê forças,*" Rylie says with a sigh while rinsing a mixing bowl.

"This doesn't sit well with me," Seth begins. "Rylie's not a cop, and you're not a detective. I don't like being dragged into the dangers of trying to solve a murder."

"You have an overprotective nature. I get it. But I have not dragged you into anything, and this is bigger than us, Seth."

He shakes his head. "Is winning that important to you?"

"Is that what you think?" I'm surprised—and angry—at his judgmental comment. "Winning isn't the reason I agreed to

Bobbi's terms. Sloane, Imogen, and Benji are—they deserve justice, and I want to make sure they get it. My goal is to clear my name completely so that I am remembered as someone who helped bring about that justice!"

"What you're doing is risking your safety. You've got to understand that, Beth. Leave the investigation to the professionals—like Detective Kane."

A pounding sounds on the outside of our truck. "Seth's right. You shouldn't be meddling in police investigations."

"The man is like Beetlejuice," I say. "You say his name one too many times and he appears." With a tight smile, I flip open the partition to the serving window. "What brings you to my truck, Detective? Again."

"Is it that strange for a man to crave chicken wings?" he asks.

"I'm sorry, but we sold out of wings. That's why we closed early. How about some Plucked and Truffled Fries?" I offer. "It's all we have left."

He gives his belly a pat. "My stomach seems to approve of that idea."

"Rylie, please get the detective his fries," I say. He raises an eyebrow at me. "What?"

"Why would you think it's a good idea to meddle in police business?" He doesn't beat around the bush.

"I'm not meddling," I squeak.

"Are you always this bad at lying?" he asks.

"Yes," Rylie and Seth chime in unison.

"Thanks for the support," I say to my traitorous brother and best friend. I look back at Detective Kane and scan the surroundings. "Where's your partner?"

"Busy," is all he says. Rylie pushes a basket of fries toward the detective, who eagerly accepts. While munching, he remarks, "I knew you wouldn't listen."

"Listen to what?" I ask.

"When I said to let the police do their job."

Seth snorts. "I've been telling you the same thing, but it's like talking to a brick wall." Narrowing his eyes, he shakes his head in disbelief. "You're the most stubborn ox I've ever met."

I jab him in the ribs with my elbow. "The police are doing their job, and I am not interfering. I don't see any problem with me reviewing video footage of the show."

"There's a reason why trained professionals handle these cases. It's dangerous, and there are legal protocols to follow. Trust me, you don't want to get entangled in something you can't handle."

How dare he and his stupid dimples tell me what I can or cannot handle!

"Look," Detective Kane says between mouthfuls, "you got lucky once, being in the wrong place at the wrong time. It's better to quit while you're still ahead."

I tip my chin up in defiance. "I don't believe in luck."

"Maybe you should. You interrupted somebody's plans once. You might not be so lucky again."

"Are you suggesting I'm the reason Imogen's not dead?"

Detective Kane gives me a lingering glare. "Maybe. Having seen Sloane first, you understand how brutal her death was. Why risk yourself?"

His words remind me of a comment made by Inga Nevarez during an episode of *Murder and Mayhem*. "Do you think Sloane and Benji knew the killer?"

Detective Kane considers my question. "Based on my experience, most of the time, there's some prior connection between attackers and their victims. Even more reason for you to stay out of this."

"What does that mean?" I ask.

"The attacks on three individuals from the same show are not coincidental." Once again, his ocean eyes turn stormy as he stares at me with a gaze that can only belong to an officer of the law. *Or my mother.*

"The other day, Bobbi shared with the contestants that the network believes Benji died of a heart attack." I'm met with Detective Kane's silent, penetrating gaze. "I don't believe it. *You* don't believe it," I add, hoping he'll mention more details. I still don't know what the inside of Benji's truck looked like. Or how they found his body.

He doesn't take the bait. Where's Hamstead when you need him?

"You're treading a dangerous path," Detective Kane tells me. "You might come across something that will upset whoever is behind all this."

"Just like the latest note we received," Seth remarks.

Detective Kane's head whips to my brother. "You got another note?"

"Right here." He fishes the piece of paper out of his pocket and passes it through the serving window.

His eyes scan the note. "When did you receive this?"

"Yesterday morning," I answer. "After we met with Bobbi about the show."

"It matches the other notes floating around set. When I said to tell me if something happens, this is what I meant." He tucks the paper inside the pocket of his tan jacket.

I knew he'd keep the note and lecture me. That's why I didn't tell him.

"You should have been more specific." I don't appreciate his tone, so I cross my arms.

"If anything else happens—threats, notes, prank phone calls—call me immediately. It doesn't matter what it is or what time of day it is."

I have to remind myself that he's only fulfilling his professional duties. "I'm not a child. There's no harm in looking at a few video files."

"Believe me, I've seen people get hurt a lot worse over far less." His words hang like a dark cloud over us. "If it were up to me, I would've had production shut down a long time ago."

"Why hasn't it been shut down?" I ask.

Detective Kane sighs. "There's *a lot* of pressure from the network to continue production. I'm not privy to everything that's been said, but the network thinks we can conduct our investigation simultaneously."

"Is it up to them?"

"Those with the deepest pockets have a way of getting what they want," Seth says.

I recall Seth's words about the way of the world.

After a moment, Detective Kane's familiar eye twinkle returns. "Watch those two," he says to Seth, gesturing between Rylie and me. "They're trouble."

"Don't I know it . . ." Seth eyes both of us. "We'll contact you if we find anything useful. You have my word."

"Thank you." Detective Kane wads up his empty fry tray and walks away.

"Hey!" I poke my head through the serving window. "You forgot to pay again!"

"Add it to my tab!" he calls out over his shoulder.

The absolute nerve!

Chapter Nineteen

In order to make the most of our time, Rylie and I start our investigation early in the morning, since filming isn't scheduled to start until the afternoon. Reviewing the files immediately seemed more productive than keeping the truck open for half a day. We forgo morning pleasantries with the crew members and head straight to the production trailer.

Tapping on the doorframe, I say, "Knock, knock," as we enter Bobbi's office. She's at her desk, hunched over a pile of papers, looking exhausted.

"I'll be there in a second," she says without raising her head.

Her plate is likely fuller than ever without Sloane and Imogen. Sloane was a big part of the show. She offered her support to Imogen, arranged for contestant interviews, and addressed any concerns the contestants had. Sloane was also always available for whatever Bobbi needed. I'm not sure how much help she'll get from Sergio. Despite being Imogen's assistant, Sergio was almost never present. Now he's taking over as head producer. That strikes me as a bit too coincidental, if you ask me. Someone mysteriously attacked two of his superiors, and he steps in heroically to help with the show.

Something isn't adding up!

Bobbi's surprise is obvious as soon as she notices us. "Beth, Rylie." She glances at her watch. "You're here earlier than expected. We still have a few hours before filming begins."

Slipping further into her office, I close the door behind us. "We figured this would be the perfect time to go through the *samples* we discussed."

"Of course." She stands up from her desk but pauses. "Before you review the *samples*, let me get you the *directions* for the *samples*." Bobbi reaches into her drawer and produces a sealed manila envelope.

Opening the envelope, I confirm the *directions* are indeed papers from an executive in the legal department confirming our team as the champions of this season's *The Food Truck Showdown*.

"Thank you," I say, closing the tab and slipping it into my purse.

Bobbi nods and takes us to a cubicle outside her office where a laptop is sitting. I observe her typing the password and subtly arch my neck for a better view, committing the sequence to memory, just in case. With a single click, Bobbi brings up segments from the show.

"Take your time, but I have a meeting in under an hour," she tells us.

"Thanks, Bobbi. If it's easier, we can take the *samples* with us," I offer.

"Unfortunately, the *samples* are property of the network. They must remain here. I hope you find the *samples* helpful. I'll come back before heading to my next meeting." Bobbi returns to her office, leaving us alone in the cubicle.

I wait until the click of her heels fades and she's safely out of earshot before I turn to Rylie. "I didn't realize how relieved I'd be not to be back in the warehouse." My gaze fixes on the desk and laptop in front of us. "Do you think this was Sloane's workstation?"

"So what if it was? It's not like she would know, anyway."

"True, but the idea of using something belonging to a dead person feels a little morbid." Grabbing a spare chair, I drag it over.

"Can you stop saying the word sample, please? Besides, it's not like she died here." Rylie reaches over and knocks twice on the desk to emphasize her point.

"Why can't I say the word *sample*?"

"Because you're saying it weird. *Sample.*"

"I'm not saying it like that. I'm saying sample."

"Well, now you are," she says. "A moment ago, you weren't. Speaking of *samples.*" Now she's the weird one saying it. "Aren't you a little concerned about the *directions* she gave us?"

"Just to be clear"—I look around the area—"when you say *directions*, you mean—"

"Yes." She stares at me like I'm a dummy. "Are you concerned about the potential consequences if her *directions* were to end up in the wrong hands?"

"I'm relieved to have a physical copy of the agreed-upon *directions* between her and me. Didn't you listen to the latest episode of *Murder and Mayhem*?"

"I was going to later when I went for a jog," Rylie says.

"Health freak," I mutter. "The latest episode discusses the importance of a proper paper trail. It's what saved a stepfather who was accused of, well, I don't want to spoil it. My point is, a clear document signed and dated by those concerned will help prevent ambiguity as to the terms agreed on, later down the line. And that is what we have." I pat my purse. "These *directions* are physical evidence of manipulation."

"Hey!" a voice shouts, startling us. "You two can't be here." An assistant to the production team is walking toward us with an arm full of papers.

"Oh," I squeak and look at Rylie, wondering how much he heard. "Are you Bert?" I ask, wondering if I've finally found the elusive mystery man.

"Who?" The guy looks more annoyed the closer he gets.

"Ignore her," Rylie answers, saving me from having to fib. "Bobbi said we could use this desk while we worked on something. Our food truck isn't exactly comfortable, and we have spotty Wi-Fi—"

"You think I care?" He drops his papers on the desk. "This is my station."

Rylie immediately doubles over, grabbing her stomach. "Beth, do you have any Midol? These cramps are getting intense."

"You know what?" The guy puts his hands up. "You can take Sloane's desk or Imogen's desk over there." He gestures toward the rear of the trailer, where there's a low partition. "The bathrooms are right outside if you need them."

"Thanks." She snatches the laptop, and we rush to the new area.

"Quick thinking," I whisper, pulling over an extra chair for Rylie.

"Cramps always work on guys," she whispers back.

With the volume as low as possible, I start with the video diaries first.

"Why are we starting with these?" Rylie asks. "I thought we wanted to see if the CCTV footage captured someone sneaking in or out of trucks."

"We'll get to those, but since we have access to everything, we should start with these. Just like Inga Nevarez says, 'Don't overlook any stone, no matter how unassuming it appears.' Who knows what we might learn from the diaries? The biggest rewards can come from the smallest clues."

Dane and Ness ramble through a dull segment. I can't help but yawn. The Jaxsons are a friendly couple, but the more I get to know them, especially Ness, the more I realize they're pretty boring. Loretta says as much in the following video diary. Her exact words are "Ness has as much personality as a wet mop."

The longer we watch, the more apparent it becomes that most contestants have nothing left to say. We're being pushed to our culinary limits, but recapping the same things each week is getting repetitive.

"Let's be honest," I say to Rylie in a low voice after we're finished watching the confessionals. "*The Food Truck Showdown* is in a rut."

We hear the trailer door open and close. Getting up, I peer over the partition. "He's gone," I say, keeping my voice low.

"*Oh meu Deus,* that was painful to watch," Rylie complains as she leans back in her chair. "I'm thinking that's why the sabotage is happening. At least it brings some excitement to the show. That's more than can be said for Dane and Ness."

"I think you're right," I say, testing a theory.

"Of course I'm right. You can find their wedding picture in the dictionary under 'boring.'"

"Not that," I say. "Okay, that is a perfect way to summarize the Jaxsons," I acknowledge, "but there are two things I noticed."

"I'm all ears," says Rylie, settling into her seat and getting comfortable.

"No matter the host, each season has something dramatic happening. A truck breaks down, or whatever. According to Seth, ratings increase with drama, resulting in higher profits for the network."

Rylie looks around and whispers, "Do you believe that someone came here with the goal of killing two innocent people solely to increase the ratings?"

"I doubt that. At least I hope that's not the case. But I suspect someone of deliberately sabotaging things to make the show more interesting. I mean, don't you remember when Ben and Bryan got into a fight over the missing flour? Ben was calm through the entire competition until that happened." Rylie taps a finger to her lips. "The production crew seems to be the only option," she says with conviction. "They can move about with ease. No one questions when they're in and out of trucks."

"Agreed. We do not know what the endgame is for people like Sergio or others who work here. Maybe they'd get a bonus, or a promotion—"

"Like Sergio just coincidently got?" Rylie points out.

"Exactly! However, Willa has filmed nothing except for videos that showcase her truck flawlessly."

"The only truck that remains safe from sabotage is hers," Rylie adds.

"I've always suspected Willa of something," I admit as I continue to bring up new files to watch. "Willa was a topic of conversation between Detective Kane and me at the Tipsy Cow."

"During your date?"

"It definitely wasn't a date, not even close! Detective Hamstead was with us and devoured all my fries. My shirt got soaked when I got a beer spilled on me."

"Sounds like a typical date for you," she mumbles.

"Why are you and Seth so rude? Besides, he doesn't have feelings for me in that way." I stop scrolling and my eyes shift to hers. "Right?"

"I don't know." She shrugs. "I've noticed his lingering glances when you're not paying attention. Or his dimple that only makes an appearance for you."

He steals glances at me when I'm not looking?

"On the other hand, his smile could be because he's planning to arrest you."

"Thanks." I narrow my eyes at her. "Anyway, I realized Willa likely isn't the saboteur. She enjoys secretly plotting and scheming, while keeping a low profile. But my theory is she knows something. Perhaps knowledge of who *is* behind things."

"Those are some pretty bold accusations," Rylie points out.

"Bold accusations for a bold woman."

We continue to watch various footage, both edited and unedited. The clips do not provide any clues about which person from the motley group of truck owners might be connected to the murders or the sabotage.

"Well, that was a bust. It's not like I expected to see a taped confession," I say as we skim through more segments, "although it would've been nice. I was really hoping for a clue or some kind of direction to guide us in our search. This is tedious work. No wonder Detective Kane is always cranky."

"Is that everything?" Rylie asks.

"The show's footage, yes. It's time to examine the CCTV recordings." I lean back in my chair. "What are you doing?" I ask, watching Rylie scour the inside of the desk.

"Chocolate." She searches a side drawer. "Playing detective makes me hungry."

"You're too much."

"What?" She side-eyes me. "If this is Sloane's or Imogen's desk, it's not like they're gonna miss it."

"It's the principle," I whisper loudly to her.

"What the?" She stops. "Beth?" She withdraws her hand from the back of the drawer, clutching two tightly crumpled notes.

We make eye contact briefly before I gesture for her to open them. As she scans the space, she smooths out both papers, and our eyes fall to the pages.

Back off unless you want to end up like your steamed buns.

Piss off!

"Whoa!" she says. "That's the note Dane and Ness received."

"And that's Benji's note," I whisper. Hastily getting to my feet, I survey the room, before sitting back down. "That's the note from the grocery store he was going to give to the Katapangs. This is the note that set everything in motion."

"Didn't Imogen promise Ness she would investigate the matter?"

"Sloane promised me the same thing," I say. "She was going to investigate the note and see if it was a threat to the show."

"But if Sloane said she would look into things, why is it crumpled in the back of the drawer?"

"Maybe that's the reason she got killed?" I gesture toward the paper. "She followed through on her word, but perhaps she dug too deep?"

"Or perhaps she and Imogen had no intention of looking into things." Pinching her chin, Rylie carefully examines the notes. "Someone hid these. That much is clear."

"What if it was Sloane who hid them?" I sit back down and scoot closer to the desk. "Maybe Imogen gave Sloane the note she received from Ness and asked her to take care of this since she was busy. Only Sloane never planned to do anything about the threats." On the screen, I exit out of my current window and start exploring the Documents folder. If those notes were hidden, what other secrets are being kept?

"What are you doing?"

"What if there's something else hidden? We're already logged into the system. Let's see if we can uncover anything here. There's no harm in checking, right?" I say, speed scanning folder after folder. After clicking around, I finally stop. "It doesn't look like there's anything."

"Did you think there was a folder marked 'Secrets'? Move." Rylie nudges me with her shoulder, and we switch seats.

I watch as she opens the file explorer from the taskbar. "What are you doing?"

"If there are any hidden files on this laptop, I'll find them." Opening the search options, Rylie changes a few settings that I don't understand. A plethora of folders materialize after executing the search command.

"Whoa! How did you do that?" I ask as my gaze zeroes in on the screen.

"Remember"—she clicks on a folder labeled "Miscellaneous"—"I'm the one who does all the software updates for your phone and the person who revamped the truck's website."

"Oh, yeah," I say, taking my phone out of my pocket. "My speaker is making a static noise. Can you look at it?"

She pushes my hand away. "Later." Clicking on the Miscellaneous folder, Rylie finds several other folders hidden inside, dated and time-stamped.

"Where did those come from?"

"When you want to hide something on a computer, if you add a period in front of the name, the file managers and other utilities will hide it from view by default."

"You make it sound so simple." I stare in awe at the screen. "These were here all along?" I ask, watching her click on the files.

"Yep. It's just a normal file or folder with a hidden option setting. It's far from foolproof, but it's a great way to hide something on a shared computer."

"What do you think is in those folders?"

"There's only one way to find out." Opening the zipped file, a folder labeled "SCRUB" appears. Rylie moves closer to me. "Why does that date look familiar?"

"Bring up the Kluckin' Clues list on your phone," I instruct her, suspecting what it might be. Rylie obeys, and we examine the screen, with our heads close together. "That's the date when Dane and Ness had their pots tampered with."

Rylie lets out a low whistle. "And look at the next set of zipped folders." She holds up her phone to the screen. "All the dates on our list of suspicious activity match the time stamps on the files. Do you know what this means?"

Glancing around the room, I lower my voice even more. "It's obvious someone doesn't want these files viewed. They're buried in a hidden subfolder."

"Whose laptop is this?" Rylie asks, picking up the laptop to examine it. "Hey, look here." She taps on the lid. "Look familiar?"

"That sticker." There's a worn red sticker with the Cooking Channel's network logo on it. It's the same sticker that was on the one we'd used before the lights went out. "Do you think it's the missing laptop?"

"What are the odds?"

"Could've belonged to anyone for all we know," I comment. "Maybe it's Imogen's or Sloane's. Could either of them have shut off the power and swiped the laptop?"

"Not Imogen." Rylie shakes her head. "Remember, Héctor told us she wasn't here that day. The only person who knew what we did that day was Sergio. He could have orchestrated things. He's also the one who gave us the laptop to use."

"This laptop here looks an awful lot like the one he gave us." We share a knowing look. Reaching over, I attempt to access the files by entering the password I watched Bobbi use to unlock the laptop. "They're locked."

"They're passcode protected. Someone—"

"Sergio?"

"—wants to ensure the safety of whatever is in there. But getting in won't be a problem," says Rylie casually. As she searches in her purse, she drops the notes inside.

"How can you find hidden files *and* unlock zipped folders but you can't cook?" I ask my partner in crime with skepticism.

"Hacking is a life skill," Rylie declares.

"And cooking isn't?"

"Here it is!" She hands me a flash drive. "You can learn anything from YouTube."

"Why did you learn to hack files? And explain why you carry a flash drive on you?"

"One. You never know when you might need one of these. This bad boy already has a preinstalled program for downloading encrypted files." She wiggles the flash drive. "Two. I didn't trust my cousin Pedro when he said he'd deleted embarrassing pictures of me. So, I went through his laptop."

"Did he?"

"Nope, he's a bald-faced liar. So, I installed software that oinks like a pig every time he tries to access a 'questionable' site." Rylie smiles, quite proud of herself. "My *Tia* Beatriz was convinced there was a wild boar living in their house."

My head falls back as I cackle, thinking about what she did to her cousin.

Rylie shushes me. "Unlocking the files is possible, just not here. But if we copy the folders to this"—she waves the flash drive again—"decrypting encrypted files is an easy process. Anyone can do it on a Windows computer. But we have to hurry. Bobbi will be back any minute to check on us."

Glancing at the time on my phone, I know she's right. Plus, we can't take any chances of someone getting curious about what we're doing. Right as she's about to insert the flash drive into the USB port, I hear a door shut.

"It's Bobbi," I whisper. The sound of her heels clicking across the floor tell me I'm right.

Rylie closes the folders and window while I quickly pocket the flash drive. Pretending that it's time to go, I push myself away from the desk and walk toward Bobbi.

"All done here, ladies?" Bobbi asks, smiling at us. "Wait." She looks around. "Did you move desks?"

"Yes," Rylie says. "Someone came in and said we were at his workstation and asked us to move."

"I see." She nods. "Did you find any of the *samples* to be useful?"

"A few of them." I smile and leave it at that.

"Well, listen." Bobbi's tone is all business. "I'm sorry to kick you out, but I have an important meeting I can't miss."

"Of course." Nodding, I grab my purse.

With a gesture toward the door, Bobbi escorts us out of the trailer. "Thanks again for reviewing the *samples* for me. I'm certain you'll persist in searching until you find the loose thread. See you back in a couple of hours."

We exit the trailer and head straight to where Rylie parked her jeep.

"What now?" she asks once we're tucked inside with the doors locked. "Do we go back and try again? And what about the notes?"

"Not we. Me." I turn and look at her. "You're gonna tell me how to find those folders, and I'll sneak back into the trailer to download them. As for the notes, keep them safe for now. We'll make sure Detective Kane gets them later."

"You are not going back in there alone," Rylie tells me. "I'm going with you."

"You can't. I need someone I trust to watch out and notify me if anyone shows up. That someone is you."

"And let you have all the fun? No way. I'm doing it."

"With your long, dark, wavy hair and tall build, you'll stick out like a sore thumb the moment you get near the trailer. The ideal candidate would be someone small and inconspicuous. Easily overlooked, someone who blends in among the towering giants. That someone is me."

"Do you even know how to download the files?"

"Nope! It's time to dust off your tutoring skills from high school. You're about to give me a crash course in hacking."

Chapter Twenty

"For today's challenge, everyone will receive a mystery ingredient to be incorporated into your dishes," Bobbi explains as the group of food truckers listen half-heartedly. "Your task is to sell the plates for ten dollars each."

It surprised me that nobody, not even Marco, withdrew from the contest. Out of everyone, he's been the most uneasy and worried about safety. The $100,000 price tag and supposed added security was probably an excellent motivator to continue. There's a sense of gloom overshadowing us, despite our agreement to stay. No amount of security measures or prizes will erase the fact that two murders happened on this lot.

Elbowing Rylie, I whisper, "What do you think they're talking about?" I tilt my head toward Willa and Sergio, who are off to the side talking. If only I were closer to hear their conversation.

"No clue," Rylie whispers.

"Don't forget, I'm counting on you to create a diversion so I can sneak back into the trailer and steal the files."

Rylie gives me a mock salute as Bobbi raises her voice, looking at Willa. "Can all contestants please return to the main area?" *Busted*. "Once everyone is present, we can distribute the mystery ingredients."

Willa receives a tight-lipped smile from Bobbi as she returns to the group.

Bobbi takes a moment to gather herself before signaling that she's ready for the mystery ingredients.

"It's him!" I point an accusatory finger at the stage. Emerging with several boxes, the young man who'd thought Seth and I were a couple appears.

"Should we tell him we're thinking of trying for twins?" Seth playfully nudges my shoulder and raises an eyebrow.

"You are *so not* funny."

"I'm a little funny."

I snort. "Yeah, funny-looking." A camera trails the junior assistant as he hands out boxes to each team while another camera moves around the area, capturing everyone's reactions.

"Well, isn't that different?" Loretta wonders while showing off a chayote squash to the camera. "I reckon it's some kind of veggie?"

"It's a squash, Loretta," Ella Mae snaps.

Some of the other drivers whisper to their partners about what they got, trying to keep their mystery ingredient a secret. The young man hesitates, unsure which of us he should approach. I must look like a rabid animal to him, because he hands the box to Seth and scurries away.

Seth opens the lid and removes the mystery ingredient. He scrutinizes the brown orb as if it were an alien artifact. "I can't believe how weird this potato looks."

"That's a jicama, not a potato," Rylie says, as if that explains everything.

"A hick a who?" His brows knit together in confusion.

"HEE-kah-mah," Rylie enunciates. "It's a bean."

"A bean?!" Seth sputters as a camera zeroes in on the vegetable. "There's no way this is a bean." He gestures with our mystery ingredient.

"It probably isn't the first thing you would think of because it looks like a root vegetable, but it's a member of the Fabaceae family. The same group that counts peas as the primary member," Rylie explains. "Jicama doesn't look, feel, or act like a pea or bean, though there may be the tiniest bit of the flavor ensconced in the crunchy white flesh." Her thumb and index finger rub together while she describes the vegetable.

The two of us gape at her. "How do you know this?" we ask in twin unison.

"*Tia* Beatriz and I are fans of Maria Flores, the host of *A Flavor Fiesta*. Jicama is common in Mexican dishes. And before you say it"—she holds up her hand to keep Seth from interrupting her—"just because I can't cook doesn't mean I don't know what it is or what to do with it. I already have an idea."

"What's your—"

The sound of a horrifying shriek makes me turn my attention from the brown vegetable to Bria Garza, who is standing a few feet away. With a wide-eyed expression, she covers her mouth in shock and disgust.

Leaning into Rylie, I murmur, "Is this the distraction you planned?"

"I have nothing to do with whatever is happening over there."

Parting the crowd of drivers like the Red Sea, Bobbi rushes over. "What is it? What is—oh my god!" Bobbi's mouth falls open as she looks inside Willa's box.

"It's a dead rat!" screams the man who just handed them the box.

"Actually," Willa says as she inspects the creature, "I believe it might be a dwarf hamster. And what's this?" She removes a white piece of paper from under the rodent. "'Drop dead,'" she reads, then waves the note in the air.

Gasps reverberate through the crowd as people exchange incredulous looks, and I step closer to investigate. Now that I'm close to Willa, I squint and attempt to read her note. It looks the same as the others, but it doesn't contain a food or cooking reference.

The baby-faced intern recoils over the dead rodent. Bria hurries past, fleeing the area with her hands still clutching her mouth. Bobbi takes the box from Willa and forcefully hands it over to the hesitant intern.

"There appears to be an issue with one of the mystery ingredients." Bobbi clears her throat. "We'll wait until it's resolved, then we can all get started with the challenge."

After a few moments, the same intern returns with a fresh box, holding it away from his body like it contains the plague. He hands it to Willa and steps back. After opening the lid, she takes out a green pepper and shows it to a camera.

"There's no way she won't win now. They just gave a taco truck a jalapeño as their mystery ingredient!" Ness shouts, a camera capturing her frustration.

"I thought you said we were safe to continue?" Marco surveys the contestants with concern. "She told us it was safe"—he points at Bobbi—"but Willa just got a note telling her to drop dead!"

"You are safe," she assures him. "I will personally investigate this matter and find out what happened."

Once Bobbi concludes her speech, Sergio guides us to the greenroom, where we express our thoughts about the challenge before we prepare our trucks. Loretta and Marco both discuss how some contestants have an unfair advantage in today's competition, and I completely agree. Jalapeños and tacos aren't exactly a challenge.

I rush through our interview, hoping to finish everything. The faster we're done, the faster I can get to those hidden zipped folders. As we pass the production staff trailer, Rylie and Seth stride ahead to our truck while I lag a little behind. Waiting is hard, but I have no choice. Our truck remaining after everyone departs could arouse suspicion.

"Cabbage and jicama slaw is the way to go," Rylie declares when I enter the truck.

"What's in it, and what dish would we pair it with?" Seth asks as Rylie puts the truck in drive and we head toward the farmers market for today's challenge.

I wonder what the other vendors at the market think about the show taking over the space while local businesses try to sell their products. I assume the filming will bring them extra business. Increased foot traffic may make our takeover more tolerable for everyone.

"Crunchy cabbage, carrots, and jicama coated in a creamy lime dressing," Rylie explains. "I suggest using the slaw on the Juan and Only Sliders."

"And you can make this?" I ask, trying to keep the skepticism out of my voice.

Rylie narrows her eyes at us. "I've seen my *Tia* Beatriz make it at least a hundred times. I think I can manage."

"You're in charge of this challenge then," I say as Rylie follows the other food trucks to the farmers market. Besides, our team is guaranteed the grand prize. If she messes things up, what's the worst that can happen?

A long-standing tradition in Clementine is the farmers market. Every week, Clementine High, the only high school in town, hosts a family-friendly event in their parking lot. With everything that's been going on during filming for *The Food Truck Showdown*, I just hope today stays family friendly. Following a brief visit to the store to pick up some essential items, Rylie successfully snags one of the last parking spaces in the packed lot. The other vendors here are already in full swing, so we don't waste any time getting down to business.

Looking through the serving window, I search for any stray cameras. "Let's avoid recording this conversation." Reaching over, I turn off the dashcam. Since the flour incident with the cameraman, Alex, the producers have given us the green light to use the dashcam for our footage. It's not possible for four people and camera equipment to move around safely in the cramped truck.

"What's on your mind?" Rylie pulls out the grater stored under the prep counter.

"What do you think about Willa's ingredient?" I ask, watching her shred the jicama.

"Which one? The dead rat or the jalapeño?" Seth snorts as he drops a basket of wings into the fryer.

"Dwarf hamster," I correct him. "Willa's reaction seemed a little too composed, if you ask me."

"How did she know it was a dwarf hamster and not something else?" Squeezing a couple of limes, Rylie adds the juice to her mixing bowl. "That was a very specific piece of information to share with everyone."

"That's a good point!" Wearing nitrile gloves, I mix a generous amount of paprika and garlic salt into the ground meat before shaping the patties for our Juan and Only Sliders. "Not sure if you saw it, but her note wasn't the same as the others. There was no food or cooking pun."

"Maybe the saboteur ran out of threatening puns," Rylie says while adding salt to the bowl.

"Isn't it ironic?" Seth wonders out loud.

"What?" I ask as I shape the patties and slap them on the flat-top grill. The sound of beef sizzling fills the truck.

"Bobbi fixed the competition so we would win. But it looks like someone else is trying to fix things. How else would you explain Nacho Momma's Tacos getting such an easy ingredient?"

I cook the slider patties, which are sizzling to perfection. "Willa receives a threatening note after being sabotaged in the most absurd manner." Shaking my head, I transfer the slider patties to their waiting baskets. "Something isn't adding up. It felt like someone was going to extreme lengths to make a point."

"You think Willa did this to herself?" Rylie finishes mixing her jicama concoction. "Why would she? She's not the type to care what people think"

Twisting around in the tight space, I look at her. "True, she doesn't care about people's opinions, only her business. What if she staged the sabotage to make herself look like a victim and grab attention?"

"You're saying it was a marketing stunt?" Rylie raises a skeptical eyebrow.

"Maybe." I shrug, flipping a slider onto a bun. "Think about it—a wave of new customers showing up, curious about the drama. If her note makes the final cut for the show, the buzz could make her sales skyrocket. What better way to grab attention?" I pause, sliding the basket onto the warming station. "I bet she did this to herself, and I'm going to prove it."

"How?" Seth asks, dumping a basket of wings from the fryer into a bowl of spices. "She won't talk to you about anything."

"I'll find a way," I say, already brainstorming.

"The slaw is done!" Rylie puts her bowl into the mini fridge. "Keep it in there until it's time to use it. The longer it sits, the more time the flavors have to marry."

"So the flavors can marry? Who are you, Julia Child?" I joke, "Where is my cooking-impaired assistant?"

"She's right here and has spent her entire life watching the women in her family cook."

"And yet, you didn't learn how to cook anything?" I ask.

"You're welcome for coming up with an idea to save us during this challenge," she says. "Or would you have preferred we leave it to Seth, who thought it was a potato?"

"We didn't need saving," my brother points out.

Rylie glares at Seth with fiery chocolate-brown eyes before slipping into her chicken costume.

"Thank you, Rylie." I push open our serving window. The aroma of freshly cooked food mixed with the earthy scent of ripe fruits and vegetables creates an inviting atmosphere for both locals and tourists alike. With an air horn in hand, Sergio makes his way toward the center of the food truck area. "It's showtime," I announce as he blares the horn.

"The jicama slaw is a hit!" Rylie yells, her wings fluttering in excitement as she rushes up to the serving window with an empty tray.

"Your idea was genius!" I tell her while grabbing the empty sample tray. "You could be a cook. Who knows!"

"Let's not get our hopes up." Rylie takes another tray of samples before continuing her rounds.

We're only halfway through the two-hour competition and we're close to selling out. Even though our team is slated to win, I want us to earn it through our own efforts as much as possible.

Peering out of the serving window, I glimpse two familiar figures maneuvering through the crowd. I'm not sure why Detective Kane and Detective Hamstead are here, but I can't help noticing how Detective Kane is stylishly dressed in a navy-blue button-down shirt, with the sleeves rolled up, and pressed khakis. A few unruly strands are falling over his forehead, and his widow's peak is highlighted by his otherwise slicked back hair. He may have annoying tendencies, but there's no denying he's a good-looking man in blue.

As the crowd pushes around them, I see they're heading straight for my truck. Despite his bulky frame, Detective Hamstead navigates the crowded area with surprising agility. Holding a crumpled fedora, he leads the two of them in my direction. I've always felt his deep-set, thoughtful brown eyes provide a contrast to his salt-and-pepper hair and weathered face. A grin spreads across the detective's face as he and I make eye contact.

"It's the chicken girl!" he says while approaching the serving window.

"Here I am," I say, looking from him to Detective Kane, who is the epitome of nonchalance as he approaches with his hands in his pockets.

Sporting a smile, his right dimple in full view, Detective Kane asks, "What's up?"

"Oh, nothing much." I try to mirror his relaxed demeanor. "Just trying to win a challenge. How about trying a Juan and Only Slider with zesty jicama slaw on top?"

"Jicama slaw?" he asks.

"Jicama was our mystery ingredient."

"Sure," he says with interest. "I'm game to try something different."

"I'll take a basket as well," Detective Hamstead says. "Don't want my buddy eating alone." He laughs, giving his partner a shove.

Snatching the baskets of truffle fries and sliders that Seth had just prepared, I set them on the counter. "I'm afraid you'll have to pay today." I extend a hand to Detective Kane. "That'll be twenty dollars."

"You got this, right, Officer Pretty Boy?" Detective Hamstead takes a basket from off the serving counter.

The use of his nickname earns me a smirk. "What? No discounts for law enforcement?" he asks.

"Nope," I say while making a grabbing motion with my fingers. "Today is a competition, so every dime counts."

"It's not easy being a cop," he says, teasingly holding a twenty-dollar bill just beyond my grasp.

Balancing on my toes, I stretch through the window and snatch the bill from his hand. "Save it for your tiny violin," I say, handing him his order.

After biting into the slider, his blond eyebrows rise. "This is tasty," he remarks, taking another bite.

"Indeed," his partner agrees, devouring his second slider in one mouthful.

"Is this your creation?" Detective Kane asks.

"Thank you for the feedback, but my assistant, Rylie, made the slaw."

As he eats the second slider, he speaks with his mouth full. "Delicious!"

Pointing toward the camera focused on Bobbi, I suggest, "You should tell her that. She enjoys hearing customers' thoughts on the food sampled during the competition."

"Will do," he agrees and glances back to where Bobbi is interviewing someone else on camera.

He shifts his attention back to me and asks, "What's the current situation on set?"

"What do you mean?" I signal for him and Detective Hamstead to step aside as I assist the next customer.

After the customer leaves, Detective Kane inspects the parking lot for cameras, but there are none trained on us. "The owners of a barbecue truck mentioned that a contestant had a dead rat as their mystery ingredient and that she also received a threatening note," Detective Kane says.

"I wanted to talk to you about that. Step to the back of the truck." I nod and switch spots with Seth so I can have a chat with them. Exiting the truck, I lead the detectives to a tree just a few feet away and stand under the shade. "Willa Garza received a dead rat, or dwarf hamster, as she called it. But I think she did it to herself."

"And why is that?" Detective Hamstead asks. "We already talked about her, and you recognized that it would be too obvious for her to sabotage herself."

"We did," I admit. "And I agree, I don't think she's the one to blame for everything that's happening on set."

"Then what's your point?"

"Rodents don't bother me at all. But discovering one as my mystery ingredient would have freaked me out. Willa appeared unnaturally calm."

"Perhaps rodents don't bother her either," Detective Hamstead suggests.

"And how did she know it was a dwarf hamster? Her note looked like the others, but why didn't it reference food or cooking?" Crossing my arms, I shake my head. "I don't buy it for a minute. I think she was trying to make it look like she's finally being targeted, that what's been happening to the rest of us is now happening to her. Or maybe she thought a camera filming her being 'sabotaged' would make viewers sympathize with her and drum up new customers. I don't know, but I don't buy what she's selling!"

The detectives exchange a glance, and I wonder if this is what Seth and I look like when our twin telepathy kicks in.

"That seems suspicious," Detective Kane says. "Thank you for sharing this with us."

Remaining under the shade of the oak tree, I watch the two men make their way toward Bobbi, who's conducting customer interviews outside Chowder Bowl on the Roll.

As the challenge concludes with the sound of the air horn, I wait a little longer before going back inside the truck. I watch as Detective Kane speaks animatedly with Bobbi. Judging by his expression, it seems he's providing us with a fantastic evaluation, and I'm crossing my fingers that it makes it to the final recording.

After we return to the lot and I put the truck in park, Rylie whispers, "All right, *irmã*. Get ready. Things are about to happen." Stepping out of the truck, still in her chicken costume, she struts with confidence, shaking her tail feathers.

"What's going on?" Seth asks.

"Why are you asking me?" I say and chase after her.

Once we're in the middle of the lot, Rylie declares, "We're not here to pluck around!" She relentlessly pecks at the other contestants who are trying to dodge her. With a cluck, she struts back and forth, jutting her neck like a rooster in heat. She comes at me, flapping her arms and squawking, and pecks me in the face.

"Rylie!" Cupping my nose, I let out a shriek. I hope her plan doesn't involve giving me a bloody nose, although I'm uncertain.

Wasting no time, I rush off toward the bathrooms next to the production trailer to check. Luckily, my nose isn't that bad. It takes only a minute to stop the minor bleeding. With the crew bustling around the lot to prepare for post-competition filming, I take advantage of the commotion and slip into the trailer. The area appears empty as I look around, but momma didn't raise no dummy.

"Hello?" I call out to confirm there's no one else around. I can easily explain my reason for being here: *I need a fresh shirt because there's blood on this one.* When I get no response, I head farther into the trailer, looking for the laptop I previously used.

Each desk in the trailer has a laptop on it. The one Bobbi gave us had a red sticker with the Cooking Channel's network logo on it. The same one Sergio gave us.

"Bingo!" I give a little victory fist pump when I find it on a desk in the middle of the room. It's not on the same desk as before, but that's not important. Crouching down, I open the laptop and press a key to see if the laptop is on. It is, but it's password protected.

As kids, Seth would make fun of me for reciting things repeatedly until I memorized them. Thank goodness I did, because I know how to access the computer. As soon as I type the sequence FTSD90210*, I gain access to the desktop. But I feel too exposed here in the trailer, so I grab the laptop and find a more secluded spot behind a partition. I pull out the chair, sit down, place the computer on my lap, and hunch over the keyboard as low as possible. Inserting the flash drive into the USB port, I follow Rylie's directions, locate the zipped folders, and begin copying them.

Just in case someone passes by, I minimize the window, set the laptop on a desk, and hide the flash drive with papers. Rylie estimated that copying everything would take about four minutes, so I need to find a place to disappear. Looking around, I realize being vertically challenged is finally benefiting me. Curling into a tight ball, I should be completely unnoticed so long as no one takes a seat at this desk.

No sooner do I hide than the trailer door opens and closes. My heart races as heavy footsteps draw near. I feel like I'm on the verge of being discovered as my throat moves up and down. The footsteps stop just outside the cubicle. I'm jolted by the sound of a drawer opening and closing, but I remain silent.

As the footsteps move away from me, I hear the trailer door creak open and close. A sigh of relief escapes me now that I'm alone again. I peek from under the desk, praying I'm not spotted by someone I didn't hear. Once I realize the coast is clear, I unfurl and maximize the window to see the progress of the file copying. I need to finish two more zipped folders before I can leave. Minimizing the window again, I retreat into the cubbyhole under the desk. As I try to get comfortable, my phone vibrates.

Rylie: Hurry! You have only five minutes before someone comes looking for you.

Me: I'm going as fast as I can. Start pecking people or fake laying an egg if needed.

Three dots appear, vanish, then materialize once more. I don't have time to worry about messaging, so I slip my phone back into my pocket, hoping that the files are almost complete. After a full minute of waiting, I check the computer again and see that the last set of files is almost done. Just as the progress bar shows a successful transfer, the trailer door opens again.

"I'll be right back. Just need to print something."

Sergio!

What is he doing here?

Closing the window, I snatch the flash drive and slide back under the desk. My heart races as the cold metal presses against my side.

The trailer door creaks open again before slamming shut. "Take your time. I'm in no rush to get back out there."

Is that Bert?

Oh god! Panic floods my veins. *What is Bert doing here?*

Wait!

I know that voice from somewhere.

"Let somebody else film the mascot squawking and flapping around. I've captured more than my fair share of her."

Alex the cameraman!

Since he stopped filming inside our truck, I haven't seen him. *Why is he here too?*

"Gotta admit . . ."

I squeeze my eyes shut as I hear Sergio walking closer to where I'm hiding.

"It's a good gimmick. The ratings are showing fans love them. After each episode, they're trending on X, #KluckinGood this, #KluckinGood that."

Stashing the flash drive in my cleavage, I squeeze my eyes tighter. His voice sends shivers down my spine.

"Yeah, that's great for them," Alex says. "But listening to her flap around and cluck constantly is getting annoying. Good thing she's easy on the eyes."

How dare he! Rylie is more than just easy on the eyes. She's intelligent and compassionate, among other qualities that escape me right now. She's more than just some object of attraction.

Straining to keep my breathing steady, I resist the urge to peek from my hiding place.

"You should ask her out, man," Sergio says. The two sets of feet are clomping closer to where I'm hiding.

Alex chuckles. "Already tried, buddy. She shut me down hard, said she's involved with someone else."

Did he just say Rylie is seeing someone?

The small space reverberates with Sergio's laughter. "So that's why you find her annoying. Did her rejection hurt your ego?"

My eyes widen in the darkness under the desk, and I tune out Sergio and Alex's converstation. *Rylie's in a relationship?* No. That can't be right. She was probably just trying to fend off his unwanted advances. She would've told me if she was seeing someone.

"Where's my laptop?" Like a knife, Sergio's voice cuts through the tense air with sharpness. "I swear, if someone messed with my stuff again—"

"Relax, Sergio. It's just a laptop," Alex, says. "You can use any computer to print the roster. Don't let it ruin your day."

"That's not the point." His voice moves around the trailer. "Someone is always messing with my things. Within the past week, my laptop and car keys were moved twice."

My mind races with panic. Sergio needs to print something, and he wants his laptop. The one sitting on top of the desk I'm hiding under. Is he going to search for it? If he does, he'll discover me instantly.

As quietly as I can, I check my phone and notice Rylie texted me three minutes ago. Seth also sent a message with a bunch of question marks. I need to get out of here, but I'm trapped until they leave.

The shrill sound of a phone ringing startles me, causing me to drop mine. Frantically, I try to grab my phone as it tumbles and manage to catch it.

"Hello?" Sergio's harsh voice rattles my already frayed nerves. "All right, I'll be right there." Shuffling fills the room, footsteps drawing closer to where I am. "That was Bert."

Bert just called him?

"I don't have time to keep looking." His voice sounds incredibly close to the other side of the partition.

Squeezing my eyes shut again, I try to steady my breathing while the sound of clicking on the keyboard fills my ears. How would I explain this if they found me?

Cursing to myself, I try to think of a way to get out of this situation. The typing comes to a halt, but I'm too afraid to move or make a sound and risk being caught.

Squinting open one eye, positioned halfway between me and the hallway, I can just make out two sets of shoes. They don't move. Squeezing my eyes shut tighter, I wait, convinced I've been spotted.

The sound of the printer spewing out pages stops me from leaving my hiding spot.

"Grab those, will you?" Sergio asks. The sound of Alex snatching the papers echoes in my ears. "Let's go. I'm ready to end this show and move on."

As their voices fade, I hear the trailer's front door creak open, then slam shut.

Quickly, I scurry out from under the desk, check the computer, confirming everything is closed, and exit the trailer from the back. I'm barely around the side of the trailer when Sergio slams into me.

"Where were you? We've been looking everywhere for you."

No you haven't.

Without waiting for a response, he guides me toward the section where Bobbi is waiting to speak to the participants. Everyone, including Bobbi, watches me as I approach, likely wondering where I've been. Standing beside Rylie, I give a slight nod to signal mission accomplished.

Chapter Twenty-One

Holding her microphone, Bobbi takes up the small stage with her usual liveliness. Sporting a sleek ponytail, she flashes a smile at the crowd.

"Ladies and gentlemen," she announces, her voice carrying through the air, "we have witnessed some remarkable culinary creations today."

A camera pans around, trying to capture the excitement on the faces of the remaining contestants.

Bobbi pauses briefly, extracting the paper from the envelope she's clutching. Fixing her dazzling gaze on the group, she smiles. "Porked 'n' Rubbed." Bobbi greets them with a wide grin. "The crowd at the farmers market was blown away by your creative use of chayote squash in two ways: pickled and deep-fried. Great work selling today! Porked 'n' Rubbed . . ." She pauses again, but I think I know where this is going. "You are the winners of this week's challenge!"

Ella Mae gives Loretta a warm hug while she wipes her eyes. Those two women are finer than frog hair split four ways. *Yes, I looked up Southern phrases, and I don't regret it.*

"Everyone deserves a round of applause for their work today." Bobbi takes the lead with enthusiastic clapping. "Unfortunately, every competition has its trials."

Bobbi takes her time scanning the crowd before eventually looking directly at Willa. "Nacho Momma's Tacos." Bobbi's voice is devoid of any emotion. "Throughout the competition, you have tried nothing new or challenging. Today presented an opportunity to elevate your cooking abilities. You made no changes to your menu, except including sliced jalapeños as a garnish. Nacho Momma's Tacos . . ." Bobbi pauses dramatically, as I'm sure the cameras zoom in so close to Willa you can count her nose hairs. "It's time for you to leave the wagon trail."

This can't be real—Willa, the self-proclaimed taco queen, recieved a *jalapeño* as her mystery ingredient. It was a guaranteed win. *But she lost!* I'd been expecting Willa's smug victory, but as the words sink in, I can't stop the victorious smile from spreading across my face.

"Hold on just a minute!" Willa exclaims, her voice quivering. "Eliminated for lack of creativity? Are you kidding me? We put our heart and soul into those tacos!" All eyes are on Willa as she stands up, her shoulders squared and glaring at our host. "Jalapeños as a garnish might not have been 'creative' enough for your taste, but let me tell you, those tacos were a masterpiece of flavor!" Willa's eyes blaze with intensity.

"I expected a lot more from you, Willa." Bobbi doesn't mince her words. Sergio and a security guard appear, guiding Willa and Bria to the greenroom for postshow interviews.

Once Willa departs, Bobbi's characteristic wide smile returns. "Congrats!" Bobbi's face lights up as she announces, "You guys are the top four teams of the season! There are only a few challenges left, so bring your A-game for the next round, everyone." Bobbi smiles into a camera before addressing the viewers. "Join us for an incredible flash challenge next week featuring our top four teams."

"Cut!" The clapboard slaps, and Bobbi walks offstage, heading straight to her office.

"We did it!" Sofia applauds everyone before we leave for the night.

Brooding, Seth sprints ahead, leaving Rylie and me behind.

"He knows about you downloading the files, and he's not happy," Rylie says.

"I'm sure he's not that upset," I say, following Seth to the truck.

Boy, was I wrong.

As I step inside, the cramped space feels tense and uncomfortable. Seth is sitting in the driver's seat, gripping the wheel. Hard. *This is not good.*

"Let's talk about what happened," he snaps. "Did you get what you wanted?"

He starts the truck before I can respond.

"You promised you would keep me in the loop." I'm not even seated when he throws the gear in drive, hits the gas, and speeds out of the lot, causing me to stumble.

"Would you slow down a little?" I say, almost falling into Rylie's lap.

"You don't seem to care about your safety. Why should I?"

"You're not being fair, Seth," I say.

"Yeah, well, your selfish attitude isn't fair, Bethany." I brace myself as he takes a sudden left turn. "A killer is on the loose, and I didn't know where you were!"

"Seth, I was fine—"

"You act like nothing will happen!" he yells over me. "You need a reality check: You're not a vigilante who's impervious to danger."

"Obviously. If I were a vigilante, I'd wear a cool cape and mask and talk in a deep, husky voice to hide my identity."

"Ooh, you should have a bow and arrow," Rylie says.

"What about nunchucks?" I gesture with my hands in mock play.

Based on the look Seth is giving us, it's not the right time to be making these jokes.

"Watch it, Seth. You're starting to look like Mom." I motion toward his current expression.

A couple of murders happen and he loses his sense of humor.

"I'm not kidding, Beth," my twin growls, taking another corner too fast on our way back to our parents' house. "You were reckless. Again."

"No one saw me. I stayed hidden under a desk the entire time. I didn't even breathe when Sergio and Alex came in the trailer."

"What?!" I collide with the counter as Seth slams on the brakes at a red light.

"Ow, that's gonna leave a bruise." I scold myself for not holding on tighter to the wall behind Seth. "They didn't see me. Rylie knew where I was—"

"But I didn't," he cuts me off.

"Because you'd try to stop me!"

"Of course I would! You didn't tell me because you knew you shouldn't have broken into the office."

"There was no 'breaking in' to anything," I clarify. "The trailer door was unlocked, and I memorized the laptop password and logged in."

"Are you going to argue with me over semantics?" Seth asks.

"I got what I needed and covered my tracks." Rylie side-eyes me as I shove a hand into my bra. "I'm confident that this USB stick holds all the answers," I say, handing it to her.

"That's a no-go," she says, throwing her hands up in the air.

"Why not?" I shake it at her.

"I don't know where your boobs have been."

"They've been nowhere!" I feel the need to defend my cleavage.

"Says you." Rylie gives me a once-over.

Seth grumbles under his breath and pulls into our parents' driveway without hitting the mailbox. He parks the truck at an angle, but at least it's far enough away from the dead hydrangeas.

Reaching over Rylie, I pump a generous amount of hand sanitizer, slathering my palms and a bit along the outside of the flash drive before offering it again. "Better?"

With a smile, she plucks it from my fingers. "Much!"

"How about this?" I say, squeezing my brother's tense shoulder. "I'll help you study for the bar and pick up your favorite cake. After Rylie unlocks the files, she can come over and we'll all review them together."

Seth grunts but doesn't answer.

"Six o'clock?" I ask.

Without acknowledging me, he gets out of the truck.

"Six it is, then! See you soon!"

"Sour cream!"

"What in the world are you doing?" I stare at my brother as he turns around, a meat-laden spatula at the ready.

"Get over here and try this." He motions for me to join him in the kitchenette.

Locking the door behind me, I join my brother, and that's when I notice the mess that has erupted in here. His countertops are littered with ingredients. Pots and pans are scattered everywhere. Pushing a few items to the side, I make room for the pink bakery box I'm holding.

"Here, try this." Seth shoves his strange-looking concoction toward me.

"Um, what is this?" I sniff the brown mixture hovering near my mouth.

"A new slider recipe I'm testing for the truck. Creamy garlic sloppy joes."

Leaning a hip against his dishwasher, I raise my palms. "I think I just became vegan."

With a big smile, Seth offers me the sample. "Try it," he encourages.

"I came here to help you study for the bar. Not find you wearing an apron in the kitchen channeling your inner Rachael Ray."

"If you don't like what I made, I'll take a bite of that raw onion."

"Like an apple?"

"Like an apple."

Opening my mouth like I'm a baby bird, Seth spoon feeds me the sample. I chew, pause, swallow, then pause again.

"Well?" my brother prompts.

"Awful." I point at the peeled onion. "Start chomping."

"You're lying." Seth snatches the spatula back.

"I am. That was delicious."

"I knew it." Seth fist-pumps the air.

"The garlic might have been a little heavy-handed," I tease to rile him up.

Seth scowls at me. "Impossible. If anything, it could use more garlic and onion."

"I half expected you to lecture me again when I walked in, so this is a pleasant surprise."

Shrugging, he scoops a spoonful of the beef mixture into his mouth. "I calmed down on the drive home."

Seth adds a bit more seasoning to the pan and offers me one more spoonful. "Mmm, still delicious," I comment while eating. "So, are we gonna study, or are you gonna keep pretending to be Rachael Ray?"

"I got hung up on a part in my book," Seth answers as he unties his apron. "I thought a snack might help, and then, well, a snack turned into this." He gestures to the chaos of his kitchen.

Onion and garlic skins litter the countertop like confetti, and his sink is stacked with dishes. Hamburger meat wrappers dangle over the rim of the overflowing garbage can.

"All right, now that you've made a snack, are you ready to study?"

My brother ignores me as he sweeps onion skins into his hand.

"What is it?" I ask, noting something seems off.

"You love the food truck, don't you?"

"You know I do," I answer, trying to figure out what's going on.

"Even with all the craziness of these last few weeks?" he asks as he busies himself in the kitchen.

"Do you think I often work in places where murders happen?" I joke. "Before the show started, everything was calm. Sure, it was intense during school," I admit. "Balancing classes, running a business, and being a boss to my best friend was a lot."

"Perhaps it would have been easier had Rylie been an actual cook," Seth teases.

"Perhaps, but we have fun. I enjoy my job."

He starts to say something, but stops himself, muttering, "See, that's just it . . ."

"Seth," I say as gently as I can. "Are you not happy?"

He shrugs his large shoulders and prepares two creamy garlic sloppy joes without answering. I wait for him to say something. We may be twins, but we couldn't be more different. What I can process in thirty seconds takes Seth days.

Placing his palms flat on the counter, he answers me. "I don't want to take the bar."

"You mean next month?"

"I mean at all. Being a lawyer is not what I imagined. I don't enjoy the game. But this"—he turns around, handing me a plate—"this is exciting! Stepping away from my chaotic life made me realize how I felt."

"What is this? A midlife crisis two decades too early? Have you considered going on a European vacation and dating a model instead?"

"Midlife, no. Crisis, yes."

"But this is what you've always wanted," I say, making sure he's really considered this.

Seth sighs. "As people change, so do their goals. Like you, I want to enjoy my job. At the firm, I've never felt as happy as I do on the truck. It's different when I'm working with you and Rylie. I spent my life running on a giant hamster wheel until you convinced me to help you with the show. I felt suffocated."

"And now?" I ask, needing to hear his answer.

It's only now that my twin really looks at me. "It's like I'm experiencing the taste of fresh air for the first time in ages."

"Oh, Seth," I say, moving closer to hug him. "Nothing matters more to me than your happiness. Running the truck together would be great, but I think you should take some more time to consider this. You've worked too hard on your studies to just walk away now. Sure, you're enjoying the truck, but that might change in a few months. Maybe talk with your boss and see if there's something you can do to offset your workload?"

Seth nods, but his eyes tell me he's already decided.

"Let's ditch studying and play detective," I say. "Rylie texted me when I was on my way over and said she finished unzipping the files. I told her to join us. What do you say, Watson?"

"Why are you Holmes?"

Crossing my arms, I assert, "I get dibs because I'm older."

"Two minutes, Beth." Seth bumps my shoulder as he walks past me. "And legally—"

"Yeah, yeah, I know, seven years younger."

The front door creaks open and in steps Rylie. "Oh, perfect! You're both here," she says, taking off her shoes. "Are you ready to see what's on this bad boy?" She waves the flash drive in the air.

"I'll set this up while you go get yourself a creamy garlic sloppy joe slider from the kitchen," Seth says, taking the flash drive from her. "It's a new recipe for the truck."

Rylie gives her tummy a pat. "Yummy, can't wait."

Seth plugs the flash drive into the side of his smart TV. "You all right, sis? It looks like you're thinking too hard." He taps the crease between my brows.

"Huh?" I look at Rylie in the kitchen, happily humming as she puts together a plate of sliders for herself, then back at my brother. "Yeah, I'm fine."

I remember locking his front door.

Chapter Twenty-Two

"When are you going to let me replace this ugly thing?" I complain as Rylie and I sit together on the brown plaid sofa with heavy oak arms.

"It may be ugly, but it's comfortable, and best of all, it was free," Seth says.

"At least let me replace that." I gesture to the worn-out mustard-yellow beanbag chair.

"And break up my furniture set?" Seth says, aghast. "I would never."

"It's a relic of the seventies."

"It's vintage."

"It's disgusting."

"It's perfect." He plops into the leaking beanbag. "Comfy cozy." He smiles at me and presses Play on the first set of files from the flash drive.

Despite the hideousness of the sofa, I'm thrilled to be watching these files with my brother. It feels like a real bonding moment for us. Plus, Rylie and I were likely near the killer when we tried viewing them the first time. The thought of how differently that day could have gone makes me shudder.

"Are these segments from the show or CCTVs?" Seth asks as we work our way through the first folder.

"This is from the CCTV camera," I answer. "The show's segments are high definition and full color. What we're watching," I say, gesturing toward his TV, "is grainy monochrome footage."

"What's that?" Rylie sits up a little straighter as we watch Imogen walk out of the production trailer with the open box of cookware Dane and Ness won. She's heading toward the refreshment tent.

The screen turns fuzzy with static just as Imogen nears the tent. "What just happened?" Seth asks.

"How would I know? Try the next file," I suggest.

The next file begins with an aerial view. "This must be the CCTV in the tower," I say aloud.

"I thought Sergio said that the camera was glitchy like the rest and probably out of commission?" Rylie recalls Sergio's words on the day I'd insisted on watching the footage.

"You're right," I say. "I guess this was one of the rare times it was recording."

"If you ask me, everything that's happened is all too coincidental." Seth expresses what we're all thinking. "Considerable effort was made to conceal the files that you and Beth found on the production team's laptop. How convenient is it that two murders happen on a lot where the security cameras are so out of date?"

"The odds of this are uncanny," I agree. "It's difficult for me to understand why a property owner would let their security system deteriorate in today's technology-driven world." There has to be another camera somewhere that caught something. Maybe everything.

The footage captures Imogen and Sergio having a brief conversation just outside of the refreshment tent. Amid some static, we witness Imogen handing him the box, tucking the flaps shut.

Just like she said she did. If only there was audio. According to the time stamp in the upper left corner, it was seven thirty in the morning.

While Sergio still holds the box, Sloane approaches from the warehouse as Imogen walks back to the production trailer. Sloane greets him while holding a cup of coffee in one hand, waving with the other.

Sloane motions to the cup she's holding. Immediately Sergio places the box on the ground and walks away. While still holding her cup, Sloane looks at her smartwatch and swipes at it with her index finger.

"Wait a minute," Seth says, pausing the TV. "I'm confused. Didn't Imogen say that Sergio delivered the cookware to Dane and Ness? Why would he leave the box with Sloane?"

"She did, but according to Sergio, Sloane offered to do it for him," Rylie explains through a yawn. Her eyes blink slowly.

"He didn't give us any explanation other than it was in her nature to be helpful," I add. "He said he had a backlog of tasks for Bert, so he took her up on her offer."

"Who's Bert?" Seth asks.

"That's what I want to know!" I say, frustrated that I still don't know who this Bert person is. "Every time I ask, no one answers me."

Seth restarts the staticky video, and we observe Sloane studying her watch for a few more minutes. After glancing around, she puts her cup on the box before stooping over to retie her shoelace.

Rylie's head bobs next to me. "Wake up." I nudge her shoulder. "How can you be sleeping at a time like this? Don't you understand the importance of watching these files? Even if the footage is choppy, we might be able to piece together something important."

"Ugh," Rylie grunts, repositioning herself. "These are the boring bits of detective work."

"It's not always high-speed chases or lurking under the cloak of darkness," I chastise her. "Seth, can you please rewind that part?" I ask.

While Rylie coils herself into a ball, my brother picks up the remote to back up the footage. Despite me shooting her a glare, Rylie remains oblivious in her drowsy state.

"What are you looking for?" he asks after the third time.

"Did you see that?"

"See what? A woman retying her shoe for the fourth time?"

"It cuts out at the *exact* moment we need." Getting up from the ugly sofa, I approach his TV. "The box is now in Sloane's hands, and the cup is nowhere to be seen."

"She threw away the cup," Seth says.

"Except the footage doesn't flicker when it restarts, like all the other moments when there's a time gap. It's a clean end, then a clean start."

"Is it possible someone altered the footage?" Rylie says from her spot on the heinous couch like a curled-up cat. "The cameras are a joke, but what if someone is leveraging them for their benefit? If there's any messed up footage, it would be blamed on the faulty system."

"But why bother going through the trouble of tampering with footage?" I ask. "Why not just get rid of it?"

"They can't," he says.

"What do you mean?" I ask.

"Security camera laws in California are strict."

"All right, Mr. Lawyer," I say. "Tell us what we need to know."

"It's complicated, but I'll break it down in a nutshell." Seth adjusts himself, causing a tiny cloud of styrofoam beans to float up. "The network is renting the facility. We'll call them 'the Tenant' and the owner of the building, 'the Landlord.' Installing cameras throughout a rental property is within the rights of property owners, but there are restrictions. The act of installing outdoor cameras to safeguard your personal property does not infringe on privacy rights. Where it gets murky is how someone uses security cameras and its video footage. California's security camera laws forbid recording in places where tenants can reasonably expect privacy."

I raise my hand. "Is that why there are no cameras inside the warehouse?"

"Correct." Seth nods. "The warehouse building has an office-style setup, allowing for individual spaces to be leased. Renters anticipate having privacy in these areas. I'm not sure why there are no cameras in the hallways that lead to the private offices. Perhaps the landlord didn't want to spend money installing them or never considered it."

"How does this information help us understand why the files weren't deleted?" Rylie asks.

"I'm getting to that." He's in full lawyer mode now. "In California, CCTV footage belongs to the landlord unless private areas were secretly recorded, or public surveillance wasn't disclosed. Since the warehouse cameras are clearly visible, the footage is legally the landlord's property. However, the tenant can request access during their rental period, especially in cases like suspected vandalism. They can view the footage but not destroy it."

"Well, there's our answer in legalese," I say.

"It would be too improbable for no footage to exist," Seth adds. "The network would be vulnerable to a lawsuit, especially after the Wiz Tech specialist confirmed that the cameras do work sometimes."

"So there are two plausible answers. The faulty footage could be from the lousy security system. Or someone might have manipulated it to conceal their role in the matter."

"I bet it was Sloane. She had a background in film editing," Rylie speculates. "She and Imogen used to manage the edits for the show."

"Anyone familiar with computers and the software could have altered the files," Seth says. "*If* that's what happened."

As Seth and Rylie discuss the ins and outs of film editing, I think about what she said earlier. *What if someone is leveraging the faulty cameras for their benefit?* "I think Rylie is right," I realize.

"Of course I am! About what, exactly?"

"It was Sloane," I say. "She's the one who tampered with the pots and delivered them."

"Are we sure it wasn't Imogen?" Seth asks. "She's the one who gave the box to Sergio, after all. And we know she worked on editing the show's episodes."

"Why would Imogen do that?" I ask. "Sergio was her PA before taking over her role on set. It's logical for Imogen to have assigned the task of delivering the box to him."

"Is there a chance she was planning to frame him?" Seth proposes. "I'm just considering all possibilities."

"I agree with being thorough," I say, "but I don't think Imogen had anything to do with this."

"Beth's right," Rylie agrees. "The news of what happened to the box set left Imogen in shock. Plus, here, Sloane suddenly appears and insists on delivering the box for Sergio. Whatever was in that cup, I bet it wasn't coffee."

The monochrome still frame of Sloane on Seth's giant TV leads me to a conclusion. "I'm pretty sure Sloane wasn't working alone."

"Don't keep me in suspense," Seth says as he rises from the beanbag, causing another small cloud of white beans to float in the air. "Speak loudly. I'm getting a slice of cake." He goes to the kitchen to satisfy his sweet tooth.

"Sloane couldn't possibly handle all of this alone with so many things happening at once. Did you notice how cagey she looked while scanning the area before tying her shoe?" My voice is loud enough for my brother to hear me in the kitchen. "Besides, she kept looking at her smartwatch. I bet that's how she communicated with her partner."

"Maybe messages about what to do?" Seth shouts his theory from the kitchen.

"During the first challenge, I saw Sloane at the grocery store," I recall.

"Is this trip down memory lane important?" Seth returns and hands Rylie and me each a slice of cake, then sinks into his well-worn beanbag chair, causing another cloud of white beans to fly up.

"What if Sloane didn't want to sabotage the contest?" I ask. "During the first challenge, Sloane confided she had a coworker she despised and wouldn't mind seeing dead. I assumed she was making a passing comment." I watch my brother shoveling cake into his mouth. "Seth, I say this with all the love in my heart, but I've wished countless times that I had absorbed you in the womb."

He swallows the mouthful of buttercream he just licked from his fork. "Come again?"

"I don't actually mean it, but I don't mind the thought when you annoy me." I pause and consider the numerous times he's been a nuisance this week. "Too bad we didn't share a placenta."

"What?" he says around another forkful of cake.

"Nothing! All I'm saying is, we've all said things like that. Is it possible that someone coerced her to do this?"

"I'm sorry?" Seth's words are muffled by the cake in his mouth. "Sloane said she wanted to kill a coworker?"

"That's what you focus on?" Rylie asks. "Not your twin wishing she had absorbed you in the womb?"

With the fork in his hand, Seth gestures. "Pfft! Look at us. I'm a foot taller than her. It would've been me doing the absorption."

"Sloane didn't say it in so many words . . ." I pause, recalling the events in the grocery store. I gasp. "It wasn't Benji!"

Looking puzzled, Seth asks, "What wasn't Benji?"

"My missing spices!" I shout.

"Uh, *feminina*," says Rylie. "I know it's making sense up there"—she taps her head—"but it's not making sense to us. Can you please explain what you mean?"

"Remember when I slammed into Benji and dropped my spice bottles all over the grocery store floor?"

"Mmph," Seth grunts as he shovels more cake into his mouth.

"I accused Benji of taking the spice bottles, but he wasn't the culprit. It was Sloane! My frustration with Benji was so consuming that she startled me when she approached me from behind. My bottles fell again, and she helped pick everything up. Or, at least, that's what I thought. But now, after seeing this"—I point at the TV—"I'm positive it was Sloane." Turning away from the screen, I chew my bottom lip. "Do you still have the notes, Rylie?"

"What notes?" Seth asks.

Rylie sets down her cake and digs through her purse.

"You kept them in your bag?" I ask, taking the paper from her.

"What notes?" Seth asks again.

Shrugging, she picks up her plate. "I forgot they were in there."

"What, no—"

"These ones." I show my brother the papers we found. "This is the note Benji dropped. At first, I thought it was meant for the Katapangs, so I gave it to Sloane. She told me she would look into it and see if it was a threat related to the show. I assumed that meant she was going to talk with the other producers about it. But now I realize Benji actually *received* it. Now the question is, who gave it to Benji?"

"Is this the Jaxsons' note?" Seth asks, taking the crumpled papers from me.

"Yep."

"Maybe Sloane did pass it along to another producer, and that's why she got killed." Rylie scoops the last bit of cake into her mouth.

"And maybe Imogen passed her note to Sloane, asking her to look into the matter," I say.

"Why am I just now seeing this?" Seth asks, passing the notes to Rylie, but I swiftly grab them away.

"Nope, you don't get these back." I fold the papers and slide them into my front pants pocket. "I'm disappointed in you, Rylie. Rule number 24 from *Murder and Mayhem:* Always keep important documents secured."

"Actually, that's rule number 17," she says, pointing her fork at me. "And I told you I forgot the notes were in there. After all, my focus was on creating a distraction for you to return to the trailer. You're welcome, by the way."

"Someone could've stolen them," I tell her.

"Who would have taken the notes?" she asks.

"The killer!" I toss my arms up in the air. "I can't believe I have to explain this to you."

"Can we focus here?" Seth interrupts us. "Where did you find those notes?"

"Crammed in the back of a desk drawer in the production trailer," Rylie says.

Seth gives her a long, calculated look. "Were you looking for chocolate?"

"Detective work makes me hungry!" Rylie balls her fists into the jank couch. "But be glad I was hungry. Look what I discovered." She flings her hand in my direction.

"This is the first note that set everything in motion," I say. "It was a threat *to* Benji."

"We know Sloane's the one behind the notes," Seth says. "What we don't know is why."

"It's clear she had a partner," Rylie says. "Working alone would have caused everything to stop once she died."

"Those notes look so fake," I say, thinking back to the first time I saw Benji's note. "Like something out of a movie. I should've known better. I should have pushed Sloane harder about it. Asked her if she talked with anyone. Maybe if I had, she and Benji would still be alive."

"It's not your fault," Seth says. "None of us expected any of this to be dumped in our laps. Even if you had immediate suspicions, it's doubtful you could have prevented anything."

I know he's right, but it doesn't change the guilt I suddenly feel.

"You intercepted the note," Seth says. "Was it a threat? Clearly. But you couldn't have known the severity of it or done anything differently at the time."

"Here's what we do know." Rylie wraps a curl around her finger. "Sloane was the saboteur and now she's dead. There's a small possibility that Sloane killed Benji if we consider the idea that he was blackmailing her. But you found her dead beside Imogen, who was barely alive on the warehouse floor."

"Why would Benji blackmail Sloane?" I ask. "Benji was a lot of things. He was a spot stealing, antagonistic, misogynistic—"

"Stay on topic, Beth," Seth reminds me.

"Right." I clear my throat. "Benji was the confrontational type. He was shouting at someone inside his truck. He even threatened the person, saying, 'You won't get away with this!' What's the reason behind doing that, if he was blackmailing Sloane?" I shake my head.

"I agree. It's not characteristic of Benji." Seth strokes his chin. "Just because Sloane sabotaged the contest doesn't mean she committed the murder. It's reality TV. Maybe she was sabotaging for better ratings. Suppose she wanted to escape the role someone forced her into?"

"If Sloane was pushed beyond her limits and confronted her puppet master," Rylie says with a pensive expression, "that person could have viewed her as a loose end that had to be eliminated."

"The problem remains that the sabotage continued after Sloane's death," I say. "The individual who was working with her is still on the loose, and that's who has continued the sabotage and who I believe is our killer."

"But how do Benji and Imogen fit into all of this?" Rylie asks.

"Benji got in their way," I state with unwavering certainty. "He received the first note and figured out what was happening, and based on what I heard in his truck, they needed him gone."

"Could someone else have learned what was happening, and instead of coming forward to the network, they tried to increase their own gain?" *Someone like Willa?* I pause, attempting to figure this out. "But if that's the case, why not kill whoever that person was too?"

"You can't just keep killing people without raising suspicion," Rylie says. "Two deaths and one attack is enough attention. How much worse would it look if suddenly everyone was dropping dead?"

She's right.

"As far as the files are concerned, it's likely the police have them," Seth says. "Don't expect Kane to give you a list of evidence."

It'd be helpful if he did.

"But you should give him those notes to add to his evidence," Rylie says.

"Yeah, yeah, stop nagging me."

"*If* our theory is correct and someone is using the faulty CCTVs as a mask for video tampering, then it's likely there's still a set of original video footage," Seth says. "Typically, there are backup files, and based on all the scrubbed folders you found, it looks like someone was erasing their tracks."

"If there are original files, how do we find them?" I ask.

"I don't know," Seth admits. "The person who has them might not even be on the show. Who knows where they are?"

Standing up, Rylie stretches her arms overhead and yawns. "Without those files, this problem is too big to solve in one night. I'm not sure about you two, but I require my beauty sleep. Let's take a break and resume tomorrow after getting some rest."

She's right. There's too much to unravel tonight. But I have a hunch that might lead me to answers tomorrow.

I think I see Seth's fingers graze against Rylie's as he walks us to his front door, and my eye twitches as severe cognitive dissonance overwhelms me. I decide I didn't see what I saw and opt to overlook it for now. I have bigger concerns to focus on.

Seth's skepticism aside, my gut feeling is that someone tampered with those files. And this time, Seth can't blame my gut feeling on recently consumed baked goods. We need the original CCTV footage. Those files hold the key to identifying the saboteur. Sergio seems to be hiding information.

On the way to our cars, I stop Rylie before she hops into her jeep. "I have an idea, but I need you to come with me tomorrow."

Leaning against the door, she raises an eyebrow. "Why do I feel like you're about to drag us into something?"

"Because that's what I'm about to do." Walking around her, I get into my car. With a couple of cranks of the key, Audrey sputters to life, releasing a small plume of smoke before I shift gears and drive home.

On *Murder and Mayhem*, Inga Nevarez always emphasizes how important it is to keep valuable items in a concealed location. At home, I put the flash drive and the two notes in a plastic bag and go to the last place I'd think of looking.

Removing the lid, I tape the baggie to the inside of my toilet tank.

Chapter Twenty-Three

As the lunch rush subsides, I wipe my hands down the front of my apron and turn to my brother. "Hey, Seth, can you take today's earnings to the bank for me? Rylie and I have an errand to run after work."

"You do?" Seth says.

"We do?" Rylie says at the same time.

"Yes, Rylie." I stress the words, giving her a look and urging her to play along. "We have that *thing* later. Remember?"

"Oh, right." She smacks her forehead. "That *thing* we planned after the last thing we did together. How could I forget?"

"What is wrong with you two?" Seth asks.

"Nothing," I reply. "Can you go to the bank for me?"

"Um, I guess. What kind of errand are the two of you going on without me?"

"Well, I'm having these terrible . . . uh . . . cramps."

"Nope, nope, nope! I don't want to hear it! La, la, la!" He's acting like a small child, plugging his ears with his fingers.

"Seth, come on, it's not that bad." Reaching over, I pull his fingers free.

"I'm serious, Beth! I have a delicate constitution!" Once again, he covers his ears.

"Go to the bank!" I yell at him.

"Fine," he says, lowering his fingers cautiously. "In the future, if you need a favor that's anything to do with . . . *that*, Rylie's your gal."

"Whatever you say." I slap him on the arm and walk past to get my purse from behind the driver's seat. "Be sure to get a receipt."

Seth rolls his eyes. "I know how to make a deposit, Beth."

"Of course you do." I slide my jacket on and sling my purse over my shoulder. "Be sure to go to the merchant line."

"Will this be a regular occurrence when we work together?" he asks.

"What? You mean me telling you what to do? Yes!" Swinging open the truck door, I step outside. "C'mon, Rylie, we've got places to be!"

"Are you sure this is the right address?" Leaning over the steering wheel, I peer through the windshield. "I thought Google maps showed that Willa has a white house with green trim, not bright yellow."

"*Oh meu Deus,* you're on the wrong street!"

"What?" The visor smacks me in the face as soon as I lift my head. "Ouch!"

"Look." Rylie shows me her phone with the Google listing for Willa Garza. "It says she's on San Marino Drive. You're on San Mardo Drive."

"How do you know?" Rylie points at the blue street sign in front of us that says San Mardo Drive. "Oh." I try to start my car, but nothing happens, "C'mon, Audrey, don't do this to me now," I plead.

"I've told you a hundred times, this car is a lemon. You need to get a new one."

"She's not a lemon, she just"—I crank the key—"sometimes takes a few tries." I try again, and the engine coughs weakly, a feeble attempt at life, before returning to its stubborn silence.

"See? Lemon."

"Ignore her, Audrey," I tell my little red Volkswagen Rabbit. Gripping the key, I make another attempt. With a shudder and a series of protesting sputters, the engine comes to life, coughing and revving unevenly. "Audrey needs a little time to warm up." I rub the dash with my hand before shifting the car into drive. I circle the block until we spot Willa's house, and I park two houses away.

After unbuckling, Rylie twists in her seat and faces me. "So, what's your plan?"

"Do you remember last night when Seth said the person who has the files might not even be on the show?"

"You think that person is Willa? Why? There have been several contestants booted from the show. Why not suspect one of them?"

"Very true," I admit. "But all of them were sabotaged during the competition. How is it that Willa remained unscathed for so long?"

"You think she knew something about the show and used it to her advantage?"

"Willa once stole Benji's food truck idea. How can we be sure she didn't overhear something while on set, then search for evidence herself?" I suggest. "I'm not saying she has the files in question, but I think she knows something about what's been going on during this season. And I'm going to find out what it is."

"And how do you plan on that?" Rylie scratches at a spot on the weathered dashboard. "The woman dislikes you with a capital D."

"She can get in line with the other food truck owners. I'm going to tell her I have evidence of her self-sabotage. That if she doesn't confess and tell me what else she knows, I'll reveal my evidence to the network. This will cause her permanent exclusion from all future shows."

"You don't have any physical evidence," Rylie points out.

"True, but she doesn't know that." Getting out of the car, I look at Rylie over the faded red roof. "The power of suggestion is all I need to make her sing like a canary. It's a common tactic on *Murder and Mayhem*." Slamming my door, I head for Willa's.

We pass her neighbors' and climb the three small steps in front of Willa's house. Rylie knocks on the door, but there's no answer.

"It seems quiet," she notes, peering at the window to the left. "A little too quiet. With all these cars, you'd think someone would be home."

"You're right. It doesn't look like anyone is in there." I squint through the front window, shading my eyes with my hands.

"Stop that!" Rylie delivers a hard slap to my arm.

"Ouch!" I quickly rub the spot where she hit me.

"You look like a burglar."

She's right.

The way I look, cupping my hands around my face and staring through Willa's front window like a prowler, doesn't look good. Out of the corner of my eye, I think I see movement in the house. Willa? A cat? I hold the doorbell, hoping someone will answer. We freeze when we hear the sound of glass breaking.

"What was that?" I whisper.

"Don't look at me. I touched nothing!"

"Something just happened."

"No kidding, Sherlock!" Rylie rolls her eyes. "What do we do?"

"Do you think it came from Willa's?"

A gate creaks, and we instinctively glance toward the side of the house, but there's nobody there. Suddenly, there's another loud bang. Spinning around, we catch sight of one of Willa's neighbors, dragging cans to the curb.

"It was probably just him." I nod toward the older gentlemen walking down his driveway. "Tomorrow must be trash day. Look." I point at the can with the blue lid. "The sound we heard was most likely bottles being dropped in the recycling can. C'mon." I start toward Willa's backyard.

"What are you doing?" she asks.

"The only logical thing," I declare as I dash around the house, with Rylie in pursuit. "If no one is going to answer the front door, we'll make them answer the back door."

She ducks through the open gate and murmurs, "Detective Pretty Boy is for sure going to arrest us."

"Where's your sense of adventure?" I question as I drop, do a roll for flair, and begin crawling in the grass.

"For once, could you *please* be a touch less dramatic?" Rylie whispers. "Now you really look like a burglar. The neighbors are going to call the cops on us!"

"Fine." I huff as I stand and wipe my pants. Rylie has a tendency to ruin my fun. I tiptoe across the grass and position myself directly under the window next to the back door. "But there's no way Detective Pretty Boy will find out. Willa lives in Greendale. That's out of his jurisdiction."

"Oh, he'll know!" she whisper-shouts at me.

I peer through Willa's kitchen window, my nose pressed against the glass, and my heart sinks. *This is bad!*

"Meu Deus," Rylie swears under her breath as she looks through the window next to me. "We need to call the police."

I take in the scene as Rylie calls 911. The kitchen is in complete disarray. The dining chairs are toppled, and the cabinets are wide open. I take deep breaths, trying to push away the horrifying memories of finding Imogen and Sloane in a pool of blood. A crunching sound comes from under my shoes as I take a step back. Looking down, I see Willa's lawn is littered with shattered glass. Stepping back once more, I notice a smashed window to the right. I guess the sound we heard did come from here.

The police arrive within minutes. Rylie and I are giving our statements when I hear someone shout, "You've got to be kidding me!"

"What's he doing here?"

Rylie nudges me. "See, I knew he'd find out."

"Ms. Lloyd." The sight of Detective Kane standing with his fists on his hips, glaring at me while his partner smirks, shouldn't surprise me.

"Detectives." I nod at the men approaching me.

"What are you doing here?" Detective Kane's nostrils flare.

"Since when is it a crime to stop by and have a chat with a fellow food trucker?" I ask.

"When you're in someone's backyard without permission," he states.

With crossed arms, I lift my chin defiantly. "What gives you the impression that I'm back here without permission?" His eyes shift and mine follow, landing on my grass-stained knees. "Those green spots prove nothing. It's possible I was playing tackle football before I stopped by."

"Were you?" Detective Hamstead asks.

I avoid eye contact. "I plead the fifth," I grumble.

"Why are you here?" Detective Kane rolls his neck.

"I could ask you the same thing. Isn't Greendale out of the jurisdiction of the Clementine Police Department?"

"Meu Deus." Rylie cups her forehead. "Why can't you shut up?"

Closing his eyes and pinching the bridge of his nose, Detective Kane lets out a deep breath. "Not that I have to explain myself to you, but if a situation in a nearby town could directly impact an open investigation, it falls within our jurisdiction."

"Oh." I guess that answers my question.

"Are you arresting us?" Panic-stricken, Rylie lets out a shriek as Detective Kane reaches for something near his backside.

"Against my better judgment, no." He takes out his notepad and pen. "But both of you should be arrested for obstructing an ongoing investigation."

"I don't see how my presence is impeding your work." Pointing at him, I say, "If anything, I think I've made greater progress than you," prompting him to growl in disapproval.

"Shut up, Beth," Rylie warns while Detective Hamstead laughs.

"Yeah, I like her," he says as he chuckles to himself.

Detective Kane gestures between Rylie and me. "I want to know everything you did and saw prior to calling the dispatcher." He clicks his pen. "Start at the beginning."

"We came to speak with Willa about the show," I explain. "We knocked on the front door, but there was no answer, so we tried the back door after noticing the open gate."

"Did you touch anything?" he asks without stopping his note-taking.

"No," I answer. "Rylie dialed 911 the moment we noticed the mess in the kitchen."

Detective Kane clicks his pen again and puts the notepad back in his back pocket. "Shall we have a look, Jerry?"

"Not sure if it's the best idea," his partner says, glancing at us. "You think we can trust Lucy and Ethel?"

"Good point. Officer Barnes!" Detective Kane summons a woman with a tight French braid who abandons her task and walks over to him. "Would you mind escorting Ms. Lloyd and Ms. Cortes back to their vehicle?"

"What?!" I shout as the officer leads us out of the backyard.

As Detective Kane and his partner climb the steps of Willa's back porch, he yells over his shoulder, "I appreciate your time!"

"Well, that went according to plan," Rylie says after the officer escorts us off the premises. "What now?"

"We go back," I say.

"You really are a crazy chicken if you think he's going to let us in there," Rylie scoffs.

"All he said was we had to be taken back to our car. He didn't say we weren't welcome to return." I pull out my phone and dial Detective Kane's number.

"It was implied," Rylie remarks as the line rings.

"What is it, Beth?" he snaps as he answers.

"Hello to you too," I reply.

He heaves a heavy sigh. "In case you've forgotten, I'm a little busy at the moment."

"That's why I'm calling," I tell him. "There's something I have you'll want to see."

The line fills with mumbling before he says, "Yeah, what is it?"

"Did you look at the video footage from the show?" I ask instead of answering.

"We've examined some of it." There's a rustling sound, almost as if he's readjusting the phone. "I'm busy, Beth. What's your point?"

"I have footage of Sloane Owsinski you'll want to see." I pause to see if he'll respond. When he doesn't, I continue. "Can I share it with you the next time I see you?"

"Fine," he says, ending the call.

Smiling at Rylie, I close my call app. "We've just received an invitation to come back!"

"We're so getting arrested." Rylie sighs as she follows me back to Willa's.

I approach the same officer who'd spoken with us earlier when the police first arrived. "Excuse me. I just spoke with Detective Kane." I shake my phone. "He wanted to discuss a few more things."

The officer steps aside. As we climb the back porch, I whisper, "And you don't think I can lie?"

Inside, police are processing the scene. The kitchen is a mess. There are scattered food boxes and overturned chairs.

"Detective Kane?" I ask when an officer becomes suspicious of us. "He's about this tall," I gesture with my hand a foot above my head. "Wearing a black jacket, and he's with his partner, Jerry Hamstead. He's expecting us. We're the ones who called the police." Nodding, he guides us toward the living room.

"Detective Kane," the officer calls out to him despite the detective being in the middle of something.

While he's still occupied, I do a quick examination of the living room, which resembles the kitchen. Broken picture frames litter the carpet, and the leather couches have three different slits. With a nudge and a head tilt, Rylie directs my attention toward the TV.

"What?" I whisper.

In a hushed tone, she says, "Look at the size of that smart TV. Those are expensive, so why wasn't it taken?" I approach the wall-mounted TV, noticing there's a small flash drive still plugged into the USB port.

"What are you doing here?" We jump apart, hearing Detective Kane's frustrated voice boom from behind us.

I compose myself and smirk at him. "You told me I could share what I had with you when we see each other again."

Detective Kane blinks at me.

Have I rendered him speechless?

"And you thought I meant for you to come back to an active crime scene?"

No, I have not.

"It's important," I insist. Pointing at the wall-mounted screen, I say, "There's a flash drive in the TV."

"So," he says, as if it's nothing important. "They were likely watching some home videos."

"You don't get it," I say as I step closer to him. "I have a feeling the security footage has been manipulated. I'm sure the original files likely reveal the mastermind behind everything."

"And how are you aware of this?" he questions. "You seem to be in possession of important information that you shouldn't have."

"I'm trying to clear my name and stop a killer!"

"You have nothing to be cleared of," he says. "We didn't charge you with anything."

"You interrogated me! You tarnished my good name in the court of public opinion!"

"Go home, Beth."

"Doesn't it strike you as odd?" I continue. "Willa is eliminated from the show, her house gets ransacked, there are missing video files that might have all the answers, and conveniently, we find a flash drive in her TV?"

"There is no *we.*" He gestures between us. "*We* are not processing the scene. *I* am. And *you* need to leave." Detective Kane uses a two-finger motion to signal someone.

I turn to Rylie. "What if Willa knew about Sloane's sabotage?"

Rylie's eyes widen as she freezes. "Do you remember what Willa said when Benji died?"

"What are you two talking about?" Detective Kane asks.

Rylie ignores him. "Willa said, 'Running a business is a lot like Hollywood. Do whatever it takes to get ahead.'"

"That's right!" I snap my fingers, remembering our confrontation in the refreshment tent when Willa tried throwing me under the proverbial food truck. "What if that's what she was doing here?"

"Doing what where?" Detective Kane asks.

"What if Willa was doing whatever she had to in order to get ahead?" Rylie says. "Even if that meant blackmailing Sloane for sabotaging the competition."

"It would explain why she wasn't targeted like the rest of us," I say.

"Hang on a second," Detective Kane says, putting his hands on his hips. "Do you have proof of what you're suggesting?"

I give a nod as another officer comes over, but Detective Kane sends him away as I explain, "Our theory is Sloane was sabotaging the contest, and it's the motive for her murder. We believe the same person killed both Sloane and Benji. And that person was also Sloane's accomplice."

"Earlier when you called . . ." He pauses. "You weren't joking when you mentioned having files on Sloane?"

Frustrated, I throw my hands in the air. "Why is it that men don't listen when women speak?"

He matches my raised voice when he says, "Please refrain from suggesting that this is a gender inequality issue. You called me while I was processing a crime scene that may or may not be associated with a homicide investigation. I find your implication disrespectful."

"Apologies," I say. "My profession is male-centric. I've grown accustomed to fighting to make my voice heard."

"Let's move on," he suggests. "How did you come into possession of these files?" Detective Kane squints, as if it will help him understand me better. "And why are you just now telling me about them?"

"Bobbi Taylor asked me to investigate some things. Hang on!" I raise my hands, attempting to ease the storm clouds in his gaze. "She came to me. She has a personal connection to this. Sloane and Imogen were her colleagues. They were her friends."

He narrows his eyes. "Where are the files now?"

"Safe," is all I reply. "Look around," I say, pointing at the surrounding chaos. "Someone was searching for something here. I don't think it's a coincidence that the TV has a flash drive plugged in. There's something important on it. I just know it."

"All right," Detective Kane says, donning a glove. He takes an evidence bag out of his pocket. "I'll see what's on here," he says, removing the flash drive from the TV. "And you're giving me the set of files you have. Now."

Once he puts the evidence bag in his jacket pocket, he places his hand on my lower back and leads me outside.

"Let's go, Ms. Cortes!" he shouts to Rylie, who was still in the living room.

As we walk down the back steps, Detective Hamstead chuckles and says, "Well, well, well. If it isn't Lucy and Ethel again."

Detective Kane reaches into his pocket and forcefully slaps the evidence bag against his partner's chest. "Tag it and log it. It came from the living room TV. We'll review it after I take Ms. Lloyd and Ms. Cortes home."

His partner's gaze falls to the bag. "The place was staged, so I'm not sure what you're looking for."

"What makes you say that?" Rylie asks.

"The glass." He motions to the broken fragments on the lawn. "When a house is broken into, we find glass shards on the inside. Not on the outside."

"Thank you, Jerry." Detective Kane tugs at my sleeve, but I don't budge.

"Whoever did this wanted it to look like a home invasion," I say. "Was anything of value stolen?"

"Let's go, Beth." Detective Kane pulls me along with him.

"What about the jewelry in the master bedroom?" I shout over my shoulder as I'm escorted to the gate. "Wait, wait!" I twist out of Detective Kane's grasp to glimpse what an officer passing by is holding. "What's that?"

"A cage for a mouse?" The young beat cop looks at me with a confused expression.

"That's not for a mouse!" I shout as I point at the bright, colored cage. "That belonged to a dwarf hamster!"

Detective Kane's left arm wraps around my waist, and his right hand grips my shoulder. "Time to go, Beth." I'm forcibly led out of Willa's backyard. "Where did you park?" He stops on the sidewalk.

"Over there." Rylie points. "The red jalopy."

"Audrey isn't a jalopy. She's a lady!"

"Yeah, a lady who's been around the block more than a few times and smokes worse than my *Tia* Vero," Rylie comments.

Detective Kane releases his grip on my waist but maintains a strong hold on my arm as he guides us toward my car. "Where are the files?"

"Back at my apartment," I say, digging in my purse to find my keys.

"Get in," he orders. "I'll follow you. Then you're going to hand over the stolen evidence."

"It's not stolen!" My protest is futile as Rylie's laughter and cough reveal my secret.

"Umm . . ." Rylie raises a finger. "I need to get dropped off first."

"Why?" I ask, unlocking the passenger door. "What are you doing?"

"It's nothing. I just have plans," she says.

"With whom?" I cross my arms. "This is the second time you're ditching me for your 'mysterious plans,'" I say, with air quotes.

"Oh, stop making a big deal out of this. Just drop me off, okay?"

Detective Kane interrupts us. "Ladies, could you maybe finish this in the car? I don't have all day."

We climb into Audrey, and with a quick silent plea to the car deities, I give the ignition a hard crank. The engine coughs weakly, so I give it a good rev.

"Seems like this old rust bucket still has some fight in her," Rylie comments as I pull away from the curb and Detective Kane follows.

"Here we are!" I swing open my front door. "Home sweet home." With a sweeping motion of my arm, I invite Detective Kane inside.

He glances around my small yet tidy living room, examining everything, and lets out a laugh. "I was expecting something different." He casually hangs his jacket on the hook next to my front door.

"What? Were you expecting a giant chicken costume in my chair?"

"Actually, yes," he says with a smirk. "Or at least some chicken paraphernalia."

I narrow my eyes at him. "It stays in the truck."

"Too bad. I was looking forward to seeing it again," he comments as he walks around me and browses the books on my shelves. "You enjoy the classics."

His statement comes across as a question. "I do. Oscar Wilde is my favorite."

Detective Kane checks out my *Wizard of Oz* collector's editions before shifting his gaze to my Jane Austen novels. His shoulder holster strains against the muscles of his back and shoulders as he bends over to examine my collections.

With his muscular stature, sharp jawline, and piercing eyes, this man appears to have been sculpted by the gods of Athens!

Clearing my throat, I take a deep breath and focus on the task at hand. "Don't take this the wrong way," I preface, "but I'll get those files for you and you can be on your way." I can't quite explain it, but having Detective Kane in my apartment feels strange.

He raises an eyebrow as I return from the bathroom.

"What's this?" Our fingers graze as he takes the sandwich baggie, and I feel that same shock as before. *Ugh, so annoying.* "Why is it wet?" He shakes the bag.

"You don't want to know," is all I offer as I flex my fingers, trying to shake the tingling. "That flash drive contains the files I lifted off a laptop in the production trailer the other day. I'm certain someone tampered with the video. It cuts at the exact moment we needed, then picks up immediately afterward. There's no static or flickering at the time gap. It feels too intentional. Also, do you remember that list I gave you of all the strange occurrences on set?"

"Yeah."

"The flash drive has multiple folders that correspond to the dates on the list. Here's the twist: All the folders are empty. Someone is erasing their tracks."

Detective Kane exhales a harsh breath. "Are you admitting to stealing evidence?"

I neither confirm nor deny.

"What's with the folded papers inside?"

"Those"—I point at the baggie—"are threatening notes. One was Benji's and is the very first note that set everything in motion. Rylie found them in a desk while searching for chocolate."

"She was looking for chocolate?"

"Detective work makes her hungry."

"You're not detectives." Inspecting the wet bag, he asks. "Did you hide this in your toilet tank?"

"What? No!" I squeak.

He arches his eyebrow and stares at me.

"All right, yes. It's the one place nobody would have expected to find it."

"It's the first place people look," he informs me. "It's common for criminals to stash things in toilet tanks."

"Did you just call me a criminal?"

"You're the one with the stolen evidence, not me."

"Touché," I remark to the smug right dimple winking at me. "Once again, I believe that whoever ransacked Willa's home had a specific item in mind. I'm convinced that the flash drive you took from her TV was the perpetrator's target they just didn't find it in time."

"You have good intuition, I'll give you that."

"Thank you," I say, following Detective Kane as he walks toward my front door.

"Beth, we've already discussed this, but we're going to revisit the conversation. You've officially done enough. Please let me handle the situation from here and stay out of it."

Our gazes lock for a moment longer than I intend. Leaning in, Detective Kane lifts his left hand. To graze my cheek, maybe? I feel the spark between us again and lean in too. Only my aim is slightly off, and my forehead collides with his cheek.

"Oh!" I exclaim, pulling back with a mix of embarrassment and surprise. I can feel a deep pink blush spreading across my cheeks. "I . . . I'm so sorry. I didn't mean to—"

His soft chuckling interrupts me as he reaches past me for his jacket on the hook. "It's fine, Beth."

The spark I thought I'd felt was just a misunderstanding—he was reaching for his jacket behind me. Not leaning in to kiss me. *Of course* he wasn't leaning in to kiss me. I have a sudden urge to melt into the floor.

Detective Kane's professional composure returns. "I should get going. I have a lot of work to do."

"Of course," I say, clearing my throat. I step around him and open my front door, willing the awkwardness to fade. "By the way, are there any updates on how Imogen is doing?"

He sighs, leaning against the doorframe. "She sustained a traumatic brain injury. We've been told she may stay in a vegetative state for several weeks."

"And what happens if several weeks pass and there's no change?" I'm filled with dread just thinking about the answer.

"I'm no doctor, Beth," he says, his voice full of empathy, "but I imagine if she continues like this, it will only worsen."

"Thanks for the update," I tell him, grateful to at least know something.

Detective Kane nods and walks away, following the path we took to get here. I wait until he's gone before closing and locking my door. Letting out a soft sigh, I look around my apartment. Between almost kissing him and hearing the latest update on Imogen, the atmosphere feels charged with a different kind of energy now.

Burying my face in my hands, I can't help but laugh at what I just did. "Of course he was reaching for his jacket. He's *not* interested in kissing me," I say to my empty apartment. "I'm pretty sure he doesn't see me as anything more than the crazy chicken girl."

My thoughts take me back to when I discovered Imogen, tied up on the cold cement floor of the warehouse building. There's a possibility she won't wake up after what was done to her. In need of something stronger than water, I grab my keys, phone, and jacket and make my way to the Tipsy Cow. The bar is within walking distance. Maybe a stroll in the evening air will help me forget everything for a while.

I'm almost a block away from my apartment when my phone vibrates. Glancing at the screen, I notice missed calls from Bobbi and Sergio as well as a message from Seth.

Just got a call from Sergio Romare. The network has opted to push up production and wrap up the season earlier than planned. Tomorrow afternoon is our last day of filming.

After having a plate of nachos, a whiskey sour, and two glasses of water, I feel better about what happened back in my apartment. I'm pretty sure Detective Kane is used to women making fools of themselves around him. What's one more to add to the list? Settling my tab, I exit the Tipsy Cow's warm embrace and enter the chilly night air. The dim glow of streetlights creates a cozy fall evening, painting pools of light on damp pavement. Wrapping my coat around me, I shiver as a gust of wind pierces through my thin jacket. Despite the temperatures shifting with the seasons, fall is my favorite time of year.

I notice movement in the darkness under the canopy of old oak trees across the street. A car door shuts, and a pair of headlights blink to life, casting an eerie glow on the damp road. Straining my eyes to see better, the blacked-out car's headlights suddenly intensify, startling me and forcing me to look away. Maybe Seth is right about my obsession with true-crime podcasts being excessive. I'm becoming paranoid.

Forcing myself to walk, I head home. *It's just a coincidence,* I tell myself. That car was probably just starting up for its own reasons.

"If I look over my shoulder right now, that car will be gone," I reason with my inner niggling voice.

I give a quick glance back and come to a stop. Just a few feet behind me, the car stops too. A few steps forward, and I look back to see the car has crept forward too. It's now that I realize my worst fear.

I'm being followed.

Turning around, I hurry back to the safety of the Tipsy Cow. As the hostess looks at me, I scan the large open room. *It figures that there wouldn't be any cops in here tonight.* I call for a taxi and wait inside for the driver to arrive. My gaze remains fixed on the black car parked along the curb across the street.

The moments drag on until I see that my taxi has arrived. A yellow Prius pulls up alongside the curb and parks in front of the Tipsy Cow. Stepping outside, I make a beeline for the rolled-down passenger window.

"Who are you here for?" I ask.

The woman looks at her phone. "Beth Lloyd?"

"That's me." I check the child lock on the door before getting in the back seat.

"Where to?" the driver asks, pulling away from the curb.

Glancing back, the blacked-out car that was parked is now following us. "Um . . ." I hesitate.

"Driving you around all night isn't possible," the driver snaps. "I have other places to be."

Going back to my place where I live alone on the first floor is not an option. I shoot off a quick text and give the driver the only safe address I can think of. "672 West Chester Street, please."

The five-minute drive to my parents' house is a blur of anxious thoughts. The moment the driver turns onto my parents' street, I text my mom to come outside. Paying the driver, I get out and sprint up to the porch where my mother is waiting.

"Well, isn't this a pleasant surprise?" I sink into my mom's embrace, feeling her warmth surround me. "Your dad and I were just talking about how we hardly see you now that you've moved out."

"I'm a fifteen-minute walk from here, Mom," I say when the sound of burning rubber stops me. Turning around, I watch the blacked-out car from the Tipsy Cow race away.

It's a Tesla.

"Do you know who that was?" my mom asks.

As the taillights fade away, I whisper, "Possibly."

"These teens have taken over this neighborhood! I'm so glad you and your brother weren't into crazy stuff like joyrides when you were younger." Urging me forward, she guides me to the front door. "*Wheel of Fortune* is about to start!"

My phone pings with a message.

"Is something the matter, dear?" my mom asks, pausing at the screen door.

"What?" I shake my head and blink in confusion.

"I asked if something was the matter?"

"It's fine." I wave for her to go ahead. "I'll be right inside." The screen door slams shut while I stare at my phone and try to process what I'm reading. My stomach bottoms out as I reread the message once more.

The level of everything blowing up in our faces is at an all-time high. She's figuring things out. The charade won't last much longer, and I'm tired of all the lies. If this goes south, I stand to lose the most. After the show ends, we have to handle this mess. See you in an hour at our usual spot. We'll talk more then.

Chapter Twenty-Four

Winnie's wet and slobbering kisses jolt me awake. I have no memory of falling asleep on my parents' couch, yet here I am.

The events from last night are slowly coming back to me, and I can't shake the feeling of betrayal and confusion. My phone, still on the coffee table, serves as a cruel reminder. The message from Rylie last night lingers in my mind like an unwelcome guest. Opening my messages, I'm half hoping it was all a terrible dream. The cold reality, however, stares back at me from the screen.

Immediately after that message, she'd sent a second one that made me want to gag.

A whirlwind of emotions and racing thoughts consumes me. How could Rylie, my *best friend*, and Seth, my own twin, keep such a massive secret from me? My heart is torn between anguish and disbelief.

"How could they keep something like this from me, Winnie?" Winnie's stub of a tail wags back and forth as she barks, begging for a scratch. As I stroke her cheek, I weigh my choices. "I could ignore the message and pretend I didn't see it."

"Arf!"

"You're right." I rub Winnie's ears. "I've been doing that for weeks and look where it's gotten me." Winnie quickly starts biting at a spot on her back. "I'm tempted to express my anger and never forgive them for their deceit. I can't believe they lied to me!"

Winnie ceases her biting and lets out a quiet growl. "I know! It's not that they're dating. Okay, well, yeah, that's pretty gross." Winnie and I shiver at the same time. "It's that they lied to me. I'm not some small child who can't handle knowing the truth. As adults, we should be capable of engaging in mature discussions."

"Ruff, ruff!"

"Thank you! You see it just like I do, right? How can I find it in myself to forgive them after being deceived? I have no idea how long this has been going on, but they should have told me earlier."

Winnie whimpers and nudges her snout into my palm. "I can't forgive lying. And I can't forgive them!"

Winnie tilts her head at me. "Oh, who am I kidding?" I mutter, my head falling into my hands. "Of course I'll forgive them. They're my best friends. But this is just all so . . . icky! Does Rylie even know what Seth is like? His toenails, when he cuts them, come back like boomerangs. If you're too close, there's a chance you could lose an eye when he trims the big toe. He never allows you to speak while watching a movie. Even when you're asking valid questions like, 'Why is she going in there? Doesn't she know she'll die?'"

Winnie gets a case of the zoomies and leaps off the couch. Within thirty seconds, she's left panting and drooling, before plopping at my feet. "I guess what really has me upset is how oblivious I was. Yes, they lied, and that was wrong. But I ignored the signs of their relationship. Maybe, somehow, I made them feel like they couldn't just be open with me."

"Ruff!" Winnie pants with her tongue sticking out to the side.

"You're right. I'll talk with them when I get to work. Work? Shoot, I don't have my car," I say to the pudgy Boston terrier struggling to climb up onto the couch. Winnie barks again, begging for another scratch. Rubbing the side of her cheek, I look at the time and sigh. I forgot it was Rylie's day to pick up the truck and slept right through.

I have two choices: call for a taxi or ask my parents to drop me off at the food truck. Our location today is the antique fair in the historic district, a perfect stop for our parents on their way to work. My mother would be willing, but Seth wouldn't be thrilled to see her. He told me he still hasn't broken the news about his possible career change. Our mother is always boasting about her baby boy becoming a hotshot attorney. It's difficult to say who will struggle more with the change. Him or her.

Even though he hasn't made an official career switch, I'm proud of my brother for having the courage to chase something that brings him joy. As long as Seth and Rylie save any gross smooching for after-work hours, everything will be fine.

I really need to call a team meeting.

"All right, Winnie." I give her one last scratch behind the ears. "Dad it is!"

I catch my brother's skeptical gaze as I climb into the back of the truck. "Why is Dad dropping you off?" Leaning against the prep counter, he stands next to Rylie as she uses the french fry cutter.

"Because I needed a ride." Shucking off my jacket, I drape it over the driver's seat.

"You should have given me a call," Rylie says, forcing a piece of potato that's too big through the cutter. "I would've stopped and picked you up."

Seth continues to eye me. "Did your lemon of a car break down again?"

"I've told you to stop calling Audrey a lemon. You'll hurt her feelings." The moment of truth has arrived, and I should just tell him. Rip off the Band-Aid and be done with it. "I visited Mom and Dad last night and dozed off on their couch. I overslept and missed Rylie by ten minutes."

All right, I'm as big of a chicken as the suit.

"Why didn't you drive yourself to work?" Seth asks.

"Didn't have my car." Pouring myself a cup of coffee, I pray he'll drop it.

"Why not?" he asks.

"Because."

"Because isn't an answer."

"Sure it is," I say. "'Why don't you like your brother? Because.'" Smirking, I sip from my cup.

Seth knows me too well and isn't buying my excuses. He narrows his eyes and stares me down, just like he did when we were kids, waiting for me to blink first. It's like we're back home, and he's attempting to get me to admit to eating the last cookie.

Crossing his arms and widening his stance, he intensifies his stare.

"Fine!" I crack. I can't handle it. I set my coffee down on the prep counter. "I went to the Tipsy Cow last night. As I walked home, a black Tesla with tinted windows turned on its lights. When I looked at the car, something didn't feel right. My suspicion was correct—the car was following me. I went back inside and ordered a taxi to take me to Mom and Dad's."

Seth unfolds his arms while Rylie moves to stand next to me. "Why didn't you call me?" His tone is a mix of worry and annoyance. "I would have gotten you."

Now is as good a time as any to call them out. "I think it's time to address the elephant in the room. You were on a date with Rylie last night."

"How did you—"

"Seth, please." I raise my hand. "You're not as clever as you think. We share the same genes that make us as subtle as a moose." I tick their indiscretions off on my fingers. "Ogling eyes, hushed conversations, Rylie preparing your coffee."

"My coffee is easy to make. Two creams and no sugar," Seth says, trying to defend their actions.

"Let's not forget how she let herself into your apartment. Twice." Rylie looks down at her feet as I glance at her. "I know for sure I locked the door when I came over with the cake. You must have given her a key. Things are serious, I'm assuming."

Rylie avoids making eye contact with me while my brother blushes.

"I'm not mad," I reassure them. "Okay, maybe a little. But I'm not as mad as I was last night. Do I wish you guys had been straight with me? Sure. But I'm not that mad anymore."

Just creeped out.

Seth releases a ragged breath. "How did you figure out that we were on a date last night?"

"I may have accidentally sent her a text meant for you," Rylie confesses.

"Oh my god!" Seth covers his face.

"You have almost the same names!" Rylie tries to defend herself. "You were both texting me, and I got the chats confused! It's not a big deal. I didn't say anything dirty."

"That would explain why you asked me about making a cilantro lime dressing," Seth says.

"She actually sent me two messages last night that were intended for you. The first one was her wanting to put an end to the lying. The second one, well, allow me to read it." Pulling out my phone, I clear my throat. "'I can't wait for you to try my new lip gloss.'" I dry heave.

"Beth, I know you're upset—"

"Upset?" I cut Seth off. "That's one way to put it. Also betrayed. I've calmed down since I learned everything, but I want to know why. Why all the lying? Why couldn't you be honest with me?"

Rylie exchanges a nervous glance with Seth before speaking, "Beth, we never meant to hurt you. It just . . . happened."

"You don't 'just happen' to date my brother and not tell me."

"It kinda did 'just happen,'" she says. "Kinda like you 'just happened' to find a dead body. You didn't mean it, but it can't be undone."

"Did you just compare dating me to discovering a corpse?" Seth folds his arms. "I don't know how I feel about that."

"Beth." Rylie's eyes are full of regret as she looks at me. "I never meant to hurt you or break your trust. We were, I mean, *I* was scared of how you would react. I worried about losing you, my best friend, if you found out I liked your brother."

"Lying wasn't the solution," I tell them. "Does it gross me out thinking about the two of you together? *Of course!* But will I support you? Absolutely! You're my best friends, and I love you!"

"I know," she says. "And I'm sorry."

"No more secrets, Rylie. No more half truths. That goes for both of you."

"Can you . . ." She chews her bottom lip. "Can you forgive me?"

"Rylie," I say with a sigh. "You're my *irmã*. Of course I forgive you!" Moving closer, I hug her tightly. "Seth on the other hand . . ." I pull back and look at my brother. "You owe me big time!"

"We were going to tell you after the competition ended," Seth says, massaging his temples. "I swear, we were going to tell you everything."

"No! We don't need to discuss the gory details." *Gag.* "The matter at hand is a team meeting to discuss how the three of us"—I motion with my fingers—"move forward in the truck."

If they're distracted, we can avoid talking about why our dad drove me to work.

"You were being followed," Seth says. "That takes priority over me and Rylie dating."

Drats.

"You're not gonna let this go, are you?" I ask my brother.

"Nope." Seth and I exchange hard stares. "Tell me what happened, or I sit on you like old times."

"You wouldn't!"

"I had a black bean burrito this morning. Try me."

As kids, Seth would sit on me and fart in my face until I gave him what he wanted. It's amazing there was no permanent damage to my sense of smell.

"I waited inside the Tipsy Cow until the taxi arrived. After realizing a car was following us, I had the driver take me to Mom and Dad's instead of leading them to my place."

"Did they follow you there?" Rylie asks.

"Yes," I reply.

Raking his fingers through his hair, Seth lets out a long breath. "Did you tell Dad?"

"I didn't want to worry them. Mom has been against the show since she found out about it. Once the murders started, she's been begging me to quit. She would have stayed up all night worrying if she had known someone was following me."

"You were smart not to go home." Rylie squeezes my arm.

"But you should've called me. You're my twin, and your safety always comes first." His eyes dart toward Rylie. "No offense."

"It would bother me if you didn't feel that way." Rylie knows better than anyone how close Seth and I are. According to her, it's what she loves most about us.

After nodding at her, he turns back to me. "Why didn't you call Detective Kane if you didn't want to call me? I'm sure he would have come."

Now it's my turn to blush.

"Remember, Beth," my twin says with a cocky smirk, "subtle as a moose. It's easy to see that you like the guy."

Yeah, but after headbutting him, I doubt he likes me.

"Look," I begin, hoping to steer away from my nonexistent romantic life. "All that matters is I'm safe and nothing happened."

"Wrong," Seth argues. "Last night proves just how unsafe you are. Someone is after you."

"At least that means I'm close to figuring this out," I say, trying to stay positive.

"That's not comforting," Seth grumbles.

"The unidentified car didn't show up by chance," Rylie says. "The discovery you made of the flash drive at Willa's is recent."

"Wait." Seth looks between us. "You found something at Willa's?"

I nod. "Don't forget about production suddenly being expedited," I add. "Why now? Why was no action taken once they learned of the first murder? Or the second?"

"According to Bobbi, the network still believes Benji died of a heart attack. Why would they end the show because of that?" Rylie says. "Not that we can blame them for believing it. That is what the news was saying after he died."

"Regardless, they should have taken action after Sloane and Imogen," I say. "Why wait until now?"

Rylie scoops a few spoonfuls of ground coffee into the filter. "Whatever it is, it happened in the past twenty-four hours. Otherwise, someone would have followed you much sooner."

"Willa's house," Seth says, his eyes boring into mine. "You called the police, and the ransacking was all over the news."

"I was gone long before any news crew arrived," I tell him.

"It doesn't matter," he says. "It's easy for whoever is behind everything to put two and two together."

"Maybe." I think back over the past few weeks. "But it doesn't matter. Other than noticing the car was a black Tesla with heavily tinted windows, I couldn't distinguish any noteworthy details because of the glare from the headlights."

"There are several Teslas on the studio lot with tinted windows," says Seth as he leans on the prep counter. "I've spotted them while waiting for you guys to arrive, but I've never seen who drives them. I'm assuming it's the higher-ups, maybe even someone from the network. If we can find out who drives that specific car, then we'll find who was following you."

"But here's the thing—production halts right after I find something at Willa's." I shake my head. "What are the chances?"

"We're not going to the final taping," Seth says, pacing the small truck and shaking his head.

"What gives you the right to make that decision?" I snap at him.

"I'm half owner."

"Until recently, you had no interest in the business. Your say means nothing." No sooner do the words leave my mouth than Rylie gasps in shock.

What I said was true, but I didn't need to say it with such ferocity. As I try to apologize, Seth holds up a hand. "You're right. I wasn't interested before. Although my feelings toward running the truck together have changed, you make a valid point. My opinion of leaving the show doesn't carry as much weight. But I'm standing my ground. We're. Not. Going." He punctuates every word.

"And I'm standing *my* ground. We're. Not. Quitting," I say back.

"You're in danger!" Seth paces once more, throwing his arms up. "What's wrong with you? What happened to not being willing to risk things because our lives are more important?"

"And you think not showing up to the final taping will change things?" I ask. "Someone is keeping tabs on me, and not showing up doesn't change that. I don't have the luxury of walking away."

"Don't be a martyr, Beth." Seth stares at me, his eyes pleading. "The person responsible is connected to the show, and they won't let you uncover whatever it is they're trying to hide."

"I'm not being a martyr, Seth. I think I know who the—"

Three loud bangs on our back door brings our conversation to a grinding halt. The truck falls into an eerie silence, and concerned glances are exchanged.

"Are you expecting someone?" Rylie whispers, hedging herself closer to Seth and me.

"No," I whisper back. "It's not even time to open yet."

Three more loud thuds strike the door. "Beth, are you in there?" Never has Detective Kane's voice brought me as much relief as it does right now.

"I'm wondering if Detective Kane might have more than just a professional interest in you," Seth comments.

"Seth," I warn.

"You have two options," Seth says. "Drop out now, or I'll talk to him about his intentions with you."

"Don't you dare!" I whisper-scream at my twin.

"Wrong choice," he says with a smirk, making his way toward the door.

"If you do this," I warn him, "Rylie will be entertained by the video of you lip-syncing 'Wild Thing' in my polka dot bikini after you lost a bet."

My brother pauses. "You're bluffing."

A few taps on my phone and then, *"Wild thing, you make my heart sing."*

"Bethany!" With a scream, Seth tackles me to the ground, trying to grab my phone.

I struggle to keep my hand out of his reach as the song plays *"You make everything groovy."*

"Wild thing. Wild thing, I think I love you."

"Give me the phone, Bethany!"

"Never!" The floor of our food truck becomes a battlefield filled with screams as we wrestle.

"Pare com isso!" Rylie shouts. "Cut it out, both of you!"

Right as Seth almost gets the phone out of my hands, Detective Kane barges into the back of the truck, pulling him off me.

"What is wrong with the two of you?" he shouts while holding on to Seth's arms.

"She started it!" Seth points at me.

"Liar!"

While Seth tries to escape from Detective Kane's hold, his elbow accidentally hits a glass mason jar on the counter, causing it to fall and crash.

"Oh meu Deus." Rylie gasps and looks at me. "That sound! Beth, do you remember when we thought the sound of glass breaking was coming from Willa's neighbor? It wasn't! We were there when someone was in her house. Our knocking scared them off, but they waited for you afterward. Luckily, Detective Pretty—er, Kane—escorted you home, otherwise you would've been followed sooner."

Detective Kane releases my brother and swiftly turns his attention to me. "Were you being followed by someone?"

"It's fine," I try to tell him. "I was smart. I didn't walk home. I went to my parents' house instead."

"It's not fine." His expression turns serious. "I need you to come with me. Now."

"Is this the moment you arrest me?" I ask, bracing myself for the familiar sensation of cold cuffs clamping around my wrists.

"Don't tempt me," Detective Kane says, and I can't tell if he's joking or not. Most likely not. "Can you step out for a few minutes so we can talk?"

Rylie gives me an enthusiastic thumbs-up while Seth scowls.

"Sure." I grab my coat. "You guys can hold down the fort, right?"

"*Sim,* I've got everything under control. And what I don't, he will." Rylie smiles at my brother.

After exiting the truck, Detective Kane asks, "What did I break up back there?"

Heading toward the bakery down the block, I chuckle. "Seth thought I was going to show Rylie a video of him singing 'Wild Thing' in one of my bikinis."

"Were you?"

"No," I say, tightening my coat around me. "That video of him was lost years ago when I accidentally dropped my phone in the toilet. Besides, Rylie has already seen it at least a dozen times. I was only playing the song. Google's amazing."

Detective Kane stops at the bakery's entrance. "You're evil."

Grinning, I open the door. "Thank you!"

The sound of the bell announces our arrival. After grabbing our muffins and coffees, we settle at a small table near a window. "What did you want to talk to me about?"

Before answering, he scans the room. Despite the place being empty, he's still cautious. "First, what's this about you being followed? And why didn't you call me?"

My eyes glance at his lips, and I quickly avert my eyes. "Because I didn't need to." There was no chance of me calling him after misreading the moment and nearly kissing him.

"Someone followed you. That's not a trivial thing."

"I am aware." I idly toy with the mug resting on the table.

"Why won't you look at me?"

"What are you talking about?" I pick at the muffin, then look up. "I'm looking at you," I say, locking my eyes on his chin.

With a gentle touch, he raises my chin so our eyes can meet. "Now you're looking at me." He pulls his fingers away. "You're acting weird. Weirder than usual. Is this about yesterday?"

"Noooo." I hastily cram a piece of muffin into my mouth and turn my head. "Why should I be concerned if I completely misinterpreted the situation and mistakenly believed you were leaning in for a kiss? Who cares if I leaned in too? You were reaching for your jacket. What's a headbutt between friends?" I lean back, crossing my arms, trying to appear relaxed. "Pfft! I don't care at all!"

"I see . . ."

My head snaps back in surprise as I look at him. *What does that mean?* Am I supposed to take that as disappointment? Or am I to interpret it as him being glad I don't care so we can move on? What's that smell? *Sniff.* God, he smells good! Is that sandalwood? *No! Focus, Beth! Stop sniffing the air like Winnie does around an open can of meat.*

Detective Kane clears his throat. "You still should have called me. What happened to you last night was dangerous and not okay."

His concerned voice helps ease my embarrassment. "I was smart. I carry pepper spray on my keychain, and I was aware of my surroundings. When I realized a car was following me, I hurried to a crowded area and ordered a taxi to take me to my parents' house. My mom was waiting for me outside. The moment I stepped onto the porch, the car sped away."

Detective Kane's jaw is so tightly clenched he could crack a molar.

"I am not someone who needs to be protected like a porcelain doll. I promise to call you immediately if anything else happens." I reach over to pat his hand but think better of it and clasp my hands. "What did you want to talk to me about?"

"It's about the flash drive—"

"I knew it!" I celebrate with a tiny fist pump. "Willa discovered what was happening and got evidence to support it. Didn't she?" He takes a sip from his coffee cup, saying nothing, so I keep talking. "She used it as a bargaining chip, blackmailing Sloane, so her team wouldn't be sabotaged." It doesn't surprise me. Willa is a person who will stop at nothing to win, even if it means taking questionable measures. She admitted as much when she said she'd do whatever it takes. "So, what's on Willa's flash drive?" I'm hoping he'll spill everything.

Detective Kane laughs. "Nothing."

"Nothing?" I ask. "How can that be?"

"The flash drive you saw at Willa's house had nothing on it. Well, nothing that mattered to our investigation. It was a slideshow of family photos."

"How can I be so close, and yet . . . not?" I say, slumping in my chair. "I was so sure she had the files."

"Hey." He reaches for my hand before stopping himself, likely thinking better of it. "Your instincts were spot on. And based on how the inside of her house looked, you're not the only one who thought the same thing."

"So what now?" I ask, perking up a little, knowing I was at least on the right track.

"Remember those files you stashed in the toilet tank?"

"That was a good hiding place!"

"No, it wasn't." He sips from his cup. "But they contained valuable footage. Thank you."

"Would you be willing to share how it contributed to the investigation?"

Shifting in his chair, he casually drapes his arm over the back. "We compared the files you stole—"

"Acquired." He raises his eyebrow, challenging me to correct him again. But I'm not that dumb. "Continue," I say, mimicking a zipper closing my mouth.

"The files you *stole*, particularly the tampered ones, were compared against CCTV footage from another camera on the lot."

"Another camera?"

"Well, that zipper didn't really keep your mouth shut, did it?" he comments, reaching for his cup again.

"I heard rumors there was likely another camera in the vicinity, but I never found it. Plus, I assumed that's what your partner was about to discuss that day at the Tipsy Cow before you cut him off."

"Jerry is a great cop, but he tends to be too talkative," Detective Kane says, sipping his coffee. *I never pegged him for a latte man.* "Hidden cameras are called hidden for a reason. But there is one specific camera on top of the warehouse building. A motion-activated rotating owl cam."

My eyes widen. "You mean Hoot Jackman?"

"Hoot Jackman?" He blinks at me.

I process this information. Hoot Jackman isn't real? I feel like I've lost a friend. Looking back, though, our relationship did feel very one-sided.

"No. He's a hyperrealistic, hidden security camera. The owners of the lot were out of the country and were extremely difficult to reach. After we explained the events that had taken place on their property, they immediately cooperated. Sent us everything they had."

All I can manage to say is "Wow." I recline in my chair. *When had I even leaned forward?* "Anything else?"

"Did you know that Marco Bartolini installed a new dashcam on his truck?"

"He mentioned he was going to."

"Contestant trucks use the show's dashcams solely during the competition. Marco's camera system has a hard-wired connection to the truck and a battery backup, ensuring continuous recording. Including everything around his truck."

Sipping my hazelnut coffee, I nod. "Maybe I should think about doing the same."

"Couldn't hurt. His camera captured a lot of footage around his truck. Footage that he gave to us. Between his dashcam, your USB drive, and the confiscated CCTV footage from the warehouse building, we have everything we need."

"Need for what? And why are you telling me all this?" He's never been this forthcoming before. I pause, considering something. "Where's Willa? You don't think Willa is . . ." I pantomime a throat-cutting motion with my finger.

Detective Kane shakes his head. "What happened with Sloane was personal. Besides, we talked with her neighbors. They said the Garzas took a weekend trip to visit family."

"Some neighborhood watch."

He snorts, and we share a fleeting moment. "Ms. Garza wasn't exactly thrilled when we called to inform her about her house. Or that she would need to come to the station to discuss a few things."

"Is that all?"

"No." He fiddles with his cup. "We got word the show is wrapping up today."

"This afternoon is our last day of filming," I confirm. "I may have been wrong about Willa having the files, but I've been doing a little online digging—"

"Of course you have."

I give him a sharp look. "I have a strong feeling about who's behind everything."

"So do we," Detective Kane says as he leans in close to the table. "Plans are in motion. We need a confession, and I'm going to need your help."

"You're asking me for help?"

"Well, you by way of your chicken suit."

Chapter Twenty-Five

I'd asked to be deputized, not to wear a wire while dressed up as a giant chicken. Detective Kane explained the details as we finished our coffee and muffins. "You'll need to dress in character. Wear the chicken suit," he explained.

"Rylie usually wears it, not me."

"Even better! That will give us the element of surprise."

"But the show is wrapping up," I said. "Wouldn't it be odd if I showed up without Rylie and Seth?"

"If someone asks, you say you came early for an individual interview."

"While dressed as the chicken?"

"The costume serves as both a distraction and an extra layer of protection."

"Why? Will I have a vest on underneath?"

"Yes," he said, totally serious. "Also, a wire and tracking device. Jerry and I will be close, but I won't put you in any more danger than necessary."

I guess this is my life now. Disguised as a giant bird, trying to secretly catch a murderer. It wouldn't surprise me if the show included footage of me dressed as a giant piece of poultry in the final cut. And just wait until the papers catch wind of all this. I can already see the headline: *Crazed Chicken Girl Strikes Again!*

As I approach the security booth, I receive an odd look. "Morning, Héctor." I tilt my head up, allowing him to see my face through the beak. "Just getting into character. Today's the last day! Isn't it exciting?" I try to sound enthused rather than terrified. "I'll be quick. Had to come in early for an individual interview."

He mumbles something about people in showbiz. "I'm not in *showbiz*, Héctor," I say to myself, gripping the wheel tighter as I carefully inch past him. The oversized chicken head wobbles every time I hit a bump, and the narrow eye holes feel like I'm looking through a blurry tunnel of feathers. The gloves make it feel like I'm driving with oven mitts. How does Rylie do this without driving straight into a ditch?

When I finally reach my regular spot, I attempt to park but immediately clip two orange cones, sending them tumbling like bowling pins. I overcorrect, and now the truck is taking up not one but *two* spots.

Great.

Sighing, I tug at the sweaty suit. "I'm just your average woman dressed like a chicken trying to help catch a murderer. Literally nothing out of the ordinary."

Unbuckling, I take a deep breath and tilt my head down. "I'm in position," I whisper to the wire beneath my suit.

According to the officer who helped wire me up, the listening device will not only record everything I hear and say, but it's also pinging my location. As long as the police stay within range of me, that is.

"Won't it be noticeable?" I asked, watching as the wire got taped to my chest.

"Your outfit is distracting. No one would even think you're wearing a wire," Detective Hamstead told me as he watched. "Besides, it hides the ballistic vest well."

"You mean Kevlar right?" I looked at the cop helping me suit up. "I feel just like Kaley Cuoco in *The Flight Attendant*."

Detective Hamstead turned to Detective Kane. "And we're sure this is a good idea?"

"It's the best option we have," he said.

"Ready to move out!" I say to my chest now. Shaking my wings, I leave the truck.

It's amusing to think how absurd I must appear as a giant white chicken rushing through the vacant parking lot. Just for fun, I stop, flap my wings, and say, "Bock-Bock-Bock!" before I run up the steps to the producers' trailer. Despite Detective Kane's and Detective Hamstead's reassurances, I'm certain that the chances of me being maimed—or dying—are high. Benji, Imogen, and Sloane are the reason I'm doing this, I remind myself. They deserve justice. Even Benji. Yes, he was a Grade A jerk, but he didn't deserve what happened to him. So, I'm making the most of this moment as I look for Sergio.

Opening the trailer door, I march in and check every cubicle. I swear into my concealed wire when I realize he isn't here. I thought he would be here by now. While I'm considering my next move, Bobbi's voice surprises me from behind.

"Rylie, what are you . . . oh!" As I turn around, I can see her surprised expression.

"Sorry to disappoint you." I offer her a small smile.

"I didn't realize both of you wore that outfit."

"I wear it every once in a while, and sometimes I even attack other food trucks while doing so." Bobbi gives me a tight-lipped smile, clearly unaware of what I mean.

"The wrap-up won't begin for a few more hours. Is there something I can do for you, Beth?"

"I was looking for Sergio, actually. Have you seen him?"

"Sergio . . ." She thinks for a moment. "Maybe. Why? What do you need from him? I'm sure I can help you."

"I wanted him to look at this." I unfold a wing. "Have you seen him?"

Bobbi inches closer while staring at the flash drive in my outstretched wing. "What's that?"

"Just something I wanted to discuss with him, but it looks like he's not here." I fold my feathers back over the flash drive.

Bobbi's gaze shifts from my hand to my face. "He might be in the warehouse. How about we look for him together?" Without waiting for my answer, she rushes out the back door, leaving me with no option but to follow.

When I arrived, the sun was bright and warm. Now, ominous clouds drift overhead, slowly covering the sun's rays.

"The wind is picking up," I say. "It feels colder." My spine tingles as a gust of wind passes by.

Bobbi squints up at the darkening sky, then looks at me. "I heard there's a storm coming." She continues walking, the muted sky casting unsettling shadows on the pavement.

I hesitate a moment, my gaze drawn upward by the sound of a haunting caw. As I tilt my head back, I strain my eyes against the fading light and observe a flock of birds ominously circling overhead. The sight makes my skin prickle with goose bumps.

"That doesn't bode well," I murmur, my voice barely audible over the gusting wind.

Bobbi stops, gazing up again at the sky. Her casual manner stands in stark contrast to the unsettling atmosphere. "Vultures," she remarks, her tone nonchalant. "They only show up when something's about to meet its end."

My eyes widen at the grim observation. Bobbi must see the concern etched on my face because she offers me a warm smile. "Don't worry, they don't attack humans. They might look scary, but they're harmless. Shall we?" Her heels clack against the pavement as she walks ahead.

Despite my instincts screaming at me to run, I press on. I've come too far and need to find Sergio. As my feet move of their own accord following Bobbi, my gaze flicks to a tree. Hoot Jackman sits silently perched on top of the building. His piercing eyes watch over the desolate parking lot like a silent sentinel.

Pausing at the warehouse, Bobbi glances back at me. "After you." The metal door groans as she pushes it open, revealing the cavernous interior draped in shadows.

"You're sure Sergio is in here?" I ask, looking into the darkness. Tucking my head down, I mumble into my chest. "The warehouse building."

"He wasn't in the trailer," she says. "He must be in here."

"It's pretty quiet," I say, walking into the empty building. "And dark. Why aren't the lights on? Shouldn't everyone be here since it's the last day of production?"

"We're conserving energy. There are only a few of us working right now, and we have a couple of hours before anyone else shows up."

The all-consuming darkness engulfs us, devouring our presence. Bobbi flicks a switch and a lone yellow bulb blinks to life, lighting our path down the hallway. With every step, the tension inside me becomes heavier, burdened by unspoken accusations. Shaking off my feathers, I feel my resolve solidify, a potent combination of fear and righteous anger propelling me forward.

This ends today.

She swings a door open and looks back at me. It's the same room that Rylie and I were in when the lights went out. This is the last place I want to be.

"Where's Sergio?" I ask from my spot in the hallway. The police were counting on him being here with me. So was I.

"He's not here," she muses, tapping a manicured finger to her lips. "But I'm happy to take care of you." An unsettling smile emerges on Bobbi's face. Reaching out, she brushes her fingers against my feathers. "It's the least I can do."

"That would be great," I squeak. "How about we go back to your office?" As I turn to leave, her grip tightens.

"I have a diagnostic running on my laptop at the moment. It won't be usable for at least an hour. Why not use the one here?"

Craning my neck, I peer into the room. "I don't see any computers in there."

Dragging me by my wing, she pulls me into the room and points to the cabinet. "There's one in there."

She walks me over to the cabinet and removes the laptop, setting it on the desk. "I'll take it." She motions for the flash drive.

According to Detective Kane, an IT guy configured it so that when it's plugged into the USB port, a folder from Hoot Jackman would immediately appear. As I pass the flash drive to her, I hope he's right.

"What's this?" she asks, squinting at the screen.

Looks like his trick worked. "Click on it."

I've watched the files twice already. Both in the café with Detective Kane and later in the truck with Seth and Rylie. The video footage begins with Bobbi and Sloane engaging in a heated argument with an enraged Benji just outside the warehouse. Bobbi's animated gestures and anger are evident as she emphatically points at Sloane, encouraging her to go after Benji.

As Bobbi registers what she's seeing, her dark-brown eyes transform into a thunderous black, stripping away the cheerfulness I've always seen. "I already promised you the competition. What more do you want?"

I smirk at her from behind my chicken head. "How about the same deal you offered Sloane? What was it? Did you offer her a restaurant? Or . . ." I pretend to think, tapping a wing against my face. "I'll take my own show, *Kluckin' Good Cookin' with the Lloyd Twins*. Has a nice ring to it, doesn't it?"

The truth is, I don't know what Bobbi offered Sloane. My goal is to get her talking as soon as possible. Starting with an accusation seems like a good way to begin. *And the less I have to lie, the better.*

As Bobbi continues to watch the footage, the tension in the room becomes palpable. The next video captures her skulking around the back of Benji's truck. She's seen sneaking through the unlocked back door in a grainy image, vanishing into the darkness inside.

The seconds tick by, and static starts to distort the video, but it still clearly captures Bobbi emerging from the rear of the truck a little while later. Her movements are quick and secretive as she sprints across the parking lot in her signature heels.

I'm breathless, waiting for her response as the undeniable evidence unfolds before her eyes. The sound of my pounding heart is so loud, I'm sure anyone listening over the wire can hear it thumping.

With a tilt of her head, Bobbi unleashes a sinister laugh. "Looks like I underestimated the little chicken girl." She steps away from the laptop, coming closer to me. Her heels click with each step. "You solved the puzzle faster than those dimwitted cops." She takes another step. *Click.* "But are you sure figuring things out is such a good idea?" *Click.* "There are consequences to asking too many questions."

And I just recorded my first threat. Keep talkin', Bobbi!

"Solved the puzzle? I'm not sure what you mean?"

"Don't play stupid with me," she says. "You know we're both talking about Benji."

"You told us he died of a heart attack," I say and watch her eyes narrow at me. "But he didn't, did he?"

"His heart gave out." She gives a dry laugh. "I'm pretty sure that's the definition of a heart attack."

"How?"

"Gaining the upper hand becomes effortless when you wear sky-high heels," she says casually, as if discussing the weather. With a swift motion, she raises her foot, revealing her iconic black stilettos. But then her smirk widens into a sinister grin. "Let's not dance around it, Beth," she continues, her voice low and menacing. "His heart didn't just give out. I ensured it did. I forcefully pushed the needle into his neck until there wasn't a drop of potassium chloride left." The cold, calculating stare that accompanies her words leaves no doubt.

"Why'd you kill him? What did Benji do to you?" I need to know. He's the only part that doesn't add up. The longer she rambles, the more it works in Detective Kane's favor. Plus, the longer she talks, the sooner the cops get here.

The original plan had involved Sergio joining me as I confronted Bobbi. Safety in numbers, particularly after the police excluded him as a suspect based on verified alibis. Sergio had agreed to help, but it seems like he had a change of heart.

Where are you, Sergio?! Looks like I'm on my own.

It was made very clear over coffee that Detective Kane didn't like the idea of involving civilians in this. All night long, he and Detective Hamstead had tried to come up with a different way to get Bobbi to confess. Ultimately, it was their boss who'd decided I was their best opportunity. The key factors were their time constraints and my preexisting relationship with her. While I was told it wasn't ideal to involve a civilian, the potential benefit of catching a killer with minimal risk to my safety, outweighed his concerns. Detective Kane was less than thrilled, and Seth threatened to sue the precinct if anything happened to me. But I didn't care about the risks when Detective Kane proposed the idea. Justice needs to be served, and seeing this through is a matter of pride for me. Even if I have to finish this without the safety of an extra person.

"I don't want to talk about Benji," Bobbi says.

"All right. Then let's talk about Sloane. Why did you kill her?"

"She wanted out," she says flatly.

"Out of what?" I need her to be crystal clear if this confession is going to be admissible.

Bobbi gives a dramatic sigh. "Everything. The lying, the cheating."

"How long had Sloane been doing your dirty work?"

"Long enough to hate it, but it was Benji and Willa who pushed her over the edge." She sneers. "They ruined everything!"

"Willa was blackmailing Sloane, wasn't she?" I ask. "How did she figure it out? Did Willa discover a copy of the files I was about to see when the lights mysteriously went out?"

"Flipping a circuit breaker isn't a mystery." Bobbi laughs at me. "But yes, Willa was blackmailing Sloane. She caught Sloane snooping around her truck."

"So, Willa wasn't immune to the initial sabotage?" I say, shocked. "I've been wondering how she avoided it for so long when the rest of us couldn't."

"Sloane's carelessness is the only reason Willa escaped being targeted," Bobbi says, irritated. "Sloane knew the importance of waiting until the contestants were a safe distance from their trucks. Still, she was in a hurry. Her rushing had consequences, and Willa started following Sloane. She confronted her, claming to have proof of Sloane's actions."

"And did she?"

"All she had was a picture she had taken of Sloane leaving the Dough Brothers truck," Bobbi states matter-of-factly. "But she said she had more. Willa was bluffing, and it worked. Despite my assurance that there was no video evidence, as Willa alleged, Sloane didn't believe me. She never worked well under pressure, and Willa's demands for her silence were burdening Sloane."

"How could you assure Sloane there was no video?" I ask, trying to understand how that would be possible. "There are cameras everywhere in the studio lot, including CCTV cameras. How could you confidently claim there was no proof?"

"Who do you think prohibited filming outside of the show? The network may front the bill, but I call the shots on my shows." Her tone is dripping with smugness. "The CCTV cameras here are a joke. Their recordings are sporadic and often glitchy. The system in this building is traditional analog. It was easy to access the network video recorders. But accidents happen with on-site video storage. Oops." She presses her fingers to her mouth.

"It's illegal to delete them!"

Like she really cares when she literally committed murder.

"I deleted only what was necessary. Anyone reviewing the footage wouldn't question the absence or alteration of a few files. I told Sloane I handled things, and I did. I took care of the files before the police were called out for Benji."

"But you didn't." I point at the laptop in the middle of the room, still playing the proof of her crimes. "If you were part of the contract process for renting this facility, you would have been aware of the hidden rotating owl camera. California law requires that lease agreements disclose the presence of *all* security cameras." *Thank you, Seth!* "You had no idea about the camera hidden in plain sight, capturing your every move."

Bobbi's eyes narrow into thin slits while she silently fixes her gaze on me.

"You may call the shots on your shows, but the network handles your contracts."

"I found out about the cameras," she finally says. "I just hadn't found all of them yet."

"That's why you broke into Willa's house, isn't it?" I ask. "With her elimination, you couldn't take the risk of her having evidence. You needed to destroy anything she might have."

"If it wasn't for someone pretending to be Nancy Drew and ringing the doorbell, I would have found them, if she had them. I made my way down the block and waited. Eventually, I watched you go into the house with that cop friend of yours."

"Detective Kane? You were watching us?"

"And following you. Almost immediately after Detective Kane left your apartment, you also left. I had no other choice but to follow you to the bar and patiently wait."

I absorb this information, thankful I'm capturing it all. "All right," I say slowly, "but why did you kill Benji?"

Bobbi makes a noise of disgust. "He was a pain from the very beginning, even before filming started. During studio auditions, someone mentioned that his traditional sexist attitude would bring a good mix to the show. The higher-ups brought him on board. Not me."

"So, they overruled your decision on who to cast, and you killed him as a result?" As I ask, I realize how petty this woman is.

"He found out what Sloane and I have been doing with other shows. A previous contestant had confided in him about suspicious occurrences and unfair treatment they'd experienced on a previous show with me." She avoids my direct question. "After Benji received the first note, he came to confront me. Only he overheard my private conversation with Sloane about the first targets of the season. He got angry and threatened to reveal the manipulation occurring behind the scenes."

"I don't understand why you needed to kill him over that. Everyone knows that reality TV isn't free of manipulation. Why couldn't you talk to him, pay him off? Or pretend like everything was a big misunderstanding?"

"Don't you think I tried?" Bobbi laughs at me. "Sloane tried too, and when that failed, I tried again. He was a liability, a loose thread that needed to be snipped. The show getting canceled was a risk if he exposed me. I couldn't have that."

"Why would that matter to you?" I ask, genuinely curious. "The host changes every season."

"I've built a name for myself," she says. "Despite still having a loyal fan base, the show's viewership is dwindling after nine seasons. The network's theory is that enlisting a regular, recognizable figure—such as myself—will create a stronger connection with viewers and increase ratings. They've offered me a contract to be the permanent host of *The Food Truck Showdown*. The new role comes with a significant salary, but it hinges on achieving excellent ratings and generating a profit *this* season. The repercussions of

Benji exposing my secret would have been worse than just getting fired. All the networks would blacklist me."

"You prioritized money and ratings over our suffering." Disgusted, I shake my head.

"Suffering? Look who's being dramatic! Those stunts I pulled helped your business. Don't deny it. How many new customers did you get each week because of the show?"

"It's not about the money, Bobbi—"

"It's always about the money!" She slams her hand on the desk, making me jump. "It's about image and money. A better image brings more money. With more money comes more opportunities. More restaurants, more personal appearances, another line of cookware."

I roll my eyes at her. "Is it always 'more' with you? You're a celebrity chef. It's not like you don't already have enough money. Who cares if one of your shows gets canceled?" The thought of the lives she took for more money haunts me. For me, the prospect of a vacation and buying a secondhand car makes me feel content. No amount of wealth or possessions would ever make me consider taking someone's life.

"I care," she spits out venomously. "It's not about *more* money. It's about having *any* money. I'm nearly broke. One of my restaurants had to be sold and the others are barely scraping by. This season wasn't my fault. We weren't even going to pull our typical stunts. Sloane convinced me that since this was going to be a permanent position, we should let things happen organically between cast members. That was our plan."

"What happened?" I ask. "Why the change of plans?"

"All of you happened," she says. "Had casting done a better job, it would've prevented all of this! There wouldn't have been a need for me to spice up the show for better ratings. Viewers are no longer attracted to amateur chefs cooking in trucks and discussing their dishes every week. Drama, bickering, and complex love stories are what appeals to the audience. When I read your contestant profiles I realized how dull all of you are, it forced me to come up with something creative."

"Creative? You call threatening people creative?"

"You have to admit, the wording on those notes was certainly creative."

She inches closer, but I stand my ground. "If this is what you did with this show, I can only imagine what you did to your other shows. Is that why you killed Sloane? You couldn't risk the years of dirt she had on you coming to light? You told me you loved Sloane. What happened to her was personal. Was that just another lie?" I accuse. "What about Imogen?"

I want her to confess everything before Detective Kane arrives with backup. I imagine him and Detective Hamstead in a nondescript van with surveillance equipment and headphones, listening to my every word like the FBI.

"Imogen wasn't supposed to be there and see what I'd done, I had to take care of her. But *you* had to show up. You have a knack for always ruining things." Bobbi's contemptuous gaze almost makes me step back. But I don't. I won't grant her any more power. "I've tried to get to Imogen in the hospital, but she has a guard watching over her all the time. It's fine. Her head hit the floor so hard that even if she wakes up, it's unlikely she'll even remember her own name."

"How could you do this?" I don't even bother trying to hide my disgust. "They were your friends!"

"They were, and I loved Sloane," Bobbi whispers. "She was like the sister I never had, and then some. No one else ever understood me the way she did, and no one ever will. What she did to me was personal. But I still loved her."

"What did she do that justifies murder?"

"She lied when she said she would always stand by me!" Bobbi spits the words. "We supported each other in this career, through good times and bad. I had faith in her. I trusted her. But she turned her back on me!"

"I know what it's like to feel betrayed when your best friend lies to you." I think of Rylie and Seth keeping their relationship a secret. But I would never kill them over it. "It's normal to feel hurt, but killing is not the answer."

Bobbi scoffs. "You can't understand."

"Then help me understand," I say. "What about Imogen? What did she do to you?"

"Imogen was an accident," Bobbi admits. "It was her day off. No one was supposed to be in the editing room besides me and Sloane. But I guess Imogen had some film segments to catch up on."

"And that's when she heard the yelling?"

"Sloane was yelling, not me. She was worried Willa would ruin her career in the industry and wanted to come clean to the network. I offered to handle Willa like I did Benji."

"Was that out of your love for Sloane? Or were you in self-preservation mode?"

"What does it matter?" Bobbi says. "When Sloane learned what had happened with Benji, she snapped. She showed no appreciation for my efforts to help her in this industry. The favors I gave, the strings I pulled. All so she could have her dream job as a top producer at the Cooking Channel. We started from scratch as amateur cooking vloggers and worked our way up together. Even when I found success, I never forgot about her. I brought her with me, spent years caring for her, mentoring her in the business, and connecting her with the right people. It was all for nothing! Sloane said killing Benji crossed a line. One I could never come back from."

Bingo!

"Then what happened?" I ask.

"I loved her, but she betrayed me! She abandoned me!" Bobbi angrily jabs her chest.

"Sloane knew too much," I say.

"She wanted to go to the police. She claimed to have video evidence that she threatened to use against me unless I confessed.

I told her she was bluffing. I already took care of all those CCTV files. She laughed at me."

"Why did she laugh?"

"Because I forgot that one of her jobs was managing contracts for the show. It was then she told me about the hidden camera on the lot, documenting our every move. *My* moves. She claimed to have downloaded every incriminating thing we had done since the show began to a flash drive. All I need is to find any hidden cameras and erase everything." She murmurs that last part to herself.

Thank you, Hoot Jackman!

"Did it never occur to you to inquire about the camera situation? How did you think you could get away with all this on the set of a TV show?"

"I did my best to cover my tracks and tie up any loose ends. But I also knew if I left one here or there that the network would protect me. I'm their biggest star."

I gasp. *They wouldn't do that! That would be wrong!* Then I recall Seth chiding me for being naive to the ways of the world. I think this is what he meant.

"I never expected Sloane to betray me!" Bobbi all but spits the words. "I trusted her! Sloane laughed as I tore the editing room apart, searching for the flash drive. But it wasn't there. She confessed to hiding the files in the last place I would think to search. I couldn't let that flash drive fall into the wrong hands." A wicked sneer twists across her face. "I guess Sloane's not laughing anymore."

"And you thought Willa had the flash drive?"

"It made sense," Bobbi shrugs. "Sloane told me she hid the files in the last place I'd look. I knew Willa didn't have anything—or she'd have used it against me. But what if Sloane hid them there, knowing I'd assume that?"A sudden thought comes to mind, so I ask it. "Did you check the toilet tank in Willa's house?"

"What?" She looks at me like I've sprouted a second head. "Why would I check the toilet?"

"Because," I say, like it's obvious, "people rarely think to check there for things."

"Have you ever watched a single episode of *Cops*?" she asks. "The toilet is the go-to hiding spot for criminals."

Why am I the last person to know this?

Focus, Beth!

"Why did you kill Sloane? Couldn't you have talked to her? Or let the network protect you since you're their star chef."

"I tried," Bobbi's voice cracks. "But Sloane wouldn't listen. It was an accident—everything was an accident!" She swallows hard, her eyes shining. "She walked away, and I got so angry. I grabbed a piece of filming equipment Sergio left lying around—he never put things away—and swung it. I didn't mean to hit her so hard. I loved her!"

My chest tightens, but I force my voice to be steady. "That doesn't sound like love to me."

"She made me angry." Bobbi sounds like a child who only cares about herself. "Despite years of hard work, love, and friendship, one mistake was all it took to ruin everything between us. She said she could never look at me the same way again."

I don't know that I would call murdering someone one mistake.

"But why didn't you kill Imogen?" I press on, needing to know the truth.

Bobbi gives me a smile that complements her sinister laugh. "You weren't supposed to be in the warehouse looking for Sergio—you interrupted me." That face and those words together are terrifying. "You've been getting in my way since day one, when you stumbled upon Benji's note."

I was right! Benji *received* the first note. It was a direct threat that initiated the chain of events.

"Thank you for sharing. Confession is good for the soul." I step back, now praying Detective Kane walks in any second.

"The only thing left to do is take care of you, chicken girl." With arms outstretched, she springs toward me, ready to claw out my throat. Flapping my wings in her face, I create a distraction, causing her to step back and swat. With all my strength, I use the opportunity to peck her face with my chicken beak. Bobbi stumbles for a moment but recovers and punches me in the jaw. The taste of coppery blood overwhelms my senses. With a hard kick to her shin, I turn and make a run for the door. That was a colossal mistake. Bobbi comes at me from behind, slamming my head into the doorframe, causing me to black out.

As I regain consciousness, three things catch my attention. First, my head is pounding. Second, Bobbi has restrained my hands and feet. The rope is cutting into my skin, making it feel like it's on fire. And third, Bobbi has moved me to another room and I'm currently lying on my side. I'm still wearing my chicken suit and hopefully the concealed wire is okay and the GPS isn't affected. Where are the police? I'm in serious trouble!

I scream for help, but it's useless. There's nobody around to hear me yell. Regardless, *I will not lie here like a sacrificial chicken.*

"These are tight," I hiss, struggling against the ropes.

The more I wrestle with the cords, the worse the pain in my wrists becomes. The rope feels like it's soaked in blood and I can feel a liquid against my skin. I squirm on the smooth concrete floor like a serpent, looking for anything to scrape my wrists against and cut the rope. This dark room has nothing I can use.

"Think, Beth, think. What would Liam Neeson do?" I replay scenes from *Taken*, searching for a solution. "That's it!"

I never thought that staying up to watch a movie with my dad would end up saving my life.

"The next part is very important. They're going to take you," Imagination Liam says.

"Well, I've already been taken, Liam," I say to myself.

"Tell me everything you see," Imagination Liam says.

I'm uncertain if my wire is being monitored, but I provide as many details as possible about the room, hoping someone is listening.

My head jerks to the side as the door creaks open. Bobbi steps into my line of vision, carrying a needle.

"What is that?" I try to wiggle away as she comes closer.

"Potassium chloride," she responds, coming to stand in front of me. "Having a sister for a nurse is fantastic. Hospitals are negligent in monitoring things. No one paid attention when I did a celebrity charity visit, then used my sister's badge to slip inside the ICU medical supply closet." Twisting the needle in her hand, she admires it. "This stuff gives the appearance of a heart attack. It was successful with Benji. Other than the resistance he showed prior to injecting him." She absentmindedly rubs at a spot on the side of her head. "It'll take you out quickly, and with your family history of heart attacks, it all adds up." With a wicked smile, she kneels next to me and slaps my face firmly.

"You don't have to do this."

She tears off my chicken head and grips my face tightly while I struggle to get away.

"How did you know it was me?" she asks, twisting my face from side to side as if she's looking for something.

"I didn't." I try to break free of her hold. "I thought it was Willa or Sergio. Willa had a questionable history with Benji. And being unnoticed was one of Sergio's talents." My squirming only results in her grip tightening even more. "Plus, the files I found were on his laptop. He had scrubbed folders and altered footage from the security cameras."

"You've met Sergio. He's not smart enough to discover those himself. I strategically placed those on his laptop to set him up as the patsy, to make it look like he was tampering with footage and deleting evidence of his sabotage. He had no idea about anything that was happening. I couldn't risk having things linked back to me, now, could I? I needed someone naturally elusive who can be occupied with trivial assignments and raise doubts about their whereabouts. Sergio was a perfect choice."

"I guess you thought of everything," I say. "Sergio is tall and has dark-brown hair."

"It was a petty move of Benji to pull my hair." She squeezes me tighter. "I've had to keep my hair in a constant updo until that area grows out. Everyone was gossiping about Sergio and his frosted tips, completely unaware that I also changed my hair color."

"Can you blame us?" I struggle to put space between us. "He resembled a relic from the turn of the millennium."

"But is that all you figured out?"

"You were the one following me the other night, and that was when everything clicked."

She shakes my head when I stop talking. "Go on."

"I remember when Rylie and I came to view the footage. There was a black Tesla with tinted windows parked in the lot. Then when the lights went out, Sergio asked us if we'd seen Bert."

"So?"

"After you offered to guarantee my truck the win, I did some investigating, which is when I discovered your real name is Roberta Taylor. Turns out you and Sergio go back almost as far as you and Sloane did."

"Get to the point, chicken girl."

"Before this season started, Sergio posted an old picture of the three of you. He captioned it, 'Blast from the Past with Bert and Sloane.' I looked it up online. Turns out, for your very first television appearance, you went by your given name, Roberta. Just like you did when you were vlogging about cooking."

"What's your point?" Bobbi's voice is more curious than angry now. "This is California, everyone drives a Tesla."

"Yes, but a friend at the CPD ran the plates from the studio lot for me," I say, silently thanking Detective Hamstead. "Your name and address were tied to the Tesla."

Bobbi's eyes widen, her composure cracking. "You had no right—"

"Second, Roberta has two common nicknames: Bobbi and Bert. Nice to meet you, *Bert.*"

With a malicious grin, she taunts me. "I didn't think you had it in you, little chicken girl." My screams are silenced as Bobbi covers my mouth with her hand. "Now, now, we don't want to cause any more trouble, do we?" The harder I try to escape, the tighter her grip becomes. "It looks like the chickens have come home to roost!" She raises her arm holding the needle.

I'm bracing myself when a bright glowing light suddenly fills the room.

"Bobbi Taylor! Drop the weapon and move away from Ms. Lloyd!" As I squint toward the door, I can barely make out shapes rushing in our direction.

Even though I can't see Detective Kane, I hear his deep voice. "Bobbi Taylor. You're under arrest for the murders of Benji Mayhew and Sloane Owsinski and the attempted murder of Imogen Comestible and Bethany Lloyd."

Bobbi refuses to look away from me. Detective Kane is probably noticing this because his voice sounds closer and softer. "Drop the weapon," he encourages. "I don't want to hurt you."

Her arm lifts higher in response to what he said, causing her to snap. My eyes shut tight as the needle aims for my neck, and I brace for the puncture. But it never comes. A gunshot fires, and a thud lands beside me, but I keep my eyes closed. My wrists and ankles are untied, but I can't bear to watch the nightmare that's happening. When two warm hands cup my face, my eyes flutter open.

I see a pair of familiar stormy blue eyes staring back at me. "Am I dead?"

Detective Kane's eyes soften. "Not today you're not."

"Is she?" I try to turn, but he holds my head in place.

"No," he whispers. "I shot her in the shoulder. She's being taken into custody. You can relax. You're safe."

Detective Kane calls for the medic as he helps me up. The sight of my wrists makes me gasp. "Rylie cannot wear the suit again until it's dry cleaned."

"Or maybe you can buy a new one? This one doesn't seem to like you very much," he jokes. "I'm sorry it took so long to find you. You moved out of range. We couldn't hear you. And your location stopped tracking. We were searching everywhere."

"It's not your fault. She slammed my head into the doorframe. I don't even know if I was still recording after that."

As Detective Kane tenderly touches the knot forming on my head, I wince. "That doesn't matter, Beth. You being safe is all that matters."

I grimace in pain. "It's you I'm worried about. After Seth sees what happened to me, he's gonna sue the pants off you." I chuckle. "Ouch, laughing hurts." I lift a hand to my head.

He pulls me into him and wraps an arm around my shoulders. "I know it does," he says. "We need to get you examined."

I was right. Detective Kane gives good, strong hugs.

Epilogue

Three months later.

"It all worked out as I predicted." I smile at my twin.

"Are you kidding me?" Seth snorts. "You did no such thing."

"Remember," I say to my brother, "I said taking the truck would be an adventure. And did we not have the best adventure ever?"

"Two homicides, aggravated assault, kidnapping, and attempted murder are not what I would classify as an 'adventure,'" Seth responds while dropping a basket of wings into the deep fryer.

"We can't all go to Disneyland," I deadpan. "My prediction came true—everything worked out. Even better, really."

"How so?" Seth shakes the basket in the oil to move the wings around.

"My two best friends are now part of the team in the truck with me." My brother and I exchange grins.

After the truth about Bobbi was revealed, the network decided to cancel the show. They divided the hundred thousand dollars among the four remaining teams and had everyone sign NDAs. It was their way of apologizing, coupled with asking us not to sue.

At that point, I don't believe anybody had any intention of suing. We just wanted to leave and never return to that lot or warehouse building ever again. I was going to miss Hoot Jackman, though. He may not have been real, but he was real to me.

Even though it ended in a bloodbath, I'm glad I joined the show and made new friends. Marco invited Seth, Rylie, and me to Oregon to visit him and his family. Even though Ben and his brothers live in another part of the state, we're already making plans to collaborate on a food truck festival. We're thinking about naming ourselves Sticky Feathers. *It's still a work in progress.*

Loretta and Ella Mae went to Texas to test their skills on the chili circuit. Dane and Ness are starting a family and settling down. The whole time, she had a little lobster roll in the oven and didn't tell anyone. Can you believe it? It's no surprise she was cranky about a little fake urine in her pots and pans. Don't mess with a pregnant woman.

Three days after Bobbi's arrest, Imogen woke up and gave crucial information to the police. After Sloane confided in Sergio about Bobbi's unreasonable behavior, Sergio told Imogen, and the two grew suspicious. Sergio's sketchy behavior was because he was conducting his own investigation. He's the one who had the original files, only he didn't know it at first. The day Rylie and I showed up at the production trailer, it was Sloane who was talking in hushed whispers with Sergio. She was unraveling the depth of the situation and needed someone she could trust.

Bobbi was pressuring Sloane to erase the security files and cover their tracks. Sloane rejected the idea, expressing that deleting footage would attract too much attention, regardless of the system's glitches. Bobbi, in a frustrated state, accidentally admitted that she would once again get her hands dirty and handle the job herself. Distrustful of Bobbi's pressure, Sloane downloaded the glitchy files before Bobbi deleted anything. Later on, she stumbled upon a secret DVR tucked away in a utility closet at the rear of the warehouse building. The DVR was connected to Hoot Jackman. Sloane hid a secret set of files in case she needed them.

Sergio agreed to help the police set up a meeting with Bobbi. However, upon discovering the truth about Bert/Bobbi, Sergio ran away on the last day of filming for fear of meeting the same fate as the others who'd looked too closely into her. The police ended up tracking him down, and he spilled everything during their questioning and provided the original files he found hidden in his car. Beneath the shifter boot, Sergio found a concealed tiny envelope. Within was a flash drive with unedited files and a confession note from Sloane exposing Bobbi's control over her. The note instructed Sergio to run if anything happened to her, as Bobbi was likely to be responsible. Which is exactly what he did. With the evidence gathered, testimony from Imogen and Sergio, and Willa's admission of blackmailing Sloane, the DA had a strong case against Bobbi Taylor. But according to Detective Kane, it was my work, especially getting Bobbi to spill so much during her recorded confession, that made it airtight. It was the irrefutable evidence that the network couldn't make "go away." Otherwise, who knows what shenanigans they would've pulled to protect Bobbi and themselves?

Our truck's business has been booming, but Rylie thinks it's mostly because of the news article that ran after everything happened.

Crazed Chick Gets Plucked and Feathered in a Showdown with the Food Truck Killer.

I was relieved to see the pictures of me in the paper this time were more flattering. Not much, though.

After discussing things with his boss, Seth decided to take the California Bar Exam and passed with a score of 270. *Woot Woot!* He didn't quit his law job after all. Instead, he decided to switch his focus from media law to general law. Seth made a deal with his firm to work part-time hours but also take on more work as required for bigger cases. He now balances his time between being a lawyer and working on the truck with Rylie and me, and he couldn't be happier. Mom's reaction to his career change surprised us. According to her, I run with a risky food group and Seth can keep me safe, or act as my legal counsel. *Whatever.*

Seth and Rylie are still together, and their love for each other is nauseating. *I really need to call that team meeting.*

As for Detective Kane, nothing's changed. He's still coming around sponging free meals off us. At the moment, his tab comes to $217.68. It's not like I'm counting or anything.

Oh! I purchased a new chicken costume, but it also hates me. The zipper snagged my shirt the last time I wore it, and Seth ripped it in half while trying to free me. I'm thinking about purchasing a cow costume to advertise our sliders.

I hear cows are friendlier than chickens, anyway.

Recipes

The Kluckin' Greek

4 servings

Ingredients

3 pounds frozen chicken wings, thawed
6–8 garlic cloves, crushed
1 small garlic clove, finely grated
1 cup extra-virgin olive oil (reserve half)
2 Tbsp cracked black pepper
1¼ tsp kosher salt
½ tsp cayenne pepper
2 tsp dried oregano
¼ cup chopped parsley
3–4 Tbsp fresh lemon juice
Zest and juice of 1 lemon
Feta cheese crumbles (optional)

Preparation

Step 1
Whisk lemon zest and juice, crushed garlic, half of the oil, black pepper, salt, cayenne pepper, and oregano in a large bowl to

combine. Add wings and toss to coat. Cover and chill at least 2 hours and up to 12 hours.

Step 2
Place racks in upper and lower thirds of the oven. Preheat to 375ºF. Line two large rimmed baking sheets with foil. Set a wire rack in each one if you have them as it helps them crisp better, but it's not necessary. Remove wings from marinade and arrange on baking sheets. Bake wings, rotating baking sheets front to back and top to bottom halfway through, until deeply browned and crisp, about 1 hour.

Step 3
Whisk remaining oil, lemon juice, and grated garlic in a small bowl. Season dressing with salt and pepper if desired. Set aside.

Step 4
To serve, stir parsley into dressing. Arrange wings on a platter, drizzle dressing over them, and sprinkle crumbled feta on top.

Mac-and-Cheese Poppers

Servings 30–36

Ingredients

Special equipment: Two or three mini-muffin pans (for up to 36 muffins), mini-muffin liners

Nonstick cooking spray and mini-muffin liners
Kosher salt
1/2 pound elbow macaroni
1/2 cup heavy cream
4 ounces cream cheese, at room temperature
2 large eggs
1 Tbsp yellow mustard
1/2 tsp sweet paprika
1 small clove garlic, finely grated
2 cup shredded mild cheddar cheese (about 6 ounces)
2 Tbsp breadcrumbs
1 Tbsp unsalted butter, melted
Hot sauce, ranch dressing, or marinara sauce for serving (optional)

Preparation

Step 1

Position oven racks in the upper and lower thirds of the oven, and preheat to 400ºF. Line two or three mini-muffin pans with liners, and coat the liners generously with cooking spray.

Step 2

Bring a medium pot of salted water to a boil. Add the macaroni and cook according to the package directions until al dente. Drain the macaroni and rinse under cold water until cool. Drain again and shake off any excess water.

Step 3
While the noodles are cooking, put the heavy cream, cream cheese, eggs, mustard, paprika, and garlic in a large bowl. Beat on low speed with an electric mixer until combined. (The mixture may have small lumps.) Add the macaroni once cooked and drained. Add cheddar and stir until combined.

Step 4
Drop heaping tablespoonfuls of the mac and cheese into the prepared muffin liners. Combine the breadcrumbs and butter with your fingers in a small bowl until the mixture is the texture of wet sand. Sprinkle the top of each mac and cheese mound with the buttered breadcrumbs.

Step 5
Bake until the cheese is melted and the bites are golden brown, 25 to 30 minutes. Let cool for at least 5 minutes before serving hot or at room temperature. Serve with hot sauce, ranch dressing, or warmed marinara sauce on the side, if desired.

Acknowledgements

Once this book went from a concept in my head to a manuscript, countless people played a part in its journey. I'm filled with gratitude for their support and encouragement, which helped bring this dream to life.

To my incredible agent, Lindsay Guzzardo. You are not just an extraordinary agent but also a dear friend. You saw something special in Beth and guided me with unwavering belief, turning this story into something beyond my wildest dreams. Thank you for being my greatest champion, even when I doubted myself. Our "momversations" have been invaluable, and I am so grateful for you.

To my brilliant editor, Faith Black Ross. I'm so glad you love food trucks as much as me and thank you for recognizing the potential in my crazy food truck idea. Your insightful edits and guidance have made all the difference. I'm honored to be a part of the Crooked Lane family.

Thanks to the amazing team at Crooked Lane Books: Mikaela Bender, Dulce Botello, Stephanie Manova, Megan Matti, Rebecca Nelson, Thaisheemarie Fantauzzi Pérez, Doug White, and Matt Martz, your patience, answers to my endless questions, and steadfast ssupport have been integral to bringing this book to life. Thank you for everything!

To my best friend of twenty years, Elisabeth Din. My fellow crazy cat lady and partner in cheese-eating therapy sessions—you have always been my support. Whether I needed a sounding board, a shoulder to cry on, or someone to act first and ask questions later, you were there. You're stuck with me for life!

To my bestie, Jennifer Natanauan, the real-life Rylie. Your unwavering belief in this story from the start kept me going. I hope you're ready to strut your stuff because your chicken suit is officially on the way!

To Irma Perez. Thank you for being a constant cheerleader for my writing and for inspiring Imogene with your fabulous green mohawk. You've brought so much life and love to this journey.

Karina Villalobos, the world's best babysitter. I can't thank you enough for keeping my boys entertained and for gently pushing me to write instead of running errands. Your support ensured I met my deadlines—and my sanity stayed intact. Mostly.

To Julie Georges and Melissa Alcorn. Your thoughtful feedback on my manuscript was invaluable, and I am endlessly grateful for your time and insights.

Shoutout to my good friend Ashley Brown. Your medical expertise brought authenticity to my stories, especially the murders (in fiction, of course!). Thank you for sharing my excitement and always being ready to brainstorm the wildest ideas.

To my critique partner and fellow author, Michele Skaggs: What began as a buddy read years ago blossomed into an incredible friendship. From swapping cat pictures to complaining about life, you've been a constant source of support and inspiration. Thank you for reading every iteration of this book and for being on this journey with me. Here's to many more buddy reads!

To my Mastermind Writing Group: Though our writing has changed over the years, your encouragement and camaraderie have meant the world. Thank you for always being there with advice and for celebrating this milestone with me.

Mom, thank you for loving everything I write, even when it's awful, and sharing your passion for mysteries with me. Dad, thanks for watching endless true crime documentaries and engaging in murder mystery discussions with me. I hope this book makes you both proud.

I want to humbly thank the devoted cozy mystery readers. Thank you for giving this series a chance. As a lifelong fan of cozy mysteries, it's an honor to share Beth and Seth's story with you. I hope you enjoy reading it as much as I enjoyed writing it.

To my sons, Levi and Lucas. Your boundless imaginations inspire me daily. I've loved you first, and I will always love you the most.

And finally, to my incredible husband, David. Your endless encouragement, honest feedback (even when I didn't want it), and unwavering belief in me made this possible. Thank you for being my rock and my everything. You were right—it happened!